MINDGAME

Also by Yang-May Ooi

THE FLAME TREE

MINDGAME

Yang-May Ooi

Hodder & Stoughton

First published in 2000 by Hodder and Stoughton
A division of Hodder Headline

A CIP catalogue record for this title is available
from the British Library

ISBN HB 0 340 71233 3
TPB 0 340 76813 4

Typeset by
Phoenix Typesetting, Ilkley, West Yorkshire
Printed and bound in Great Britain by
Mackays of Chatham plc, Chatham, Kent

Hodder and Stoughton
A division of Hodder Headline
338 Euston Road
London NW1 3BH

To ANGIE,
for rescuing me

PART ONE

Body

肉體

Chapter One

'Mrs Wyndham has been waiting for you, *mem.*' The guard at the gate gave Fei directions across the grounds. She turned off the air-conditioner and wound down the window. The warm smell of the night blew in, heavy with salt from the sea. She shifted her executive model Proton into second and cruised to the car park.

She should have arrived here at the Wyndham Centre for Mental Health and Excellence by late-afternoon. The sudden night of the tropics had come hours ago. She had left Kuala Lumpur after lunch and turned off the north-south highway near Ipoh three hours later. She had then got lost along the old trunk road, stuck behind local traffic: rusty Toyotas swerving into her path, a bullock yoked to a cart, school children cycling four abreast. Finally, she had found the turning and for the last half hour her car had been the only vehicle on a narrow road through undeveloped jungle. It had emerged into the delta of a mangrove swamp as she approached the coast, rising at last to the higher ground that cupped the Centre like a natural fortification.

She parked on the edge of the rise and stepped out into the night. Below her, the white colonial-style sanatorium was warmly lit along its verandahs. The shapes of coconut trees fanned out against the sky. The stars were bright over the dark curve of the sea. It was rare that Fei was ever out of the city these days, work and urgent meetings always the priority. She stretched and tried to relax.

She followed the lit gravel path, leaving her briefcase and overnight case in the car. From the architect's plans she had seen, she knew that the path was one of many along the wooded slope, linking the staff bungalows. If she stayed on this one, she would reach the Wyndhams' residence. But after her long drive, she wanted a moment to relax and the lure of the waves drew her down towards the sea.

Lights from the residences dotted the woods behind her. Bright bulbs festooned along the path across the lawns cast a criss-cross of shadows about her feet as she walked. It was like finding a beach-side Shangri-la in the wilderness. She felt free suddenly, as if she had left her old self with her life back in the city. There her clients clamoured for her: contracts and joint ventures, judicial reviews and planning applications piled up in her tray; bills, budgets and the administrative demands of her law firm battered at her time. Her mother was complaining again about Anita's behaviour, her youngest sister starting up arguments all the time at home. There were the family's bills for a new air-conditioning system, repairs to Kit-Li's car, a bridging loan Johnny needed to expand his construction business – her other sister and elder brother both working but always somehow short of cash. And there was Sam.

She did not want to think about Sam tonight. They had had another argument that morning. *Why do you have to go to the Centre the day before? Why not go tomorrow like all the other guests?* Sam had slammed away from the breakfast table. *It's always business first with you, isn't it? Never mind about us.* That bitterness echoed still in her mind. Fei had tried to explain. But what had there been to explain?

The Wyndhams were her most important clients. Ginny Wyndham had asked her up the day before, gentle but firm in her persuasion. 'Come up early. You work too hard. A day by the sea will be good for you. In my professional opinion.'

'You always know how to get your own way,' Fei had laughed.

'Besides, I want you to myself for a while.'

Three years before, Ginny Wyndham had come to Fei's firm

4

with deeds to the vast tract of coastal land the Wyndhams had acquired and a detailed proposal for building a mental health sanatorium there. She and her husband, Piers, had bought the property cheap from the holiday resort company that had gone bankrupt after years of troubled development works at the site. Piers, a neuropsychologist, had developed a revolutionary form of community-sensitive and culturally based therapy for mental health treatment which would be the basis for the Centre's work. He left the administrative and PR matters to Ginny, focusing his energies on research and patient care.

In the time Fei had worked with the Wyndhams, she and Ginny had become good friends. Outside their business relationship, they often had a meal or a drink whenever Ginny was at the Wyndhams' apartment in KL. Fei had finally told Ginny about Sam. Perhaps it had been the cosy European decor, the wine, Ginny's relaxed affection, as if they had been friends forever and outside was London and not Asia. It had all poured out: how Fei couldn't get through to Sam anymore, how they were always fighting now, how things had changed after four years together. Ginny had listened quietly and taken her hand. At last someone understood, Fei had thought, and the secret she had shared with Ginny had drawn them closer over the last months . . .

Rasping breath rushed up suddenly behind her. Something clawed hard into her shoulder. She sensed the warmth of another body close to hers, the grip digging deeper into her flesh.

'What—'. She tried to twist round but could not free herself.

A terrified voice in her ear, hot breath and saliva spraying her cheek. 'Out of the sea, I saw beast rising. Had ten horns and seven heads. They . . . the missing link . . .'

Fei pulled away with a cry. She stumbled with the sudden momentum. Her heart lurched in her chest. She could not find the breath to scream. He came after her, grabbed her arm.

His face was up so close, she could see the sheen of sweat and stubble even in the sallow light. His breath was rank; saliva ran from his lips, speckling into froth. His left eye was closed, that side of his face hanging slack. Fei felt his weight swaying against her, his grip tightening. He shuffled, favouring his right side, dragging his left arm and leg. He wore white, sheened yellow by the electric light.

'The number of the beast – six six six. There are seven angels with seven plagues. They are the missing link. Mighty Babylon, your doom is struck. Warning you . . .'

Fei pushed at him. He staggered but did not let go. She slammed her fist into his face, the contact sending a jolt of pain up her arm. His head jerked back but otherwise he did not move.

Running feet. Voices. People around her, pulling the man from her. A blur of activity, three men and a woman surrounding her attacker. Fei saw a syringe thrust into his arm. He was struggling against them, subsiding into stupor. Fei staggered, her mouth dry. She was shaking.

Piers Wyndham stood beside her, tall and straight-backed. 'Take him to the Secure Unit.'

One of the other men looked up. He was in jeans and a T-shirt. 'But he's not a high-risk patient.'

'He is now.' Piers glanced at Fei, his tone crisp. 'One of you stay with him tonight and in the morning, work out a rota. We can't take any chances with the ceremony tomorrow.'

The group, whom Fei took to be nurses or orderlies, walked away from the main building with their sedated patient. They were all dressed casually. Piers turned to her. He wore a Malay-style high-collared tunic and dark trousers. His European features were angled with shadows, blond hair gleaming against the darkness. 'Why didn't you go straight to our residence, Fei-Li?'

His abrupt tone startled her. 'I – well, the sea . . . the view . . .'

'Come with me.'

Fei had to hurry to keep up. She felt cold suddenly. Her legs felt like slinkies pouring their way down stairs. She gasped, 'Who was that? What was he talking about?'

'He used to be the keeper at the Sanctuary down the road. You'll have passed it on your way.' Piers spoke as if describing a clinical study. 'The isolation broke him. He never took a

6

holiday. Loved the orang-utans like his own family. He was reading the Bible day after day – religious man. He knows the *Book of Revelations* by heart. That's what he keeps quoting to anyone who'll listen. The end of the world and so on.

'We don't have a uniform for patients or staff but Deng likes to wear white, the Chinese colour for death. He was one of our first patients, and usually our therapies work with him. He's not so morbid now. But once in a while he gets over-agitated – we've been disrupted by the preparations for the ceremony all week so no doubt that upset him.'

'Will he be all right?'

'He'll be fine once he's calmed down.'

'He – he didn't seem well.'

'Stroke. Paralysed the function on one side. He gets about, though. Strong-willed.'

Ginny was waiting for them on the steps of the bungalow. She looked tense. She said, almost like a complaint, 'Why didn't you come straight up? I've been waiting all day for you.'

Fei didn't like the way that they both seemed to treat her like a child. She said, 'Sorry.'

Ginny seemed to notice her husband for the first time then. She stiffened, her voice formal. 'Thank you for bringing Fei, darling. What happened?'

He told her in his terse tones. Ginny took it in without a word. Fei looked at Piers by the light from the porch. There was something about his gaunt severity that discouraged friendliness. His hair was too neat and his gaze seemed always clinical. Near his collar was a tiny badge, an abstract swirl of silver and red-gold. Fei recognised the logo of the Asian Values Alliance.

<hr />

Fei and Ginny sat at the table on the back verandah. The Wyndhams' bungalow was set at a distance from the other accommodation on the seaward slopes of the ridge. The sanatorium was to the south and out of immediate vision. All Fei could see were palm trees dark against the stars and sea.

By flickering candlelight, Fei ate fried noodles that Ginny had heated up in the microwave. She hadn't realised how hungry she was. Ginny did not eat but shared a Tiger beer with her.

'I was looking forward to spending some time alone with you.' The petulance was still in Ginny's voice.

Fei nodded. She had imagined a pleasant and amusing evening with her friend, like they usually had. She had looked forward to it, too, she wanted to say now. Why was Ginny being like this?

'You're here, that's the important thing.' Ginny smiled but her lips were taut. 'Even if you're late.'

Fei attempted conversation. 'Piers didn't come in.'

'He won't be joining us.'

'Does he always work this late?'

'Great scientists never keep mere mortal hours.' Ginny drank her beer. She looked at Fei and seemed to soften. This time her smile was genuine. 'Are you okay now? Poor Deng – he must have given you such a fright.'

Fei laughed. 'I thought some demon had got me.'

They talked more easily again, their fondness for each other dispelling the first awkwardness. When Fei had finished eating, Ginny showed her round the empty house. In the three years of their friendship, Ginny had always used the Wyndhams' apartment in Kuala Lumpur as a base. The continuing construction work on the Centre had been the excuse for not having visitors to the bungalow here. This private invitation now before the official inauguration ceremony felt special to Fei.

The bungalow was a traditional long-house-style wooden building on stilts. Verandahs ran its length at front and back. Each room inside opened into the next. The guest room was at one end. Ginny and Piers had their rooms at the other, one large room divided into a suite of two. Ginny's room faced the sea, colourful rugs on the wooden floor and saris hanging on the walls. The soft furnishings on the rattan furniture hinted at her English origins. There was a Laura Ashley spread on the bed. They stood there awkwardly.

There was no hint of Piers's presence in this room. It was as if Ginny wanted Fei to see that she and her husband no longer slept together. She seemed to expect a response and finally Fei said, 'It can be easier like this.'

'I knew you'd understand.' Ginny slid her arm through Fei's. 'But, please, no one else knows.'

Fei's heart went out to her. The Wyndhams stood for healing and wholeness to the outside world but it seemed their own relationship had failed them. Fei suddenly understood Ginny's previous agitation. She had wanted to share this pain with Fei, talk to her from the emptiness of her marriage. Her unhappiness was echoed in Fei's heart.

They strolled along the verandah back to the table. The candle was burning low now. Ginny opened two more bottles of beer from the fridge as they sat down.

She said gently, 'How are things with Sam?'

'A bit fraught.'

Ginny touched Fei lightly with her fingertips. 'Do you want to talk about it?'

Fei shook her head. She didn't want to think about Sam. Not now.

The rejection made Ginny brittle again. She withdrew her hand. 'I thought we could be close. Especially after you told me about Sam. I thought you'd understand the position I'm in. I thought you were a friend who could help me through it instead of . . .' She broke off.

Ginny's voice had risen to a staccato, her movements jabbing with tension. Fei stared at her in confusion. 'Help you through?'

'I hate it all — all this. The fund-raising, the polite smiles and constant chat, the PR spin on everything. Everyone knows me as Ginny Wyndham, Director of the Mental Health and Excellence Centre — and no one knows me at all. I thought you of all people might understand! I thought I could be close to you.'

Fei had never seen her like this. Ginny had always seemed so poised and confident, a perfect representative for the Wyndham Centre. It was as if this was a different woman.

Ginny pistoned on 'How do you think I get through it all? All those meetings with health officials and CEOs, begging for money and support, charming my way into their coffers? You think I'm damn' good at it, don't you?'

Fei said nothing.

Ginny seemed about to go on then looked stricken as if she had already revealed too much. Finally, she said, 'I thought you could make things different for me.'

'Me?'

'You're my friend. My only friend.'

'You have lots of friends. And Piers . . .'

Ginny grabbed Fei's hand. 'I started out working on the computer – algorithms and microchips, that's what I wanted from life. They don't judge you: they're at your mercy, not you at theirs. Piers made me into this smiling people-person he needed for the Centre while he got on with the real work. They brought in Ricky Teong and his computer team to work under my supervision. He's at it with his guys round the clock while I get sucked out there to lecture tours, fund-raising, PR dinners . . . They'll have no further use for me on the graphics side soon, I know it, I taught Ricky too well. The joke is, I feel like a wind-up doll with the spring coiled too tight most of the time. Don't you see that?'

'I'm sorry if I haven't been a very good friend.' The intensity in Ginny's eyes made Fei uneasy. They seemed to be pleading with her to go down a road she did not yet want to take. Ginny's neediness startled her, like the sight of a raw wound. And yet fascinated her. Fei promised, 'I'll try to make it up to you.'

Ginny seemed to relax then. She took Fei's hand. The display of gratitude embarrassed Fei. 'You'll be fine tomorrow, I know it,' she said.

Ginny nodded, tears glistening in her eyes. It touched Fei that out of everyone in her life, Ginny had turned to her. It was only Fei who could help her, make her safe again. But Fei could not stop herself from instinctively pulling back. She took a swig of beer to camouflage it, tilting the glass to her friend in a toast.

Fei slept little that night. Her mind raced. She kept seeing Deng's crazed face shouting at her. His senseless babble churned in her mind. It had been a long day – and a long stressful drive: his sudden appearance had shocked her, she told herself, that was all. But even as she battled down that disturbance, another plagued her. Deng transformed himself into Ginny, his manic behaviour becoming her nervy tension, his voice her tight staccato complaints. Fei opened her eyes with a start.

Her heartbeat was loud in her ears. She was sweating. Fei sat up. It was as if Ginny's need and loneliness had darkened the shadows in her own heart. Fei thought back over the last few years with Sam, tried to find the moment when it had all started to go wrong. The mosquito net over her bed felt like a cage. She gathered it up and draped it over its frame. There was no point in trying to sleep. It would soon be light. She went out on to the verandah.

The rhythm of the sea ticked away the night.

The last time Fei had been by the sea had been with Sam a few weeks before. It had been a disaster. She had taken Sam to Pulau Tioman for the weekend. The island was famed for its white beaches and four-star luxury amid a tropical paradise. All she had wanted was for them both to be happy again but Sam had seemed tense throughout Saturday. After dinner, they had gone down to the beach.

There had been a full moon. They had walked wordlessly through the shallows. When Sam tried to take her hand, Fei pulled away. The setting might have helped them if the quarrel had happened earlier in their relationship. But they had had this argument too many times in the last year.

Sam said, 'Why pay for all this romance and luxury if you won't let me touch you anymore?'

To make up for all the times I've let you down, Fei wanted to shout. But aloud she said, 'You know we can't.'

'There's no one here to see.'

'Just in case someone . . .'

'And what if someone saw us? So what? We're just friends, aren't we? That's what you tell everyone. Your family and friends. Business contacts you won't let me meet. This is just friendly hand-holding – who would say otherwise?'

'Please keep your voice down.' All Fei's hopes were unravelling before her eyes. She did not know how to save them.

Sam swore and turned away.

Fei pleaded, 'We've been through this before. But this isn't London. What you can do in the West, we can't do here. You've lived in Malaysia now for almost four years. When will you ever understand?'

'So I can't touch you outside the four walls of the hotel room on our romantic weekend?'

'I have my career to think about. And my position in this society. Don't you see?'

'You never used to be like this. Remember? In the first year I came to KL, you used to be proud to be seen with me.'

Fei turned away. 'Things are different now.'

'Or is that just the excuse?'

Was Sam right? Was all this just shadow boxing? Fei felt the breeze on her face. Was she creating these arguments, anything to engage with Sam again?

Sam said softly, 'I love you so much, Fei. But what's happened to us? This last year – it's all been going wrong.'

Fei blinked against the tears. It was as if her heart had grown numb. Her frustration burst into the silence. 'In London, we could live how we liked. But Asia is different. In London, we could forget that we're different from the rest. But not here. It's easier for you, this isn't your home. You have no stake here. If it all falls apart, you can always go back to London . . .'

Her last words had hung in the air between them.

They hung there still in Fei's mind. *You can always go back to London.* Sam's contract at the National Hospital of Malaysia would come up for renewal in ten months' time. They had not talked about it. Somehow they had forgotten how to talk.

The first grey light of day began to appear. The sky brightened but the sun behind the ridge would not be seen for a while yet. Fei began to distinguish the colours of the landscape she had only seen by night. The sea was metallic grey, deepening moment by moment into olive. Blue gave way to pink and purple on the shoreline, green washed into the lawns and vegetation.

Monkeys whooped across the jungle slopes behind, their calls echoing over the bay. In the stillness of the morning, Fei could just make out the deeper tones of the waking apes in the Orang-Utan Sanctuary two miles away.

She had passed the turn-off through the jungle the night before, the sign boldly proclaiming: 'All-Asia Orang-Utan Sanctuary and Research Institute'. The orang-utans had hit the international news some years before when they had been discovered during land clearance in the Titiwangsa mountain range. These apes were a sub-species never before known to man, according to the media reports, dark grey where the better known Orang-utans were rust red and smaller in size.

Fei remembered the national excitement at the opening of the Sanctuary eight years before. She had just come back from England to start as a trainee in one of the major law firms in KL. The grey orang-utans had been the pride of Malaysia while the red apes of Indonesia declined because of deforestation in Borneo. To world acclaim, an anonymous benefactor had opened the Sanctuary exclusively for the Malaysian species. The apes seemed to symbolise a defining moment in the country's history and they appeared in ad campaigns and politicians' photo opportunities, emblazoned children's school bags and pencil cases, populated every tourist brochure and souvenir item.

Malaysia stood on the verge of what was touted as the 'Asian century', the era when Asia would rise to eclipse the West as the dominant global player. The new millennium would see Asia leading the way in international affairs, business, industry, trade, culture and social change, the pundits declared. The grey orang-utans stood for all that was new and hopeful and yet were as ancient as the hills from which they had come. They were brought out of the jungle to meet the modern world in an ecologically protected environment. The apes and their new habitat were monitored and managed with the most progressive ecological techniques and the best forestry and veterinary technologies. They stood for the best of Malaysia – its traditions and heritage, the vast beauty of its rainforests, and also the nation's coming of age, its modernity and its future, most of all its uniqueness. Fei understood such hopes and optimism, felt the energy and ambition in her own blood.

She had met Sam in London. They had been happy in the cool, orderly atmosphere of Europe. England had been such a safe, easy place. Fei had loved it for that, loved its patchwork fields and clean pavements, its reasonableness and tolerance. It was a country that had only one deadly species, the adder, which was a rarity anyway – and that summed up everything she loved about England. Fei had tasted freedom there: the freedom to talk and argue, to step out of tradition and custom and be whoever she wanted to be. She had felt a curious sense of safety and peace in London that she would never feel in Asia.

And yet this was her home. Not just the teeming jungle and quiet sea, but also the clogged, manic city she had left that afternoon. She loved the conflicts of Malaysia: the wild landscape that harboured cobras and tigers and bright birds, the thrusting monuments to pride and ambition in KL, the battle of its dusty traffic snarl ups, the *atap* villages with their palm-thatched houses among the coconut groves. She felt alive here, jostled by the myriad colours and cultures: Chinese, Malay, Indian, aboriginal, Eurasian, white and migrants from all parts of Asia, all with their own religions, cultures, customs and dialects, mingling their cuisines in an exotic mix of spices and flavours, bound together in a common drive to make good. She was one of them. She belonged. And yet she did not.

Fei turned away and went back into the room. She showered and began to dress, putting on the armour of her professional self. The uncertainties of the night dispersed in the brightening day. She became Qwong Fei-Li again, partner in the rising firm of Ming, Siap & Qwong. She was thirty-two and already netting an annual personal profit of a quarter of a million *ringgit*, excluding income from her investments. In the business community, her reputation was increasingly formidable. She would not let herself be overwhelmed by intangibles. She was in control of her life and her future. And nothing was going to knock her off course.

Chapter Two

Ginny accompanied the dignitaries through the sanatorium and its grounds. Fei studied her in amazement. Today Ginny was dressed in a pale pink linen suit, her brown hair styled and sleek. A touch of make-up softened the angles of her otherwise plain face. Her public persona was poised and charming. No one seeing her now would have guessed at the brittleness that had marked her the night before.

It was a bright, clear day. Cotton-ball clouds drifted across a lapis lazuli sky. The palm trees shimmered with sunlight. Beyond the lawns, bursting with the colours of bougainvillaea, hibiscus, fast-growing yellow flame and frangipani, the sea foamed white against deep jade. The main sanatorium was cooled by jacaranda and pine trees. Verandahs running the length of its several storeys shaded rooms where ceiling fans turned endlessly. On the central lawn, a stage had been set up, covered by a marquee-style awning. Catering staff had laid out a buffet table and dining facilities beneath the coconut trees.

Among the guests were regional chief executives of major health and education charities – from Mental Health Asia, Education for All International to the Asian Values Alliance. Health officials from Thailand, Philippines, Singapore and Malaysia were all represented. Multinational companies keen to show their community face and encouraged by tax breaks had sent directors from their boards. Ginny knew everyone by name and found a moment to chat with each of them.

Fei realised it was a major coup to have got the Wyndhams on to her client list. They had originally come to the firm through one of her partners, Stanley Siap, via a large commercial client. Stanley had been bursting with self-importance as the Wyndhams had already got the backing of well-known corporations and charities for their venture. They were also personal friends of Siew Kei-Win, the CEO of Enlightenment International, a lighting and utilities conglomerate, and President of the Asian Values Alliance. It had been as if Stanley had seen strings of lights illuminating his career path towards the rich and powerful. Fei remembered Ginny standing at the boardroom door looking at her with curious eyes. Speaking across Stanley's triumph, she had requested Fei as the Centre's lawyer.

She had taken over all the Wyndhams' files from their previous legal firm, Teck & Co, a one-man band that had been wound up following the death of the sole practitioner. Teck had negotiated the acquisition of the site on which the Centre now stood and had pushed through all the legal paperwork. He had subsequently suffered a nervous breakdown after a financial scandal, according to the talk Fei had heard, and one night had blown his brains out, sitting in his car in the garage.

Fei had steered the Wyndhams through the complex legal work involved in construction of the Centre. She had handled negotiations with government departments, local authorities and environmental committees to obtain the appropriate licences and permissions. She had also set up a charitable trust for the Centre's finances, taking advantage of tax exemptions and incorporating strategic flexibility for the expanding international aspects of the Wyndhams' work. Ginny never quibbled over her bills and Fei's fee income had almost doubled.

Her work for the Centre had been one of the best challenges of her career. It had brought her into contact with many government officials and judges. The Centre's high profile had also increased hers. Ginny's contacts were already opening up a network of new clients for Fei. The celebrations today brought her naturally into the circle of the elite. Fei made herself focus.

With confident charm, she began to work the VIPs, handing out her business cards at every opportunity.

The press trailed the proceedings, photographers and TV cameramen hurrying ahead of Ginny and her guests. With media representatives of many of the South East Asian countries were two or three journalists from Western international weeklies. Fei noticed a tall, blond man. He had the broad build of an athlete, poised lightly like a cat about to spring. He was wearing a denim shirt and khakis, an old tie carelessly giving the required touch of formality. A camera with a telephoto lens hung from his shoulder. His gaze caught hers. She looked away.

Fei saw that the independent satellite news station, N-Sat, had also sent a camera crew. N-Sat stood for Nanyang Satellite and was the new twenty-four-hour information and entertainment satellite network, owned by a Hong Kong telecommunications tycoon. Its programmes were beamed to Asian countries from Pakistan to Japan. Its catch-phrase was 'The best of Asia for the best in Asia', capturing its aim to broadcast only Asian programmes and films and to cover news from a purely Asian perspective. No American or Western programming or product advertising appeared on N-Sat channels.

The dignitaries were filmed in the sanatorium, chatting to patients with schizophrenia, depression and anorexia. With patients, Ginny was reassuring and calm, prompting them with gentle directions.

The guests were not permitted access to the Secure Unit located on the headland to the north of the Centre's grounds. It housed psychotic patients who posed a danger to themselves and others. 'The few we accommodate there are the ones most in need of care and protection,' Ginny said with compassion and grace. 'Their best interests would not be served by an invasion by media and visitors.'

A video link showed the patients in a comfortable amenities room, attended by friendly staff. In one corner, Fei noticed Deng watching television. He was smiling as he stared at the cheesy images on the screen – they seemed to be an extended ad for a happy family holiday. At first, Fei assumed his state to

be the product of tranquillising drugs. But there was a natural-
ness in his movements that belied that suspicion. He seemed alert
yet composed. Deng's transformation astounded Fei. Seeing
such results, Fei thought, the Centre's techniques had to be truly
impressive.

Outside again, Fei emerged a few paces behind Ginny. She
could see Piers waiting for the guests, catering staff by his side
bearing trays of iced drinks. Security personnel shepherded the
guests in his direction. The press fell away from their formation
round the VIPs as everyone relaxed.

Without seeming to, Ginny drew Fei into her wake and
inched her out of earshot of the other visitors. She slowed her
pace to let the group pass them. Fei sensed Ginny's easiness with
her, the tension of last night gone. She felt relief like the hit of
a drug.

Fei kept her eyes on the group of VIPs as they moved ahead
of her and Ginny.

Ginny bent her head close to Fei's, her manner serious, as if
discussing a legal problem. But her voice was low and intimate.
'Thank you for last night. I'm sorry I've been neglecting you
today. Are you all right?'

Fei stared after the group ahead. Something made her uneasy
as she watched them. She tried to match Ginny's manner,
murmuring, 'You've all this to deal with. It's difficult for you, I
know.'

'Thank you.' Ginny seemed moved by this acknowledgement. She touched Fei's arm lightly, as a friend might. But stayed
a moment too long. 'May I call you?'

Fei nodded.

And Ginny was gone, taking the arm of someone from the
Thai health ministry and asking after her children.

Fei caught a figure out of the corner of her eye. It was then
that she realised they had been observed. Looking round, she
saw the blond man, standing some distance away. He was staring
at her and did not try to hide it. That was what had been bothering her – she had not seen him in the main group as it had
passed her and Ginny.

Suddenly, he swung his camera up and took a photograph of her. He grinned and walked away.

'Hey!' Fei began, but he did not stop. She looked after Ginny and saw her deep in conversation. When she glanced back, the blond man was nowhere to be seen.

Piers stood with Siew Kei-Win in the shade of a jacaranda tree as the latter sipped iced tea. They were some distance away from the festivities. Siew was a handsome man in his fifties, tall and fit for his age, his hair still untouched by grey. Piers's stance was straight-backed and still, both hands in his pockets. His smile belied the tension balling his fists beneath the well-cut cloth. 'Another week, that's all we need,' he said, trying not to make it sound like a plea.

'This is the second postponement.' Siew's eyes were hard. A muscle jumped in his jaw.

'The new generation have not yet reached maximum growth capacity. The process is a natural one, using H cultures for optimum reactive results, you know that. We can't control these cultures as you would a synthetic product.'

'The delay had better be worth it,' Siew said grimly. His voice had a slight Australian lilt.

'You won't be disappointed.'

Siew looked away and beamed at another guest by the buffet table. Turning back to Piers, he made a show of congratulating him then walked away without another word.

The knot tightened in Piers's gut. He made his way back to the crowds. A blond man intercepted him, reaching out to shake his hand. He wore a denim shirt and khakis. 'Carson Dean, *Global Weekly News*. Great work, Dr Wyndham.'

Piers did not shake his hand but smiled as he knew he should. All this PR schmoozing was tedious. It had been Siew's idea to go for the high profile. The gamble was working, entwining the reputations and interests of the Asian establishment with the fate of the Centre. For the sake of their long-term ambitions, Piers would have to endure today and all the other public appearances that would be expected of him. But his primary objective awaited him in the labs and the sooner he could be left alone to work the better. He tried for an amiable tone. 'Thank you, Mr Dean. You're American?'

'Yeah. You ever been to America?'

'No, but I'd rather like to. You're doing some interesting therapeutic work over there.'

'You sure you've never been to America? New York, maybe?'

Something in the journalist's insinuating tone warned Piers. Dean wasn't just making conversation. He tried to move past him but Dean kept pace. 'You remind me of someone,' the journalist went on. 'You ever know Justin Lovelace?'

Piers did not break step. He kept his expression neutral and shrugged. 'Should I?'

'I swear, you look just like him. He was in New York – well, New Jersey, actually – back in the eighties. Scientist, just like you. You never came across him?'

'Not that I know of.'

Dean stopped in front of him. He dropped his 'naive American' act and said, 'If you do come across Lovelace, I think he'd want to talk to me.'

Piers's mouth was dry. He had never thought to hear that name again. Not after all these years. So far as he was concerned, Lovelace was dead. He met Dean's gaze. 'I have no idea who you're talking about but I assure you, Mr Dean, if I come across Mr Lovells, I will pass on your message.'

'Lovelace. Justin Lovelace.' Dean offered him a card but Piers did not take it. Dean reached over and slipped it into Piers's breast pocket.

'Whatever.' He pushed past the journalist. This time Dean did not try to stop him.

Piers stood for a moment by the buffet table. His breathing was shallow in spite of himself. He signalled to a security guard. 'Tell Ong to keep an eye on that American over there. And have someone run a check on him.' He took out Dean's business card and stared at it a long moment, finally handing it to the guard.

***

Han Lee-Ren crouched in the undergrowth by the boundary on the ridge overlooking the Centre. Around him, the cover of trees kept the shadowy air cool. He was not far from the entrance gate, alone but for the scuttling, humming creatures of the jungle. Through the two lines of fencing, he could see the stage and the milling crowd down in the bay. From its appearance, Han knew that the outer fence was electronically sensitive and judging from the sophisticated overall design, both boundaries were likely to be dug deep into the ground to prevent tunnelling. For a civilian institution, these defences seemed curiously over-cautious. Han adjusted the device he had installed on the ground, careful to stay out of range of the CCTV cameras placed at intervals along the fencing.

He was dressed in black, his face and hands darkened with mud. He carried a small pack on his back. His automatic pistol dug into his hip in its concealed holster. Han tightened the noose on his frustration. He had had short notice of the inauguration ceremony, and then only by chance through a call to a local contact. There had not been enough time to plan this job properly. He and Raul had only arrived in KL in the early hours of the morning. They would not be able to penetrate the Centre now to place the devices. But at least the small but powerful surveillance camera he was setting up would glean them some information. Han swore silently. They couldn't afford to fuck up, especially with the Suits looking for an excuse to pull the plug.

He murmured into the mike of his body set, 'Try it now.'

Near the turn-off from the trunk road inland from the mangrove delta, a closed van was parked under rambutan trees. In the back, Jose Raul watched the gritty television screen. The picture was coming up at several frames a second, giving the scenes of celebration at the Centre a static, disjointed quality. He adjusted a control on the panel of switches and electronic displays by the screen. The camera had 180-degree vision but it was too far away from the activities on the lawn of the Centre to pick up any dialogue. The picture on screen changed perspective as the remote signal swivelled the device several miles away.

'It's set.' Raul's voice crackled in Han's concealed earpiece on the secure radio channel.

Han nested the device under a camouflage of branches and leaves, working slowly to minimise noise and movement. He moved away, inching his way along the perimeter, recce-ing for a possible point of penetration through the defences for a future incursion. He had a second surveillance device he needed to install to cover all angles of the Centre. Through the dense trees, the sea shimmered brightly in the far distance.

In the van, Raul eased the zoom up. The Filipino recognised Ginny Wyndham among the moving figures from photographs of her in the press. She seemed of medium build for a white woman, with an athletic form beneath her elegant suit. She was talking to a Chinese woman, their heads bent close. They were smiling as if they shared a feminine secret. The Chinese was of a more delicate build, her sleek hair cut gamine-style. Her tailored trouser-suit gave her an air of authority in spite of her petite frame. Raul dredged his memory. She was the Wyndhams' lawyer – he had also seen her in press pictures, accompanying the Wyndhams to a planning hearing. And they were the best of friends, too, he noted from their manner. Could be useful, he thought.

<hr>

Ginny introduced Fei to Mei-Hong, the wife of one of the doctors at the Centre. Fei was touched that in all the buzz of the festivities, Ginny kept coming back to see that she was all right. They would share a few private giggles and then Ginny would make sure Fei met all the right people. Now she said, 'No more networking. Have some fun with someone our own age!' And was gone, after squeezing Fei affectionately on the arm.

Fei sat with Mei-Hong at a table with a group of other women, eating *satay* and chillied prawns from the buffet and sipping fresh guava juice over crushed ice. Palm trees and frangipani shaded them from the sun and perfumed the air with sweetness. The other tables were filling up with guests. Chang Mei-Hong was slim and pretty, in her late-twenties, a primary school teacher and beamingly proud of her husband, Ben. 'He stays here at the Centre because of his work. He's doing really well. If everything goes well, he hopes to head a team for the Centre based in KL and that's when we plan to start a family.'

Ben sat at another table. He was good-looking – in his early-thirties, clean-cut and smart. A good catch by any standards. He was sitting beside Siew Kei-Win, Fei noted. At his table, there were only men. It struck her that many of the other guests had grouped themselves by gender. This segregation was not deliberate – it never was in Malaysia. There was just a natural gravitation of the sexes towards each other at events like this. Men had their own talk, deep voices resounding with discussion of business and politics and current affairs. Women sipped sweet, iced beverages and talked about their homes and families.

'Are you married?' Mei-Hong asked.

Fei shook her head. Her heart sank. This was a question she was often asked. At thirty-two, she was getting close to being an old maid by Asian standards.

'You career girls, you mustn't forget you're a woman also-lah.' Mei-Hong's concern was genuine. 'You all think a husband can wait but, I tell you, having a man of your own – it makes you feel like a whole woman. Why don't you come to one of our meetings? AVA guys are special, you know, with old-fashioned values.'

It was only then that Fei registered the abstract swirl on her lapel. The AVA logo was based on a human figure metamorphosing into flame, body and arms curling like fiery tongues around a head that might also have been the heart of the sun. This was the latest fad to sweep across Asia. She knew people who were members but none of her friends – mainly cosmopolitan professionals – took AVA types seriously. The Alliance were a pan-Asian organisation rallying Asia to old-fashioned values which they believed made Asians superior to westerners: hard work, thrift, responsibility to the community, family values – as against the selfish, corrupt individualism they attributed to the West. Fei's circle called them dorks. Paul, a lawyer friend, would mimick a sing-song small-town accent: *Mummy's boys, no mind of their own-lah, they all never stay out late, never try anything new, only like what Daddy tell you to like.* Fei smiled at the memory. But ideology made her uneasy, no matter how well-intentioned.

Mei-Hong went on, 'I'll call you when we have the next meeting. You must come, no need to be shy.'

Fei remembered with dismay that she had given Mei-Hong her card. She thought of Sam and how the AVA people would condemn her for such a relationship. But Ben worked for the Centre and Fei's rule was never to offend a client. She said, 'Sure.'

Later, the formalities began. Piers stood at the podium on the stage overlooking the tables. His clear, English voice carried over the loudspeakers across the grounds. He introduced the scientific concepts behind the Centre's work and outlined his research project. Ginny sat with the other dignitaries to one side of the visual-aid screen. Fei watched her as she watched Piers, fondness evident on her face. He had an intense, uncompromising aura, eyes unreadable behind his wire-framed spectacles. He was in his early-forties but looked younger.

On the screen behind him were computer-generated slides of the neural networks of the brain as he talked about receptors, transmitters, hormones as a complementary messaging system to the functions of the central nervous system. The technical jargon meant little to Fei but she followed the gist of it. By manipulating the bio-chemical status quo in the brain and body with natural herbs; hypnosis; computer-assisted visualisation or external stimulii such as low electrical currents, heat and massage – Piers postulated – the chemical and biological conditions in the body as a whole that gave rise to mental disorders could be modified and controlled to restore mental health. So far as Fei could understand, this was what traditional medicine and complementary health therapists had been doing for years but Piers and his team were trying to document definitively the scientific basis for such treatments.

Ginny spoke next, exchanging warm looks with Piers as they passed on stage. She talked about the cultural bias of Western psychiatry and how the Centre's aim was to redress that balance by taking into account the social and cultural context of their Asian patients. The Centre took in patients from all over South East Asia, with specially trained multi-lingual staff and cultural advisors to meet the diversity of their patients. The Centre had a capacity of almost a thousand patients. The first thirty were thriving and there were already scores more due to arrive over the next few weeks. She went on to outline the educational outreach work of the Centre. She and some of her colleagues travelled the region on lecture tours, conducting seminars and workshops with the aim of dispelling myths about mental illness and breaking the taboos that cloaked such conditions in silence and shame.

Ginny returned to her seat, leaning close to Piers to exchange a few words. They were both smiling and seemed a couple happily in love. Fei watched their public performance curiously and thought suddenly of Sam. She had trained herself so well that her mind almost believed that Sam was just a friend. *Just* a friend. How dismissively she set aside the one person who knew every part of her. A rush of shame washed over her. She and Sam played a similar game to Ginny and Piers, only they had pretended so well not to be in love that the disguise had hardened into reality.

───>●<───

Mei-Hong led Fei to Ben's table. They settled in chairs close to him, careful not to disturb the men's conversation. Fei recognised government officials and prominent businessmen from

various Asian countries among the group surrounding Siew
Kei-Win. There were other younger men she did not know,
diffidently attentive, AVA badges in their lapels. Ben Chang
looked strained and pale.

One of the older men was challenging Siew good-
humouredly. 'We all think the Wyndhams are doing valuable
work. But how can you, Mr Asian Values, support whites? Why
not use your money to fund something run by Asians?'

There was laughter as others nodded. The younger AVA
men looked offended. Fei smiled. These guys needed to relax.
The mock-antagonistic debate was a familiar feature of the Asian
social gatherings she attended.

Siew's reply was amiable. 'It's a good point but based on
wrong assumptions. Asian Values for us is not about race. We
reach out to everyone in Asia. I say, leave the West to destroy
itself with its wrong-headed muddle of ideas about being free.
Look at all their crime and poverty and problems with drugs,
their teenage pregnancies and homelessness and AIDS. Some
foolish Asians choose to live by Western values. They prefer
McDonald's and Coca-Cola to their own tasty Asian food and
call that progress. They think that American movies, pushing sex
and violence and body worship, are freedom of expression. That
they, little individuals that they are, are more important than
their families or community. They want to sexualise our children and make our women as aggressive as men, all in the name
of being modern.'

'Look at the Spice Girls,' a young AVA follower spoke up.

Everyone shook their heads and tutted. Fei shifted in irritation. Siew's statements were simplistic and blinkered by
prejudice. But she said nothing.

'Such foolish Asians are deceived by the propaganda of the
West. They're yellow on the outside, white on the inside – like
bananas. They don't know who they are or where they belong,'
Siew went on. 'Asian Values is a state of mind. They are
universal values – love your family and community, work hard,
respect your elders and betters, don't waste anything, live a
healthy life. Whites can uphold and live by the values we impart

as well as any Asian person. It's a question of whether they want to or not. Dr Wyndham, for example, is a valued member of our community.'

'Ginny isn't an AVA member, is she?' Fei blurted out.

Ben Chang glanced at her, startled, then looked away. Siew turned his penetrating gaze on her. Fei realised she had spoken against form. She had not been introduced to him, let alone the group. She was acutely aware of her alien female presence among them. Siew replied graciously, 'No, she is not. But the Alliance judges the spirit of a person's actions.'

'Well said.'

'Very wise.'

The elite around the table murmured their approval. Siew's young acolytes gently applauded. Ben seemed to rouse himself and nodded. He kept his eyes fixed on his glass of beer.

Siew kept his gaze on Fei. 'You are . . .'

Mei-Hong leapt up, flustered. 'Brother-Elder Siew, I'm so sorry, please excuse my rudeness. This is Miss Qwong Fei-Li, she is the lawyer for the Centre.'

Fei stood up and shook Siew's hand while he remained seated. She felt like a child again, made to meet an important grown up. Siew said, 'I have heard of your good work for the Centre. You've done well to bring your clients through all the legal processes.'

'Thank you, Mr Siew.' Fei blushed in spite of herself. He had the manner of an emperor bestowing his favour on her, she thought, and somehow it carried her along. She glanced round the table at each of the VIPs: at least Siew's plug was good for her profile.

'You're a partner in your own firm?' he said.

'Ming, Siap & Qwong.' Fei beamed and presented him her card with both hands, Asian-style.

'You must be a remarkable woman.'

'You're very kind.'

'It's a pity you have had to sacrifice so much for your achievements.'

Fei stared. 'What do you mean?'

He smiled paternally. 'Forgive me for saying so, but your feminine qualities – charm, modesty, family-mindedness, home-making, lovingness. You've had to give all those up to succeed in the aggressive, masculine world of business and money, haven't you?'

'Not at all!' Fei could hardly believe what she had heard. Her earlier irritation turned to anger.

Siew looked at Mei-Hong who took the cue. 'Brother-Elder Siew is only concerned for your happiness. We are not backward-looking. The AVA believes women are equal to men-lah but we have our special role to play just as men have theirs. Of course, we women should fulfil our potential, whether it's making a home for our families or going to work. But there are certain jobs more suitable to us women-lah – like teaching and nursing where we can use our caring skills. And public relations, charity work, some types of sales . . .'

'A pretty woman with a gentle voice, nice manner – we all want to see her and listen to her,' another AVA follower chimed in. 'She can sell anything to me-lah.'

The men laughed deep, manly laughs. Fei felt her hackles shoot up.

Mei-Hong went on. 'But business and finance it's better to leave to the men, they know how to fight and argue. It's like battle-lah, men are stronger – better at it.'

Siew put in, 'Asian Values brings together the best of all the great teachers of the world's religions and philosophies. We want society to be a happy place where each person belongs and has a special part to play.'

Fei couldn't stay silent and polite any more. 'I've never heard such rubbish! You men want the biggest share of everything – power, money, respect, the best-paid jobs. That's what this is really about. You treat women like children and keep them poor, uneducated and powerless so you won't have to face any competition. You can dress it up in nice words but it's still the same old selfish bigotry by another name.'

Mei-Hong looked shocked. Silence lay like lead across the table. The men stared at Fei with stony, affronted eyes. Ben turned to look at her. He seemed to take her in for the first time. Fei felt a pang of horror. She had offended some of the most important guests of her clients and sullied her own good image in their eyes. All because her pride wouldn't let her keep her opinions to herself. But the arrogance and contempt in what she had heard infuriated her.

Siew's lip curled, as if she had just proved everything he had said. 'You're not married, Miss Qwong?'

'No.' Fei bit back her anger.

'There, you see what you have lost because of your ambition. Be more gentle and sweet and maybe a good man will want to marry you and make you a proper woman. You know, in Chinese tradition, you can never be a woman until you are married.'

Fuck tradition! Fei wanted to snap back. How dare he presume to comment on who she was and how she chose to live? She didn't need his pity for all the offers of marriage *she* had turned down. She didn't need to be made a woman by any man. She was a woman here and now and proud of it. Her blood boiled. But she said nothing. There was no point. She would never win any ground in this gathering, especially when the only other woman there seemed to parrot everything Siew taught.

Feeling sick inside, she decided to go for damage limitation. 'I apologise for my outburst. I will think on what you have said. Thank you, Mr Siew.'

After all, she told herself, he was an important figure in Asia – as were the other men at the table. There was no point in making enemies where she could make friends. Fei realised she was still standing. She returned to her chair, aware of Siew watching her. She flashed him her most sincere and respectful smile.

———⊶●⊰———

Han crouched in the undergrowth. His painstaking progress had taken him most of the way round the landward side of the

Centre. He had seen no easy area of penetration through the double fencing and CCTV circuit.

Raul's voice came over the channel. His relaxed manner was deceptive, Han knew. 'There's that white man – he's come up before. Hair used to be longer and he was bearded that last time. But it's the same guy.' Han felt a prickle of excitement. At last, something that might vindicate this operation.

Inside the van, several miles away, Raul made the camera track the white man through movements of the joy-stick control. He was moving away from the lawn and up the slope towards the headland. He seemed casual but occasionally cast quick glances around him. He took photographs of the views his ascent was opening up to him on all sides. Raul described it all to Han, speaking into the mike. 'The same journalist from Hong Kong.'

Han's murmur came back to him. 'He was hunting a contact with the AVA director there.'

'He's here today. Siew is here today. Coincidence?'

Raul pulled the camera back into a wide-angle shot. He panned up to the headland and zoomed in again. The terrain was densely covered in trees. He described what he saw in a practised patter. A path edged with rocks cut along the southern side of the promontory. Here the grass had been mowed. The path led to closed gates in double wire-mesh fencing, twice the height of a man. He could make out the words 'Secure Unit' on a sign on the outer gate. The fencing ran along the width of the headland, cutting it off from the rest of the grounds. Deep inside the secure section, Raul could make out a low building under cover of trees. To the north, boulders pushed out of the long *lalang* grass and undergrowth, the terrain clearly impassable. The white man's figure came into view, out of focus. His image sharpened as he moved along the path towards the building, back to the camera.

'What's he looking for?' Han said.

'Just snooping. Like we would do if we'd got inside.'

'You think he's a spook?'

'Maybe.' Raul saw the security guards before the white man

did. He talked Han through it. Two men were coming up behind and grabbing the journalist's arms. The white man struggled but there were two more guards ahead of him, coming from the trees. Another man appeared, a senior security official. He took charge and began to question the white man, who was all smiles and shrugs as if he hadn't realised he'd been trespassing. He handed over what looked like a passport and a press card.

At a nod from their boss, one of the guards took the camera from the white man and pulled out the spool of film, tossing it to the ground. The white man made a show of protesting.

'He doesn't seem too bothered about losing his film,' Raul mused.

The guards began to frogmarch the man away from the headland.

Han worked his way back towards the main gate. He moved as quickly and as noisily as he dared, keeping an eye alert for the CCTV cameras in the trees.

'Look at Singapore,' Siew declared. 'In the thirty years since Independence, it transformed itself from a little-known mosquito-infested backwater into the financial hub of South East Asia. Everyone now has a place to live and good health. Every household has a television set. There's little crime, the streets are clean, there's virtually one hundred per cent literacy. Singapore is what the whole of Asia can become. Singapore is the future. The West criticise and ridicule Singapore – why? Because they envy it.'

'They envy all of Asia,' a Thai businessman said. 'But they also call us "the tigers". It's a mix of respect and fear.'

A rumble of consensus. The discussion had widened around the table, with the older men airing their views and the younger ones listening. Mei-Hong sat silent as was appropriate for a woman. Fei could not bring herself to leave, held as if by a strange fascination. Their talk of the rise of Asia touched a chord within her – echoed much of what she hoped for her own career, excited her with its bold ambitions and its confidence in the ability of Asians to better themselves. Their concerns about crime, prostitution, drug-taking and violence were the concerns of every citizen. Between them they painted a picture of Asia in stark contrast to Singapore – thronging in chaos and un-controlled energy for the lack of strong morals. It was as if a single mind had been divided, Siew said, by the conflict between old and new. Change was happening too fast and Asia's spirit was struggling to meet the future even while its body seemed one. In a world where you could suddenly have everything, he said, you could destroy yourself in the glut of excess.

In an age of rapid progress, there were those who were being left behind – in their frustration, they were turning to robbery and rape to get what they wanted, a Filipino busi-nessman said. The young were shunning the old religions, an Indonesian man said, they chased only money and their own selfish desires. Computers were changing the workplace and how people related to each other, the old family and social ties breaking down because of modern employment patterns, a Malay millionaire added. They were looking at an Asia that might yet go the way of the West, losing all the ground they had gained and spiralling into degeneracy, alienation and disintegration.

'Asian Values has the power to make us all one,' Siew said. 'One mind, one spirit, one body.'

The rising fervour made Fei uneasy. These men were not all AVA members but as Siew guided them through his phil-osophies with so light a touch that none saw his manipulating hand at work, the talk grew more inflamed and intense.

'We are entering the Age of Asia,' he said. 'And we must be ready to take the lead. Ahead of China, ahead of Hong Kong and India and Pakistan, we in South East Asia, we will take the helm through the new millennium.'

His evangelical manner held his listeners in thrall. He spoke with the control and style of a master. Fei remembered a profile of him she had read in a magazine. He had once been a fervent 'born–again' Christian in Sydney, where he had grown up, the only child of a Chinese father and white Australian mother. He had formed an Asian youth group in a stand against racial harassment from the whites in post–war Australia. It had been transformed into the AVA in his thirties as he had begun to make his first millions in the lighting industry. He had then settled in Singapore. His company was now a global player in utilities, infrastructure and property development, his personal assets worth billions of *ringgit*. The Alliance he led now encompassed hundreds of thousands of members across Asia, with branches springing up in Australia, New Zealand, North America and Europe where there were pockets of Asian immigrants.

There was an energy about Siew that was impressive. Fei knew that his family had not been wealthy in his youth. His father had been a teacher but had not worked after racist bullying had broken his mental health. His mother had supported them by nursing. Siew's success had bought his parents a huge estate outside Sydney, bodyguards and round–the–clock care in their old age. He embodied for Asians the single–mindedness and hard work that carved out wealth, power and influence as if from nothing. In spite of herself, Fei felt admiration for all he had achieved. Listening to the AVA President at first hand, it struck her that this was not a movement of dorks and sad cases as her friends liked to think. They were potentially a powerful and influential force across Asia – and the world – whose energy and drive could mould the future of the region.

But as Fei tried to picture the new order that Siew was conjuring, she felt a cold uneasiness. He talked of a society ordered by an ancient hierarchy of elder before younger, men before women, senior before junior, collective before individual; men in the workplace, women in the home; worthy and wholesome books, movies and plays to entertain the educated masses; a world that was crime–free, drug–free, dissent–free; a society of good citizens and model humanity.

It'll never work, she wanted to say. Such naivety was almost laughable. It was as if the AVA had taken the basic

ideas of decent, human values and somehow stretched them
to their logical, literal conclusion. These were not Asian values
as most people in Asia would understand them, Fei thought.
But instead an extremist tract for a paradise on earth that
would be impossible to achieve in the real world, given the fail-
ings of human nature. And yet here were educated, grown men
falling under Siew's spell, nodding along to his idealistic statements, adding their more and more clamorous agreement to
each point.

'Asian Values can be part of our children's education. Then
they'll learn from young the right values, the right way to live.'
An official thumped the table to enthusiastic acclaim.

'Children are our future.' Siew looked at Ben Chang. 'Eh,
Ben? You've been very quiet. What do you say?'

The doctor blinked and stammered, 'Y-yes, children – they
are the key.' But he looked strained and sick.

Siew turned to the group. 'Ben is my star. I chose him out of
hundreds of bright youngsters many years ago. Now look at
him: a young man with a great future here in the Centre.
Soon he will run the new associate centre they'll be setting up
in KL. By then he is likely to have a very senior role in the
Alliance too.'

Ben seemed embarrassed. 'I don't know . . .'

'Don't be so modest.' It was a command. The younger man
flinched. There was a hard edge to Siew's words now. 'Of course
you can do it all. I have put my trust in you. You won't let me
down, I know it.'

Ben managed a weak smile. Fei watched the exchange curiously.

An aide strode up and whispered in Siew's ear. Siew excused
himself. 'A phone call,' he said. But as he walked away, talking
to the aide, Fei saw Piers in the distance coming to meet them.
A security guard was with him – she guessed from his manner
and the style of his uniform that he was a senior officer. They
clustered together, an air of tension about them even though
they were evidently trying to appear casual.

Fei squinted in the bright light. What had happened?

Han hastened his retreat out of range of the tree-mounted CCTV cameras. But as he moved down the slope, the sudden crashing of bodies through the undergrowth told him the Centre's security teams were on to him. Han swore. No time to think about the white man now. He must have been caught on one of the cameras in spite of his caution.

Han picked up his pace, letting the downhill momentum take his feet. Behind him, figures fanned out to intercept him down the slope. He changed direction, stumbling on treacherous roots and ferns underfoot.

They were gaining on him. Han pushed through the trees, his vision blinded by branches and the flashing of shadow and light through the leaves. The road, there, winding down the hill towards the mangrove delta. He leapt the last few feet down, landing heavily. A shout behind him. He took the width of the tarmac in two strides and was back under cover of the trees. The slope here was steeper than he had anticipated and he fell, skidding the length of the wooded stretch to thud on to the tarmac below. He was badly winded but heaved himself across. He slid down the next slope into the muddy soil at the edge of the swamp. Gasping, he dragged himself under the cover of mangrove, groping for his Beretta. He held it above the surface as he submerged himself neck-deep into the water. The air roots of the trees weaved about his legs and groin like eels. He suppressed the urge to beat them off.

Clinging to the trunk of a mangrove tree, he worked to control his breathing as six or seven figures thundered out on to the road. They charged about for a few minutes. He slipped into shadow, cursing under his breath. He expected professionalism from his partner and perfection from himself. Now the spectre of failure kicked him in the guts. Bad karma had dogged this whole operation, twisting each development out of his control, almost as if his target was laughing in his face.

He shook himself mentally. Anger had no place on the job.

He swam cautiously into the swamp, away from the road. The guards began to make their way back up the hill, radios squawking. He would have to make it back to the van via a detour.

Chapter Three

Sam had joined the men playing *sepak takraw* in the garden. Fei could see them from where she stood on the verandah outside her mother's kitchen. Mrs Qwong lived in a Malay-style wooden house in Titiwangsa, an old residential neighbourhood in north KL. Fei had come up with Sam that morning to spend the day with the family. A compound of grass and bougainvillaea fronted the house and Johnny, Fei's brother, had set up their old badminton court for the game. Her mother and sisters were busy laying out tables and chairs for dinner in the garden. Some friends and neighbours had already arrived with their 'pot luck' offerings of curry, spicy fried chicken and sweet *kueh*. Mrs Qwong was fussing over the spread of food, enjoying the bustle and laughter.

The late-afternoon sun cast the day in turmeric. Beyond the neighbouring houses, the ridges of the Titiwangsa hills shimmered in the heat. The turret of a mosque gleamed in the distance, overlaid by palm trees curving out above the rooftops. The air was hot and still. Fei waved an ink-dot midge away. She did not know how Sam found the energy to play the ball game.

Sepak takraw was similar to volleyball but instead of their hands, players used bare feet and heads to pass the rattan ball. Johnny played on one team with two other men. Sam was on the other, her slender figure modestly clad in tracksuit bottoms while the men played in shorts. She was slight for a Caucasian, her black hair tied back more bunny-tail than pigtail. Her movements were swift and balletic, the prime skills of the game.

Seeing Sam's exhilaration and skill, Fei forgot the difficulties between them – the tension on the drive up, the long silences, the way they didn't meet each other's eyes. She found herself staring as if hypnotised. Sam was swifter than the men and took shots they had not thought possible, tapping the ball over the net with her foot as she flicked herself sideways and up off the ground. This round, the ball stayed in the air for almost two minutes, shuttling between the players, sustained only by their precision and daring. Sam's team finally scored with a hit just out of reach of their opponents.

Fei laughed out loud, applauding, unable to take her eyes off Sam. Her mother and the others glanced round.

'Fierce shot, man!' Johnny cried.

The game erupted into laughter. Sam exchanged banter with the men in Malay, her voice soaring above their deeper pitch. Her team slapped her high-fives, whistling. The party on the lawn turned to see the cause of the excitement.

Sam broke away from the court. She flew up the steps, grabbing Fei and spinning her with the momentum. Sam was damp with sweat, her eyes bright. Her laughter swooped around Fei. She smelt of milky musk and vanilla. Fei found herself drawing into Sam's hold, longing to nuzzle into the hollow just beneath her ear. It was so natural to her, a familiar moment from a long time ago. They had been so easy with each other in London, touching as they moved around the kitchen preparing a meal or curling arms around each other while out with friends. Fei had not been afraid then and for a heartbeat now, forgot where she was and succumbed to the intimacy they had almost lost.

Sam bent her head towards her and their foreheads touched.

Fei pulled away. The heat of the afternoon; the men's voices in the garden; her mother and their neighbours turning round to glance at them. Her sisters – Anita and Kit – pausing with bowls of curry in their hands. They crowded in on her. Fei pushed Sam from her. 'Well played,' she said.

She saw Sam's look of hurt before she turned away. Fei stared at the floor. She heard Sam move slowly down the steps.

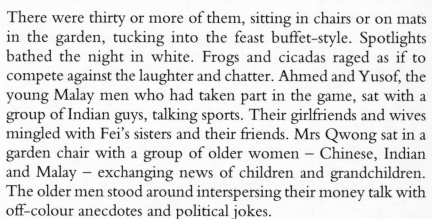

There were thirty or more of them, sitting in chairs or on mats in the garden, tucking into the feast buffet-style. Spotlights bathed the night in white. Frogs and cicadas raged as if to compete against the laughter and chatter. Ahmed and Yusof, the young Malay men who had taken part in the game, sat with a group of Indian guys, talking sports. Their girlfriends and wives mingled with Fei's sisters and their friends. Mrs Qwong sat in a garden chair with a group of older women – Chinese, Indian and Malay – exchanging news of children and grandchildren. The older men stood around interspersing their money talk with off-colour anecdotes and political jokes.

Her father would have been so happy, Fei thought. She pictured him here tonight, presiding over it all from his favourite rocking chair. She sat on the steps with Sam and a couple of Kit-Li's friends. Her brother Johnny sprawled on the grass in front of them, his boisterous friends beside him. They all balanced plates piled high with food, swigging beers. Johnny was joshing Sam that the English were too clumsy to play *sepak takraw* well. She was holding her own, their banter steeped in affection. Sometimes, Fei thought, Johnny seemed to get on better with Sam than he did with her.

Their father had died when she had been twelve, wasted away with cancer. The family had found a savings account book, written over in his shaky scrawl: 'Fei-Li's education fund'. In it had been ten thousand *ringgit*, money that might have given him a few months' more treatment. Ever since she had been four, he had said, 'You're going to Oxford University, the best in the world!' He had risen no higher than senior accounts clerk in the local authority in all his working life, her mother supplementing the family income by working as a teacher. He had always talked of his children as their hope for the future, of Fei-Li as the one who would make it for all of them.

She had won a scholarship to Oxford but the award had only

covered the fees. Her father's savings had helped but after conversion into sterling had not been enough. Her family had had to meet her living expenses. Johnny had left school at sixteen to work in the construction business so she could take up her place. Her mother had tutored Maths privately after school and at weekends. Even her two younger sisters had worked at Saturday jobs to bring in extra cash.

'I'm no good at books,' Johnny had said to Fei at the airport. 'It was easy for me to go and work. Don't cry. You are meant for something better-lah. You can have the good life for all of us.'

And when she had had to put in capital for her share in the partnership of Ming, Siap & Qwong, her mother had mortgaged the family home and Johnny had taken out loans to cover the amount.

They had made her father's hope a reality and it was an obligation that still bound her to them. She had repaid each of them in money many times over by now. Had set Johnny up in his own construction business; seen her sisters through university; given her mother a huge allowance; paid off their mortgages; still gave them money at every opportunity. But it seemed to her that she would always carry the debt. She owed it to her father and to her family never to fail them.

After four years of living with Sam, going on holidays with Sam, visiting her family with Sam, doing everything together with Sam, Fei realised that her family knew the real nature of her relationship with her 'friend'. In their own way, they let her know their feelings about Sam – making her welcome in their home, always including her in everything they did with Fei, treating her in all but name as Fei's partner. But they never spoke of it and Fei did not force the issue. Words did not always tell the truth, she told herself, so what was the need for them to hold down what was already known?

Among this group of friends lounging round the steps, she felt at ease. These men and women were all in their thirties, with careers and their own businesses, too involved in the buzz of life to make judgements on others' personal preferences. There was a vigour and an air of enjoyment about them that was generous and all-encompassing. There were Chinese, Malays and Indians among them, all speaking the common language of thirty-somethings: the difficulties of juggling work with personal lives.

But Fei remembered in spite of herself that beyond this cosy night there was a reality that was darker. To most Asians, homosexuality was a disease and, when manifested in men, a sign of criminal insanity. It was a social evil more shameful than paedophilia and a corruption thought to threaten the equilibrium of society. Fei knew of lesbians who had lost their jobs when outed – maliciously by a colleague, or inadvertently overheard on the phone to a lover or seen kissing at a private party. Men had been imprisoned for their private sexual conduct. Across Asia, there were stories of harassment and abuse, assaults and death threats. One woman had been raped by her boyfriend when she had tried to end the relationship because of her feelings for another woman. He had never been charged. A lesbian couple had been dragged through the courts in a rural part of the region on a succession of trumped-up charges, their intimate conduct gone over again and again in minute detail. A father had beaten his son to death rather than live with the shame of the boy's sexuality.

Fei and Sam had lived together in London, openly a couple to friends and colleagues. Now, they had to choose their close friends with care, ferreting out the underground homosexual community with painstaking discretion. A password, changed every month, let them into private gatherings where women could dance with women and men could touch other men. But these were not always safe. Word would get out, rumour circulate and the authorities sometimes acted on a tip-off.

Fei remembered a raid in the back functions room of a club. Even now, two years on, she felt sick with fear thinking about it.

A bell had gone off over the music, a warning from the front desk. There had been a scramble, lawyers, accountants and other professionals all jostling in the confined space. At first she stood frozen in Sam's arms, both of them not knowing what was happening. The room did not empty, there was no time.

Suddenly a gay man, an Indian doctor, grabbed her. She just had time to see his partner, a Chinese architect, pull Sam in front of him as the police burst through the door.

And there they were, men dancing with women, shuffling from foot to foot to the blasting music. The regulars looked up in a semblance of surprise, their safety riding on the fragile roles they played. Fei did not glance at Sam, the blood ringing in her ears, her mouth parched. She could hardly breathe. Someone turned off the music and in the terrible silence the police officers stalked the room, staring into each face as if to find the mark of their evil. A small man glared at Fei, lips thin, eyes filled with cold loathing. She held his gaze, terror churning in her gut.

There was no evidence of criminal behaviour and the police grudgingly left.

As the music blared again, Fei had vomited in a toilet at the back of the club.

'Hey, Anita!' Sam now saw Fei's youngest sister at the buffet table. She waved her over before Fei could stop her. Mrs Qwong had been nagging Fei to speak to Anita for weeks. 'Nothing is good enough for her now she got that new boyfriend,' Fei's mother had wailed. 'She look down on me, she tell us we live our life all wrong. She always talking back, so rude to me, her own mother. If your father was still alive, he wouldn't let her get away with such things. Talk to her-lah, Fei.'

Fei was tired of being the heavy in the family. She had been avoiding Anita all evening. Besides, she knew that if she got involved, it would only make her sister worse. They had never talked about it but Fei knew that Anita, of all her family, found her relationship with Sam distasteful.

But Sam seemed determined to make friends with her sister in spite of Anita's obvious antipathy.

Reluctantly, Anita joined their group around the steps with her boyfriend Jackson. He was a gawky young man with a *kwai chai* haircut – that unimaginative forties schoolboy style favoured by 'good boys' in their mid-twenties. As he sat on the grass, slipping a napkin under him, an icon on his collar flashed in the spotlight. The AVA logo.

Johnny's friend, Yeow, was talking about starting a family with his wife Sally. 'It's going to be tough-lah, with both of us working. We can't depend on our folks, they all getting old. And baby *amahs* are expensive nowadays . . .'

'You got to be careful if you get these import maids,' Jackson cut in. 'From Philippines or Indonesia? You make sure the contract says they don't leave the house.'

'What do you mean?'

'You mustn't let them leave the house by themselves. Don't give them the day off.' There was an urgency in Jackson's voice.

Yeow said, 'Once a week on Sundays is the normal thing, isn't it?'

'Not with these ones. Ask the agencies to make sure. You let the maids go out and they fall into bad company – get pregnant, get into drugs. They bring home their bad-hat boyfriends into your house when you're not there. Your kids will suffer, you will suffer. It's better not to risk it, man.'

The group stared at him in stunned silence. Fei could not believe what she had just heard. Someone coughed. In London, there would have been a chorus of voices taking issue but here, Fei knew, no one wanted to be rude. She glanced tensely at Sam. Johnny tried to change the subject.

Anita came to Jackson's defence. 'You would only be protecting her for her own good, isn't it?'

Sam said, 'You can't just lock someone up like that. Especially if they haven't done anything wrong. These women are human beings, too.'

Jackson turned to her as if she were a child. 'Of course, *you* would say that as a white. You don't understand Asian ways. We want a safe and clean environment for our children. If these people want to come and work here, they have to behave properly.'

'But domestic servants have a right to their own liberty. They're not your slaves!'

Jackson clucked like an old man. 'It's in their contracts. They agree to it so they do have a choice. We're not fascists, you know.'

Sam's voice was rising in outrage. 'But the balance of bargaining power is such that they have no real choice. Their own financial situation . . . unemployment in Indonesia . . .' She turned to Fei, eyes blazing. 'Will you explain the whole "unfair contracts" thing?'

Anita was glaring at Sam and Fei, her lips hard with fury and panic. Fei felt the hatred gore into her. Ever since Jackson, Anita's coolness to her and Sam had been fuelled into active dislike. It struck Fei now that Jackson had not picked up on her relationship with Sam in all this time. Anita would probably never tell him and nor would the rest of the family. Fei stared at her sister and saw the pleading behind her eyes. She did not want to be tainted with Fei's corruption in Jackson's view. The realisation crawled up Fei's spine. If Jackson knew about Fei, he would dump Anita — and probably do everything in his power to ruin them all.

She said brightly, 'Anyone want some more curry?'

Sam's face froze. A mask of cold anger shut Fei out. She turned away.

Jackson's lips curled in triumph. He said, 'We Asians try to prevent evil, we don't invite it into our homes as you Westerners like to do.'

'What right have you to control another person by force, however you rationalise it? Such arrogance is what real evil is!' Sam cried.

Jackson shrugged and looked around as if to say: What a mad woman. Anita stood up and grabbed his hand. As she led him away, she beamed at him. 'Come and meet some other people . . .'

Behind his back, she threw a glare of loathing at Fei.

———⟫●⟪———

N-Sat was the first channel to broadcast the item in its prime-time evening news: an attempted assassination attempt at the Wyndham Centre inauguration ceremony during what was thought to have been a staged diversion. The newsreader said, 'An American purporting to be a journalist distracted security guards while an unidentified gunman hid in the woods outside the Centre.' A blurred photograph of Carson Dean printed from the Centre's security cameras at the main gate flashed up.

'Tight security around the Centre thwarted the gunman. He was pursued from the scene by guards. The chase was captured by security cameras.' Footage of a man running through the trees flashed up, time and date counters running in the corner. The viewpoints changed as each new camera picked him up. His face was darkened and unclear. There were few distinguishing features on his black outfit. He was carrying what looked like a rifle. 'The gunman remains at large and is believed to be very dangerous. If they sight him, members of the public are advised not to approach him but to call the police immediately.'

An AVA spokesman was interviewed. 'It is highly likely that the target was Mr Siew Kei-Win, our President. There have been a number of death threats against him. We believe that the gunman is part of or hired by anti-Asian elements. The Wyndham Centre is a flagship of Asian achievement. The choice of time and place for this attempt was not accidental. These anti-Asian elements want to see the downfall of not just the Alliance but all Asian successes.'

A relaxed Siew spoke confidently on camera. 'I am only one member of the AVA. If I'm no longer here, there are thousands more who will step into my place. We stand for Asian Values, and Asian Values are what make our societies healthy, strong and ordered. Our enemies are those who want to destroy Asian Values because they are trying to destroy our societies.'

Cut to a security expert who had analysed the film. 'We see him first when he triggers the off-fence camera – here. He's moving in classic style for covert action in this terrain. Then he's running – fast, assured, tactical. Obviously in peak physical condition.' The expert declared that the intruder was probably a member of the army or security forces.

Sam and Fei were watching the news at home in Fei's condo. They had been tense with each other for a few days, ever since the argument with Jackson. Sam had accused Fei of never standing up for her principles. Fei had accused Sam of fighting battles for the sake of it. *You can never win against people like that so why waste your energy?* Sam had refused to speak to her after that.

They had negotiated a truce of sorts, more from having to live together than any conscious effort. They were managing civilities this evening. It was a kind of progress. Shocked by the news bulletin, Sam made to take Fei's hand. 'This happened while you were there?'

She sat forward out of Sam's reach, her eyes on the set. 'My God, that was what called Siew away.'

Sam moved so that she could put a hand on Fei's back. Concern and relief made her want to touch Fei. For the first time in a while, she felt the simplicity of her true feelings. Faced with the knowledge that Fei might have been in danger, every-thing else seemed burned away. Only the steadfast reality remained. She loved Fei and wanted her safe, did not know what she would do if anything happened to her. Nothing else seemed real – not the arguments and frustrations and silences, not the difficulties and half-expressed emotions, not the long tiring struggle of the last year. Maybe they could forget all that and start again, in the next moment embrace each other as they used to, and then somehow start talking as they once knew how to do.

But Fei stood up suddenly and went to the phone. Sam's hand fell to the cushions. She stared after Fei, hurt and confusion stirred up again. Why hadn't she turned round? Acknowledged Sam. Seen her concern. Who was she calling? Who so pre-occupied her mind at this crucial moment?

Fei's voice was soft and intimate when her call was answered. She had her back to Sam. 'Are you all right? – Yes, I saw the item – I can't quite believe it – do you know who – no, not yet, huh? – I just wanted to check that you were all right.'

Pain gripped Sam. Seemed to squeeze the life from her. There was someone else. Had been for – how long now? How had she not known it? Fei telling her that Ginny Wyndham had wanted her at the Centre the day before the ceremony, to stay the night. Fei always meeting Ginny for a meal or for drinks, talking on the phone for ages like the best of friends. Best of friends . . . As Sam and Fei were supposed to be 'best of friends'. She might have laughed had she not felt so sick.

'Nothing happened between us.' Fei did not know how many more times she could repeat that phrase.

Sam was stalking the room like a wounded cat. She would not let Fei near her. Her eyes were dark with pain and suspicion. Then, suddenly, she stopped.

She seemed to collapse inside. Staring at Fei across the distance of the room, she slumped, beaten. 'Maybe I don't care if anything happened. Maybe this is just the excuse that we need.'

'What do you mean?' Fei's heart was pounding. Her life was unravelling. She had been stupid: in her concern for Ginny, she had not seen Sam's concern for her. She didn't know what she felt for Ginny. Hadn't wanted to come too close to that. But it was undeniable that being with Ginny had always been fun, charged with something more than simple friendship. She enjoyed herself too much, laughed too much, talked too much, played the fool too much. It had been a change from all the difficulties with Sam, a respite. A relief. And now – what?

'Ever since you've been back in Malaysia, you've changed,' Sam said. 'Your career and making money are all you think about. Everything has to give way to your work – our holiday plans, evenings we might have spent together. You hide me away from your life out there. What's the point of going on pretending we have a relationship?'

Hurt turned to anger at the injustice of Sam's words. Fei said, 'You used to like my ambition. You called it drive and determination then. I thought you understood? I'm not the only one in the equation – I have a duty to my family . . .'

'They're all adults and capable of looking after themselves. Besides, you told me yourself, you've given them back everything and more.'

'. . . a duty to my father. Don't you see? I have to fit in to make a success of our lives. I need to belong. This is my home and I want to be a part of it.'

'And belonging means making money at all costs?'

'I want to make the most of my life – is that so wrong? What is this thing you have against money? Whenever I've talked to you about investments and stocks, you behave as if I'm trying to steal your soul. It's only making the most of your savings!'

Sam laughed bitterly. 'You used to think that was integrity and you loved me for it. "I love your passion," you used to say. "You're not afraid to fight for what you think is right." You used to admire that. Now, I'm an embarrassment at parties.'

Fei said nothing.

Sam went on, '*I* want to make the most of my life, too. I thought we could make the most of it together. But somehow the things we used to love about each other are ugly and hateful now. I feel as if I've been losing you moment by moment. I thought I could hold on but the more I tried, the more I said or did, the more you slipped away from me. I know everything there is to know about you – I know how much you need to belong and how much you want to prove yourself to your family. But my heart still hurts too much because, in all of that, you leave me out. I can't hammer away anymore to be let in. I can't go on anymore. Fighting, not talking, making up . . . and then it starts all over again.'

'What are you saying?' After months of baiting each other with inconsequentials they had come at last to the real issues. Fei felt cold horror. Had she meant to bring them to this all along?

'I don't know. I gave up my job, my flat – everything. I moved to Malaysia because of *you*.'

'Don't you think I know that?' Fei cried. They were talking to each other at last. The confusion of pain and frustration was unbearable. 'You gave up everything because I asked you to.

I've repeated that like a mantra this last year as if it might save us. But it's turned into a curse.'

Sam said, 'I can't be the good consort you'd like me to be, making superficial chat at dinner parties. I can't drum up an interest in share markets and finance. I can't shut up when I meet arrogance and nastiness. Someone has to speak up. How else can you change what's wrong?'

'Why does it have to be you that changes the world?'

'Someone has to stand up . . .'

'Yes, but why you!'

'Why *not* me?'

They stared at each other across the floor.

A band seemed to tighten Fei's throat. 'I don't have the courage you'd like me to have. I've let you down so many times and I know I'll let you down again. I can't fight the battles you want me to fight. And perhaps I shouldn't expect you to jump into my warzone of money-making and business. I just want to go on quietly, fitting in, being moderately successful – ordinary ambitions like everyone else's. It's not the same for you. You need the light, you need to be bold and fill every corner of your life. You don't have everything to lose. There's always London for you. This is my home.'

Fei sat in the living room as Sam put a few things together in a tote bag. The programme after the news focused on the forest fires raging in Indonesia. They had been lit over the last months to clear land for development and agricultural use. But in the unusually dry, hot season resulting from the El Niño effect, the undergrowth had been like a tinderbox. The fires now burned ferociously across Sumatra, destroying villages in their path, fanned by warm winds and devouring more and more pristine jungle. Plumes of smoke rose out of the rainforests, filmed from a helicopter. On the ground, smog drifted across a blasted landscape as the reporter picked his way through charred logs and blackened tree stumps. Fei felt as if she was watching a projection of her emotions on the screen.

Sam stood by the door with her things. Fei moved towards

her. Was this what it felt like after a terrible disaster? They did not touch. She said, 'Where will you stay?'

'I called Jean and Paul. They said I could go over.' Jean was a lesbian who had married Paul Wee, a gay man, for the sake of their families and reputations. Their partners had the apartment next to theirs, also masquerading as a happily married couple. 'I'll come back for my stuff when I've got a place of my own. In the next few weeks, hopefully . . .'

'No hurry,' Fei said as if in a dream.

Later, alone in the condominium, she wandered from room to room. She and Sam had done it up in a pre-war style with carved Indonesian furniture, timber floors and ceiling fans. Books and magazines were everywhere, photographs of the two of them, their friends and families sprawled across the walls. A mosquito net draped hazily over their bed even though up here, on the tenth floor, the apartment was insect-free. 'It's romantic, silly!' Sam had insisted, laughing as she had made Fei help her put it up.

Fei stood on the balcony for a long time, her heart tearing apart, oblivious to the sobs that shook her. Beyond, the stark spears of condominium blocks loomed over Bangsar. The nearest was still unfinished, cranes and scaffolding jagged against the sky. Within its skeletal frame, wires, concrete, rubble and steel frames hung like torn innards. A sheet of canvas hung across one face of it said: Happy View Luxury Condominiums. The irony made Fei laugh, coughing against her tears.

⟶➤●◀⟵

Over the next few weeks, the regional and international media picked up the N-Sat item on the attempted assassination of Siew Kei-Win. For the first time in decades, Asia was making a serious impact on world news reporting. Everyone was interested in the 'tiger' economies of Malaysia, Singapore, Indonesia and the rest of South East Asia. Asian tycoons were buying up businesses and properties in London, Vancouver, Queensland, the United

States. The world wanted to do business with Asia, cash in on the 'Asian miracle'. In Malaysia, prestige projects made the headlines: the Bakun dam development, the building of an administrative capital to outshine Washington DC; the race to complete KL's gleaming new international airport in time for the Commonwealth Games and ahead of Hong Kong's Chek Lap Kok; the creation of Cyberjaya, a city of the future and centre for the Multimedia Super Corridor.

The West's spin on Asia seemed to be a mixture of grudging admiration and sceptical reserve. There was much still to be done on human rights, the freedom of the press, individual liberties, they said. Sour grapes, Asian pundits retorted. And the debate began on Western ideals versus Asian values. Any Western commentator writing in the West in support of Asian values was often ridiculed as naive and blinded by the hype. An Asian speaking out for Western ideals was lambasted in Asia as a pawn of the West, corrupted and brainwashed by Western media. The accusations made by the AVA against 'anti-Asian elements' threw a firecracker into the hornet's nest.

Speculation exploded as to who or what organisation might have been behind the attempt on Siew's life. One theory was that it was the Americans – in particular, the CIA – intent on destabilising Asia and disposing of their fiercest critic in one blow. The involvement of the American seemed to support this until he was verified as a bona fide journalist working for a bona fide publication with no connections to any political or intelligence or para-military organisation. The police released him after brief questioning and issued a statement clearing his name.

Another rumour was that there was Asian involvement at government level, focusing on the 'security forces' reference made by the expert who had analysed the footage. The argument went that Asian governments were concerned by the influence of the AVA, considering the movement extremist and dangerous to the stability of the region. The Alliance was an unelected minority group and their vociferous call to their vision of an Asian Utopia alarmed many in the mainstream. Their increasingly successful recruitment, especially among the younger generation, was seen as potentially dangerous by the authorities, so the theorists said. There was talk of several Asian governments banning N–Sat broadcasts into their countries from the channel's transmitter in Hong Kong – on the basis that its bias had been seditious and an incitement against the authorities by implying government involvement in such a heinous crime. The AVA also seemed to be under threat for the bold statements it had made in that N–Sat broadcast.

'There won't be a ban,' Siew said to the AVA board at an emergency meeting. He was proved right in the following weeks. As he had gambled when devising the release of the footage to N–Sat, a station controlled by another high-ranking member of the Alliance, Asian values was too hot an issue to be threatened by any Asian country. He assured his colleagues, 'Any move to ban or censor or curb the Alliance in any way would bring into question the commitment of those authorities to Asian values and their pride in being Asian. The anti-Asian tag will find its way to anyone opposing the AVA. We are on the way to becoming untouchable because the Alliance is the icon of the best of Asian morals.'

'How close are we – or the police – to identifying the unknown man?' An AVA director spoke up.

'That is our one problem.' Siew's face was grim. The group had been tailed over the last few years by shadowy figures, junior members approached for information. Once, an infiltrator had got close to an AVA director based in Bangkok. Fortunately, the director's aide had become suspicious but the infiltrator had disappeared before they could swoop on him. Siew suspected government forces were keeping tabs on the Alliance, chasing up rumours of fraud, corruption and murder. But they would never pin anything on him or the movement, he would make sure of it. He was determined that, this time, he would win the skirmish and hopefully turn the war around. Taking the moral high ground, he was already beginning to gain the advantage. He said, 'This unknown man might not matter in the larger scheme of things.'

The next move was the definitive one, he thought, so long as Wyndham delivered on the experiment they were all waiting for. It would be both a preparation for the Final Phase and a public relations coup that would win him the following of all Asia.

Chapter Four

The safe house was an apartment above a coffee-shop over-looking Pudu market in Kuala Lumpur. In a bare room, the windows were shuttered against the early morning. The stale air was stifling. Han leant against a wall, tension coiling inside him. It had been over ten days since the operation at the Wyndham Centre.

The television and VCR were the only equipment visible in the room. Other electronic and insurgency hardware was stashed in hidden cubby-holes. On the table were maps and papers. The only other furniture was a few battered chairs. Raul sat by the table, his face expressionless. A low-wattage bulb cast a sickly light over the room.

Mokhtar sat in the only armchair, his face grim. He was a stocky Indonesian with a pencil moustache, in his late-fifties. Han clenched his jaw. They had fucked up and that was why Mokhtar had come in person from Jakarta. His Beretta nudged into his left hip in its concealed holster. He shifted to ease his weight off it.

Mokhtar flicked off the TV and VCR by remote. The tape had been playing clips of the N-Sat bulletin and the subsequent news and commentary that had flowed from it over recent days. He lit a *kretek* cigarette, its sweet aroma of cloves filling the stuffy room. 'The Suits are panicking.'

'They gave the job the green light.'

'Not an assassination attempt!'

'I was not carrying a rifle.'

'How do you explain the footage?'

'The image must've been doctored. We were not on a shoot-to-kill.'

Han and Mokhtar spoke in *Bahasa*, the Indonesian form of Malay. The older man studied Han through a haze of smoke. 'The Suits have their reputations to protect – they are answerable to the people. The Family does the work that the Suits need done outside the "conventional options" open to them. No one but a handful of men knows we exist. This fiasco has put Family business at risk.'

Frustration tightened in Han's gut. 'There are no identifying elements on that footage . . .'

Mokhtar cut across him. 'The image of an armed Family Snake is out there in millions of homes, whether or not the rifle was digitally superimposed. Siew is piecing it together – who we are, what we're after. Before long, the people on the streets will know. We can't risk exposure. This and the other bungled jobs have made the Suits jumpy.'

The Family net over the AVA had been cast four years ago. Snakes tailed senior AVA members across Asia, worked to get close to those targeted as likely key players. The snake was cunning and deadly, an apt name for the men and women who carried out the Family's work, Han thought. But the AVA had detected some of the Snakes, raising an outcry about harassment by sinister forces. This had heightened the Alliance's profile and added to it a cloak of martyrdom that only increased public sympathy. Two of the identified Snakes died subsequently, one in a suspicious fire at home and the other apparently knifed in a street mugging. The perpetrators had never so far been found. Another Snake had got close to an AVA director but been exposed by an unreliable informer. A tip-off that his cover was blown gave him enough time to disappear but the woman who had warned him was found a week later, raped and murdered in the back streets of Bangkok. Han felt a rush of impotent rage. Those Snakes had been his friends, the woman a bystander who had tried to help. And all the Suits cared about was their fucking reputations! It was almost as if they had been bought by Siew's spin.

Mokhtar went on, '*Bapa Tua* has reviewed the whole damn' thing at the request of the Suits.'

This was it, thought Han. He exchanged a look with Raul, his face impassive. Rage and humiliation cut him.

'The Old Man has decided to terminate.'

'Fucking . . .' Han shot away from the wall, biting back his words with an effort. He stood very still, every muscle coiled. His breathing was harsh as he mastered his temper.

Raul spoke for the first time. His voice was conversational but his dark eyes were intense. 'We've had a report that a key general in Myanmar has been replaced by a figure with close links to the Alliance. The general died after a sudden illness. You know of the other Alliance gains in influential positions – CEOs of media conglomerates resigning at the height of their careers in favour of AVA people, citing "personal reasons"; government officials dying in car crashes or from heart attacks to be replaced by those whom we later learn have AVA associations.'

Han interrupted, 'And what about the AVA links to the Red Tiger triad? The editor of *Asia Report* was slashed by gang members last year. We got information that he had been going to publish an investigative piece on suspect finance deals made by a leading AVA member in Indonesia. After that they never published, of course.'

'Nothing but speculation,' Mokhtar said. 'Not enough to get the handle on the AVA the Suits need. Siew and his organisation are gaining support and a respected profile now. They've got the Suits by their balls with their media war on Asian Values. They don't quite make the accusation direct but the message is there: shady government forces are trying to destroy Asian values. It's just the seed they want. The AVA want the current order in Asia to be seen as corrupt regimes and whipping boys of the West. You've just walked straight into their hands.'

Han scraped a chair across the floor and sat astride it, arms against its back. He cursed under his breath. He was determined to prove himself to the Family and each dead-end mocked his ambition. His frustration and anger intensified with each failure. 'Piers Wyndham is an AVA member . . .'

'That doesn't mean a thing. Many prominent public figures are members.'

'Yes, but the Wyndhams appeared on the scene eighteen months ago, apparently with no traceable history. The defences they put up round the Centre – para-military-style fencing with motion detectors, CCTV along the boundary and in a buffer zone beyond, highly trained security teams. As for sea access: I used a fishing trawler for cover and checked out the bay. There's a string of buoys set up to trigger an electronic warning system. The moment we went through, a private security launch headed across to move us out. The personnel were armed . . . For a touchy-feely institution, it's fucking paranoid unless they've *really* got something to hide. Something's going on, goddammit! In the last few days we've been checking their financial dealings – all legit, but a disproportionate amount of their funding comes from AVA-associated corporations or individuals.'

Mokhtar interrupted. 'Being security-conscious is no crime and they have all the correct licences for their firearms. Besides, the AVA donates millions to charity every year. You're not trying to tell me Save the Children, Oxfam and the Red Cross are AVA puppets?'

Han spoke fast. 'That American – Carson Dean. Our checks place him in Hong Kong, Taiwan and Shanghai. This ties in with information from our Snakes there that he may have had dealings with AVA people in those locations. I reckon his pieces on the *Global Weekly News* are fronted by staff writers – they don't correlate with his known movements over the last two years. What's with the sudden interest in the Wyndhams now? Does he work for the American government? If so, what the hell are they after?'

'Our Snake in Beijing reported six months ago that a Caucasian couple was working on scientific experiments in Shanghai under the protection of the Red Tiger,' Raul added. 'We keep getting the same players, the same locations.'

'We don't know that those two whites were the Wyndhams.'

'We don't know that they were not.' Han was desperate. 'At least let me check it out – if only to eliminate that possibility?'

Mokhtar looked thoughtful. 'Two weeks ago news came in of Chinese interest in the Wyndham Centre at the highest level. An undercover approach was thought likely.'

'The Americans, the Chinese . . . Whatever they're after, we have to get hold of it first.' Han sat forward on his chair. 'The Old Man *can't* fucking terminate now.'

Mokhtar said in measured tones, 'If the Suits want to stay on top of the game, they need to hold whatever it is the Wyndhams have got, and they need to do that before the Americans or the Chinese or the Alliance get to it.' He seemed to come to a decision. 'I'll handle *Bapa Tua* if you keep tabs on the Wyndhams. Stay clear of the AVA – at least till the dust settles from this fiasco. A new angle of approach may be no bad thing. Focus on Dean: find out what he wants from the AVA. What is the US up to, stalking prominent Asian citizens and a successful Asian sanatorium?'

Raul added, 'Dean could be our lead into the Alliance, Han. We can't be seen checking out Siew but it would be legit for us to keep tabs on the American – and to find out what *he's* trying to find out.'

'Now we're talking.' Han grinned.

Mokhtar said, 'Only you. All other Snakes are called off.'

'What?' Han slammed his hand on the chairback. Even Raul started from his customary coolness.

'Passive surveillance. No infiltration, no covert action, no direct contact.'

'A fucking gumshoe?'

'Keep it low-level, do you hear? You've got two weeks to wrap it up and then I've got another job for you.'

Han stared in furious disbelief. 'I can't run this like a part-time contract . . .'

'The Family can't afford any further embarrassment. Unless you come up with something live, I won't be able to keep digging you out of the shit.'

'You want results but you don't give me any time or back-up or even any bloody room to manoeuvre.' Han shot to his feet, the chair flung aside with a crash. He ground down hard on his rage. Raul sprang up, ready to pull his friend back if he needed to.

Mokhtar stood and stared Han down. Finally he said, voice calm, 'You need a break from this one, Han. Look at you.'

'I don't need a fucking break!'

'You'll do what I tell you.' Mokhtar moved to the door. 'And a word of advice, Han: keep a lid on your emotions if you want to make it in the Family.'

Then he was gone, slipping out of the shophouse into the alleyway.

'Shit, man.' Raul reached out one hand but thought better of laying it on Han's shoulder. He began to tidy the papers on the table.

Han went into the bathroom. He relieved himself, scowling, and washed his hands. Stood in front of the glass above the basin combatively. There was nothing wrong with him. Tall for a Chinese man. Broad-shouldered and muscular. Not a hint of fat. Or weakness. A hard face, angular in the way that peak fitness renders the features. No distinguishing marks – that was a condition of the job. He jerked his head to relieve the tension. He was damp with sweat. A muscle jumped in his jaw. His eyes were too cold, his mouth too stern maybe. But fuck it, that's how he looked when he was pissed off – what else had Mokhtar expected?

Twenty minutes after Mokhtar, Raul left. A nod, an exchange of looks: no more. Han waited for ten minutes more then walked out into the alley. By then the morning was hot and muggy even though it was still early. The alleyway stank of vegetables decaying in the drains. He dodged puddles from the rain the night before. Out on the central square, he left the row of shophouses behind, the coffee-shop and its neighbours just opening up their metal doors. Trucks and vans jostled for position on the roads around the covered wet market, unloading baskets of squealing piglets, sweet potatoes, plastic household goods, crates of live chickens and dogs. After the shuttered room, the stink of animals, blood and salted fish was like a blow to Han's senses. He cut through the dank interior of the market, passing blocks of severed cow's heads and hanging pig's intestines. Through a corridor filled with gunny sacks of garlic, curry powder and spices, he emerged into open-air stalls shaded by multi-coloured umbrellas. He found a fried noodles vendor. Sitting at the counter to the side of the wok, he ordered a plate of food.

This was the Asia he had come from. The energy of the place and its gritty reality always gave him a kick. People doing business, scrabbling for a living, shoving for a life for themselves and their family. This was what he understood. What the fuck did the Suits or Siew know about these lives down in the street? From their air-conditioned towers and mansions, they made decisions that pushed these people this way and that. Han had not moved too far from the dirt and stink. They were in his blood, they were the reality of living. The Family had given him a chance after three years in the dead-head army, taught him how to use his furious energy for something more than smashing up cars and beating up on rival gangs. They had moulded his violence into a weapon, made a Snake out of a street-wise kid. He got good money but that wasn't why he was in the game. They had given him a cause.

He knew the hype about the New Asia: full of progress, riches, power and bullshit. He didn't buy into it for one fucking minute. It was the same old battleground he had known as a teenager. Those with the power – whether they wielded it with money, land, broken bottles, razors or sheer fucking size – *they* were the ones who got to the top and stayed there. Everyone else got screwed or had the shit beaten out of them. Nothing had changed. Siew, the Suits, the rich and powerful in their swanky cars and fine clothes . . . they were no better than the thugs on the streets. Siew goaded Han in a way that no other target had, almost as if he embodied every evil Han loathed: the smugness of the rich; the smoothness with which they controlled the spin and worked the system; the ease with which they bought power and influence. And behind that mask Siew presided over fraud, extortion, blackmail, intimidation, corruption and murder. Han knew this in his gut but nothing ever stuck to Siew. Against this shifting horror, the AVA's message chilled Han – it divided the world into the worthy and the damned by the random moral code which the Alliance dictated. And in the scramble to be thought worthy, the life force that drove Asia would die.

Han looked round at the mix of Chinese, Malays and Indians bustling through the market. They did business with whom they pleased, hung out with whoever they chose as their friends. They ate together, talked, argued, fucked who the hell they liked. Nothing would change in the new AVA world – only there would be those sly enough to hide what they did, and those not quick or smart enough to do the same. The sly would be thought worthy. And worthiness would join the list of weapons alongside switchblades or money to squeeze the spirit and soul out of those the AVA damned.

Han scowled. Mokhtar's orders had hog-tied him to the American. It pissed Han off that he could no longer take the lead in the op but had to sniff around the tail of the white man. All he could do was hope Dean would get close enough to something real that Han could snatch for his own purposes. He didn't give a shit what agenda the American was working to. So long as Han could turn it to his own use, that was all that mattered. He didn't care about politics or any of the moral niceties the Suits droned on about. Western values, Asian traditions, liberal sentiments, right-wing dogma – they were all a smokescreen for the same fucking thing: Power.

<hr />

Ginny stood behind the desk in her office at the Wyndham Centre. The room was large, on the first floor of the sanatorium. It was decorated in pastel colours, setting off the view of the sea through the picture windows. She reached for the video-intercom. Ong, the security chief, waited. As the screen bipped on, Piers's face appeared, looking tense.

'That journalist is here again. He's been at the KL apartment, too – the head porter there phoned yesterday,' Ginny said into the monitor. She did not like disturbing Piers but did not know what else to do. She was aware that something had happened between him and the American but did not know what. All she knew was that ever since their brief exchange, Piers had been strung out to breaking point. 'He wants an interview. We've had a pile of letters and phone messages from him in the last week. I've told him "no" in more ways than I can remember.'

Ong leaned closer. 'He was the one we found snooping around.'

'Did you run those checks on his documentation?'

'They confirm he is who he says he is.'

Piers nodded with strained irritation. 'Get rid of him! I don't have time for this. Siew's expecting results in the next few days. We've had to postpone the extraction once already. I don't care how you do it – just get rid of him once and for all.'

The screen went black. Ginny knew what had to come next and it filled her with dread. She could not meet Ong's eyes. She said, struggling for breath, 'Throw him out. And make sure he understands that this time it's for good.'

When the men had gone, Ginny did not move for a long time. Then she turned and drew the blinds on all the windows. She would see nothing of Dean now. She wanted to know nothing and hear nothing. She flicked on the television and an N-Sat music-video station filled the room with pop versions of Asian folk melodies. Switching on the desk lamp, she sat down and picked up the lecture notes she'd been preparing. She shuffled them in agitation over and over again.

Two security guards escorted Dean out of the gates, each twisting one of his arms up into a tight half-Nelson. They jerked him on, forcing the pain. Ong followed with Dean's bag of equipment: camera, tape recorder and notebook. They moved off the road on to rocky ground, dragging him towards an outcrop high above the sea until he could see the drop beneath his feet. The rocks were loose and he slipped, the pressure on his shoulder blades a tearing agony. He cried out.

'No interviews. No trespassing,' Ong recited as if by rote. 'The best interests of our patients are top priority.'

Dean watched as Ong took the camera out of the bag. He flipped open the back and pulled out the spool of film, flinging it out to sea. Dean struggled as he would if the film had had any significance. The guards yanked his arms again. He swore. But the film was a decoy. The photos he had taken this visit – and at the ceremony, of the patients, VIPs and grounds – were embedded in the camera's digital memory. Ong let the camera fall, the lens cracking on impact. Dean winced. The machine was a custom-built digital model that had the appearance of an ordinary SLR, specially designed for his undercover work.

At a nod from Ong the guards let Dean go. He stumbled, pulling himself back from the edge. His arms hung by his sides even as he tried to use them. One of the guards tripped him with a kick to his legs. As he fell, Ong swept down and grabbed his hair. One powerful lunge and Dean's head cracked into a rock. Blood oozed. He tried to move and could not, his co-ordination sluggish. He was breathing hard, pain pounding his skull. He lay on the rocks, groaning.

Ong said, 'Be careful how you go-lah. You could fall and hurt yourself, sneaking around this rough ground.' He dropped the bag on Dean, the weight winding him.

Dean was aware of Ong and his men moving away. There was the sound of a gunning engine. He struggled up on to his elbow, the bag sliding from him. Someone was driving his car. It swung away from the gates. Screeched towards him. Dean froze in horror. The front bumper rammed at him from a distance of a few yards, accelerating in seconds. He scrabbled to move but his body failed him. He pivoted his head away as the car shot towards impact.

Dean slowly turned back. The car's licence plate stared at

him from within a centimetre. He felt dizzy, realised he was holding his breath. The hand-brake was ground on and the driver stepped out. Dean gasped for air. The door slammed and footsteps crunched over the rocks onto gravel, fading as the guard headed back to the Centre.

Chapter Five

Piers brought the extract to the electron microscope in the laboratory. He wore surgical robes and cap, his cheekbones and fierce eyes visible above the mask. The laboratory was sealed, recirculatory ventilation with modulated air pressure ensuring zero exchange of atmospheric contamination between the lab and the rest of the complex. Reinforced and heat-sealed glass on one wall allowed observation from an adjacent technical support laboratory.

At the observation window, Siew stood beside Ben. Siew was watching intently. As Piers placed the extract on the specimen stage of the microscope, Ben switched on the auxiliary monitor in the viewing lab. They would see a duplicate of the image on the main screen in the sealed lab. At the microscope, Piers controlled the resolution with dials along the electron gun, a tall cylindrical column above the grid on which the extract had been placed. Using an electron beam instead of a light, the electron microscope would enable them to see matter that was up to ten thousand times smaller than the smallest particle visible to the naked eye. In place of a glass lens, focus was achieved through the control of magnetic coils along the path of the beam. The image was produced when the electron beam hit the specimen on the grid and was scattered by the structures within it.

Piers stared at the screen beside the microscope. 'Beautiful.'

He had been right to postpone extraction for a few more

days, he thought. The increased thickness and volume of the compound showed that he had timed it to reach maximum growth capacity. The specimen had been prepared by sucrose gradient centrifugutian and had taken the Congo red dye stain perfectly. He could not have done better to impress his patron. Piers felt an adrenaline rush.

'Ben,' he prompted.

Ben Chang cleared his throat. Over the intercom, his voice sounded distracted. 'The extraction and distillation process of all the cultures will take five days to a week to complete. That gives us another week in which to prime the subjects with the resulting product before Dr Wyndham and I meet with them for the therapeutic work.'

He faltered. Piers looked up at him through the glass. Ben stared back, blinking rapidly. 'I can't . . .'

Siew shot him a glance, eyes narrowed. Piers knew he had been aware of Ben's conflict ever since he had arrived late last night. There was an emotion behind Siew's tight-lipped anger that contrasted with his usual icy control. Like a father betrayed by his son.

'Generation 105,' Piers prompted. Cold, hard data. That had saved him long ago. He had hammered it home to Ben the night before. *Go back to the science, it's the only thing that's real. Everything else is an illusion.*

Ben continued, 'This version of the Cure is the 105th generation, using SPrp33.' His eyes darted left and right, following the autocue in his mind. He struggled to master his rapid breathing. 'Generation 105 has been developed alongside generations 104 and 106 to 110. This simultaneous cultivation of the different versions of the Cure has speeded up the production process to meet the tight scheduling of the various Phases. Gen105 is the most stable version to date. We propose to combine this batch with HPrp33-gen98 to reduce rejection of the Cure.'

'Why not use HPrp entirely?' Siew cast his hawk-like gaze back over Ben. Piers stopped himself from stepping in with the answer. At Siew's instructions, he had been grooming the young man to take the reins. Piers wanted to shake Ben. *This is the future you've longed for, grab it with both hands.*

Ben seemed to struggle back from a long way away. Siew's question had thrown him. Piers frowned. Siew and his associates were pouring millions of *ringgit* into this work and the AVA President's patience had already been strained by the last postponement. The relocation to Malaysia and new high-profile strategy had bought them all a little time but the threat of exposure still hung over them. How much did that American journalist know? How had he traced them here? And the assassin lurking in the jungle beyond the gates – what forces did he work for? The uncertainties shook Piers. They were not safe yet and it was up to him to get the Cure right before disaster struck. This was no time for Ben to be getting the jitters, whatever his personal feelings about the experiment.

Finally Piers said, 'Previous trials have shown that HPrp, although proportionately more stable in the long term, lacks the effective binding capability of SPrp – that is, the suggestivity capacity is weaker . . .'

'The trance induction doesn't work so well. Is that what you're saying?'

Piers nodded. 'To achieve maximum trance-state in the subjects, SPrp in combination with HPrp is the only current solution. We are working on a version of HPrp that will be both stable and trance-effective but that is several generations down the line.'

Siew said nothing. Piers looked at Ben but the younger man seemed distracted, his face taut. He was agitated, as if he longed to be elsewhere. Sweat dampened his brow although the air-conditioning maintained a constant cool.

Piers kept the lid on his anger. He continued clinically, 'A subsidiary issue is that we do not have sufficient HPrp cultures for the number of subjects we are proposing to work with. Combining SPrp means that the appropriate quantity overall is produced . . .'

'How many more H cultures do you need?' Siew cut in. Piers noted wryly how they all avoided everyday nomenclature, preferring instead the objectivity of scientific terms. Even Siew. Or perhaps, especially Siew.

'For this project – double what we've got.'

Siew's face set hard. 'I don't like compromise, particularly for work of this significance. It's too late for this experiment. But, in future, get all the H cultures you need – whatever it takes.' He moved up closer to Piers. 'It's a little late to be held back by sentiment, don't you think?'

'Not sentiment, practicalities. You want more H cultures, you give me the means to do it. More men, more trawling.'

Siew eyed him. 'You got it.'

'I need some air.' Ben started for the door suddenly, sweat sheening his face. Siew did not stop him. Piers held Siew's hooded gaze through the glass.

Siew found Ben as dawn broke on the beach. Siew's speedboat was anchored not far from shore, a guard standing on deck. The deep water of the cove, cut into the northern face of the headland, was ideal for the secret visits he had made over the last few years. The natural harbour could not be seen from the grounds of the Centre, hidden by the headland. It was obscured from the mangrove swamp by the jagged boulders that had tumbled down from the cliffs a thousand years before. From the sea, the arm of the headland and rocky islets hid any craft anchored here from the view of passing traffic. The Centre's own security vessels patrolled the waters to the south of the headland, dissuading the curious from coming too close to the private stretch of coast.

Two security officers stood at the foot of the steps cut into the cliff behind them. Siew sensed their curiosity. He looked at them and they turned away. The air was still in the shelter of the cove and voices seemed to be amplified by the wall of cliff and rocks. Although it was early, Siew felt the muggy heat dampen his shirt.

'But children!' Ben turned on him. 'How can we risk children? Even if it's for the greater good?'

He was flushed, sweat drenching him. His tie was askew and his chest heaved. Siew said, 'We'll be helping the kids, giving them hope and ambition. A future. Things they have a right to.'

Their subjects would be boys at a school in Johore Bahru, at the southernmost tip of the Malaysian peninsula. The boys were aged from nine to sixteen, troublemakers who were on the edge of expulsion. Their crimes in school included disrupting classes, threatening teachers, bullying, theft and vandalism. A combat knife had been found on one of them. Truancy was habitual and the likelihood of serious juvenile delinquency if they were expelled was high. Research into their family backgrounds had revealed broken homes, alcoholism, physical and sexual abuse, and other family members already on a criminal path. They had been an ideal subject for the experiment.

'How do we know this Cure is stable? Only by trying it out – and then it's too late!'

'These are the kids who most need Asian Values. They have a right to believe in themselves. You'd be failing them if you walked away now.' Siew wanted to shake Ben. The boy's panic disgusted him. He hated weakness. Weakness was destructive. But Ben was young, Siew told himself, and this emotion just the passion of youth. Such passion could be directed, made useful in time. He grabbed Ben by the shoulders. 'We fail in order to learn, Ben. Learn and go on. There's no going back.'

Ben was whooping for breath. 'The subject – gen13 – he – oh, God, he deteriorated so fast. The spasms . . . screaming . . . He was dying, man, as we watched and took notes . . .' Gen13 had been Ben's first involvement in Wyndham's experiments. Three years before. Siew hit him. Hard, back-handed, across the face. Ben staggered. Thudded into the sand. Siew stood over him. 'That's enough!'

Through his shock, Ben focused on him. Blood trickled down his jaw. Siew hauled him up and held him close, lifting him to tiptoe. 'You're like a son to me, Ben, and it hurts me to hurt you. But understand this: what I do, I do for your own good. Asia is like a child to me and what we do, we do for the good of all its people.'

Ben blinked.

'You owe it to me to give me your all.' Siew enunciated each word. 'You owe the Alliance. We gave you that scholarship for the best secondary school education in Singapore – or have you forgotten? I gave you a clothing allowance so you wouldn't feel out of place. Bought your textbooks. Put you up with a respected AVA family during term-time. Paid for your train tickets home to your family every holiday. The Alliance paid your university fees in Hong Kong and got you started in the best hospital research facility in Asia. Do you remember?'

Ben nodded but it was more like a spasm of shame.

'And how did you get your smart new house in Lower Damansara?' Siew asked.

'Because of you.' It was a mumble.

'I can't hear you!'

'You gave me a loan.'

'A personal unsecured loan at half a per cent interest.'

Ben looked as if he wanted to bury himself in the sand. Siew said, 'And Mei-Hong. Tell me how you met her?'

'Mrs Siew introduced us.'

'Sang your praises to her. Had her in love with you even before you met her. Isn't that right?'

Ben nodded.

Siew pushed him away. The boy stumbled but stayed on his feet. Siew softened his tone. 'Tough decisions have to be made in what we're doing. I depend on you to make tough choices for a better world – for the future we all believe in. Or have you forgotten everything you stood for, too? Have you forgotten personal loyalty, paying back what you owe, community, doing what is right? Have you forgotten the Alliance way?

'Fear and anxiety are normal, Ben, but you don't have to make them your masters. That's what we Asians pride ourselves on. We don't give in to every whim because we feel like it – every lustful, greedy, selfish, mean desire. That's what makes Asia superior, isn't it? You are the future of Asia, Ben, young men like you. Are you going to give in to your feelings? Look at the young people of the West, making nothing of their lives, scrounging off social security, out of their heads on drugs and sex, spreading disease "because they feel like it". They think they are more important than God. They worship their feelings, don't care about community and value nothing. Is that the kind of Asia you want to live in? That you want your kids to live in?

'Because that's where the future is heading. That's where the boys in that school are heading. I can't promise you complete success with this experiment. We won't know till it happens. But we have to try, whatever the risk, if we want to bring about the birth of a new world.'

Ben had started to weep. He was shaking.

'All or nothing, Ben. That's what the Alliance wants from you. It's what the Alliance expects of all its people. You have a choice. You can go on and be a part of Asia's reborn future. Or you turn your back on everything you owe me and everything you believe in – and you are nothing. Do you understand me?' Siew spoke the words like a warning: 'Nothing. We do not forget. The Alliance made you into family. You are blood now. Blood can never be severed.'

Siew watched Ben digesting what he had said. The boy was hiccuping for air but the sobbing had stopped. He went white and then flushed. The Alliance had created his soul and they owned his body. Siew had known it all along but it was only now that Ben understood what all that money and education had bought. Shock and then terror played across his face. In a moment he seemed to age forty years as, finally, the truth hit him. With all that he knew, about the scientific work, about Siew's intentions, about the Alliance's methods, about the Centre . . .

'There *is* no way back.' Ben's voice was hoarse. 'Is there?'

'No.'

Then Siew turned and walked up the beach.

He heard Ben hurrying behind him. 'Let me complete the run-through of the Johore Bahru experiment for you,' he said. With an effort, his voice was firm. He held himself straight in spite of his dishevelled state. He indicated to Siew to proceed back to the labs, his outstretched hand caught by a moment's tremor.

Siew eyed him for a beat. It satisfied him to see Ben's courage. He put an arm around the young man. 'We all fail and fall short. That is the curse of being human. It takes courage to conquer the weakness within our minds. I knew you would choose well out of the dark night of your soul. Those who freely choose to journey with Asian Values, we honour them, whatever their past failing. Life for them will be good. Those who fight us –' Siew shrugged with a deliberation that underlined the threat. 'They will not stand in our way.'

The scene was like mission control after a successful touchdown. Ginny stood on the raised walkway at the back, taking it in. In the pit, where the computers were banked in rows, the programmers clustered in a loud, laughing group. They wore jeans and loose shirts over T-shirts. Some had long hair, all were unkempt and unshaven. There were some whites among the Asian faces. All of them were men, none older than thirty. In the centre sat Ricky Teong, slugging beer in his swivel chair and jiggering his leg. He was twenty-four but had the look and manner of a kid.

Music blared from the speakers around the room. It was a wall of sound, electric guitars slamming, a rasp passing for voice and lyrics. On screens all over the room visual representations flashed to the beat – abstract shapes pulsating, changing. Faces, people, scenes intercut, morphing into each other. On the giant screen at the front, above the viewing partition into the sound stage behind, the images played with the brilliance and contrast turned up. Ginny's nerves felt raw. The band was Juicer, an English 'indie' band that was Ricky's favourite. No one who knew him could avoid knowing that. He played their music digitally from the computer, synced to his own compilations of imagery. When she had run the control room, they'd worked to silence. Under Ricky, there was always noise – rap, house, techno, indie – anything that his programmers wanted. Except when they were doing a 'shoot' – the psych team insisted on that.

The psychology team and their actors were down with Ricky, passing round drinks. Ginny moved past their monitors and headsets on the upper deck at the rear. Sheafs of notes spread across their unit, typed scripts and some handwritten dialogue. The knot in her stomach tightened. Although Piers had been spending days on end in the labs, frantically working to meet the deadline he had promised Siew, she had not been down here for the last few days. Her part of the experiment had been ready, the digital images and backdrops stored in the bank of computers.

She had not known till a short time ago that Piers had asked Ricky to review her programme. He had reworked the software to give the images more texture and depth, smoothed some of the transitions which he had considered jerky. He had also played with the sound, upping the cinematic feel with dramatic music and constant background accompaniment. It had been Ricky who had demonstrated the whole package – psych team, actors, computer input and all – to Siew. Anger and humiliation made her flush. She wanted to scream at these cackling boys, find Piers and lash out at him. Tears of frustration and panic surged. But she held them down hard. She and Piers ran this Centre, she told herself. She could not let these kids see her breaking. Not now. Especially not now.

She was being manoeuvred out of control of the graphics. Ginny was more use in her PR role, Piers and Siew said. She did not know whether to believe them. Ricky was working on projects he kept from her. Some of the team were distant with her, as if they guarded a secret. Ricky had access to everything she did but she suspected she did not know all the projects he was working on. The humiliation hurt like a cramp.

Ginny had designed this room, set up the first scenarios, produced the first workable programmes. She couldn't give it up. In spite of the problems with Ricky, she felt safe here in this windowless cocoon, even with his screaming music and the marks of his domination – the newest technology and equipment, the mess of personal effects she would never have allowed, the informality. Here you could control a world of your own creation, make contact through unseen barriers with lives and feelings you might never touch in reality outside. And you would be safe, always in control, always able to escape and re-boot at the touch of a button. The PR world Piers forced her to move in terrified her, devoured too much of her energy, and she needed contact, no matter how fleeting and how humiliating, with the magic she had built and loved.

'Hey, Gin-jeanie, come on over-lah!' Ricky waved at her. 'Give the lady a beer!'

Ginny approached but declined a drink. It was nine in the morning.

'Siew loved what we'd got set up for the experiment,' Ricky shouted above the music. 'He's only just left. To him, we're fucking long-hair louts . . .'

His team cat-called, clapping each other on the back and laughing.

'. . . degenerate youth . . .'

More proud laughter.

'But he fucking needs us-lah. I had him kissing my arse once he was sitting there at the screen.'

Someone mimicked an Australian accent. '"It's remarkable. How do you do that? I've never seen anything like it."'

'"You're a god, Ricky Teong!"' a pony-tailed Indian programmer joined in. Someone else waggled his tongue obscenely.

'He fucking needs us degenerates,' Ricky crowed. 'Screw his pure Asian principles! Hey, Gin and Tonic, it's not my fault your programming needed work. Be glad for me, no hard feelings.'

She hated his comic tags for her. He always found an opportunity to rub in his growing ascendancy. She started to move away. 'I've got work . . .'

'Need your morning fix, ha?'

His laughter rose above the others'. She flushed with anger and humiliation. For once, she was thankful for the deafening music. She slipped through a side door, walked down the corridor and entered a room off it.

The trance suite was furnished with armchairs and giant cushions on thick carpet. The lighting was restful and the decor cosy. There was a huge screen on one wall and electronic equipment that might have been a hi-fi stereo, only larger and fitted out with control panel, keyboard, hard drive and voice-recognition software. A headset for enclosed trance lay beside it, shaped like a visored motorcycle helmet and wired for stereo sound and 3-D vision.

Ginny came here every morning for what Ricky called her 'fix'. Years ago, she had developed the first prototype as an aid to relaxation. Images from her camcorder transferred into digital form and overdubbed with a script from a self-hypnosis tape: sunny meadow, trees, lake, a soothing voice telling her to breathe deeply, relax, feel the grass under her feet, the sun on her face. Working to Piers's specifications, she had improved on the format and technology through all their moves from one secret location to the next. Of all the components of their scientific work, the computer imagery was the most advanced and the aspect that achieved the highest rate of success. She had not wanted to go further at first, to follow Piers down the road of his obsession. Ginny felt the familiar guilt twist inside her. But she owed him more than her life.

It had happened so fast. A moment's inattention and their lives had changed forever. Ginny felt the old panic seize her. She was back there again in that terrible, uncaring crowd. Her heart pounded in her chest. She could smell the meat frying for the hot-dog vendors, its stench making her retch. She could hardly breathe. Families with children. Tourists scanning the park with video cameras, posing for photos. The bright sunlight off the Hudson River blinding her. She was running, screaming, searching the crowds. The ferries to Ellis Island and the Statue of Liberty loomed above her; the thronging queues watched her. No one seemed concerned, their eyes glazing in detachment even as she grabbed them, begging their help.

Ginny forced herself to control her laboured breathing. It had happened a long time ago, she told herself. Battery Park was a long way away – a lifetime away. She sat down in an armchair beside the bank of controls and dimmed the lights. She was no longer the person she had been back then. She shivered. She was sweating. Adjusting the thermostat, Ginny tried to relax. The panic attacks had never left her in all these years; in the last few months they had become more intense and more frequent.

Her life belonged to Piers, she could give him that at least. But it was not enough. It would never be enough. He had become like fury possessed, emotions burned away by his fanaticism. Asian Values was the one true cause for him, his science the Alliance's weapon in the control of chaos and humanity's ills. Order, civility, safety: the ramparts of a perfect society. Its model the clockwork precision of Siew's adopted home – Singapore. Such hideous violence could never have happened there, Piers would rant in his fever of despair. *He* – Piers could give no name to *him*, the demon who still haunted them both – *he* could never have been created by that rationalised environment. *He* was the monster born of a society enslaved to desire, lust and the gratification of every need. Piers's ravings had frightened Ginny. He never spoke of such things now but she knew they fed off his blood every moment.

Since that terrible day, she had tried to make it right for him, done everything he had asked of her and more, given up her own life and future for him. And still Katie was dead. Ginny could never change that. Piers in all his driven passion could not change it either. She tapped out a command on the control panel, entering passwords through the levels of entry clearance. The main screen blipped on. She had accessed their private archive which Piers had carried with them from country to country.

It was an old home movie, transferred into digital form from a camcorder. Piers, young and happy, playing with Katie, her blonde hair streaking across her face. They had been in the yard at home in New Jersey, a bleached summer day, new tans highlighting the gold of their hair. Katie had been precocious as an only child, picking up the language patterns of her parents. She and Piers chatted together stretched out on the lawn, her every remark wisdom in his ears. Then they were up, Piers flinging her into the air, spinning her round as she squealed with laughter. She had been six. In his eyes, even on the shaky tape, Ginny could see a brilliance she had never seen again in him after Katie died. The film had been taken a week before that day in Battery Park.

Ginny stopped the film. She let her grief overwhelm her, claw tears from her and crush her heart. She needed to remember. Keeping the pain alive was the only way she would be able to get through this time. She had to remember whom she loved, whom she owed.

She accessed the latest trance sequence. Over the years, working with her team – and with Ricky – she had transformed computer-aided hypnosis into a state of being, the experience of it like a fourth dimension to physical reality. She flipped over to voice-activated control and slid the helmet on. The 3-D screens in the visor had been improved to remove any peripheral vision and the images played as if she had plummeted into the world beyond the LCD veneer. The sound lived inside her head from the stereo speakers at her ears. The trance induction was abstract at first, images of a vortex within spinning, swirling mist, the music no more than four notes, matched to the rhythm of her heart. A soft voice, hardly audible, told her she was being drawn out of herself, leaving her body behind, falling into the endless tunnelling void. Normally, it did not take her long to drift into a deep hypnotic state, her breathing full and regular, her body relaxed. But this time, Ginny remained detached, her mind working to a beat of its own.

She watched the life correction sequences as if from a distance. They were images of her as she needed to be – confident, glamorous, warm, open and in control – meeting endless streams of people, chatting with them, making them trust her, believe in her, speaking with conviction and charisma. The production values were perfect, as if filmed in real settings with real people instead of on the sound-stage and digitally manipulated. The focus was always on the image of Ginny, brighter than the surrounding scenes, more detailed in texture and nuance. She had been played by one of the actors, her face implanted afterwards and smoothed into a seamless whole. The view-point shifted, magnified, zoomed in, pulled back. At each moment, the accompanying voice described how she was feeling, who she was, what she believed in, what she knew of herself. It was her own voice, engineered through voice-stimulation software to deepen its tone, enrich its resonance and empower it with a persuasive confidence.

There had been a time when she had only needed the 'fix' once every few months. She had willingly absorbed the fictions of the correction sequences, devised together with Piers and the psych team. They controlled her panic and shifting distress by transforming her sense of herself. The effects were temporary, of course, a veneer over the truth of who she was. Still, with little but her work to absorb her, they were able to maintain the equilibrium for increasingly longer stretches without a relapse. She would absorb the Public Contact sequence before a lecture engagement, or the Negotiation Control sequence before a meeting, the Ginny Identity sequence to still disturbing memories. And all these years, she had succeeded in living the lie.

She longed for peace. The stillness of mind that came from the harmony of acceptance. She would never have that until Piers's experiments produced a stable version of the Cure. She had waited all these long years and with each incremental day, she might have succeeded in burying the last remnants of her emotions. She had not known intimacy and affection for so long now, she almost fancied that she might have endured without the Cure forever. Over time, she seemed to herself an empty body, functioning well enough but hollow inside. Her mind, too, devoid of memory and hope, given over to her work and filled only with logarithms and programming technology. She had been safe then. But now, she needed the Cure to be perfected more than ever.

Ever since she had met Fei, the 'fixes' had begun to lose their power. Fei's call shortly after the N-Sat newscast, her voice catching with concern for Ginny's safety . . . the memory flipped her heart. Ginny shifted with tension. She desperately needed the Cure. Then she would be safe. Safe from her own desires.

She had not watched the newscast. Did not like to be reminded of the state of siege she and Piers had lived under for the last ten years. Nor of the debt they owed to Siew and the AVA. It had been Siew who had decided the slant of the press release to N-Sat. She had worked on the CCTV footage at his demand, imposing the rifle image into the unknown man's hand. 'It's ideas that win wars,' he had said. 'Communication and ideas. They are the weapons of the modern world.' She did not want to be told his tactics, did not want to be a part of his manipulation. But he owned her as he owned Piers. Whatever he required of her, she had no choice but to perform.

Agitated, Ginny pulled off the headgear. The sequence was playing simultaneously on the main screen. She stared at the images without seeing them. She said, 'Sound to main speakers.'

The music and voice came up on the quadrophonic speakers around her. She would never forget the first time she had seen Fei. It had been at the offices of Ming, Siap & Qwong, Stanley Siap introducing them both in an air-conditioned meeting room. Fei had been seated at the table, looking through some papers, her delicate features still with concentration. When she had looked up, her eyes had found Ginny's at once and her face had danced into a confident, friendly smile. Ginny had felt a dizziness, forgetting Siap beside her, unable even to reply to Fei's greeting. She had grasped Fei's hand as if in a dream and the touch of her had drained Ginny of breath.

She said out loud, 'Display sound menu.' A dialogue box appeared in the corner of the screen.

'Display character tones.' A subsidiary box appeared. It listed a range of voice files by name and type. There was 'Piers.xqp', 'Ginny.xqp', 'Suleim.xqp' among those labelled for age, class, gender and inflection. Running these files with any voice text enabled that text to sound as if spoken by the voice-type of that file. Ginny said, 'Run "Fei".'

The voice on the speakers began to mutate like a singer shifting notes and vowels in a moment's drunkenness. The tone deepened and softened, the vowels rounded into a perfect Oxford accent, a flutey breath heightened the resonance. Fei's familiar voice filled the room. 'You are Ginny Wyndham, at peace with all, holding yourself tall, unafraid . . .' The words of the correction sequence, spoken by Fei, seemed more intimate, charged with eroticism. Ginny was breathing in short shallow breaths. Her mouth felt dry. She had kept some of the messages Fei had left on her voicemail over the last year and run them through the voice analysis programme. Extracting its essential characteristics, Ginny had written the 'Fei.xqp' file, giving colour to the qualities she was most drawn to – Fei's gentle manner of speech and sensuous tones.

In the last year, Ginny had felt as if overwhelmed by a drug. Everything she did, every moment, each waking thought, she carried Fei within her. In the barrenness of the last ten years, she had thought her heart parched and dead. But that, too, had been a lie. Fei had given it life again, watered the cracked soil with her voice, lured out a garden with her friendship. Ginny had made herself believe that that was all it was – friendship. But she had begun to depend on seeing Fei week after week, working intently over the legal transactions in the days; in the evenings, talking, spending time, being with her. And when Fei had told her about Sam, her sexuality so softly revealed, her eyes shy, with unexpressed pain, Ginny had heard nothing of her sadness at the failing relationship nor her devotion to Sam. She had felt only the joy burning inside her: Fei might yet love her in return.

But it was Sam whom Fei loved. The thought cut her like broken glass. Sam. Ginny had never seen her. It hurt her that Fei was hurt by this woman, and yet there was a shameful satisfaction in it. The pain Sam caused was Ginny's way to Fei – through friendship and concern and always being there. It was only a matter of time, it had to be. She remembered how Fei looked in her distress, her gaze turned inward to Sam. Ginny felt a spasm in her heart. How she longed for Fei to feel with such intensity for her! Irrationally, she felt hatred for Sam, as if Sam had hurt her personally. The power of it surged with a sudden violence that alarmed her. Ginny clenched her eyes shut as if wrestling down the tumult with all her strength.

She had grown used to the aridity of the past. Now, she was living a storm of emotions and it frightened her. But more than anything else, her desire for Fei was a betrayal of all she owed to Piers. Such a love had broken them both once before, and now there was so much more to lose. Ginny could hardly force down her panic. She had reached out that night Fei had come to the Centre, showing too suddenly her need for her, trying to grasp what could only be touched with gentle hands. Fei had withdrawn like a startled deer but Ginny had not been able to hold back. Even as she had heard the desperation in her voice and seen her own clumsy manner, Ginny had not been able to stop herself. It was as if knowing Fei's sexuality had unleashed all the desires and loneliness she had tried to contain for so many years. Ginny loathed herself for it, feared it. But she could not fight it.

She said, 'Close sequence image. Display video application. Run Inauguration file.'

The images faded out. There was a moment's pause. Then footage from the inauguration ceremony played. Ginny had edited the tapes taken by the N-Sat film crew, extracting only clips where Fei featured. She fast-forwarded to a long segment where Fei was caught in middle view and close up. The voice from the previous sequence continued to play on. Ginny stared at the screen, Fei's voice embracing her like a physical presence.

She stood up, the headgear falling to the ground. Fei's beautiful features were huge on the screen, her long eyes bright. Ginny knew every curve of her face, the sweep of her lips, the delicate line of her jaw. She watched transfixed as a breeze played over Fei's dark gamine-cut. Ginny's voice was hoarse when she spoke: 'Freeze the image.'

Fei glanced at the camera and straight into Ginny's eyes. Hardly aware of what she was doing, Ginny moved towards the screen, an ache of desire impelling her, gaze locked with Fei's unmoving gaze. She longed to hold Fei in her arms, feel her breath on her neck, smell her soft skin. Ginny reached out her hand and touched Fei's cheek with gentle fingertips. She felt only the cool surface of the screen.

Chapter Six

The offices of Ming, Siap & Qwong were on the fifteenth floor of *Menara* Loy, a block away from the internationally renowned Petronas Twin Towers. Loy Tower was one of the most prestigious locations in Kuala Lumpur and Fei and her partners footed an impressive rent to prove it. In addition to Stanley Siap and Ming Goh-Teng, there were two other partners: Ahmed Zulkir, a Malay, and Krishna Anapurti, an Indian. The firm's business was commercial work, the three Chinese partners bringing in the most billable work, Siap doubling as their tax expert and Fei covering commercial property, construction and development. Anapurti's caseload was business litigation and court appearances. Zulkir's role was client development. His family were established in KL society and his presence gave the practice weight.

Like most professionals making names for themselves in the capital, Fei and her partners had been educated overseas, she and Siap in England and the others in Australia and New Zealand. Their law degrees were recognised in Malaysia but had been supplemented by Malaysian professional qualifications. Lawyers emerged as both advocates and solicitors. Malay was the national language and that of the courts and government documents. Daily transactions and private contracts were conducted in English, the language of business.

The partners took profit in return for capital investment, other staff being paid a salary. They had a legal team of ten, Fei

supervising three, including the trainee. There were six secretaries, one of whom doubled as the computer systems
manager, two office boys, a financial accountant and his book-
keeper. Everyone was squeezed into half the office space, the
other half given over to a grand reception, fitted out in pink
marble with a cupola, and ornate conference rooms with
mahogany tables and leather suites, all dazzlingly lit.

At this early hour, the office was empty. The splendour of
the hall always gave Fei a boost. It never failed to remind her of
what she had achieved – the clicking of her heels on the marble,
the air-conditioning just so, the whole setting exuding confidence and success. All those salaries, all those expenses, all those
interest payments back to the bank, she thought, and the firm
still made an immense profit.

The office area was open plan, desks pushed close to each
other. The few individual rooms were reserved for partners,
cramped with just a desk and chair, walls lined with books, a
computer terminal to one side. Files were ranked in cabinets in
the centre of the main area. A small library of statutes, text books
and journals was squeezed into one corner. Secretaries and
support staff were partitioned away to cut down on the noise of
their WP machines.

It was seven in the morning and the other lawyers would not
appear for a while. Since Sam had moved out, Fei had started
coming in earlier than usual. She liked the quiet, she told herself.
Driving in early also meant that she could avoid the traffic that
gridlocked KL at rush hour. But the truth was that she could
hardly bear to be at home.

She did not know how she had got through the last ten days.
Without Sam, the apartment had been silent and empty. The
stillness unnerved her. It was as if her home had crumbled and
there was nothing to keep the uncertainties of the outside world
at bay. When she had first moved in, she had installed a security
alarm to the windows and front door even though the apartment
was on the tenth floor of a serviced block. Out there was the self
she needed the world to see. Out there, she brought male dates
to business functions, flirted with men at important dinner

parties, courted the attention of male lawyers, entrepreneurs and professionals. Some had asked her for dates, a few had even proposed marriage. She had declined each time, letting them down with a coy smile. No one who mattered for her work knew about her real life.

Whenever she left the apartment, Fei religiously bolted everything and set the alarm. Sam used to laugh at first. Then Fei's paranoia exasperated her. 'People are not as malicious as you think,' Sam would say. It became another issue they'd argued about. Sam had not understood – this was Fei's sanctuary against the world. Here, she needed safety to unfurl her true self. Photographs of Sam and Fei were everywhere: arms around each other, cheek to cheek. There were more in photo albums, details of their life together in London, their lesbian and gay friends, Gay Pride. In a drawer were love letters from Sam in London when Fei had first moved back to Malaysia and e-mails Sam had sent, de-encrypted and printed out. Fei had lesbian novels, books on homosexual social history, lesbian lifestyle magazines from London. Any intruder who found all these owned her life. Or even if they did not, she thought in terror of the police swarming through her home after a burglary, asking questions, rooting through her most private self. Without Sam, she had nothing to hide, Fei thought, but the locks and bolts had somehow lost their promise of security.

The alarms had gone off a few days before. The block's doorman, Hassan, had phoned her at work but there had been no actual intrusion, the burglar scared off when the siren had gone. 'Don't call the police!' she had cried. She had rushed home. In the corridor, Hassan hovering behind her, the alarm tearing her nerves, she had seen the marks on the door where the burglar had tried to tamper with the locks. Alone in the apartment later, she had sat trembling uncontrollably.

Over the past week, she became aware of all the news stories of people who had gone missing without their absence being noticed for days or weeks. These were usually single people living alone in the city, without family or having lost touch with them. They might have jobs or be part of the underclass of casual workers. The investigative piece in the *New Straits Times* drew together anecdotal evidence from around Asia, highlighting dislocation and alienation in modern urban environments. The sentiment touched a chord and other media took it up in reports and television debates. People wrote in to the papers, gave vox-pop opinions to news crews on the street, talked about it across dinner tables and in bars from KL to Tokyo. Asia was losing its old sense of community and neighbourhood, fragmenting into lost and lonely individuals all in the name of personal independence and economic progress. On TV, an AVA spokesman commented on the need for traditional values, the role of the family in preserving identity and a caring environment. Fei felt the loneliness and pathos of all those lost souls eating meals for one in their empty flats, or wandering the streets of the capital talking to no one for months on end. They were special to no one, loved by no one. They might live a whole sixty years or more and still no one might notice. The thought terrified her, goaded her ache of loss.

The AVA spokesman derided personal greed at the expense of communal good, pointing to the effect of currency speculation on the previously robust KL Stock Exchange. He handed over to a business expert, graphs and figures flashing up on the screen behind. The *ringgit* was down to a low of 2.65 to the US dollar for the first time in three years. In the weeks before, the Thai *baht*, the Singapore dollar, the Filipino *peso* and the Indonesian *rupiah* had also fallen. What did this mean for the economy? As the expert talked on, Fei frowned. She thought of her investments and the partnership loans, the firm's business that was dependent on the robustness of their clients' prospects. This uncertainty after so many years of boom was a shock and fed her mood of anxiety. There had already been a number of high-profile business collapses in Korea and Indonesia early in the year – at that time, most people had viewed them as one-off misfortunes. That could never happen to me, everyone thought. Now, Fei was not so sure. She thought of her family being poor again, struggling for everything the rich took for granted – everything she had now.

Satellite news reports on the forest fires in Sumatra followed. The fires were raging unchecked across the jungle, a blanket of smoke covering much of Indonesia. Other flash fires were reported in surrounding areas. Steady winds blowing east to west were beginning to lay the blanket over parts of the South China Sea. Haze was expected in Singapore and parts of West Malaysia. The footage of yellow-grey fog enveloping villages and billowing over scorched earth was like scenes of Armageddon. Fei felt a suffocating powerlessness. Those trees had taken hundreds of years to reach their resplendent maturity and now in a moment's rashness, they were gone forever. They seemed to her an icon for this moment that Asia had come to. They were not just trees but all the pride and ambition and hard work that had grown into the dynamic, thrusting region of which she was a part. And they were all that she had made of her life and her love – all the moments of struggle and care and detail. All the hopes she had planted and tended with Sam. Her grief was like a shaft of pain, tears blinding her as she stared at the television. Gone forever. Sam was gone forever.

In her tiny office that morning, Fei fought her emotions. She had to stop indulging in self-pity. They were doing the right thing, she told herself. They would be happier this way in the long run. No more hurt and anger and frustration. If only she could believe it.

She put down her briefcase. Her desk was clear except for pens, paper pad and a hand-held dictaphone. She liked to have nothing on it but the matter she was then working on – it kept chaos at bay, focused the mind. She pulled out the consortium agreement she had been working on. Drafting was easiest when the office was quiet. This was a joint venture for luxury retail outlets and residential apartments above, to be built in the new administrative capital a few miles out of KL.

Beyond the tinted window, the city skyline rose like the fortifications of an ancient army, helmeted and breast-plated against all comers. The warriors were bold and powerful, jagged with pride and soaring with glory. The field of battle where they stood was gashed with red earth from land that had been cleared for new developments. The Twin Towers loomed so close she might almost have touched their gladiatorial armour. The morning seemed more choked with smog than normal, she thought. Even allowing for the tint of the glass, the sky looked a dirtier grey than she'd seen it for a long time. On the drive in, there had been a pervading smell of smoke in the air.

She worked till ten most nights or else, as she had last night, met friends for drinks and dinner, anything for distraction. These were her straight friends whom Sam had never liked: lawyers, bankers, stockbrokers, accountants, people in the money business. 'I don't care who or what the hell they sleep with,' Sam had said when they had argued about it. 'They just talk about money all the time: who earns what, how much their houses and holidays and cars cost. Everything is an excuse to brag. They're just so crass!'

'Like me?' Fei had retorted.

Sam had rolled her eyes and let out an angry groan. She had slammed out of the room, but to Fei, the answer had been clear.

Fei always went with her smart set to the new bars and restaurants opening up across the city, each one trendier and more expensive than the last. The venues had names like *Wall Street, Maugham's, Beverly Hills, FooTSE Index* and *White Raja*. The in-themes this year were money – with mock-ups of stock exchange trading screens, bar staff in trading jackets and cocktails named after hot stocks – and colonial chic: the male staff in starched tunics and the waitresses dressed as sing-song girls in tight Chinese dresses. Last night they had gone to *Old Malaya* and in spite of her determination to enjoy herself, Fei had hated the whole evening, surrounded by straight couples talking about weddings and children, and a few single men trying to chat her up. When she had got home, the apartment had seemed even more lonely.

Ginny called that night as she often did now, trying to cheer Fei up with her fond jokes and sympathy. It had helped, the teasing voice in her ear easing the tension, dispelling her wretchedness. Fei had begun to look forward to each call now. Ginny was the friend she needed. A good friend. That was all.

She made herself concentrate on the document, focusing on legal phrasing and the framework of the law. She began to draft.

Soon the office filled up with lawyers and she had pages of draft clauses. The frantic business of the day began. Lawyers came in to consult her on legal points – an international jurisdiction issue, a restructuring problem, a planning query coupled with a funding risk. Amid all this, the phone rang with calls from clients and other lawyers. Fei wore a light headset that allowed her to move around and freed her hands to juggle documents. The call that made her day was one from a contact she had made at the inauguration ceremony – a Korean software company looking to set up a distribution network in Malaysia. At the partners' meeting she was up-beat from the high of it, cracking jokes and working through the agenda with gusto.

In the afternoon, as she was scrolling through the billing accounts on her computer, the lights went out. The screen blinked off. The offices were plunged into semi-darkness. Fei felt a jolt of panic. First, the lurking assassin at the inauguration ceremony. Then the attempted break-in at her apartment. Sam gone. The equilibrium of her daily life seemed to shake still from the after-effects. The sudden darkness alarmed her for no reason. Fei tried to steady her nerves as she stepped out into the main area.

One of the receptionists came through. 'It's happened on the whole floor. Short circuit-lah.'

'There's an electricity board fellow doing routine maintenance in the basement.' Fei's secretary spoke up from a call she'd made to the ground-floor lobby. 'He must've blown a fuse-lah.'

Secretaries sat away from their terminals, stretching. Lawyers wandered to each other's desks for a chat. The air-conditioning fell silent.

After a few minutes, the lights flickered on again. Computers whirred on. There was cool again as the air-conditioners started up. Fei went back to her desk. The computer was on but showed an error in the application. Tension ground her. It alarmed her, this lack of control that seemed to have permeated the last few weeks. She didn't like chaos, it disturbed and upset her. She heard one of the secretaries call, 'We need to re-boot the server.'

'Faridah's on holiday,' someone said. Faridah was the systems manager. The server was the mainframe computer that provided the digital memory and brain for all the terminals in the office. It was never turned off as re-booting involved a specific procedure in the operating system that underpinned the everyday Windows applications. The short-circuit had crashed it. 'Who else knows how to start up the server?'

No one did and Faridah's emergency folder with the relevant instructions could not be found. They would have to call the computer service contractors to come out to start up the system. Fei swore to herself. This was a mess. She tried to ease the tension inside her. She would speak to Faridah when she got back from holiday. Set up new controls, back-up procedures against such failures in the future.

⸺►●◄⸺

In the basement, the electricity board technician closed the circuit cabinet and replaced his tools in his kit bag. He spoke into his cellphone. 'It's all yours.'

Han replied, 'Got it.' He slipped his phone into his pocket. He was at the end of the road, crouched by a telephone exchange substation. It was a hot afternoon and the traffic roaring by kicked up a haze of dust. The overalls he wore over his suit were stifling. Sweat prickled on his face but did not smear the dark make-up he wore. His jaw and cheeks were itchy under the glue of the beard, his head baking under the wig. To anyone who looked, he knew he passed for an Indian.

The technician was one of the many contacts Han had cultivated in KL over the years. The man owed him a favour for money Han had lent him to buy a car – the sort of standard family expenses Han and other Snakes paid in exchange for extending their network.

The substation door stood open to reveal a tangle of coloured wires, thin as vermicelli, set in a complex grid. Han connected the interceptor to the line from Ming, Siap & Qwong's office. It was programmed to pick up a specific number, letting all others pass. He held the palm-sized box in his hand, reading the LCD display. After ten minutes, it locked on to the number that was ringing. He picked up the receiver linked by a line to the interceptor and hit the 'accept' button.

'Blue Chip Computer Systems, can I help you?' he said. The voice-alteration device over the mouth-piece would transmit his voice as that of a woman. 'One moment, please. I'll connect you to our service personnel.'

Han lifted off the device and spoke with an Indian accent. 'Siva, here. What's the problem?'

He went through a list of questions about the law firm's server that the secretary calling would expect to be asked – its serial number, the information currently displayed on the screen, the firm's account details. 'I'll be with you within the hour, *mem*. It's better to do a systems test as well, you don't know what damage a power surge can cause.'

Han hung up and disconnected his equipment. He walked round the corner to his car, stripped off the overalls and stowed his gear in the boot. He pulled out a briefcase and put on a pair of thick spectacles. Checking his make-up, he wiped off the sweat and straightened his tie. He sat in the car and turned on the air-conditioning. Half an hour later, he pulled up to the *Menara* Loy.

He had followed up on Qwong's details after their surveillance of the Centre. Having located her firm, he had contacted the Family's Data Research people. They had the appropriate access channels to government-held data in most Asian countries and had obtained a list of the firm's employees through cross-referencing Inland Revenue records. He had befriended the firm's junior secretary at a singles bar, posing as a computer analyst. Over several dates, tanked up with pina coladas, the girl had told him all he needed to know about the firm's computer system. She had told him when the systems manager would be on holiday, had brought him the instructions folder, given him the name of the service company, all in the belief that if she could participate in his passion for systems software, she might also participate in his life.

Up in the law firm's offices, the same junior secretary walked past without recognising him under his disguise. An older woman who'd showed him to the server hovered while he fiddled with the wires and tapped on the keyboard. They were in a box-room in the far corner of the office, more walk-in broom cupboard than an office. The computer equipment sat among cartons of disks, software manuals and discarded furniture.

Re-booting and systems tests were not complex procedures if you knew what you were doing, he thought, but he made a show of convoluted analysis. After a few minutes, she was called away. Quickly, he located the modem behind the hard-drive tower. It connected the lawyers' individual terminals to the server for e-mail purposes and each socket and lead was labelled with the fee-earner's initials. He unplugged 'QFL' and fitted a tracer device, no larger than a matchbox, before re-attaching the lead into the socket via the device. The device ran off the power from the modem.

Han slid the door shut and pulled out of his briefcase the transmission box, a pair of insulated gloves, pliers and screw-driver. He climbed up on to the desk, the monitor between his feet. He did not have long. Working swiftly, he pried away a ceiling tile and slipped the transmission box into the space. He pulled on the gloves. He could just reach the wire leading to the overhead light. After a few minutes, he had connected the box to the electricity supply, by-passing the on-off switch at the wall.

When the secretary re-appeared, the ceiling tile was back in place and he had the server up and running. The tracer in Qwong's modem socket would extract duplicates of whatever passed through the modem to the lead to her terminal. The data would be sent by a secure radio channel to the transmission box in the ceiling, which was equipped with a powerful booster to transmit on. The receiving point was in a room in a low sixties building several blocks away. It consisted of a mobile commu-nications modem wired to a computer with multiple CD-ROM drivers. Qwong's daily communications would be recorded there for Han's review. He had rented the room under his cover of one-man insurance broking agency.

Fei glanced up from her dictation as the Indian man shuffled through the door. 'I have to systems test your terminal, *mem*,' he mumbled. For him to access the computer, she had to leave her desk. She moved past him, taking tape and files to give to her secretary. But there was something unusual about him. Fei glanced back. He was athletic, the muscles in his back outlined under his light jacket. Yet he moved with marked self-consciousness. His expansive male presence filled the poky room in spite of his deferential manner. She felt uneasy, her earlier sense of alarm returning. She watched as he huddled over the keyboard, trying to quell her anxiety. He was just doing his job, she thought as she left the room.

Han slid a bugging device out of his pocket and reached for her phone.

'Any problems?' Qwong stood at the door.

'No, *mem*.' Han pushed the phone aside as if to give himself more room, pocketing the device again. She moved to the desk to study the screen. He ran the standard checks. She did not move away till he had finished and then only to let him pass. He glanced back at the door to find her busy with papers on the desk.

When the man had gone, Fei checked her drawers and looked over the phone and terminal. Nothing missing. She sighed. Perhaps she was getting too paranoid. The patient who had attacked her at the Centre had not hurt her. No one had been injured by the 'assassin' at the inauguration ceremony. No one had managed to get into her flat. The blackout had just been a short circuit. Why was she so jumpy? There was nothing here that could give her away. She massaged her temples. She needed to relax, she told herself.

Han worked his way through the office, checking the other terminals. He was tense in spite of himself, ready to take another chance to place the bugging device on Qwong's phone. But she never left her room, and he could not risk further contact with her, given her watchfulness. His presence in these offices raised a finger to the Family's orders for passive surveillance only. *No penetration, no covert action.* Han swore under his breath. They had wanted him to do his job with his fucking hands tied behind his back. But if he played it right, they would never need to know about this till he got the results he needed. Then he'd be a fucking hero and no one would weep over his methods.

He had failed in the operation to penetrate the Centre. The dressing down Mokhtar had given him still smarted. Surveillance on a part-time basis in-between other jobs and without penetration was a goddam' joke. He'd had no choice but to disobey if he wanted a shot at breaking this thing open. He had tried to access the Wyndhams' suite in KL to place recording devices but his recce of the block had revealed security at all entrances, CCTV in the underground car park, lobby and along the outside of the building. All visitors had to have prior appointments notified to security or be verified by the apartment resident over the CCTV intercom. Undetected penetration would be impossible, especially as Han was working without a back-up team. It was a luxury block for wealthy ex-pats and such security was in keeping with the anxieties of the rich. But Han's investigations had also revealed that the block was AVA-owned – a property-managing company in which a senior AVA executive had a controlling interest. It had goaded him like poison in the gut.

He had moved on Qwong in the hope that she might be the weak link in the security around the Wyndhams. As their lawyer, she was likely to have inside knowledge of their trans-actions and dealings, especially with any corporate vehicles or financial structures set up to front illegal activities. He had tried to break into her apartment but the alarms had been tripped as he had started on the locks. Bugging her lines at home and at work from outside had not been an option. Both lines came through a main switching terminal with hundreds of other calls a day to and from the other phones in the buildings. The interceptor had only worked because he had known the number being dialled at the service company. He had left it connected, programmed to pick up the few numbers he had been able to trace to the Centre and the Wyndhams. But he suspected that there were probably other lines and numbers that his targets used, either illegally or registered under names he could not track. Calls made through those connections were lost to him. Still, at least, he had planted the modem bug through the sloppy management of her law firm. Han began to shuffle across the open-plan floor. As he passed Qwong's door, he darted a look inside.

She looked up and met his gaze. He glanced away.

He rode the lift down. He would have to be satisfied with his one success. It was a matter now of sifting through the transmissions that passed to her terminal: e-mails and data transfers that might yield some tangible information about the Wyndhams and their activities for the AVA.

Han scratched his chin through the beard. He had also gained some ground on the American, he thought, in spite of not having found anything of significance in his apartment. Han had been following Dean and had broken into his apartment in an old, unsecured block of flats downtown. It had been sparsely furnished and the only items of note had been a TV, video recorder and satellite dish on the wall outside the window. A word-processor had stood on a desk nearby. The one-room apartment had had 'foreign correspondent' written all over it. Otherwise nothing of significance had turned up, not even when Han had checked walls, floor and ceiling with a radio-frequency scanner that detected pulses from hidden electronic devices and equipment. He had put a tap on the phone and a bug in the light socket in each room. This morning, Han had accessed the tapes in his 'insurance' office to which the bugs were transmitting. All of them played a local radio station endlessly. At first he had cursed − in disguising the transmission channels of bugging devices, it was common to tune them closely to the frequency of a radio station: had he mistuned the channels? Then it struck him that Dean might have done a sweep and found the bugs, re-tuning them to make them useless in a way that would mislead his surveillant. That would be what Han would himself have done. Most likely, Dean had also bolstered the security in the flat to make future break-ins more difficult. The question was: what kind of 'journalist' would do a regular sweep − or even know how to?

He would fucking break this thing open, Han promised himself. He strode out into the hot afternoon and looked up towards the fifteenth floor. Qwong would be his ticket in.

Chapter Seven

The Petaling Street night-market thronged with noise and smells. The heart of KL's Chinatown heaved with people browsing through gaudy stalls of T-shirts, leather goods and cheap watches. Music and video stalls played their tapes at full volume, the latest Jackie Chan competing with the Spice Girls. Generators powered lights and equipment under multi-coloured umbrellas. Barbecuing pork filled the air with smoke. A drinks stall sold *air mata kucing*, sugary water spiced with the cat's eye fruit. A Malay man fanned racks of *satay* over hot coals. An Indian stall poured *teh tarik*, sweet tea shooting from one jug to the next.

Fei bought iced sugar-cane juice, dangling the plastic bags from her fingers. She gave a bag to Ginny and they moved on through the jostling bodies, dodging trolleys of cheesy-smelling *durian* fruit. Ginny's pleasure was infectious as she took in everything with wide-eyed delight. Fei found herself laughing at nothing. In the last few weeks, she had talked for hours on the phone with Ginny. It had been a relief to talk about Sam, about how their relationship had ended, how conflicted she felt. Ginny had not lost the knack of making Fei laugh even when she had been at her most miserable. Before long, they would fall into their old teasing and word-play, Fei's spirits lifting with each moment. Ginny was her affectionate self again and their friendship seemed deepened by the hurt of each of their broken relationships.

Piers had gone to Johore Baru to work on a project for a week and Ginny had come down to KL, ostensibly for meetings. Away from the Centre, Fei thought, Ginny seemed to bloom, her face animated with pleasure. Pushing through the crowds, she turned and caught Fei's hand. Her grip was firm and confident. She called, 'I don't want to lose you!'

'You won't.'

Ginny held her gaze for a long beat. Her eyes crinkled as she smiled. For a while they walked very close, the crowds pushing them against each other. Fei felt the warmth of Ginny's body as they touched. Ginny did not let go of her hand. It was only after several minutes that Fei realised she did not want her to.

As if in a dream she realised she was not afraid to hold Ginny's hand in public. A blur of faces and colours and lights swirled around her but they were nothing to her. People were everywhere but they were nowhere. It was as if nothing existed but Ginny and her. A rush of voices and music made her start. A Chinese family pushed past. Malay youths laughed and puffed on *kretek*, the clove-tinted cigarette smoke blowing in her face. It struck Fei that no one saw anything out of place, they were just friends. Two girl friends looking for trinkets. She felt a strange rush of vertigo. No one saw anything strange because there was nothing to see. Two women together in Asia, touching and affectionate before all eyes, meant only sisterly feeling. Fei laughed out loud. Ginny was not Sam, and without that intensity of feeling Fei experienced the exhilaration of liberation.

They ate *hokkien mee* in a coffee-shop, the tables set under the open sky. The noodles were dense with garlic and caramelized soy sauce. Flames from the stoves flashed as the cooks tossed shrimps and pork in their woks. Sweat dampened Fei's body beneath her silk vest. She used to come here with Sam, she thought. It had always felt safe. No one they knew would come to the night-market. Most of KL's middle classes preferred the First World ambience of air-conditioned bars and restaurants to this Third World face of the city, a contrast to the film-set look of *White Raja* and *Old Malaya*. Sam had laughed once: 'This Asia is just too real for them.' It felt strange to be here with someone other than her. But also not so strange. This was Ginny after all. Fei sipped jasmine tea and grinned. 'You've been such a good distraction for me. Thank you.'

'You mean, like a stand-up comic between the acts?' Ginny pulled a face of mock-indignation.

'No.'

Ginny picked up the pepper pot like a microphone, the old teasing look on her face. She started the patter of a vaudeville entertainer, her eyes never leaving Fei. 'What a great crowd you are here tonight. Did you hear the one about the lightbulb? How many feminists does it take to change a lightbulb? Five – one to change it and four to form a support group. Boom, boom.'

'Ginny, I didn't mean . . .' Fei tried again but laughter overcame her.

'Our main attraction this evening: Ms Fei-Li Qwong – drum roll, please.' Ginny poked the pepper pot under Fei's nose.

Fei shook her head, gulping with laughter. 'Stop it! You know what I mean!' She grabbed Ginny's hand to stop her waving the pepper pot. Their laughter subsided. She was holding Ginny's hand in both of hers. Colour rose in Ginny's cheeks. She did not move. Fei withdrew, the warm touch of Ginny's hand like an imprint on her palms. She could not look at her.

Ginny's voice was suffused with breath. 'I do know what you mean. And it's my pleasure.' Then, so softly Fei had to strain to hear, 'I love being with you.'

Fei felt the white noise of confusion. It was as if the affection they had felt for each other had flipped into something else. When had it happened? Fei flashed on the times they'd spent together, their conversations on the phone, Ginny's hints at her distant relations with Piers. Fei had always thought Ginny attractive, loved her charm and confidence. She had never wanted to think of her as anything other than a friend. But then, Sam had always been there. And Fei had always thought Ginny to be happily married.

She had not wanted to read the signals. But clear in her

memory, there they all were: the way Ginny looked at her, the teasing tone in her voice, the way she touched Fei's arm, took her hand, lightly embraced her waist. She saw it now, the desire that had been unspoken but infused in every moment they had passed together. Ginny's air of grasping neediness that night at the Centre had confused her at first but now it made sense. Fei felt the rush of an electric storm on her skin.

'How – how long have you and Piers been –' she began.

'A long time. He and I, we've never – we haven't slept together in – in years.'

'What happened?'

Ginny shifted. She stared at the passing crowd. 'It's difficult to explain. We're not . . . It just wouldn't have been right.' More firmly, 'Let's say it just didn't work out and leave it at that.'

Fei nodded. 'I'm sorry, I didn't mean to intrude.'

Ginny dismissed the apology with a wave. She said brightly, 'Do you want to come back for coffee?'

Her colour suddenly deepened again and an embarrassed smile curled her lips. Her eyes flicked away but she forced them back, concentrated on Fei. The classic connotation of the question had dawned on her at the same time as it had on Fei.

She found herself unable to stop grinning. 'Coffee – or "coffee"?'

Ginny attempted casualness. 'Well, a midnight snack then. Hot milk and nibbles before bed . . .' She hid her eyes with her hand, flustered. 'Oh God, did I really say that?'

'I think you did.' Fei's smile was so wide it hurt. Warmth crept into her face.

Ginny sat up straight. 'All right, a drink. Would you like to come back for a drink? Bailey's perhaps?'

'I would love to.'

———————⇒ଚେଟ———————

Sam recognised Ginny Wyndham from her photographs in the media. She was sitting at a table in a coffee-shop, in T-shirt and jeans, talking to a woman who had her back to Sam. She wondered idly what someone like Ginny was doing in the market and something made her pause in her stride.

After moving out of Fei's apartment, Sam had managed to rent a small house in Petaling Jaya, the satellite town on the edge of KL. It was a short drive from the hospital but she often found herself detouring across town after work, unable to head straight home. She would drive for hours, skimming through the highways that tangled through the city, heading out into the dark landscape on the north-south interstate. Tonight, she had cruised through the older part of town, taking little roads that wound round residential areas and ending up here in Chinatown. Parking askew on a yellow line, she had stopped to buy take-out noodles for dinner.

Ginny Wyndham looked like the cat who'd got the cream, Sam thought as she skirted round the tables out of her line of vision. And then she saw Fei.

Sam slid behind a watch stall. Her heart felt as if it would fail. She stared at the two women through the dangling trinkets. Ginny got up, Fei following. They were both smiling. Sam had not seen Fei smile like that for so long. It was the smile of a new lover. It slashed at Sam's gut.

As the women moved away, Ginny glanced in her direction. For a moment, their gazes met. Sam held the stare unable to move or think. And then Ginny looked away, back at Fei.

Sam made her way blindly through the crowd. Somehow she got back to her car. Sitting in its silence, she felt as if someone was squeezing her heart till blood ran.

Ginny slid open the doors to the terrace. The warm evening met her, drawing her from the air-conditioned interior of the apartment. Behind her, Fei dropped her briefcase and linen jacket on the sofa and slipped off her shoes. She had been up here countless times on business or for dinner and the apartment was familiar to her. The security staff downstairs had greeted her like a resident as she and Ginny had come in. The ease with which Fei seemed at home here filled Ginny with a pleasure that was almost proprietorial. It felt good to think of Fei as a part of her life.

Fei came out on to the terrace. In her bare feet, she seemed even smaller next to Ginny. She might have been a teenage girl in her white vest and dark tailored trousers. Ginny felt awkwardly robust as if her own shoulders were too broad, her manner clumsy and mannish beside a beautiful child. Fei leaned on the balustrade and looked out over the city lights. There was a hazy sheen smearing them, as if seen through dirty glass. Away from the busy smells of the market, the night air was scented with smoke.

Ginny felt as if her heart would burst. It had been easy after all, asking Fei back here. They stood so close now. Ginny wanted to touch her, feel the warmth of her smooth brown arms, taste the scent on the curve of her throat. It was as if these last few weeks, every moment had driven her to this next move. She had not thought of what might happen beyond it. A heart-beat away from her desire, terror gripped her. She thought of Piers, working on the new experiment even now. If it was a success, the Cure might yet save her from this self she hardly knew. But there was no more waiting, she was here now, on the brink of everything she wanted and everything she feared.

The dirty yellow walls of the criminal court spun suddenly into her vision. The sea of faces staring up at her. The drone of the prosecutor's voice. So many questions, so many insinuations, the jury shifting in their seats, disgust clear on their faces. There had been an uproar in the court and outside, beneath the sentinel towers of the courthouse, the media frenzy had surged at them. Microphones and cameras thrust at them, wild faces shouting questions, goading her.

Ginny remembered screaming, terrified and furious: 'Leave Katie out of this!' Then people grabbing her, pinning her down, dragging her into the waiting car.

She moved away from Fei. In the cool of the drawing room,

she poured two glasses of Bailey's on ice. She was trembling but told herself it was just the air-conditioning. The apartment sprawled across the thirtieth floor, fitted out with meeting rooms, dining room, guest rooms and a study. It was the manifestation of her present incarnation. The past was another place, another lifetime. It could not find her, she told herself.

Outside, Fei felt the warm breeze on her skin. She could not be sure what had happened this evening, how she had arrived at this moment. It all seemed a blur of colour and half-remembered conversation. Nothing existed but being here now, enveloped by the night, the smell of smoke in the air. It was as if an electric storm had passed through her memory and erased everything. Sam was just a name, the last few years a film she could hardly recall. Ginny offered forgetfulness, a connection without responsibility or doubts. Fei realised suddenly how long it had been since she had made love with breathless excitement. Her encounters in the last year with Sam had been like the conversations of a couple who had forgotten how to talk to each other, correct in form but devoid of meaning. Being with Ginny, immersed in the other's desire, Fei felt herself awake only to the present moment, sensing each passing emotion as if that was all there was and all that mattered. She felt safe with Ginny for they both had so much to lose. It was a bond that tied them to secrecy, an understanding without words that drew them even closer. Her anxieties of the past weeks, the hurt of losing Sam, were forgotten in this fine mist of desire. It clung to Fei, hid from her everything beyond the immediate moment, cocooned her here with Ginny in timelessness.

Ginny came back out into the night. She did not know what she was going to do but in the distance between the interior of the apartment and Fei, Ginny felt as if she travelled into another consciousness. It was as if she had already decided, had always known, what she would do. She had only had to let her last defence crumble. Fei was turning to watch her – and in those long eyes, Ginny found the permission she had denied herself. Her terror fell away, memories of Katie, the guilt that bound her to Piers dispersed into smoke. There was only Fei, her smile that made Ginny dizzy, a longing that exploded from her very core.

Fei reached for one of the glasses in Ginny's hand. She said, 'I love being with you.' Her voice was like silk.

Ginny fumbled the glass. Fei caught it, the creamy liquid splashing on to her hand, ice cubes clattering to the floor. She was laughing, a sound that collapsed whatever of Ginny's consciousness that remained. Ginny took the glass from her, spilling liquid now from both glasses in her one hand.

With the other Ginny drew Fei's hand towards her. She did not take her eyes off Fei. Inclining her head, she licked the liqueur from Fei's fingers.

Liak heard the blaring music as he stepped out of the van. It was mid-morning, glaringly and hazily hot. The air smelt like stale cigarettes. They had driven to the far side of the grounds of Johore Baru. Here the bougainvillaea bushes had not been cut, the grass of the lawns straggly and tall. He recognised Anjing Engine, a Malay rock band. Their latest hit was all squealing guitars and hoarse vocals, lyrics about money and girls. Liak grabbed his tote bag from the pile on the gravel, jostling the other kids who had got out with him. The anxiety in his gut eased. This was like no hospital he'd ever been to. Anjing Engine had been banned from Malaysian public broadcast a few times for obscene and un-Muslim songs. They were the coolest, Liak thought. He'd heard an illegally taped song that someone in his class had got from Hong Kong. *I wanna fuck you from behind* – he'd chanted that line the next day at school. Made two girls cry with it. Liak grinned.

He caught the eye of one of the other guys, Salim, thirteen, a year older than Liak but in his class. Liak pulled a face as if to say maybe this place wasn't so bad but he wasn't going to relax yet. Salim prodded the nine-year-old kid, Timmy, making him stumble. 'You're in my way, worm shit.'

Timmy was scared but trying not to show it. Liak swallowed.

Nothing to be fucking scared of, he told himself. The hospital guys began to round them up, big guys in jeans and T-shirts, name badges pinned to their chest. The five boys followed them into the one-storey building, Liak jerking his head to the beat of the music to break his pent-up energy.

The dormitory already had six or seven boys in it, their stuff thrown on to several of the beds that lined the walls. At the far end, a TV was playing, a jumble of clips like a music video – only they made no sense: Mickey Mouse, then Jackie Chan, then Japanese cartoons, then Madonna. The sound was off, loud rock music over-dubbed. The kids were all guys from Liak's school, the troublemakers. Heng, sixteen, big and muscled like Stallone, had brought a machete to class and threatened the teacher. Rashid, a wiry Indian kid, always fighting, had knocked out another kid. Salim had stolen money from the secretary's office to buy 'E'. Little Timmy had beaten up some of the younger kids for their pocket money.

Liak dumped his tote bag on a bed. Among these familiar faces, he felt his anxiety fade. They were all in this together. He was here because he had been caught by the truant officer vandalising cars in a back lot by the cinema. And for exposing himself in the girls' toilets at school. And stealing – Old Beng's grocery store, Fatt the ice-cream guy, other kids' bags and desks, the school canteen: you name it, he'd taken from it. Liak was stashing it up to go find his brother in KL, then he'd be out of this shit life in JB, make a name for himself like *Tai Koh*. Elder Brother had left JB two years ago. No word since but money orders would arrive for *Ma*. She'd use it for groceries, fixing up the leak in the bathroom, boring stuff. He got a few *ringgit* more pocket money a week but that was all. Liak knew *Tai Koh* had made it big in KL – probably driving around in a Merc, girl by his side, getting respect wherever he went. Liak would surprise him. Show *Tai Koh* he had the street-smarts to get ahead too. Show all the fuckers. He'd be somebody and no one would treat him or his family like shit anymore.

The school had made *Ma* send him here. They had been going to kick him out for good. That would've been fine by him. But they'd talked her into this second chance shit. If he took part in this therapy thing, they'd keep him on at school. *Ma* had taken time off from the factory to meet the head and more time off this morning to see them pick him up. She always got pushed around, never stood up for herself or for him. His stomach clenched into a fist of fury at the thought of her anxious face. 'Be a good boy-lah,' she had pleaded with him. 'Go to school, study hard. Why you get into trouble all the time?'

He didn't know why. Liak scowled. He hated it when she pleaded. That soft woman's whine. If she wanted him to do something, she should just fucking tell him, he thought, not wheedle like she used to do with *Ba*. No fucking wonder Father left. To shut her up, Liak had attended school for the last month, leaning back in his chair against the wall, bored. At least they served a bloody good lunch – free, too, for everyone at school that month. Curry with huge chunks of meat, spicy beef patties, slabs of roast meat and plenty of iced milk. The milk had been flown in from Australia, they said – the creamy taste better than the powdered stuff he was used to. Some kind of health drive by the school. The shit part was they all had to do PE three times a week, running round that damn' field, even the girls, press-ups, squat jumps till his body hurt.

Two hospital guys came through the door with boxes of canned drinks. They set them on a table then left. The boys scrummed for the drinks.

'No fucking beer!' Heng growled.

They grabbed two or three tins each, beginning to relax. Liak got cola, orange and lemonade drinks. The guys popped all their cans over the next hour. Liak joined in joking and rapping over all kinds of stuff, swigging back the sweet drinks. He could almost forget where he was. They finished the drinks, tossing the empties on to the floor. Heng filled his with piss.

'I could fucking break out of here if I wanted to.' Heng sat on the window sill, leaning against the wire grilles. He flexed his huge arms, pulled a face. 'But the cops are out for me. It was here or Matok.' Matok was the young offenders' unit outside Johore Baru. 'So I say to myself, why not-lah? Easy life for one week, good food, watch TV all day. Only you fuckers are here and not one damn' one of you a girl, man!'

Salim gravitated towards the crowd forming round Heng. 'What you think this therapy is?'

'You're not fucking scared, are you?' Heng eyed him.

Salim puffed out his chest, hitching up his jeans. 'Just asking.'

Rashid made wild eyes. 'They gonna fuck with your head. Electrodes here and zzzt!'

'Ice pick here between your eyes – then whap! In it goes and you're a nice guy.' Liak mimed the procedure.

Timmy moved away from the group. He looked like he was going to cry. Liak thought, maybe he shouldn't have frightened the kid. But something about that sad, weak face made him angry. Fucking cry-baby, he thought.

Liak began to feel bored. When was anything going to happen? He sat on his bed, staring at the TV. Cartoons were playing. A dog with big funny ears and teeth. 'I'm sweet on you,' it said in a dumb voice. The music was a flute, tootling a melody of love. Liak was dimly aware that the rock music had faded away. Why the fuck were they playing this shit? He looked around. Everyone else was staring at the screen, some on their beds, some standing, all stopped in the middle of what they'd been doing. The bright screen lured Liak's eyes back. The dog's eyes were huge, black against white. A red polka dot tie beamed out from under his chin. The melody rang in Liak's head over and over again. Black eyes against white. Laughing mouth with giant teeth. 'I'm sweet on you,' Liak said.

He found himself standing up. He had the idea he'd go to the door. But the dog was here and he couldn't leave the dog, the sweet dog. Then the dog was gone, blank darkness in a flash. Liak heard the flute playing, the same phrase over and over. He liked the phrase. It filled his brain. He thought he'd go now. He noticed that the others were doing the same. Strange, he thought. He was vaguely aware of a voice, a guy's voice – older, tough-sounding – speaking over that sweet melody. Where was it coming from? There was only them kids. Liak walked through the door, down a corridor and through some other doors. The older guy was talking, like right beside him. But when Liak looked, there was no one there.

Ben Chang watched the kids come through the door into the hall. His assistants went through to the dorm to collect the soft drinks cans for incineration. Other staff began to fit the boys with monitoring equipment, sensors across their skulls for brain activity, pads to monitor pulse, breathing rate and blood pressure all wired up to body sets on belts strapped to their waist. The sets collected data while transmitting it to the main controls where Piers and the medical team assessed the information. The boys were quiet and still, as instructed by the voice over the speakers. Ricky had modified Ginny's version of the programme, giving the scenarios a harder edge, a streetwise jaggedness. The instructive voice had the rasp of a tough-guy, the kind of man these kids would respect. From experience, Ben could tell that the boys were in a deepening trance state. The chronotonin dose injected into the soft drinks had triggered the Cure exactly as Piers had calculated, right down to the moment. Ben felt a spark of relief. If Piers was right on this count, he was probably right about the long-term effects of this experiment. This one, of all their work, could be the one to succeed after all.

They would have these premises for a week. The buildings were part of Johore Baru's general hospital, an old sixties clinic that had been abandoned since modern blocks had been built a few years ago. Ginny Wyndham, working closely with Piers, had persuaded not only the school board but also a number of local councillors as to the merits of the experiment and they had arranged for the use of the clinic. They were told it was not an experiment as such but community-based social therapy, a non-invasive technique for rehabilitating the socially excluded through affirmation and community-related activities. Piers had issued a month-long pre-therapy programme to the teachers and parents, to be implemented for the whole school. It involved a healthy diet, exercise and communication techniques based on affirmation, positive feedback and support. In his presentation to the board and councillors, he had guaranteed success, promising that the school would go down in history as the first to implement the therapy that would change the face of Asia.

'We are at the dawn of a new age. There will be no more delinquency, no more crime, no more degenerates, no more anti-social behaviour. The Asian way of community and helping each other will win through. The children of today are the makers of the future. You will be the founders of a new tomorrow. Generations to come will look back on this school, on all of you, and know that their Asia is a better place because of you.'

They had embraced his ideas, purring at his flattery. Ben wanted to believe it all. Sentiments such as these had been why he had joined the AVA as a young kid. Science was the answer to a better life, a better society, better people. Now he was not so sure.

The hall was fitted out with huge TV screens on all the walls. Bean-bags and cushions were scattered across the floor. Ben and the scientific team wore communication headsets. The controls and screens were connected by remote video and data link to the computer and psych teams at the Centre. Piers, at the main bank of controls, sat upright and stern. There was an icy passion about his manner, precise yet invested with a hardness that might almost have been cruel.

Piers watched the kids but all he saw was *him*. The loathing surfaced like a corpse out of water. He controlled it with all his determination. These kids were like *him*, they would become *him*, if Piers did not change them now. *He* would have been better dead as a child than the monster *he* had become. So too for them.

His spoke over the network, his voice clipped. 'Standby, all teams. Proceed to Stage Two.'

Chapter Eight

The man towered over his son, his face mean and cruel. He was drunk. He swore at the boy, cuffed him across the head. The boy looked about six. He cowered in terror, crying. They were in a tatty kitchen, smashed rice bowls on the floor, chairs over-turned. The man beat the boy, fists thudding into flesh. His roar drowned out the kid's squealing. The background dissolved into a living room, cheap furniture against a cement floor.

Each blow thwacked through the hall. Liak and the other boys flinched as if they had been struck. They stared up at the giant screens, faces contorted with the boy's agony. Some turned their heads away but the bright pictures drew them back. Their bodies were immobile as if in sleep. They were sobbing. The huge figures on the screens were invading their consciousness, clawing out their own experiences, mingling fiction and memory like blood. Ben Chang could hardly bear to watch. He stared at the readings on their monitors. They showed rapid pulse rates, sweat, shallow breathing, tensed muscles. Brain activity showed stress, increased adrenaline.

Piers's voice came over the network. 'Move into Stage Three – Empowerment.' He was watching the boys impassively.

The tough-guy voice spoke. 'You can stop this. You can change what happens. You have the power.' It was a command.

The boys were breathing hard but they were listening.

'Feel the strength of your voice. It's getting louder inside you. Your voice is your power. You can stop the beating, you have the power, you *are* the power. It's bursting out to stop the beating. Stop it, stop the beating, do it now!'

The boys opened their mouths as one, throats rigid with fury. Their voices exploded. 'Stop it! Stop now! Stop, stop!' It became the scream of wild animals.

The man on the screen looked up, arm frozen in mid-blow. He stared at the boys, his face stricken. Their shouting continued. He backed away from the little boy. He seemed afraid, growing smaller. His eyes were lowered, his posture submissive. The background changed into a marble hall, dwarfing the man. The colour faded to muted shades, the little boy turning to the real boys in the hall. He grew to fill the screen, a giant now. He was brighter, more colourful than the rest of the picture, his cuts and bruises fading. He smiled and gave a thumbs-up to the real boys.

They shrieked in euphoria. Tears streamed down their cheeks. The tough-guy voice said, 'You did it! You changed how this turns out. You are heroes.'

'I did it!' each boy laughed. 'I'm a hero! I stopped him!'

Ben's relief was as tangible as a shot of liquor. The fantasy had been devised by the psych team. It tapped into similar documented experiences in the boys' lives. Those memories would reconstruct familiar locations over the disorientation that the scene changes evoked. In their deep state of trance, they experienced the drama as a real event, the tough-guy voice telling them how to feel, how to react. It was saying now, 'You will always remember this. *You* stopped them beating you – *you* stopped your father, your uncle, your brother. They could never hurt you. You have the power, you will always have the power.'

The boys were nodding.

Without the Cure, the fantasy was no more than an interactive movie. The Cure made all the difference. They seldom used its scientific term these days, the name bestowed by Siew having such emotive and heroic resonance – 'the cure for society's ills'; 'evil is a sickness and we will find Asia's cure for it': these phrases permeated all of Siew's speeches. Ben remembered how Piers had explained the science of the Cure to him.

'What are we but the sum of all our experiences read through our emotions?' Piers's eyes had flashed with excitement. The sum of our experiences, he had said, was banked in our long-term memories. In neurological terms, memory existed only as the firing of circuits of neurons across the cortex, the outer layer of the brain. A specific memory was the coming to life of a specific set of neurons in a dancing feedback between the hippocampal system, which included the hippocampus and the amygdala, and the neocortical regions. By modifying the pattern of the circuit board, Piers had postulated, they could modify the memory thrown up by it – alter it, tune up certain factors, play down others, replace it with a different version. In changing a person's store of memories, they could change the sum of his experiences and so change his life – or at least his perception of his life: which amounted to the same thing.

Ben watched the boys. Experiences were accompanied by emotional responses. Emotional functioning arose from the interaction of the limbic system – the hippocampus and amygdala again, and the hypothalamus – with the posterior parietal cortex of the right hemisphere of the brain and the pre-frontal cortex. The interaction occurred through neural firing and the release of hormones such as adrenaline. When a memory was triggered the accompanying emotion would be stirred up again. Piers had hypothesised that a modification of the emotion would additionally fine-tune the character of the person they were creating anew.

Conventional therapies such as hypnosis, meditation, visualisation, neuro-linguistic programming and bio-feedback superficially adapted memories and reactions to cure a patient of phobias, to develop self-esteem or to reduce stress. Their success depended on the willingness of the patient to co-operate and none attempted permanent and radical alteration of the patient's belief in who he was and what his life meant. The beauty of the Cure, Ben mused, was that, when activated, it put the brain involuntarily into a state of shock akin to a deep trance. In such a state, adapted hypnosis techniques and graphics-aided visualisation by-passed the will of the subject to reconfigure his store of memories and emotional responses. The reconfigured neural reactions created in his consciousness the better life and better person he had not had the chance to be in reality.

If this experiment worked, these kids would *know* themselves to have had fulfilled childhoods and contented family relationships. They would believe in themselves. They would find their strengths and talents, the motivation to achieve their best potential. They would be fit citizens for the new Asia. Ben knew each of their stories in-depth from the detailed psych reports that had been prepared and his heart went out to them. Now he and Piers and their team were giving these boys a chance for happiness and success, lifting out of the ghetto their souls as well as their bodies, making right the grim hand that fate or God had dealt them. A few years ago he might have been high on the success of it so far. But today, after all that he had seen, relief was all that he could hope for – relief that nothing had gone wrong. Yet.

Over the next week, the scientists worked intensively with the boys, using trance states induced by introduction of the trigger Piers's research had discovered. The hormone chronotonin occurred naturally in the boys' bodies, biorhythmically released in an approximately twelve-hour cycle between seven and nine in the morning and again in the evenings. Chronotonin regulated the internal body clock as an adjunct to melatonin, enabling the body's natural 25-hour diurnal cycle to correlate with the daily external cycle of 24 hours. Its decreased levels coincided with the 3-4 a.m. nadir of the human system when the body was at its most vulnerable and debilitated. In the history of espionage, the interrogation and psychological coercion of spies and war prisoners was often timed to take place during this period. Chronotonin reacted in the presence of the Cure with the boys' brains to activate the sudden state of hypnotic shock. Piers and his team took advantage of these twice-daily doses by playing consolidating sequences on the televisions in the dormitory, canteen and session rooms wherever the boys might be during the trigger periods.

For longer trance-states – of one hour to almost four – the

scientists introduced controlled doses of the hormone into the subjects' bodies through spiked drinks in sealed cans. The neural programming sequences told fables of Asian values: the little boy triumphing through study, hard work, patience, fortitude, courage and righteous anger. Painful and frightening episodes drawn from the real boys' own lives were interrupted and the outcomes transformed through interactive play with the characters on screen. The boys – through the persona of the screen boy – were able to transform dysfunctional and abusive families into loving, model relationships, eliciting praise from father, adoration from sister and mother, love and respect from his friends. Troublemakers were scorned and invariably defeated and diminished. The boys – through their projected selves in the screen boy – relived their childhoods, grew into adolescence and adulthood, good-looking strong young men, filled with compassion, grace and quiet power. The image of the boy evolved over the week from victim to the hero of archetype and embedded itself in reality through the boys living out the drama in the hall.

When the trances wore off, the boys would think little about the past. In their consciousness, new memories were setting like moulded clay. As instructed during the sessions, they cared only for the present, involving themselves in the group games, art therapy, behavioural cognitive therapy and counselling which interspersed the neural programming.

———⟫●⟪———

Every day, edited versions of the digital video recordings of the experiment were transmitted to Siew Kei-Win in encrypted data files. At the end of each set, Piers appeared and reviewed the progress made, highlighting the developments to date. Siew watched the updates on his computer monitor late at night, in the den of his colonial-style mansion in Singapore, nodding with satisfaction. The Asia he had dreamed of would yet become a reality.

He had taken a risk, trusting the Wyndhams: whites and outsiders. Siew had little respect for whites but being white was more a state of mind than a physical attribute – as evidenced in Piers Wyndham. His zeal for the cause had surpassed that of many of the Alliance's Asian devotees. He had embraced his new life and new persona freely and with passion. Not all whites would be willing to adapt with such vigour. Indeed, not all Asians understood the salvation that lay before them through Asian Values. Siew despised the arrogance of such people whatever their race. He hated their greed, their selfishness, corruption and dissolute behaviour. After the Final Phase, no one in Asia, white or otherwise, would have the will to contest the one true way.

Siew smiled. The prospects looked good. By then, Ben would be ready to take over the public role of the Alliance's Medical Co-ordinator. Wyndham would be able to retreat to the labs, as he longed to, to develop their scientific work further. Ginny Wyndham would be programmed for a better life once the serum were perfected. Her sexuality disgusted Siew but she had been a crucial factor in the development of the graphics software and was an asset now on the PR side. Each member of the Alliance was fallen once, he reminded himself, before they were shown the way of light. Siew's Christian background made him compassionate to all who tried to live the righteous life, no matter what their past, and it was a quality he fought to instil in the Alliance. The glory of the movement lay in its openness to embrace those who had turned away from their former evil and Ginny Wyndham had proved herself a model wife and woman in all the time he had known her. In fact, she had often seemed more evangelical about the Cure's potential than any of them, galvanising the scientists and back-up teams with her hope in what it could do for herself and for humanity.

Siew went out to the terrace. The house was in the exclusive District 10 suburb of Singapore. Usually, he would be able to see the lights of the city against the bay but in the thickening haze, there was only a murky darkness. It enraged him that this city state he loved was choked in the foulings of its less sophisticated neighbour. Singapore had been Siew's haven as a young man. In Australia, he had seen his Chinese schoolteacher father broken by racist taunts, ending his days washing up in a take-away. He had heard the taunting of his white mother for marrying a 'chink'. He had stood up to bullying and sneering but the cumulative abuse had begun to cow him. Visiting relatives in Singapore one summer, he had discovered a country where to be Asian was valued as the ultimate virtue. The city was growing fast, embracing modernity and progress, educating its young as if their lives depended on it. He loved the energy and ambition, the lust to be the best – and the unwavering belief that Asians could achieve anything they wanted and had a right to do it. Siew had lived here for most of his life now, giving back to his adopted country wealth, jobs, donations, schools and charitable institutes and offering to Asia a movement that could make the region the sole victor in the race to control the next thousand years. Would Asia freely embrace the power he offered it?

The question had dogged him from the beginning. Most of Asia was dragging itself into the developed world, with its new middle classes and connections to world markets. They had factories and banks, universities, computers, fast cars, highways, grand national projects like dams and towers and airports. But still deep in Asia's underbelly were parasites, vermin and scum. In the Philippines, there were squatters living amongst mountains of scrap and garbage, scratching livelihoods out of the dumpheaps. In the Indian sub-continent, millions lived in ignorance, filth and factional violence. In Malaysia, there was rural poverty, drug trafficking, prostitution. In the countries of Indo-China, the after-effects of wars, dictatorial rule and communism had left brutality, desperation and self-seeking power struggles. Most of Indonesia was still agricultural, poor and illiterate, with ethnic conflicts a regular occurrence. There was no cohesive vision for Asia, no ambition beyond the individual drive for power of each of its politicians and businessmen.

Asia could never be great without one unifying driving force, Siew thought, and he was the only man who could do it. Who *was* doing it. The AVA reached out across local politics to the whole region. Its effects and potential were more powerful than the work of any single prime minister, president or king. That was why they were all beginning to show him respect. The Alliance had not been banned – nor had N-Sat – for the many harsh comments they had made about the authorities. Reportage in other media had shifted from portraying the movement as a fringe group of laughable eccentrics, afraid of the modern world, to talking about them with a respect usually reserved for religious matters. Channels were also opening to key figures in authority across Asia – in government, the armed forces, business and religious affairs. The Alliance's campaigning over the years was beginning to work, Siew noted with satisfaction: not just in winning Asian hearts but through its unseen influences.

He had worked with the Red Tiger for years, initially with their Sydney players for revenge attacks on white thugs who had terrorised him or his friends. Now they did what he and the Alliance could not be seen to be doing. Through the triad gang, the AVA had placed hundreds of true believers in crucial positions amongst the Asian elite. In Myanmar recently, the Red Tiger had engineered a car crash to get the general out of the way and leave the vacancy to be filled by an AVA man whom the Alliance had been manoeuvring into position for years. These lynchpin figures went about their official business while underpinning every contact they had with the influential among Asia with a subtle AVA agenda. And now, the mood of those who mattered was changing at last. The Alliance was becoming respectable, even fashionable.

Asia could be great. They were now reaching completion of Phase Three with the JB experiment, and after it there would be Project Max. In under a year, Phase Four would be the real test, the dress rehearsal for the Final Phase. Siew squinted out into the smoky night. Asia's greatness would come from its people, the best spoils of any war. That was why the Final Phase had to be bloodless. But Siew was a realist. People would die before the future was won. People were dying now. But only those who deserved to die, he thought. Those who could offer nothing but corruption and evil to the Asia he loved.

The words of Christ echoed in his mind from his Bible study days: 'If you are not for me, then you are against me.'

⋖⋗⋘⋙

Liak went home the following Monday evening. He felt a rush of excitement as he came through the door. The little apartment had a cosy, safe air about it. His mother was frying noodles in the wok, her solid frame filling the kitchen. The food smelt great and Liak strode up to her with a grin. He hugged her, making her laugh with delight and confusion. She asked him a stream of questions, fussing over him. He smiled indulgently. 'Ya-lah, the kids were great. It was fun. We just played and laughed and talked and watched movies. The doctors were really cool.'

'They feed you well? You look so good! So handsome, my boy. What a smile! I haven't seen you so happy before.'

He laughed, a strong manly sound, and hugged her again. It was good to be home. He helped her make dinner. And washed up. He focused on each action, scrubbing, rinsing, placing the object on the rack. A soothing rhythm. It was eight p.m. Then he watched TV, a community channel on N-Sat which the Centre had installed as a reward for his part in the experiment.

It was a drama about a boy from a poor neighbourhood achieving his ambition to be a policeman. Liak sat transfixed, feeling the boy's every emotion, his heart quickening at the young hero's success. While he watched, his subconscious self tuned into the subliminal visuals and commands, seen only for a fraction of a second and heard only at the lowest level, scrambled with the other sounds from the show. The chemical messaging networks in his brain caught and processed them as if expanding compressed memory. The experiences were real to him, truths about himself that he felt with all his heart – he was a good boy, he loved his mother, he loved hard work and success. When the programme ended, it was nine p.m. and he recalled only the surface drama he had watched – as he had been pre-instructed to do in the programming-sessions.

Afterwards, he got his books out and settled at the table. There was a lot of homework to catch up on – the last month at school he had ignored all the work the teachers had set him. What had got into him, slacking like that? He frowned. To get ahead, he had to work hard, pass all his tests and exams. That was the way to be a real hero. Only cowards shirked their duty, ran off like *Tai Koh*. What a loser Elder Brother was, he thought, angry suddenly. People like *Tai Koh* made all the problems of this world, but for how much longer? Liak set his jaw. He would not be like Elder Brother. He would be a success, a real one, not a sham. Liak felt the pure flames of his anger, focused them on the books in front of him. Channel the energy, master it, use it. He worked feverishly. What he couldn't do, he would ask the teacher to explain. He felt no fear, no uncertainty, only confidence that whatever he faced, he would deal with.

At school the next day, he helped a girl pick up the books she had dropped, smiling into her startled face. She was afraid of him – why? He shrugged and greeted a smaller kid trying to squirm past him unnoticed in the corridor. The kid looked stunned and managed a weak smile. In class he was always first to put his hand up, whether he knew the answer or not. If he got it wrong, he shrugged and waited to learn the right one. That was what he was here for. Liak sat in the middle of the room, strangely happy. It felt good to be here with the other kids, some better than him, some more stupid. He could only do his best like each of them should be trying to do. He was part of something bigger than his own wiry frame, he was part of the class, part of the school. He belonged and it was just the coolest thing.

———◦►●◄◦———

Fei pulled down the sheets in the guest room. It was six-thirty in the morning. In her T-shirt and pants, she rolled on the bed, ground her head into the pillow, wrestled with the sheets. Throwing the top sheet aside, she sat up and moved the lamp, clock and magazine on the bedside table out of their ordered positions. She flicked part of the curtains aside to cast a chink of light into the room. Then she took a shower in the en-suite bathroom.

Afterwards, she went back to Ginny's room as she towelled her hair, leaving the guest room as if it had been slept in overnight. It had become a ritual in the last week for the benefit of the Wyndhams' housekeeper who arrived every morning at eight. Ginny was still asleep, naked beneath the flannel sheet. She lay in the middle of the bed, curled towards the space where Fei had been, one arm outstretched.

Fei dressed, combing her hair sleek to let it dry naturally. She would go home as usual to change into fresh clothes before heading into the office. The morning-after ritual of lovers was new to her and she preferred this melting away into their separate lives to conversation over breakfast. It seemed to heighten the romantic intensity of the time they had together, feed the passion of secrecy. The alternative would only remind her of breakfasts with Sam and lay down the foundations for a new relationship. Fei did not want a relationship. Not right now. She wanted only the present moment.

That first night, Ginny's desire had carried them both like wildfire. She had drawn Fei in from the terrace, her touch urgent, her lips burning. Her tongue sought out every part of Fei, her hands exploring the shape and curves of her body. In the tangle of the sheets, their skin seemed hot with fever, every contact shaking Ginny to breathlessness. Fei found herself giving in to her intensity with a curious pleasure. It had been strange at first, feeling the touch of someone who was not Sam. A part of her seemed to withdraw even as her body moved with Ginny's. The effect she was having on Ginny flattered her, she thought dimly, and its erotic power was like a high. Her body swayed and snaked as if beyond her control: heart pumping fast, breath shallow, nipples swollen hard. There was nothing else, only the present moment and the longing for climax that they were both reluctant to fulfil. She had closed her eyes against her doubts and finally given herself up to the physical senses.

Now Fei picked up her briefcase and slipped out of the apartment. Ginny was flying to Hong Kong this morning for meetings with a complementary medicine institute. Piers would be back at the Centre later today and would expect Ginny there on her return in a few days. Fei did not know when she would see her again. It struck her curiously that she did not mind one way or the other. She felt a rush of liberation. There was no responsibility in this affair save silence. Ginny had her life with Piers and the Centre. Fei had hers among her affluent friends, her soaring career and a KL that seemed to lie at her feet. It was as if all her pain and fear had been numbed by a powerful hallucinogen.

Fei found her car in the basement parking lot. She drove out into the grey morning, tipping the security guard. Automatically, she glanced round her as if expecting to be spied on. She did not know who she expected to see. It had become a superstitious habit in the last few days. Her jumpiness had returned, heightened by the secrecy that she and Ginny had to preserve. She had not thought further than a heartbeat into the future that night in Petaling Street. The thrill had carried her, shorted her rational mind. Now she thought of the journalist who had watched her and Ginny together at the ceremony. Why had he taken a photo of her? What had he been able to infer from their tête-à-tête? Fei shook herself in annoyance. She and Ginny had just been two girl friends then, there had been nothing to infer.

They would never be found out, she promised herself. There was not the same danger as with Sam. It was not a relationship in the same way with all the complexities that that state implied. Fei and Ginny lived apart, Ginny appeared to be happily married, they would never go out into the gay scene, no one else knew of their affair and it would stay that way. And, more than anything, Ginny understood the need for deceit and vigilance. She had given Fei a mobile phone. 'Land lines can be tapped,' she had said. Their calls to each other were to be made only between that phone and Ginny's own mobile. The digital signals were randomly switched across several channels and at random transmission rates. Any eavesdropping scanner had to be synchronised to exactly the same random pattern to pick up the spoken words. The chances of that were one in several million. 'We cannot afford to be compromised – even by a casual hacker.'

She could have it all, Fei thought. It was as if, for the first time in her life, she answered to no one: not her family, not Sam, not her law partners, not the authorities. Not even Ginny. The sense of invincibility made her breathless, blew away her sudden anxiety.

Fei headed home to Bangsar, the fashionable residential area for young professionals. She peered through the windscreen at the hazy day. The ferocious KL traffic had already begun although it was still early. Cars cut in front of her, motorcyclists screeched past. Flashy off-road vehicles accelerated into several hundred yards of space before slamming their brakes at the grid-lock. Fei hurled the wheel, pumped the gas, fighting for headway and ground. Horns screamed and raged. The onslaught was manic, tearing her from the cocoon she had drawn up around herself.

She squinted beyond the traffic. Was it her imagination or had the smog grown thicker? The skyline of the city from the cross-town highway lacked definition in the blue-grey haze of smoke, as if it had been coated in many layers of dust. She had not put the air-conditioning on as the morning was unusually cool. Underlying the fumes of the traffic, the air was heavy with the scent of burning but there were no fires to be seen. The acrid mist was insubstantial but its presence everywhere, in every corner, every crack, clinging to hair and clothes, sucking into lungs, creeping into eyes, gave Fei a sense of claustrophobia.

The fires in Indonesia were spreading with the hot prevailing winds. Fei had seen the news pictures. Singapore, Malaysia, Thailand and the Philippines were all swamped in the cloud of smoke. Every breath filled her lungs with its taint. There was no escape from it. Fei felt a closing-in, as if she had gone down a wrong alley. For a moment, silence filled her head. The tangle of cars and trucks surrounding her seemed to shape into the walls of a darkening tunnel. In the gloom there seemed no way forward and no way back but something like recklessness – a strange madness, even – was driving her deeper into the fog.

⇒►●◄⇐

It was a Saturday night in Chow Kit, the rundown red-light district. Traffic clogged Jalan Raja Laut, the main road through the area. The cinema on the corner thronged with crowds waiting to see the latest Hong Kong kung-fu movie. In a side street, a ramshackle night-market sold pirated videos, music and gadgets among hordes of motorcycles and cruising vehicles. The air was thick with smoke.

Fei watched Siew as he worked his way through the shifting crowds. He was trailed by the spotlights of television cameras and an entourage of AVA faithful. They were of all ages and races. All the women had long hair worn neatly on their shoulders or in a bun. The men looked like they had all gone to the same barber with their matching short back and sides. It was a week after Fei had seen Ginny. Mei-Hong, Ben Chang's wife, had called and Fei had been unable to side-step her insistent invitation to this special event. They both clutched AVA leaflets for distribution to passers-by. The Alliance, according to the pamphlets, had members all over Asia from Pakistan to Japan and China. They appealed to Asians to unite in the best spirit of Asian community, 'to create a United States of Asia in all our hearts'.

'How did you fall into this moral corruption?' Siew asked. The prostitute he spoke to wore heavy make-up on her plain face. A tight, frilly dress wrapped her stocky figure.

She shifted awkwardly in the spotlights. N-Sat had promised her that her face would be pixellated out of focus on screen. 'I need money.'

'Would you do this if you could make money another way?' She nodded obediently. Fei wondered if she was just going through the motions expected of her, giving the punters what they wanted. She had seen an aide pass an envelope to the woman inside a doorway just before the cameras approached.

Siew told the woman how Asian Values could give her a new life, embrace her into a community where she would find work and respectability. He gave her a leaflet. 'Would you like to join the Alliance?'

'Oh, yes. Thank you, sir. I come to your meetings, yes.'

Siew and his band of followers moved on. The footage would be edited into a special hour-long programme on the state of Asian morality to be transmitted on N-Sat the next day. Fei said to Mei-Hong, 'Is she really going to join the AVA?'

'Of course-lah. You saw the money, isn't it? That's just a down payment for her future, to show her we all in good faith. Someone will come to make sure she goes to the meetings, like a fellowship mentor. The AVA will help her find a job, make sure she and her kids – they always have kids, these ones – are all right. She will be one of us through and through, no changing her mind, don't worry!'

It sounded so easy. Fei tried not to show her scepticism. Something about the setting up of that poor woman alarmed her. It was the certainty in Mei-Hong's tone, that overriding sense that the Alliance had the right to manipulate the woman's life to their own advantage. Regardless of their worthy motives, Fei could not help feeling repelled by the Alliance's coercion and bribery.

Mei-Hong had manoeuvred them closer to Siew as the group moved through the street. He was talking to camera, the crew shuffling backwards in front of him. 'Here and across Asia the Haze is a symbol of the moral swamp our nations have fallen into. You all know that incidences of asthma, bronchitis and burning vision are rising in our hospitals. Schools have to close, businesses shut their doors, people have to stay at home. The Haze creeps into every part of our lives and our bodies. The West is behind the Haze. They fear and envy our success. Their conspiracy is to destroy the success of Asia by any means. Like the Haze, moral failure has seeped in all around us. If we do not fight against lust and perversion, selfish desire and greed, there will be disease, chaos and death. All true Asians must actively take part in this battle for our future.'

Afterwards, Mei-Hong and Fei sat with Siew and his closest devotees in his Mercedes limousine. Mei-Hong, as Ben's wife, seemed especially favoured by Siew and respected by the others. Fei felt a churning in her stomach. She was in the perfect position to advance her career. Siew, with his multi-million-dollar business and personal fortune, his standing in Asia and his network of contacts among the rich and powerful, would be an ideal patron. Being seen with him, especially on regional tele-vision, would be spectacular for her profile. But the dark side of the deal hovered like an executioner's sword. Fei did not want to be here. Whatever Siew's public standing, his slick fanaticism horrified her. She was frightened by the AVA's moral fervour. If they knew about her . . . if they found out . . . the possibility made her sick with fear. In their smiling mouths, decent values had become an extremist tract for the control of people's private lives. Malaysians are tolerant, compassionate and humane people, she wanted to shout. We are human, we fail – we just try to get on with our lives as best we can. What are you trying to make us into? You can't buy our hearts, you can't force us into being just how you want! But she said nothing. These were not people that reason could touch. There was only their obsession for control. She looked at the clean-cut faces in the limousine. Everyone was neatly and modestly dressed, their logo badge just so on their lapels. Fei had put on a long, unflattering skirt for the evening but the safety of her disguise seemed pathetically flimsy.

Siew said to her, 'Are you learning from what you've seen tonight?'

'Oh, yes – a lot.' She smiled as sincerely as she could.

'When Mei-Hong said she had asked you to come, I was pleased. You must not think us anti- career women. The more of you we have on board the better for us. We need your energies and intelligence. There is much work to be done – outreach, counselling, fellowship . . .'

Keeping us in our place, Fei thought sardonically.

'. . . I would like you to see us with an open heart and open mind. You will want to join us in time, I have no doubts about that.'

Fei bit her tongue and nodded, a smile glued to her lips.

'Some movements go about changing society in the wrong way.' Siew opened out his dialogue to the others, settling into a guru's tone. 'They try to get rid of social evils by heavy-handed laws and intimidation. Like imprisoning prostitutes and drug addicts, or inciting violence against homos.'

Fei felt her mouth go dry. She tried to keep her expression neutral.

He went on, 'That's just a waste of resources and of human lives. The Alliance wants to see these pitiful souls transformed. We use persuasion and brotherly – and sisterly – compassion to show them a better way. We want a society of strong Asians, and to be strong we must stand together – yes, even with the dregs of our people. Because they are still *our* people. We give them the chance to change so that they can become good and upright Asians. I look to a day when there will be no crime, no whores, no drugs, no homos, no one who does not live within the embrace of Asian Values.'

'How . . . how will you do that?'

'Social exclusion. "Perverts" – those who pervert the true nature of good – don't want to be part of society's pact. So be it. Society will not accept them. It's simple and fair.'

Mei-Hong said, 'We mark them out and have nothing to do with them.'

Fei felt sick. 'Like the Nazis did to the Jews?' *And homosexuals.* But fear stopped her from adding that.

Siew smiled indulgently. 'Those are strong accusations. Our way is not so sinister. "Perverts" want no responsibilities within society – that's fine. So: they will have no rights. As I said, it's a fair exchange. But we'll find uses for them. Waste not, want not, that's the Asian way.'

'Yes, Brother-Elder.'

'So be it!'

'Be proud to be Asian!'

The chorus was breathless with rapture. Some clapped. Fei brought her hands together. The smile on her face was beginning to hurt. Anger and fear twisted her gut.

Siew spoke of 'perverts' as if they were things to be recycled and not human beings. That ease of disassociation frightened her. They had not sniffed her out yet, these smiling monsters. But for how much longer was she safe? How long could she put up this charade? She was who she was. To cut out the part of her that loved would be to cut out her heart. Her feelings, how she experienced her life, how she met each choice, were hers alone. She suddenly felt a terror. Her emotions, her identity and her very self were all of who she was. That they might be torn away from her gave her a sense of falling.

They had dinner at a Chinese restaurant, Siew in expansive mood. Fei had no appetite but could not leave before the close of the evening. Finally, after what seemed an eternity, the party broke up. She declined Mei-Hong's offer of a lift although it was late. Hurrying down the smoky street, Fei passed an old Toyota. She stood in the glare of traffic and flagged down a taxi.

In her agitation, she did not see the white man inside the Toyota, slouched down in the dark. He had watched her from a distance all evening and tailed Siew's car here, carefully hidden among other traffic. As her taxi pulled away, he started the engine and followed, several cars behind.

Chapter Nine

Sam nudged the speedometer up past a hundred miles an hour. It was three in the morning and the interstate highway was almost empty. Johnny, Fei's brother, sat in the passenger seat beside her. He had not said anything for the last half-hour. They were heading south in the direction of Malacca. Sam had not been able to sleep again and since she had seen Fei with Ginny Wyndham, her night drives had taken on an obsessive quality. She had honked for Johnny outside the Qwong family house in Titiwangsa and he had come out for the ride. The wind blasted through the open window, its thunder beating to the roar of the engine. The air was thick with smoke. Speed was the only drug that seemed to soothe Sam. There was no time to think, only react. Taking the bend, lining up the streaking cat's eyes.

She slowed suddenly, burning rubber, squealing the Honda into an unmarked turn-off.

'Fuck!' Johnny gasped. He clutched the dashboard.

Sam dodged the 'do not cross' barriers, bumping on to the soft verge and up again on the other side. Past the half-built toll booths and on to unmarked tarmac. This was an unfinished feed-off to a dormitory town outside KL. She shot up from twenty to forty, holding the car straight.

'What the hell . . .' Johnny jolted back in his seat.

'Hold on!' One and a half turns of the steering wheel, bracing herself, the back of the car skidding round. Sam slammed on the handbrake. The car flying backwards, Sam shrieking in

133

delight. A quick glance at Johnny – he was white as a sheet – and she slipped into first, revving with the clutch down, rolling the steering wheel straight. Handbrake off, clutch off, the spinning wheels catching, the acrid smell of burning tyres. And shooting straight out at forty miles an hour in the direction she had come.

She whooped, heart racing, adrenaline pumping.

Johnny was laughing. He punched the roof in exhilaration. 'Fucking crazy woman!'

She repeated the 180-degree turn just before the toll booths, cruising to a standstill where the tarmac ended. Sam cut the engine and lights. Pumped up and breathing hard, they got out. Sam was trembling. In the sudden blackness, she sat up on the bonnet, laughing. 'Bloody brilliant!'

At sixteen, she used to take her mother's BMW out of the garage late at night and drive through the quiet roads outside Guildford. Sometimes she would pick up Diane, her best friend from school. They would find out-of-town superstore complexes and race around the empty car parks, trying out handbrake turns, weaving through mazes they devised with shopping trolleys, pushing up the speed each time. The tricks ruined the engine but her mother never said anything. Dad didn't care, he was hardly ever home, spending most nights at his pied-à-terre in the City. Sam and Diane never stayed long enough to be caught, speeding off to neighbouring towns on the motorway. A few times they parked in a lay-by and shut off the engine. In the back seat they would kiss and feel each other's breasts, climaxing through their jeans. Sam grinned at the memory. Diane was now bringing up two kids in Camberwell with her partner Monica.

Johnny leaned against the bonnet next to Sam.

It was strange out here in the smoking dark. She could not see the sky through the haze. The night was black. The sound of crickets and toads drifted out of nowhere. Johnny said, 'You not seen Fei since . . .'

It was the first time that night either of them had mentioned her.

Sam thought of Fei with Ginny at the market. 'We didn't speak. She didn't see me.'

'She's with someone now?'

'Yeah.'

After a silence, Johnny said, 'What you going to do?'

Sam thought about being back in England with its neat fields and tidy houses. It would be the logical thing to do at the end of her contract, now that she and Fei had broken up. 'I could get a job at a London hospital.'

Hook up with her old friends again, throw herself into the lesbian scene and probably meet someone. Move in together to a nice basement flat in Crouch End. A woman with the same feminist views, the same political outlook, who volunteered for Lesbian Line, didn't buy animal products, ate health foods and owned a cat. Someone who wasn't Fei. They would be happy and out, free to be themselves. But the safety of it all stretched out like boredom without relief.

After four years in Malaysia, Sam realised, she could not imagine being anywhere else. She glanced at Johnny but he was just a shadow in the dark. How could she explain how she felt? The Asian landscape was alive. Europe to her seemed frozen. She loved the noise of the tropics, its night creatures calling from the darkness, its strange birdsong in the glaring day, the bellow of street hawkers and the loud conversations of people uninhibited by English reserve. There was a dynamism about the place, an enthusiasm for hard work and good food and the best that money could buy. Its vulgarity sometimes horrified her but it struck her that it had been her English suburban sensibilities that had started all those fights with Fei. Another part of her thrived on that energy, laughed more fully, spoke more loudly, played with greater gusto, worked with a more focused drive. The disparate cultures and foods and people of Malaysia jostled together like the diverse life of the jungle that erupted from every patch of soil. Limitless, colourful, angling for light and success at every opportunity. A garden left untended, a cleared stretch of land, would be colonised by the entrepreneurial wilderness within weeks.

There was a delight in family and friendship here, in the blood of the people, and yet a shocking, naive cruelty also – children beaten for disobeying their parents, domestic disputes settled with knives, fist fights over parking spaces, maids imprisoned in the house, young girls abused, burglaries pulled off with guns and machetes, horrific accidents on the roads from furious impatience. In the relentless drive for progress, Malaysians built glittering towers of marble and steel and littered their surroundings with abandon; fought their neighbours over boundary-lines for a few feet more and welcomed them to their homes on religious festivals; bought the fastest, most expensive cars of their dreams and baked in clogged, polluted traffic jams. It felt to Sam that this was life at its most real, stripped of the veneer of Western politeness and reserve. This was life with all its contradictions and conflict that Europe had worked for generations to hide.

Sam said out loud, 'England's too orderly and efficient, you know? It's hung up on class and everything's fenced off. It . . . it doesn't have any jungle.'

And it was the jungle that lured her.

It had been Fei's contradictions that had drawn Sam. Her petite build and outwardly controlled manner framed a passionate ambition and energy that Sam had not sensed in any woman she had known before. Sam said, almost to herself, 'Fei would come down to London from Oxford at weekends and we'd get into this whirlwind of theatre, clubbing and parties. I thought she was amazing – forthright and outspoken. She shocked all our friends out of their English reserve, you know?'

Her thoughts spun with memories of the Fei she seemed to have lost. Fei warmly chatting to women they'd never met before in the WOW Bar where *sang froid* and immaculate make-up were the rule. Fei moving feverishly on the dance floor at the Ace of Clubs, wide-eyed with pleasure at the crush of so many women, then outside on Piccadilly at three a.m., kissing Sam in the cold night. They would end up back at Sam's flat in Battersea making love in the early hours of the morning, then walking across the river to Chelsea for breakfast. When Fei moved in, Sam saw her shift into high gear at work as well as play: immersed in piles of law books late into the night, volunteering as an advocate at the Free Representation Unit, debating legal points at group study sessions at home. In addition to her First at Oxford, she passed her professional exams in the national top ten.

'You give up on her too soon.' Johnny's voice came quietly out of the night.

'What do you mean?'

'You two are good together. When she met you, she became happy. We can all see that. But Fei always like things her way.' There was a smile in his voice.

'I know.' Sam grinned in spite of herself.

'You, too.'

'Me?'

'Sure. She wants you to be like how she wants. You want her to be like how you want. She don't see you, you don't see her. Trouble for sure-lah.'

Sam squinted at him in the darkness. 'We've been trying to control each other, change each other?'

'You have to let someone be who they are. We see Fei with you. My mother sad at first. She don't like it. Then she worry for Fei. You know-lah, people, they all don't like such things, they can make trouble for you two. But Mum said, Fei is Fei still. Same Fei we said goodbye to at the airport long ago. Same Fei who come home with presents.'

'The same Fei I always knew.'

'And you the same woman she always love.' Johnny's hand was warm and rough on hers. 'You two just forget, that's all.'

And then he moved away. He stretched, yawning noisily. 'It's late, man. I got work tomorrow.'

'So have I.' Sam slid off the bonnet. They would never speak about this again, she knew. It struck her that it was the first time they had ever talked so openly. The love and generosity of Fei's family moved her. They had not tried to change Fei or fight her or turn her away. She wanted to thank him, to throw her arms around him. But that would be to acknowledge that the conversation had happened. Instead, she said, 'Thanks for coming for the ride.'

'No problem.'

Perhaps Johnny was right, Sam thought. She had thrown in the towel too soon. The pain of the disintegrating relationship had been too much for her to endure. She had not understood Fei's own conflicts, had only interpreted them through her own Western perspective. Instead of exploration, there had been arguments and accusations. After a while they had no longer been able to communicate, every gesture or remark driving them further apart. It felt as if lately Sam had been trying too hard to hold them together and the harder she had squeezed, the more she had lost. Like trying to hold sand too tightly in the palms of her hand.

'I can't leave at the end of my contract,' she said suddenly. In London, she would never see Fei again. She would never have a second chance. Whatever the truth about her relationship with Ginny, Sam could only think of one thing. Her own life stretching ahead of her, fifty more years maybe, sixty even – all that time without the one woman who could engage her whole being, who knew the entirety of her.

'You stay then?'

'But what should I do?'

Johnny weighed up the question. He said, 'Nothing.'

'Nothing?'

'Just be here. Be still.'

'Siew must never find out about us.' Ginny sat up in bed, drawing the sheets tight against her as if to hide herself.

Fei did not move. They were in a hotel near the new international airport. They had been meeting secretly like this every few days in the last weeks. Ginny found excuses to come down to KL at any opportunity and they would meet at the Wyndhams' apartment, ostensibly engaged in legal business. Or they would drive to one of the satellite towns sprawling round the capital or to Ipoh or Malacca, check in to a hotel in different rooms and spend the night together in Ginny's bed.

Fei had been telling her about the AVA tour of Chow Kit. She said, 'It's okay. He thinks I'm a believer. "Be proud to be Asian" – it's the best camouflage.'

'When was this tour?'

'Couple of weeks ago.'

'Why didn't you tell me before now?'

Fei hesitated. She sat up and drew on her T-shirt. 'I was worried you'd react – well, like this.'

Ginny's eyes were hooded. Her face seemed pinched. She snapped, 'Like what?'

'That you'd panic.'

'So why didn't you put Mei-Hong off? Not go?'

'It was difficult . . .'

Ginny cut across her excuse. 'Just don't get too close to the Alliance.'

Fei started at her brusque tone. She studied Ginny, defences closing in. She said tersely, 'I have no intention of doing that.'

'Don't take anything for granted. AVA sympathisers are everywhere.'

'Sure.'

Ginny grabbed her. 'Don't you get it? What we're doing is . . . is unnatural. It's wrong! We're perverts, freaks of nature . . .' She let go suddenly and slid back across the bed. Looking wildly about, hands jerking nervously, Ginny could not meet Fei's stare.

'Is that what you really think?' She felt as if Ginny had slapped her. She could still smell their love-making on her skin, taste Ginny on her lips.

Ginny tucked her head into her chest, clawing at her hair like a child in pain. Her face was twisted with despair and anguish. 'I wanted us to be friends, just friends. It could have been so easy then. I didn't want to fall in love with you. I can't let it happen again, not after everything . . .'

'Let what happen again?' Fei moved across the bed to her.

'But you were too beautiful, too insistent. How could I resist you? You sought me out, chased me . . .'

'I – what?'

'But they'll find us out. Then they'll damn us to hell. It's disgusting what we are . . .'

Fei put her arms round Ginny. Her collapse into hysteria was frightening Fei. She had to stop it. She had to put the pieces back together. She whispered firmly but with tenderness, 'Hush now, my darling. Do you really believe that? Truly? I don't think so. How you touched me and kissed me, how you shivered when you felt my lips on you . . . Is that unnatural? How we moved together, how your body knew what it wanted, what it longed for? What you feel, what you dream of, that excitement, that happiness – is it really disgusting to you?'

Ginny began to weep. She gulped for air, tears and saliva falling onto Fei's bare arm. She shook her head, her body shaking. She clung on with fearful desperation, as if Fei might be torn away from her. 'I'm sorry . . . I'm sorry . . .'

In their subsequent encounters, there seemed a new intensity, as if in choosing Fei over her conscience, Ginny had given over her whole life. The drama of it swept them along, as of a great sacrifice made for love. Fei did not think of anything beyond their affair. Their passion was an intoxication and an adventure. She felt free for the first time in her life. She rarely contacted her family now nor returned their calls. She had been father and matriarch to them all for so long – just once, they could make their own way without her advice, her presence. Without *her*. The money she'd been saving against their need of it she at last began to spend on herself. All these years, she'd given the best of everything to them: the indulgence of her own desires felt shameful and thrilling.

Fei bought a new wardrobe of designer suits, a Bang & Olufsen hi-fi and TV. She went out to the most expensive restaurants, treated her friends to spectacular meals. A host of eligible men took her out to KL's fashionable nightspots, forlornly hopeful that their devotion might be returned. She joined an exclusive yacht club in Singapore, flying down for weekends of sailing and parties. She bought a Mercedes sports model, metallic blue. She was even able to forget Sam some of the time.

But there was a new brittleness in Ginny that made Fei uneasy. She couldn't put her finger on it exactly. It was as if fear still dogged most of their recent contacts, and not just that something would give them away. Ginny didn't like not being able to get through to Fei when she wanted to. She was unhappy that Fei never stayed for breakfast. She asked endless questions about what Fei had been doing each day, who she had been seeing. And then there were the interrogations about Sam – the tone too casual for the barrage of detailed enquiries, like that of a jealous wife.

Yet, in a strange way, these difficulties only heightened the excitement of the affair. After a strained exchange, the next contact would be more charged with emotion. Their mutual relief seemed then to explode into greater pleasure. The uncertainty as to whether there would be a row or a scene at each moment drew taut the erotic tension of every encounter. They made their rendezvous via unexpected, circuitous routes. Their secret love was dramatic and grand, a madness hidden from a world that did not understand them.

They never went back to Fei's apartment – she managed to sidestep it several times. Her home had been Sam's home. It was where her real life was lived, it seemed to Fei, and this fantastical romantic adventure had no place there. Fei felt as if she were living a hazy dream. She couldn't see clearly even if she wanted to. It was as if her doubts and anxieties and fears were numbed by an exhilarating drug.

<hr/>

Carson Dean stood behind Fei in the queue at the *nasi lemak* stall in the air-conditioned food court. She walked the several blocks to this office complex every few days at lunchtime to escape the office. It was scruffier than the ones nearer her block, an amusement arcade full of lonely men and surly youths across the corridor. She seemed to enjoy its anonymity and lack of pretension. Dean had been tailing her for several weeks. He had noted her stays at the Wyndhams' apartment in KL and her presence among Siew's entourage in Chow Kit. By now, he had a good picture of her daily routine. Today, instead of following her on foot from Loy Tower, he had parked his Toyota at this complex and come straight up. She had appeared just after one as he had expected.

'Good day at the office?' he grinned.

'Not bad.' She did not look at him but she was smiling. 'You don't give up, do you?'

'You enjoy my company, admit it.'

'Well . . .'

'Here, I'm buying.'

'No. How many times do I have to tell you . . .'

'All right then, you buy.' Dean nodded at the stall owner, indicating their two trays laden with rice and chillied prawns. 'We're together.'

Fei's eyes widened at his cheek. Then she burst out laughing, reaching for her vouchers. 'You're incorrigible.'

Dean winked. 'I love it when women say that.'

They sat at a corner table. He had chatted Fei up the week before, bumping into her as if by accident near the cutlery dispenser. She had recognised him but had not been able to place him. She had been amiable at first, till she'd learned he was a journalist. 'You were at the Wyndham Centre!' And then she had withdrawn into reticence. This was their fourth lunch together, Dean always angling to sit with her, nudging her back into warmth with all the charm he could muster.

He said now, 'I'll be straight with you. Yes, I approached you at first because of your connection with the Wyndhams – or that's what I kept telling myself. I'm supposed to be a dastardly newshound, always sniffing out a new contact, a lead, whatever. But to hell with that. If you don't want to talk about them, that's fine with me. Journalists need friends, too. We can keep business out of it.'

Fei said nothing but he could see she was wavering. She was trying hard not to smile. 'Is that on your bumper sticker – "Journalists are people too"?'

'Come on, give me a break. Have I once asked you about the Centre or the Wyndhams?' Dean stretched and glanced casually around the food court. An automatic reflex every fifteen minutes or so. Out of the corner of his eye, he noticed a man staring at them from his position by a slot machine in the arcade. Dean swept his gaze towards him, but all he saw was the man busy playing the buttons. Perhaps it had been a trick of the light, a reflection in the glass partitions. 'So, have I?'

'Well, no –'

'There you go.' Dean leaned forward, his voice serious. 'I like you, Fei-Li. I'd like to go on seeing you.'

She looked up from her meal. 'Is that American for "Can I sleep with you"?'

Dean grinned and looked away sheepishly. He turned back, eyeing her from under his brow. 'Can I?'

She laughed. 'No, of course not.'

Dean pulled out a piece of card from his jacket pocket and gave it to Fei. It was a colour print out of the photograph he had taken of her at the Centre. It was a full face shot, zoomed close. She wore a look of enquiry, lips parted, eyes facing directly into camera. He said, 'I've had that up by my desk all this time. At any function, I take shots of everyone and anyone, it's part of the job. But with you, when this frame came up on screen – hell, I dunno, I knew I just had to get to know you.'

Fei took the picture. It was not a standard photograph, the paper was thinner and had a wide margin, A5 size. The image was less sharp too, almost like a colour photocopy. 'Is this a digital photo?'

Dean nodded. 'State of the art.'

Fei handed the photo back. There was nothing she could say to his frankness. The American way of seduction was more up-front than any other she had come across. She wondered if their lesbians were just as direct with each other. She looked at Dean. He was good-looking in a clean-cut, healthy way, blond and tanned. He behaved in rejection as in any other mode: with confidence and cockiness. He had amused her each time they had met, making her laugh with his jokes and stories. He was right, she did enjoy his company. And he did seem more interested in *her* personally rather than who or what she knew. After her encounter with Siew and his Asian Values devotees, Dean's Western irreverence and wit were like a blast of fresh air.

Seeing Dean trying to charm her, it occurred to Fei that she could have him, if she wanted him. But she did not.

Friendship was so much easier with a man. Especially as she had no feelings of desire to confuse matters. Dean somehow had the knack of drawing her out, making her laugh and amusing her with an amiability that was thankfully uncomplicated. Fei had gone back to the office almost two hours late the last time, she and Dean the last people to leave the food court. The men she met through her work were often serious, conservative Asians who talked only of business or stocks and shares and computer games. It was refreshing to spend time in the company of a man who could talk about books, art, theatre and politics. It reminded her of being in England and the pleasure of talk and debate she had almost forgotten. The company of straight men could be invigorating, she thought, their opinions so certain and unafraid, their manner energetic. As a woman, Fei had to work harder to be taken note of and stand firmer not to be swayed but she enjoyed the exercise like a good work-out.

'So, Mr Carson Dean.' Fei carried on with her meal. 'Tell me about you?'

'Please – Cass.'

'Cass.'

Dean smiled happily. He had been in Asia for three years, he told her, and loved it. He had been in Taiwan, Hong Kong, Manila and Shanghai before now being based in KL. 'A long way for a kid from Cincinnati, huh? I moved to New York as soon as I could after college. I guess I just kept on heading east!'

'Do you miss America?'

He grinned. 'I miss browsing in a good bookshop sometimes. Getting the Sunday papers on the way home from a movie on

Saturday night. A real coffee – you know, black, bitter, Italian.'

Fei closed her eyes with a sigh. 'Waterstone's on a rainy Sunday afternoon, checking out the new paperbacks – then cream cakes and cappuccino at Patisserie Valerie in Soho.' A rush of emotion caught her unaware. It seemed a lifetime ago, her life in London. A stolen year with Sam. The intensity of her feelings took her by surprise. She opened her eyes to find Dean watching her. She smiled, mastering herself.

'Is living here such a prison?' he asked mildly.

'My family's here, my career is here.' Sam was here. But for how long more? 'But it's different . . .'

'No one reads those books here, do they? Written by obscure European writers, about the minutiae of doomed love affairs.'

Fei laughed. 'It's all "How to make millions before you're thirty"!'

'You can't have those conversations about art and per- formance poetry and that incomprehensible Hungarian movie at the film festival . . .'

' "Are you married? What's your tip for the hot stock of the week? How much did you pay for your condo?" ' Fei thought suddenly of Sam and their arguments about money and success. Always Sam cluttering her memory. Why could she not forget Sam?

In the amusement arcade across the floor, Han put another token in the slot machine. He had a clear view of Qwong's face from here, Dean's clear-cut profile to one side. She looked sad beneath her animated conversation, tired lines at her mouth and eyes. But it was only for a moment and then she was laughing at something Dean had said.

Han had come back to KL from another operation in Bangkok the night before. He had a week to pick up the Wyndham job before he would be expected in Indonesia to back up Snakes operating covertly there. So far, his tap on Qwong's e-mail had produced nothing of interest and he had not had another opportunity to access Dean's residence. His only tenuous hope was old-fashioned P.I. techniques like this. Slow but not unproductive – as today was turning out to be.

He had followed Dean here earlier and the meeting with Qwong had convinced him the American was after something. It was too coincidental to ring true – the journalist caught snooping on the Wyndhams' property now romancing their lawyer: Han had been in Family business too long to believe in love. Clearly, Dean had reached the same conclusion he had: Qwong was the weak link in the Wyndhams' defences.

⬤

Sam accessed the confidential directories on her computer with her password, a random set of numbers she had memorised. The terminal and stacked hard drive sat in a corner of her office on the eighth floor of the National Hospital. Reports and files filled the shelves. Textbooks on epidemiology, pathology, neurology, microbiology and biochemistry were piled up against computer software boxes and manuals. The labs where she and her team worked on their practical research and analysis were down the corridor and sealed for anti-contamination purposes. Her office, however, was not classified and the windows were open to a cool breeze.

She opened a directory marked 'Factor?' It contained data, autopsy reports, pathology test results, scanned electrographs and chemical analyses on her research project. Factor Q, designated for the Querymark, was the strange protein common to all the deaths recorded in her data, most but not all of which showed evidence of a degenerative brain disorder.

It had been a week since her late-night drive with Johnny. It was a relief to bury herself in her work. There was no place for emotion in the labs, only data and cold analysis. She had made some headway on the project, pushing her pathology contacts in Hong Kong, Delhi and Manila for the reports they had been promising her. The last one had arrived by e-mail today from Dr Ranjathi in Delhi. She switched applications and retrieved the e-mail and attached data file, moving it to the Factor Q directory.

When she opened the data file, a picture postcard of an Indian Tiger was all there was. Sam grinned. Ranjathi liked to use animal pictures. She pulled down the encryption application and tapped in her alphanumerical password. It was her private key, known only to her, that slotted into the public key that she had agreed on with Ranjathi. The two codes ran in conjunction to unlock the encrypted file. The screen blanked out as the program decoded the data. A few moments later, the path report came up in place of the tiger. It had been encoded in the digital information that made up the picture, much in the same way as camouflage melted into the surrounding jungle. Sam often exchanged information via the internet in this way for security reasons, especially where the prestige and recognition of a research thesis rested on being the first to publication. For now, the less her sceptical colleagues knew of her work the better.

When Sam had still been in London and Fei had moved back to Malaysia, they used to exchange letters via e-mail under an encryption program based on photographs of their friends. It had allowed them to write freely about their relationship and feelings without the risk of discovery. Sam smiled. It was only afterwards that she learnt that Fei had printed out the unencoded e-mails and saved them in a drawer like conventional love letters instead of keeping them encrypted on disk. No wonder she was paranoid about locking up her condo every day.

Ling, Sam's research assistant, came in with mugs of coffee. 'What have we got?'

'Take a look.' Sam shifted so that Ling could pull up a chair. She was a serious young Chinese woman in a sensible skirt and top, more interested in her work than in her doctor boyfriend whom she referred to as 'that fellow'.

Sam made herself concentrate as they both studied the screen. Ranjathi's report detailed two deaths within several months of each other. Both young men had been found wandering through the streets of Delhi in a bewildered state and taken to hospital by the police. In each case, the notes of the admitting doctor revealed that the subjects had shown clear signs of dementia. It had increased sharply during the forty-eight hours they had been retained for observation. Motor co-ordination had also deteriorated, from uncontrollable shaking such as found in Parkinson's disease to complete immobility within the two-day period. Death had occurred shortly after-wards. The pathology investigation had found evidence of vacuole and amyloid plaques in the brain. The cause of death had been certified as transmissable spongiform encephalopathy although no one had been able to identify its exact type.

Sam called up her database of Factor Q cases. Her curiosity had first been sparked three years ago by a casual conversation with a path lab colleague who had mentioned an unusual case. A young man had died of an apparent brain haemorrhage but the autopsy had revealed deposits of amyloid plaques, unknown in a non-encephalopathy-related case. Sam had obtained the file and sample brain tissue for further analysis and biochemical breakdown, which had revealed the presence of protein Q. Further informal enquiries over the next few months had thrown up other cases with the unexplained presence of a similar protein. Sam had subsequently formalised her enquiries, extending their range to pathology and histology colleagues throughout the region, and each week several new cases arrived in her e-mail.

Since that chance conversation, she had collected over a thousand reports from hospital sources across Asia. The death certificates always stated the most obvious cause of death and in numerous instances, merely 'natural causes'. Where the conflict of evidence was too mystifying, the certifying doctor usually assumed that the pathology results had produced an error or a non-significant result. That the Q cases seemed to manifest randomly all over Asia, presenting different symptoms, no doubt made their commonality more difficult to detect unless, like Sam, the doctors were looking out for it. She grimaced. Her opinion of doctors in clinical practice was low: their whole training seemed to gear them to stick to the most obvious diag-nosis and to discount what they did not know even if the evidence stared them in the face. It had been part of the reason why she had gone into research – there it was what was not known that was engaging.

The database detailed symptoms ranging from those exhibited by the two Indian men to violent mood swings and personality disorders, schizophrenia, meningoencephalocele, immunodeficiency syndromes and myalgic encaphalitis or ME. The symptoms would all progressively worsen or overlap over a short period, ending in death.

'There's no common sociology among the victims.' Ling studied the columns of facts. 'All ages of adult males and females, all races – including one or two whites: travellers. All occupations, all classes and income brackets.'

'No children,' Sam said.

'Nothing unusual in most of their case histories, no common diet, no contact between any of the victims – at least, according to what can be inferred from each report.'

'Some of the victims appear to have suffered blackouts prior to the onset of symptoms – usually weeks or months before. Apparently, they were unable to account for periods of up to several days. Do we know if this was told to the doctors by the victim themselves or by friends and families?'

'I'll follow up to clarify.' Ling moved to her own office next door.

Left alone, Sam stared out at the dirty sky. In spite of herself, and all her bravado about hard work and concentration, she wanted to see Fei again. The feeling always grabbed her unawares. She looked at the phone, the autodial button for Fei's office still undeleted. God, how many times had she had these staring matches with the phone? Sam stood up and made a big diversion of stretching.

Then she reached for the phone and punched the buttons to delete Fei's number from the settings.

Chapter Ten

The storm had been swelling all afternoon, its pent-up energy darkening the already grey light. The rising wind dispersed the smoke and by evening there was a gloomy clarity across the bay. A clattering of palm fronds and the din of the waves crackled in the air. The smell of rain lay heavy over the Centre. There was a restlessness among the patients, the disturbances of the ether catching them like sparks on tinder. Voices rose louder, tics and compulsive mannerisms escalated. Arguments and scuffles broke out. The staff moved through the wards and amenity rooms with an urgency, impelled as much by an inexplicable tension as by the demands of their patients. Shutters and doors slammed in the wind. Flashes of lightning flickered across the dusk. Distant thunder rumbled moments afterwards.

The trucks made their delivery late in the afternoon, grinding up towards the headland. Ben received their cargo, checking off quantity and squinting through the crates to assess quality.

'Not too close-lah!' the handler warned.

Ben stepped back. 'You're forty short. There aren't enough here.'

'That's all we got, man.'

'We need more.' Ben's lips drew tight. They were behind on their production target as it was. Siew would not accept this further setback.

'You better talk to Ghuna-lah.'

Ben grabbed the man's collar. 'You tell Ghuna we want what we ordered. I don't care how he does it. Get me those forty more! Do you hear?'

———————————

By nightfall, the rain had come, ghostly sheets catching the light from inside the buildings. It pounded on the roofs and smashed against the panes. The noise was frantic and unremitting. Lightning crackled, closing in. Thunder pursued in ever-mounting fury. The earth seemed to shake with the sound. The patients screamed and yelled in terror.

Ginny stood on the steps of the terrace, staring out at the lawn. The cacophony of voices and fear behind her faded beneath the relentless drumming of the rain. Cold drops at her face and arms, spattered on her blouse. She breathed in the smell of soil and damp. It felt like a blast of cocaine, clearing her head yet making her dizzy. She had been working with the staff to calm the patients and at another time might have coiled herself up into a fury of frustration. She might have cursed this tropical storm, drawn on her reserves of loathing. In the long years she had been captive here, Asia had become symbolic of all the failures that trapped her. It had been nothing more to her than a wilderness of alien peoples, disgusting smells and a violent mishmash of cultures and religions. Beneath her smiling public mask she had recoiled from the horror of it all, withdrawing into her 'fixes' and retreating into the safety of the labs. But such things did not seem to matter anymore.

Ginny stepped out into the rain. It caught her like needles, wrenching a gasp from her and soaking her in moments. White fire flashed just ahead of her, its jagged edge shooting down to the blades of grass. Thunder slammed into Ginny as if shaking her heart. She felt a wild exhilaration as she walked on in the furious dark, her vision bright with phantom light. She wanted to embrace the night, draw around her the beauty of this place

– the earth and sea and sky. For the first time in a long while, she was happy.

She did not stop walking. Palm trees creaked and lashed all around her. She was not far from the sea now. Its rushing waves could be heard just ahead, strangely soft through the ringing in her ears.

Fei had changed everything. In her dusky skin, Ginny saw the lithe, sensuous glory of Asia. In her every mannerism lay the history of these multifarious peoples. All around her, Ginny sensed Fei. She knew her in every Asian woman, touched her in the day's heat on her skin. The jungle and the earth belonged to Fei and to be a part of them was to be a part of her. The din of the street-markets and the ambitions of the city landscape were the heart and soul that made Fei.

Every part of Ginny felt the rain, breathed the electric air. Every sense sang. She stood beneath the trees and gloried in the raging sky.

In Ginny's office, Piers squinted out at the flash of lightning. They had had to cancel the shipment of H cultures by sea because of the storm. So far, the Haze had provided perfect cover from the patrolling coastguards and shipments had been regular and frequent. He could wait another day for this latest drop but the short cargo from Ghuna today had upset their schedule. Piers swore with frustration. He knew the constraints Ghuna worked under but there was no way around it: they needed his cargo to be on target if Project Max and Phase Four were to succeed.

Piers started searching through Ginny's papers again. He had to concentrate on the task at hand. He had been through all her cabinets and drawers, leafed through files and letters. He replaced the last of her documents. On her computer, he had accessed every directory he could get into. There were some she had barred through firewalls and lock-out passwords. He leaned on her desk in a pool of light from the lamp. He would have to get her to give him access or call in Ricky to hack into her direc-tories. But he did not want anyone else to know – least of all Ricky with all his unpredictability. If what Piers suspected of Ginny were true . . . He did not want to have to think of the consequences. They had been safe for ten years now. They were so close. So close to her salvation. Why did she have to risk it all now?

———⟫●⟪———

Piers stood with Ginny on a wooden viewing platform in the heart of the Orang-Utan Sanctuary. It was several days after the storm.

The Haze had settled heavily over the jungle again, cloaking the distant trees and undergrowth. Piers found himself breathing hard after the walk up the path, struggling for oxygen through the smoke. He needed to talk with Ginny alone, away from the claustrophobia of the Centre. But he wasn't sure how to start. A part of him did not want to hear what he had to learn from her.

After what had happened to Katie and Morgane, she was all he had and he did not want to lose her. It would have been so much easier to have left her behind when the police had come after him. But he had not been strong enough. Her part in their deaths had made him hate her once but in the moment he'd had to choose, he had seen the love that still bound them. She had not been ultimately to blame, he knew that. Katie had died at the hands of the man he could never bring himself to speak of. *He* had raped and mutilated Katie, dumped her in the Hudson still alive. *He* had been the cause, too, of Morgane's death. Hiding in the hold of the frigate out of Baltimore, Ginny cowering beside him, Piers had realised that if he let his hatred and anger destroy Ginny too, *he* would have won. *He* still lurked somewhere in the corruption of New York – alive

– and the thought of it turned like a skewer in Piers's stomach. But *he* would never win, nor those like *him*. That oath screamed inside Piers like a demon's mantra.

'Why did we have to come to the Sanctuary?' Ginny complained, breaking into his trance. 'You know I hate to see these creatures.'

A mother ape and its baby had swung up on to the platform and were gazing at them curiously from the deck. The baby clung to the female, its eyes wide. It was sucking its toe. The mother watched them, too, eyes dark and solemn. They were compact and fragile, grey coats short and thick. Ginny made herself look away. 'They're too human. I can't bear it.'

'What's going on between you and Fei?'

'What do you mean?' She turned back to the orang-utans.

'You've been seeing a lot of her. I've been making enquiries. She stayed the night before the ceremony . . .'

'Everyone knew about that.'

'In the week we were in JB, she slept over at the apartment six nights out of seven.'

Ginny's hands were tight on the balustrade. She turned to him in agitation. 'And did the housekeeper also mention that Fei slept in the guest room?'

'Yes.' Piers's voice was gentle. The love he felt for her was suffocating. It alarmed him but he gave it rein for a moment. 'As my wife, you're the perfect cover and as the public face of the Centre, no one could be better. We're so close, Ginny. Don't let it all slip now.'

'I've kept my part of the bargain all these years.' Her voice cracked. 'But I can't stand it anymore. I can't stand being watched and judged all the time. I can't go on with those "fixes" day in, day out, over and over again.'

'The Cure is almost perfect now. Before long, you'll get the fix you've always wanted. You'll be free at last, just like you've always longed for.'

Ginny began to weep. The words she had screamed at Piers long ago rang in her head. 'I don't want to be a queer, a filthy dyke! Change me, please, tear this disease out of me, make me normal.' She had thrown herself at him, sobbing, scratching at her face. It had been the day they had acquitted Katie's murderer. Only now, Ginny did not know anymore what she wanted.

She pulled away from Piers and gulped in smoky air. She felt so tired. Her behaviour recently had unnerved her, angry energy rising as if from nowhere. She had let go of Katie, betrayed the little girl and all of them in that moment. And because of her, they had been denied the right to justice. Horror struck her that she had opened her heart again, not knowing if she had the strength or desire to master it. The thought of her madness in the storm made her sick with panic. The intoxication was wearing off. She said with conscious irony, 'I've never been happier or freer.'

'You didn't answer my question about Fei.'

Still Ginny said nothing.

Piers was watching her closely. 'You know she's been seeing that journalist, Dean?'

It was as if he had hit her. 'What?'

'Red Tiger have been continuing their checks on Dean since that last incursion. He's been taking Fei out.'

Ginny tried to keep her expression neutral. Anger was wrestling with disbelief. Fei had said nothing to her about Dean. 'How long? How often . . .'

'Several weeks. Every few days.'

'But why? What does she get from him?' Ginny fought the jealousy from her voice.

'More to the point, what does he want from her?' Piers's face was hard now, his gaze penetrating. 'What have you told her?'

'Nothing. How can I tell her anything?' Ginny flashed angrily. 'Christ, what do you take me for?'

'So why have you been spending so much time with her?'

Ginny felt her chest tighten. She couldn't breathe. She had to keep Fei safe. Free from suspicion. Fei's betrayal of her with Dean – Ginny would have to deal with that on her own. But for now, she had to find a smokescreen. Anything to buy her time. She said, 'I've . . . I've been collecting data. On Fei-Li – she's a Double Alpha subject and we haven't had a successful trial of Double Alphas yet.'

They had classified the population into several categories according to intelligence, will and self-awareness. Most people were graded Beta down to Epsilon: Beta indicated an average mix of factors and Epsilon extremely limited capabilities. Double Alphas were those who were not only highly educated but also self-motivated with a deep reservoir of internal resources. Scientists, writers and artists, intellectuals and top business professionals were the usual Double Alphas. With most experimental subjects, the compound hijacked the neural networks without resistance – the only problem had been its stability within the subjects' systems. With Double Alphas, their awareness of what was being done to them summoned up an internal resistance against the invasion of their wills and minds, interfering with the effectiveness of the programming. They would subsequently lapse back into their original personality or leap between the two states.

Ginny felt Piers studying her. She made herself control her breathing. The silence unnerved her. Did he believe her? He said, 'I thought Fei was your friend?'

'We failed with Double Alphas in the past because we didn't tailor the programming to the specific weaknesses and belief systems of the subjects.' Ginny spoke rapidly as the thoughts occurred to her. 'Fei is my friend and that puts me in an ideal position to probe. And it's because she's my friend that I'm doing this. Look, she's assertive, modern, ambitious. She won't fit into the new world order after the Final Phase. If the Cure is stable, I'd like to see to it personally that she gets the best re-programming we can give her. With a detailed history and personality analysis, we can fine-tune it so she can really be content in her life, whatever happens. And if we do it right, she won't even know she's changed.'

Piers nodded slowly. He was gazing at his own thoughts. 'Yes, tone down that confidence to a lady-like demureness. Give her some old-fashioned values. Take away the ambition. She's, what – mid-thirties? Make her less picky about men and give her a chance for love, marriage and kids.' He looked hard at Ginny. 'Perfect! Siew's perfect woman. He'll be ecstatic. If we can do that, there's no stopping the Final Phase.'

Siew would have his perfect Asia. Ginny flushed. Treachery was so easy in spite of her love for Fei. But what else could she have done? How else to explain their intimacy? The justifications soothed her but shame sat like a dead-weight in her gut.

Piers went on, 'I'll talk to the psych team. And Ricky. Get them started on the program. Let me have your file in the next few days. That'll get rid of the security risk with Dean and finalise Double Alpha programming in one sweep . . .'

'No!' Ginny started. 'No . . . it's not ready yet . . . I don't want us to make a mistake. Besides, Fei is no risk, I tell you.' She was gabbling now, unable to stop. 'She knows only the spin we tell the world. How could I tell her anything else? How could I look in her eyes and tell her what we really do? She would be afraid of me. Hate me. And I couldn't stand her hatred. Don't you understand, Piers? Dean can chase her, flirt with her all he wants, he'll find out nothing from her because she *knows* nothing. That gives us a margin, doesn't it? If he gets nothing from her, maybe he'll give up. Anyway I need more time to get the file right.'

Piers took in all her arguments, his face expressionless. She could not tell what he was thinking. After a pause he nodded, as if he had decided to believe her, no matter what she had said. 'When will it be ready then?'

'There's another Double Alpha file I've completed.' Ginny couldn't let them work on Fei, not in reality. The lie had saved her in that moment of panic but now Piers was turning it on her. This wasn't supposed to happen . . . Ginny felt a scream rising in her. What had she done?

She said suddenly, 'I know of an excellent candidate. She and Fei-Li are close friends. I feel I know her as well as I know Fei. A doctor, female, English, non-conformer: it's all in my file. A worthy challenge for the Cure. If it works on her, it'll work on the toughest Double Alpha subject.'

'Her name?'

'Sam Ryder.'

━━━━▶◄━━━━

N-Sat filmed Siew at the school in Johore Baru, meeting the school board and awarding the Asian Values Medal for Excellence to the boys who had taken part in the therapy. Siew spoke on camera about Asia's place in the world and how their children, brought up with the right values, would make the next millennium the Age of Nanyang – an ancient term for South-eastern Asia. Europe had once dominated history with its empires; China's dynasties had ruled over the East for thousands of years; America's brief shining moment was waning. 'Our tiger economies have a chance now. All we have to do is join together not only as trading partners but in a single proud force and we will be unstoppable.'

Malaysians and Singaporeans watched the documentary in every home. In coffee-shops across Indonesia, people turned from their drinks to the sets above the counter. In Thai villages, neighbours crowded the houses of those with televisions. Everyone had heard about the miracle treatment that changed thugs to good citizens and wanted to see the boys for themselves.

Liak appeared in footage provided by the Wyndham Centre – an interview filmed the week before he had gone to the hospital. He was sullen and fidgety, hair unkempt. He wore a T-shirt with a flaming skull logo. His eyes avoided the camera as he answered the questions reluctantly. 'I dunno what I want to be. Rich-lah. Big car. Girls, girls, girls.' He snickered. Viewers across Asia tutted and shook their heads.

When he next appeared, there were cries of wonder. His hair was short and neat and he faced the camera with good-natured confidence. He wore a collared shirt and sat up straight, speaking gently and politely. 'I want to study business at college. I want to get a good job so I can look after my mother in her old age-lah. Then, also, I want to marry a nice girl and have a family.'

Some days after the broadcast, Siew threw a party for the senior Alliance directors in the imperial suite of his Singapore mansion. The rooms were furnished with leather sofas, plush carpeting and Asian antiquities and fine art. The guests were all men, as befitting of senior leadership. No wives had been invited. The hostesses were beautiful Asian women in the formal dress of their cultures, cut from exquisite material and tailored to show off their feminine attributes. Serving cocktails at low tables by the sofas, the girls knelt with their trays, showing splendid legs in silk stockings.

These were the cream of the AVA entertainment hostesses, girls chosen for their abilities as well as their beauty and charm. They could play feminine instruments like the piano and harp and recite poetry for the men. The ancient role of the geisha and sing-song girl was considered an honour among ambitious AVA girls. They also performed favours of love and intimacy if the guests desired it. In the culture of the Alliance, these were not the animal gropings of Western sleaze scandals but the valued art form of a respected tradition. The guests were powerful men who gave up their time, energy and even health for the greater glory of their cause. In Asian traditional medicine, there was a belief that a man must replenish his masculine *yang* energy through sexual ecstasy which, if practised correctly, was akin to a spiritual experience. It was a privilege for the hostesses to be permitted to assist in such a sacred ritual for the finest of the Asian elite.

Siew met Ben Chang at the door and drew him in to meet the other men. The evening was in full swing. Guests lounged on sofas attended by the hostesses. Trays of delicacies and drinks circulated. It was still too early for the bedrooms off the suites to be filled. The laughter and celebrations gave Siew a high. It had been a risk, going public with the experiment. The AVA was now linked irrevocably to its success or failure but Siew had no doubt of its success. Ben Chang had been up in Johore each week monitoring the kids and the long-term prognosis looked good. Ben had come through, Siew thought, in spite of his moment of panic those months back. He put an arm around Ben's shoulders. This boy was like the son he'd never had. Siew loved him more than any of his own daughters. They were good girls, pretty and obedient – but they were not sons. Ben would head the neural programming after the Final Phase and with Siew's passing, would one day run Asia.

Wyndham would get a generous payment on top of his release from his high-profile duties, Siew thought expansively. The white man had delivered the Cure at last. Siew had chosen the right moment to forward the AVA's public crusade. Initially, the objective of bringing the media in on the JB experiment had been to publicise Asian Values. The experiment had pushed the desirability of Asian Values and was a major step in preparing people's minds to receive the AVA message in the Final Phase. But an unexpected advantage was evolving.

'They like the idea of an Asian Values course in schools,' Siew said to Amitabharam, one of his vice-presidents, the head of a property development conglomerate, with a personal worth of four billion *ringgit*. Siew had lunched with the home affairs minister the day before. It had been one of many meetings with government figures in the region in the last month. Over the next few weeks, he would be seeing representatives of the armed forces in Vietnam, China and Indonesia to discuss incorporating an Asian Values regime into their troops' daily routines. Businesses wanted to know how Asian Values could make their employees more productive: cut back on theft, fraud and shirking; instil greater corporate loyalty and increase contentment while decreasing wages. Governors of prisons wanted advice on how Asian Values could help rehabilitation. Wyndham structured the details of the therapy but it was Siew who imparted the vision of a perfect society. The beauty of it was its apparent simplicity: good health, good food, good community and transformation through computer-aided medication.

He laughed. 'They're all inviting us in! It's going to be much easier than we had planned to set up the visual-aid infrastructure and spread the Cure into the key areas of society.'

'People want strong values to guide them in these fast-changing times.' Amitabharam helped himself to some caviar. He fancied himself an intellectual. 'We offer them a vision of themselves as strong, pure and powerful – Malaysian or Thai or whatever nation they are – and Asian through and through. Our modern, democratic governments are grounded in traditional values just as Western governments are based in Christianity. They can't suppress the AVA without appearing themselves to be anti-Asian and puppets of the West. That would undermine the moral foundation of their governance and their claim to modernity and democracy. The Alliance has got them in a double bind. We've won.'

'The glory of Asian Values is that it appeals to everyone with a stake in society.' Siew looked at Ben. 'Governments are only just beginning to see that. I'm putting out feelers to bring some of them in.'

'Government funding! The pot is bottomless.'

'Not just money. Don't forget the armies, navies and air power at their beck and call.'

Amitabharam whistled. 'But can we trust them? Something as powerful as the Cure – they might want to control it completely. Without us.'

'My approach is cautious. A few key figures at a personal level for starters. I meet with them. The Tiger meets with those they hold dear.' Siew smiled. That was the way he always handled sensitive deals. The Red Tiger were his ultimate bargaining tool. No one would refuse him with a gun held to their son's head. Siew said, 'They'll like what we have to offer. They'll have to.'

Amitabharam crowed.

Siew went on, 'We can make better citizens for them and they can help us prime the people. Once the Final Phase is through, their people won't need them – but don't tell them that.'

The two men laughed.

'All the people will need is the AVA.' Ben looked strained

but happy. He had lost weight. He probably hadn't slept much.

Siew took him aside. 'Take a holiday after this month. You and your lovely wife go somewhere relaxing – the Bahamas. I'll pay for it.'

Ben beamed but hesitated. 'Project Max is coming up. I need to be part of that . . .'

Siew eyed him. He had expected Ben to be squeamish about Project Max. The young man's eagerness to be a part of it was an encouraging sign of his commitment. Siew had not been wrong to put his hopes in him. 'That's my boy! But after Max – promise me? We need you on top form for Phase Four.'

'And then the Final Phase,' Ben said too loudly. He blinked and pushed his hair out of his eyes. These agitated tics had started when his doubts had been most severe. They seemed still to be with him.

Siew said, 'Relax, Ben. Try out some of those meditation techniques you use at the Centre.'

Later, Piers Wyndham made a brief appearance. Siew knew he had come more out of respect for the host than a love of celebration. Wyndham was stiff and reserved as the other guests came up to him. Siew had first met him here in Singapore when the *gwai lo* had been a young psychologist at the top teaching hospital. The white man had been passionate about Asian culture and values and had been researching the comparative psychologies of Eastern and Western peoples. It had been a controversial project, smacking of racism and eugenics, but as the study appeared to prove Asians superior, there was much regional interest in its findings. After Wyndham had moved back to Europe and then on to America as a neuropsychologist, Siew had kept himself abreast of the scientist's work. When he had learned of Wyndham's hypothesis for mental reprogramming, he had done everything in his power to facilitate the production of the compound. When the police had eventually raided Wyndham's lab in Jersey City with a warrant for his arrest for murder, Siew had arranged his safe passage out of America.

Siew had foreseen the Final Phase then and it could only become reality with the insidious power of the Cure. It was at the Final Phase that Asia would fall into the complete control of the AVA.

⊷⊶

Liak blinked as he stared at the exercise book on his desk. The page wavered under his blurred vision. The notes he had copied from the blackboard started off neatly at the top of the page and then ran at an angle down one side. What was happening? Liak looked up in panic but the teacher skidded in and out of view. The windows rushed in to take her place. He was too frightened to speak, his mouth dry, throat constricted. His breath came in short, shallow gasps. His head was jerking in a wide arc. He could not hold it still. His leg began a staccato jigging, his thigh hitting the desk. His hand scraped the pen across the page, ripping the paper.

He heard his teacher's voice. 'What's going on, Liak?'

I don't know. Help me. But no words came. Only a gagging sound. The muscles in his jaw seized up, twisting rigid. Sharp pain shot through his neck and shoulders. His limbs curled in on themselves, steel claws of agony.

Liak fell from his chair, hitting his head on the concrete floor with a thud. He barely felt the pain. There was screaming all around him, rapid movements as the other kids panicked. The teacher bent over him but Liak did not notice her. He was only aware of a tough-looking kid staring down at him. He had seen the kid before in his dreams – a sullen guy with wild hair and attitude. Everything had gone still and silent. Liak squinted up and tried to see the kid's face. He saw himself and a spinning, churning vertigo caught him.

He was screaming but no sound came. He was gulping in air, straining to be heard. His body locked rigid. Only his mind skidded free.

And suddenly he was the guy standing over the stiff, contorted body. He turned and ran towards the door but there was only darkness beyond. He stood at the threshold staring into black emptiness. No up, no down, no way ahead. How had he come here? What had they fucking done to him?

Liak sucked air through his rigid, drooling mouth. He felt the cold floor on his back. Heard the roar of voices and crashing of furniture, someone shouting for an ambulance. His eyes rolled sideways and he saw his own hands twisted at horrific angles. He screamed, an animal shriek of terror.

Chapter Eleven

'Someone's asking questions about you.' Johnny turned to Fei. He stopped pacing her living room.

'What?' She felt a surge of alarm. 'Who?'

Her brother had turned up late at night unannounced. He looked tired and worried, was talking fast. She managed to piece the story together. He had just had a quarrel with Anita. The whole family had got involved over dinner and it had all come out. Each of them had been approached or had heard from colleagues or friends who had been approached. Someone – or some people – wanted to find out things about Fei. He ran a hand through his hair. 'We don't know who-lah, that's the thing.'

Anita had been the last to speak to a stranger about Fei. She had been out at a cocktail bar on a girls' night out. Jackson, her boyfriend, had gone to an AVA meeting and thought her at home with her family. 'Anita-lah, you know she likes going out and having fun. I don't know how long this thing with that square-head will last,' Johnny said. 'So this guy start to talk to them all. He said he met her at a party before but she don't remember him. Somehow they get on to talking about you. He says he saw you once with some friends of his, he liked you but you look all snooty. He was afraid to talk to you. Wants to know about you, whether he got chance with you.'

'What was his name?'

'Lee or something, she said. He didn't tell much about himself.'

Fei frowned.

'She said he was big – no, hunky. Like a US football player type but Chinese. Late-twenties, maybe thirty.'

Fei shook her head. 'I can't place him.'

'The thing is he ask all kind of questions. About your work, your money. How come you so rich? he want to know. He buy her lots of drinks. He ask about your friends, business deals, everything. She started getting angry. You know Anita, what a temper she got . . .'

Fei felt her mouth go dry, remembering her sister's look of loathing that night at her mother's house.

'All he wanted to do was talk about you, she said. She was screaming and crying at dinner. She wanted to spit it out, she said. Tell him *all* the truth about you.'

'Shit! Johnny, how could she . . .'

He steadied her with his gaze, his voice deliberately calm. 'But she didn't, Fei. She said, what you are touches her, too. It's your secret but if she lets it out, she also will suffer. So she kept quiet. That Jackson – she changed when she met him. She never used to be like this about you.' Johnny sighed and shook his head.

'Did she get this Lee's address? Phone number?'

'No-lah. I ask her that also.'

Fei sank down into a chair, hardly listening anymore. She felt weak. She felt as if unseen forces out there were closing in on her. Ginny's insistence on calls only on the encrypted mobile phones, their paranoid route changes whenever they met: Fei had preferred to treat all this as a game. The darkness beyond had been too unnerving to hold in her mind for long. For weeks now she had had a sense of being trailed. Of someone watching her. It was a Chinese man, she was convinced of it. Broad-shouldered like a boxer. He was a face in the crowd at the food court where she had lunch, a familiar shape among the drivers waiting for their bosses outside Ginny's apartment, a movement behind her in the street. Yet sometimes she would sense a watcher and he would not be a Chinese but an Indian or

Malay. She murmured, 'It's still the same features, the same build, I know it.'

'Fei?'

'I think someone's been following me.'

'Have you gone to the police?'

'No – there's nothing I can tell them for sure. It's just – a feeling. Sometimes I see the man but I don't know . . . Maybe this is just proof I'm going crazy – along with everything else.'

'Everything else?'

Fei told him about the other incidents: the attempted break-in, the assassin at the Centre, the mad rantings of that patient. Her heart raced even as she remembered them. She might have convinced herself that they were nothing but her own paranoia – that she had nothing to fear, no one wanted to harm her. But for the man she kept seeing.

Johnny squatted in front of her. He took her hands. 'Tell the police.'

'Tell them what? They'll laugh at me.' Spoken out loud, the incidents seemed to Fei to have no validity. They were hardly evidence of anything other than her own state of fearfulness, she told herself. 'The police would want to know what I'm so afraid this sinister conspiracy will find out. What do I tell them then? I'd be ruined. The family, too.'

Johnny kissed her forehead. The gesture surprised Fei. It struck her then that this was the first time they had talked as if her sexuality were a given. She hugged him. She felt safe in his arms: *Tai Koh* – big brother. But the moment did not last.

'Are you involved in – in trouble?' Johnny said quietly.

'No, there's nothing.' Was Ginny trouble? Fei laughed to cover the lie. 'No drug dealers or triad clients, I swear.'

Johnny searched her face. 'You be careful-lah, okay? Promise?'

'Sure, don't worry.' Fei smiled with a confidence she did not feel.

Fei could not concentrate on the to-and-fro of the conversation around her. There were ten of them at the dinner party, all professionals, a mix of sexes, some straight, some gay. Their hosts were a married couple, the husband an architect, the wife an interior designer. The house was a luxurious blend of Western empire elegance and oriental splendour, the pool hazy bright beyond the open patio doors.

Fei kept glancing out into the spotlight night. She could not shake off the sense of danger lurking just out of sight. The Haze seemed to shift like a phantom, reaching into the elegant rooms. She had driven here by a circuitous route, taking sudden detours and U-turns. Had it done any good in shaking off whoever might have been following her? Had anyone really been tailing her? Did it matter anyway, for what secrets could be teased out of a simple dinner party? Her mind ached. She felt tired and distracted. She had not slept properly in days.

Sam was watching her from the far end of the table. Fei had not known she would be there. They had had almost half an hour alone earlier, sitting by the pool with drinks. Sam had just come back from New Delhi and had talked about her research. Fei had not really followed the details, having taken in only that Sam was not going back to London after all. She had felt ridiculously light-hearted then, although she knew she should feel nothing one way or the other, whatever Sam decided. In the darkness, they seemed to have edged closer together as they talked, their voices softening. For the breath of a moment – she felt it still with unexpected immediacy – Fei had almost touched her, run her fingers across her back, caressed her hair. She smiled brightly now at Sam and turned away to chat to the man beside her.

The talk turned to the latest buzz in town. Razali, a Malay doctor, said, 'I can't see how they changed the JB kids' person-alities without drugs or medication?'

'It's some patented trademarked new-age therapy.' Janice was a Chinese stockbroker. 'The Wyndhams are American, right?'

'English,' Fei said.

The talk clattered with differing opinions. It was quackery.

It was a miracle cure. The consequences for social engineering were phenomenal. The therapy had been sponsored by the Asian Values Alliance – what were the implications of that?

Their host, Woo, took a long gulp of brandy. 'We'd all be engineered out of existence for sure. Look at all this decadence: Western brandy, South American cigars, divorcees, couples living in sin – of all permutations, all of us exercising our Western-educated minds and offering our opinions on every topic under the sun.'

Amid the laughter, Razali said, 'Asian values with a small "v" are all well and good. But Asian Values as spouted by the Alliance – ugh!' He shuddered. 'Who are they to tell us what's acceptably Asian or not? We're all Asian in our own different ways – however we live, whatever we choose to do, whatever values we personally hold: that's *our* Asian way.'

'I'll drink to that!' There was banging on the table as they all tossed back a toast.

'Social engineering of this nature should be deplored.' Sam's clear voice cut quietly through the chatter. 'It's a breach of civil liberties and basic human rights. Who has the right to remake another person in their own image?'

'Yeah, it's creepy – like Frankenstein,' Janice agreed.

Woo said, 'You mean, the Wyndhams are playing God?'

'I don't trust them . . .' Sam began.

'What do you mean?' It came out more harshly than Fei had intended. The whole table turned to her. In the silence, she was only aware of Sam's gaze on her.

Sam's tone was mild. 'The Wyndhams are white and the AVA are ostentatiously anti-white. Yet the Wyndhams have joined the Alliance cause. There are some issues there, wouldn't you say?'

'The AVA are not anti-white. Asian Values is a state of mind. They aim to appeal across race, religions and gender.'

There was a murmur of surprise round the table. Fei blinked. Had she really said all that? Why did she feel so defensive? Other than the fact that it was Sam who was being critical of the Wyndhams.

Sam smiled. 'The Wyndhams are your clients, right?'

'So what if they are?'

The other guests exchanged looks at Fei's snapping tone. She and Sam were causing a scene. Fei glared at Sam but that only seemed to make her smile more serene.

She said, 'For a moment there I thought you'd signed up for the cause. It was very convincing.'

Fei ignored the cautious laughter of their friends. Anger spurred her on. For over a week now Ginny had been distant, making excuses to avoid meeting, being strangely abrupt on the phone. There had been resentment in her tone, almost an accusation of betrayal. But she had ignored Fei's expressions of concern. Ginny's behaviour had hurt Fei more than she had expected. It was ridiculous to be having this public argument about the Wyndhams – Ginny did not need defending. But Sam sitting there needling her, always having to be right – Fei felt the pressure gauge of her temper mounting.

It was as if they had never broken up. Whether or not she agreed with Sam, she had to take the opposite position. 'Why shouldn't delinquents be made into useful members of society? The JB kids don't know any different in their new lives – they're happy, they're part of the community. What's wrong with that?'

'They were given no choice. And that's a freedom we should all have. Only tyrants and dictators take that away from their people.'

'They had a choice. Their families signed consent forms . . .'

Sam laughed. 'The lawyer's eternal cop-out! That's not what I mean. Each moment of our lives, we are free to make a choice. Do I take brandy or water? Do I smoke or not? Do I love men or women? Do I live to the best of my potential or the worst? Who's to say what's best or worst for me? That's up to me. That's the glory of being alive, don't you see? You can persuade me, you can show me another way, you can negotiate with me . . . but who are you to *steal* all those choices from me? Who are you to say being or behaving in a certain way makes me happier? It might make *you* happier but you're not me. I'm not you. And that's a human truth that must be respected in any society that considers itself civilised.'

Fei was aware of their friends watching them like spectators at a tennis match. God, she and Sam were ruining the dinner party. But she could not make herself stop. She almost shouted, 'You're so – so – Western!'

'If by that you mean liberal and respectful of each individual, then thank you! Since when did you become such a fount of Asian Values?'

'Since you got on to your high horse of self-righteous perfection!'

Not a sound could be heard. Fei felt a flush of embarrassment. What had got into her? What had got into Sam?

Sam stared back with blazing eyes. She seemed to make an effort to control her voice, saying hoarsely, 'You mean, since I criticised the Wyndhams? I'm sorry, I didn't think you would take it so *personally*.'

At that moment Fei's cellphone rang.

The tension around the table dissolved into loud chatter as she scrabbled to answer it. Everyone was studiously changing the subject. The voice on the line caught Fei by surprise. 'Ginny?'

Sam's sardonic tone carried over the hubbub. 'Speak of the devil.'

<hr />

Ginny was hysterical on the phone. Fei was tempted to fob her off, play the game of cat and mouse Ginny had forced on her for the last week or more. But she needed to escape from the dinner party and Sam's watchful eyes. She rushed to meet Ginny at her law office.

Ginny played with a pen as she recounted the accusations made against the Centre. They were in a meeting room, the night outside opaque with darkness. Even with the air-conditioning on, the smell of smoke permeated the room. It was the same throughout the building. The Haze had hung over KL for two months, claustrophobic and suffocating. Fei tried to set aside her anger at Sam and annoyance with herself for getting into the slanging match. She made herself focus on Ginny.

Anxiety and stress had deepened the lines around her eyes and mouth. Her skin seemed taut across the ridges of cheeks and jaw. She could not stop shifting in her chair. And there was something else. Fei sensed resentment behind that tension, an accusing glare that Ginny could not keep from her gaze.

Fei avoided her eyes after a while. Instead she looked through the letters Ginny had brought with her, breaking off to jot notes on her legal pad. Ginny was jerking in her chair, leaning against the table. Her voice was tight. 'The headmaster, Zainul, wants to sue. He's got the school board behind him and now the PTA. I've been fighting him on the phone, by letter. I thought I could handle it. But I need you. Tonight, with this latest development, I had to see you!'

Fei decided to stick to the legal matters. She spoke with professional calm. 'The parents and board gave written consents to the therapy. They have very little to stand on.'

'We've managed to keep it out of the press till now – fielding all their letters and calls has been a nightmare. Liak got sick ten days ago. The JB hospital, thank God, were happy to keep it under wraps. But now more kids have got sick and we can't contain it much longer.'

'How many altogether?' Fei looked up.

'Seven.'

'All from the therapy group?'

Ginny tapped the pen. 'There's one who's not.'

Fei was alert now. 'Go on.'

'Apparently, she's a top-grade student in a junior class. Plays the violin. Last week, she couldn't hold the instrument and was hospitalised. She has spasms like the other children – rigidity, then paralysis, with intervals when they're fine.' The pen was tapping a rapid staccato.

Fei placed her hand gently over Ginny's. She let the pen fall.

Fei said, 'If she never took part in the therapy and Piers's team never had anything to do with her –'

'Never.'

'– and she exhibits the same symptoms as the other children, then we've got a weapon to fight the school with. The kids obviously caught something – say, meningitis or Legionnaire's disease. I would contend that the school board is trying to pin the blame on the Centre to save their own hides.'

Reading details of the terrible symptoms, she felt for the children and what they must be suffering. She would have to review the video tapes of the sessions to be sure of the Wyndhams' defence. She believed in her clients – whether or not she really believed in the Asian Values cause or the merits of social engineering. The argument with Sam still riled her but Fei tried to make herself forget it. The Wyndhams had done so much to improve the care of the mentally ill, she told herself, and their innovative therapies could help thousands more as they had helped the boys in this project. The school board was pursuing the wrong culprit, it had to be. 'This therapy is new and different – that scares people no matter how well it works. The Centre is a high-profile institution with money behind it. That combination of fear and money raises hopes of a huge pay-out.'

'Oh, God!' Ginny blanched. 'If there's a trial . . . I couldn't get up on the stand. Please, don't make me!'

Fei moved to touch her again but Ginny pulled away. 'There needn't be a trial. We'll kill this thing before it gets any bigger.'

Fei had wanted to call Krishna Anapurti, the litigation partner, but Ginny had been adamant. 'No! Just you. I want you to handle it.' It had been a while since Fei had handled litigation but she was finding herself firing up skills she had almost forgotten. The skirmish to come gave her an outlet for the jumpy energy she had been stockpiling in the last few weeks. It was as if it offered her control over the malign threats that lurked just out of sight. In her mind they became real flesh and blood opponents in the tangible form of her clients' accusers. She felt protective of Ginny, like a hero who would do battle for her beloved, and the feeling warmed and excited her.

Fei began to talk tactics, almost as a soldier might show off her arsenal. She outlined the legal issues – malicious libel, negligence, health and safety regulations. She talked about the contributory role of the school board and the hospital. There was a counter claim to think of, damages to claim – millions of *ringgit* for defamation. They needed to focus on medical reports from their own experts, interviews with witnesses, negotiation strategy. Fei ticked the points off on her fingers.

Ginny turned to her with frightened eyes. 'You won't make me give evidence in court . . .'

She hadn't heard much of what Fei had been saying, it was clear. She was surprised by the intensity of Ginny's terror. There was something almost manic about her manner. It was as if she might leap up and tear out of the room at any moment. Fei touched her arm. This time, the contact seemed to soothe her. Ginny did not pull away.

'It won't get to trial. And even if it does, I won't let you be called, I promise.'

Ginny seemed to calm down. She breathed in deeply, steadying herself, and nodded. Fei stood up, 'Look, there's not much more we can do tonight. I'll make a start on our plan of attack in the morning and . . .'

Ginny did not move. She stared at Fei coldly, her voice suddenly harsh. 'Are you leaving me now? You're always leaving me.'

'What?'

'You leave me so easily. All those mornings, before I woke up, you were gone.'

'I . . . I thought it best. Before your housekeeper came.'

'But slipping off like I'm a – a woman you're leaving in a brothel.'

'Ginny!' Fei felt the sting of the accusation. And its semi-truth. She flushed.

Ginny's voice was taut, plaintive suddenly with anger. 'You made me fall in love with you, you can't just walk away from that.'

'I made you . . . what?' Fei stared at her in confusion. 'But I'm here for you now.'

'Do you know how difficult it's been? I can't stop thinking about you. How can you just get on with your life as if nothing's happened? I'm in love with you, Fei – don't you feel the same way?'

'What's all this about? Why are you being like this?' She felt frustrated and tired. Two arguments in one night was too much. Sam – that was understandable maybe. But Ginny – they were supposed to be in this wild, passionate romance. Her head was beginning to pound.

'I don't lie as well as you,' Ginny snapped.

'What?'

'Are you going to deny it?'

'Deny what? It's late, Ginny. Don't play games.'

'Carson Dean.'

'Ah.' Fei took a breath. 'Is this what you've been sulking about? I was going to tell you . . .'

'Were you? Are you sleeping with him? You've been seen with him a lot. I thought you weren't into men?'

'We're just friends.' Fei felt disorientated. Had she said these words to Sam about Ginny? She was too tired to take this squabble seriously. She laughed. 'Are you jealous of him? Ginny, he's a *man*. Don't be ridiculous! He's funny. We talk about books and movies, he's urbane, cosmopolitan in the way that only highly educated Americans can be. He makes me laugh. Yes, *he* fancies me but that doesn't mean I fancy him. Besides, it makes the perfect cover for us, doesn't it?'

Fei pulled up a chair to sit beside Ginny. 'People see you happily married to Piers but they don't know you're not sleeping with him anymore. People see me with this dishy guy who follows me around like a puppy dog – they don't know that I'm really sleeping with you. They'll leave us alone because we've confirmed all their expectations, right?'

Ginny said nothing but Fei could see she was grudgingly coming round. Ginny said, 'There's something you should know about Dean. He's been trying to get a story on the Centre. We've put him off so far but he's obviously trying a new angle.'

'I was suspicious at first but I've drawn the boundaries firmly.

I don't talk about my clients' business – that's professional ethics. No one gets round that, least of all a *man*.' Fei pulled a face to lighten the mood.

Ginny managed a smile. When she next spoke, her voice was soft. 'Take me home with you tonight.'

Fei hesitated. This issue again. Ginny had brought it up a few times now. She sighed. 'You know I can't. Not yet.'

'You mean you won't.'

Fei could not look at Ginny. Her apartment was where her real life was. It was where her life with Sam had been. This breathless affair with Ginny had no place there. To take her there would be to seal it into a relationship. She did not want a relationship, she told herself again. But was she just playing with words? *A lawyer's cop-out.* Sam's words. Sam's voice in her head. Sam still in spite of everything. She said, 'Ginny, please, it's late.'

'When will you take me there?'

'I need time.'

'You do love me, don't you?'

Fei kissed her. 'Let's go back to your place.'

In the Wyndhams' apartment, Ginny sat with Fei in the living room eating cold chicken. It was four in the morning. Being back here was like being back in the web of the Centre and the Alliance. Ginny could not shake off the tension crowding in on her.

Piers had told her that the legal route was a necessary one for now. It was the expected, natural route. But Siew and his people were working behind the scenes to smokescreen the matter. Ginny knew the all-too-effective means Siew's people would use to eliminate trouble-makers through their underworld connections if the legal means failed.

Siew's rage had been palpable over the secure video-link phone from his Singapore base. Piers's team were working non-stop to review the Cure and to expedite the next generation that

Piers had not anticipated they would need. Ben Chang had been shuttling down to JB, his nerves fraying, reporting back on the children but unable to take part in their treatment without implicating the Centre further. Piers had finally confined him to the Centre for the young man's own health. When Ginny had left the Centre, Piers had not slept in days, panic and fury driving him on in the labs.

Ginny needed to be with Fei, feel her strength and love, even if Fei knew nothing of the truth. Or perhaps *because* she knew nothing. She didn't want to think about the diseased children or Piers or the Centre or their pact with Siew. Fear screamed inside her like a child. She wanted only Fei. It was so simple and yet so impossible. The talk of courts and trials had sent her into a tailspin and suddenly all she felt was a sense of being abandoned, a terrifying loneliness she could not overcome. She regretted the question she had pressed on Fei. *You do love me, don't you?* Fei's startled expression was still vivid in her memory. She could not forget that Fei had not answered her.

Chapter Twelve

A few days later, Fei left her office after eleven p.m. The streets were still busy but at this late hour traffic was flowing freely. The haze glowed from the moving streams of headlights and tail lights. Fei was tired but adrenaline from the last few days of hectic activity gave her a live-wire buzz. Running the Wyndham case on top of her other responsibilities had meant working even longer hours as she juggled the demands of her various clients. She would eat a packet of cold fried noodles at her desk for dinner and crash out for a few hours the moment she got home. She liked the frantic pace. It distracted her.

She swung on to the cross-town highway, stretching her back as she cruised along, and headed west to pick up the inter-change for Bangsar.

Headlights on high beam dazzled her in the rearview mirror. Fei frowned, squinting. The idiot was sitting on her tail. She was going sixty as it was, rushing traffic in the lanes to either side of her. She forced a space open in the nearside lane to pull in so the moron could pass. The car she cut in front of honked angrily.

The car on her tail slipped in behind her, still nosing her rear bumper.

'What the hell . . .' Fei blinked against the light in the mirror. Trying to think. Her heart raced. She thought of the man – men – she had seen over the last few months. She saw the gouges on her apartment door where someone had tried to break in. Felt again those powerful arms grabbing her at the Centre.

Fei changed lanes again, hardly noticing the screeching brakes and honking as she cut ahead of a truck.

The car tailing her swooped smoothly in behind.

Panic hit her. Cold sweat broke out. Fei tried to move into the fast lane but a Mitsubishi jeep barred her way, screaming on its horn.

Green highway signs blurred past above. An exit soon. She didn't know where to, no time to think. Fei swerved across a lane of traffic, roaring into the hard shoulder. The car behind mimicked her every move, keeping pace. She speeded up, tyres squealing as she took the turn-off. The glare in the mirror vanished for a moment then came back as the car rounded the corner. It raged up to her, touching her bumper with a jolt.

Fei jerked forward. Felt her car skid momentarily. Fought for control. Pulling in to join the new flow of traffic. The car behind had eased back after contact but was still hard on her tail.

Fei felt sick with terror. She clutched the wheel, stared blindly to left and right. All these cars, all these other people. Why didn't they help her? How could this be happening? With so many people about, why was he doing this? Help, get help. But if she stopped, tried to flag down a car – she would be out there, at his mercy. Shit. Think. Think.

Her phone . . . But it was in her briefcase. The case had slid off the seat next to her and was jammed awkwardly on the floor under the dashboard. She leaned across the gearshift, holding the car steady with one hand, her foot down on the accelerator.

Another jolt from behind. Fei was rammed against the dashboard. She pounded her foot on the brake as she felt her car go out of control. Blurred shapes shot across the windscreen. Screaming horns. Right arm aching as she struggled to keep the car in lane, pushing herself upright with the other. Then fighting the gears and clutch, down to second, feeling the tyres grip the tarmac. Shooting straight, out of danger, correcting speed to avoid a crash into the car in front. Three seconds, no more.

An opening in the outside lane. Fei yanked the wheel across, scraping cars as she accelerated into the space ahead. Foot down to the floor, shooting forward. The glare in the mirror was gone, the car tailing her caught in traffic behind. Fei took a steadying breath. Then she heard it: the crash of metal on metal. In the mirror she saw a car with headlights at an angle. It rammed its way out of a logjam. Blaring its horn, the car was fighting the other traffic, dodging in and out, gaining on her. It pushed cars out of the way, clashing metal on metal. Ground against a van until it gave way.

The headlights were back on her tail, highbeam burning into her eyes.

Fei was almost weeping with terror.

And then the car behind changed lanes. As another green exit sign cruised by, it swung towards the nearside lane and into the turn-off. Fei twisted her head to see it go. In the hazy dark and at high speed, she caught nothing telling about it. The night seemed suddenly still and silent. And dark again.

Fei found herself shaking, tears wrenched out of her. In the sealed silence of the air-conditioned interior, she sobbed aloud. But she did not dare stop. Through blurred vision, she made herself drive on. All she could think of was getting home, bolting herself in. She would be safe then. There was a security guard in the building. If anything happened, there would be help. The door to her apartment was reinforced, no one could break it down. She was on the tenth floor, sliding grilles at the windows. She usually opened them when she was home but tonight she would keep them locked in place. She would be safe at home.

By the time she parked in the basement car park of her building, Fei had steadied herself. The floor was well lit and there was a familiar air of security that calmed her. She hauled her briefcase out, locked the doors and hurried towards the lifts. There was silence but for the reassuring hum of the ventilation system.

A car door opened just in front of her. A man eased himself out, footsteps loud on the concrete. Fei hurried on. The lifts were just ahead.

The man stepped forward. He stood facing her, in front of the bonnet of his car. His weight was balanced evenly, arms relaxed by his sides. He was broad-shouldered and dark-skinned. Navy jeans, black shirt. Short-cropped hair. Angular features behind sunglasses.

It was his stillness that frightened Fei.

She glanced around her. She was alone in the empty car park. The fire exit was by the lifts. The other exits were at the far side of the floor. She kept on walking.

She stared at his face as she passed. He turned to gaze back but did not move. It was the same face she had seen over the last few months.

And then she noticed the car. Not its make or colour or number plates, but the dents and the scraped bodywork. The faint hot smell of its engine.

Fei backed away and ran, crashing into the stairwell and up the stairs towards the lobby.

⸻ ◦ ⸻

Han watched her go. He took off the sunglasses and slid back into the car. He started the engine with a roar and swung out of the car park into the street. By the time the security guard came down, he would have vanished in the traffic.

Out in the smoky night, he headed back to his lodgings. He had had enough of waiting and watching. Rushing in to KL for days at a time over the last months, in between other jobs, he had got nowhere fast. He had spoken with her friends and family, got his local contacts to sniff around. His last attempt had been to chat up her sister Anita, a ball of catty resentment who looked like she might spit out something he could use. But nothing. His tap on Qwong's e-mail had shown up only exchanges about meetings and legal discussions about the JB school case. His interceptor on her office phone lines had picked up numerous calls made to the Centre and the Wyndhams in the last few days but they too had been the usual lawyer-client communications about the sick kids. He had tried scanning mobile phone calls but nothing had turned up. Impatient for progress, he had decided to force the pace.

He had got Qwong panicked now. It wouldn't take long to shift this stalemate. A target with something to hide plus panic equalled an explosive package. Han grinned but it felt more like a snarl. Something would go off. And Han would be ready for it. It would be the break he desperately needed.

———————————

Dean was waiting for Fei by the lifts outside her offices. It was almost ten at night and she was the last to leave. It was a week after she had been followed. Since then she had made sure that she was never alone between her office and her apartment. She tipped the security guards in the buildings to escort her to her car and even to follow her on their motorbikes to her destination. Friends came to meet her for breakfast or supper and accompanied her wherever she needed to go. 'Someone's got a bit too keen on me,' she would tell them, her gung-ho manner covering her real fear. She said nothing about the chase or the violence of it, telling them only that a man she had met at a party was following her and would not leave her alone. 'Hopefully he'll get bored soon before he turns into a regular stalker.'

Fei had hardly slept that night after she had locked herself into her apartment, talking to Ginny for over an hour on their secure cellphones. Ginny had been in a state of panic, wanting to come over then deciding against it – whoever had tailed Fei might see her. Offering Fei a security guard from the Centre, then deciding against it – a bodyguard close to her at all hours might find out too much, notice too much about her relationship with Ginny. Asking Fei over and over: what had the man been after, had he been tailing her all these weeks, had he seen their assignations, spied on their affair? There was no question of going to the police. She and Ginny had not even brought that option up. Fei longed to talk to Johnny but could not involve him. He would only try to confront the man and it would escalate and she did not want to think of what the man might do to her brother.

Both Fei and Ginny channelled their energies into the work surrounding the legal action, seeing each other only in meetings and only once spending the night together. Ginny shuttled between the Centre and KL. Injunctions and court motions fired at the school board and members of the PTA had bought the Centre some time. Independent doctors and scientists hired by the Wyndhams were making examinations for detailed reports.

Ginny had come to Fei just in time. The JB story had broken in the news the next day. Over the following two weeks, it built to a frenzy. The media focused on one boy – Liak – who had appeared on the N-Sat documentary about the therapy. He had captured the public's interest and every day updates on his condition were relayed over the news. He could hardly make himself understood now, his head lolling and saliva drooling down his chin. His weakening limbs curled close to his body at times, and at others hung limply. Spasms racked him, jolting the bed against the floor. Fei had hardly been able to watch the bulletins.

There were now twenty children ill, three of them close to death. The speed with which they'd been struck and their rapid decline filled the country with horror. Liak, in particular, had deteriorated sharply and the media clamour was rising. He was slipping in and out of a coma. In his waking state, he was no longer able to speak. The spasms were giving way to prolonged periods of total paralysis. The health and education ministries were carrying out their own independent enquiries.

Fei worked late most nights, juggling the Wyndham case with her other transactions. Dean was making sure that he would be there to pick her up every evening now for a meal or a drink. His presence made her feel safe. He looked like a man who could as easily hold his own in a fight as at the latest gallery opening. 'I'll take care of it,' he had said when she had told him her stalker story. A regular all-American hero, she had called him.

'And my reward? An exclusive on the JB case?' he had twinkled.

'No work talk, I told you that when we first met.'

' "If I had to choose between my friend and my country, I hope I'd have the courage to choose my friend",' Dean had said with a grin. 'E. M. Forster.'

He was covering the school story, going to the hospital in JB regularly for an update on the children's conditions and trying to get a parent or doctor to give him an interview. But so far Dean had not broached the subject with Fei, loyally adhering to his promise. Hospital staff had been ordered by the health department, backed up by the education department, not to talk to the media until investigations could determine the cause of the illness. It was a wise move to defuse the situation – there was nothing more emotive than sick children. Covering her clients' position, Fei had talked with a spokesman for the authorities, expressing concern regarding any unfounded allegations against the Centre that might be made by the official investigative team. She had fought her corner and gained an assurance that no statements would refer to the Wyndhams unless the investigations proved conclusively that they were at fault.

Dean took Fei to a bar/restaurant in the fashionable Bukit Bintang area. They had grilled fish with their drinks in a corner booth of the American-style dining room. Dean was flirting with her again. Tonight, Fei found it tiresome. The underlying tension of the last week did not help. She found herself glancing round every few minutes, checking the exits, and the other diners. 'Carson, please, I've told you: just friends.'

He pouted. 'I know I'm in trouble when you call me Carson.'

'It'll be Mr Dean soon if you don't stop.'

'I can't help it, I find you too attractive.'

Fei rolled her eyes. But she tried to relax.

'Don't you find me even a tiny bit hunky and gorgeous?' He ducked his head and crinkled a smile. 'Most women I've met don't have your self-control.'

Fei burst out laughing. 'And you're modest, too!'

Dean waited like a little boy. Fei shook her head. He really was too cute for his own good. 'All right, I'll tell you the truth.

I've just come out of a long-term relationship and I don't want to get involved with anyone right now.'

He looked concerned. 'I'm sorry, I didn't know. God, I've been crass. Consider the asshole well and truly booted.'

'Okay.' Fei smiled. 'I'll tell you when you can try your luck again. Till then . . .'

'I'll wait, I swear.'

Fei liked Dean for his curious mixture of sensitivity and macho confidence. It gave him an energy that lifted her spirits in spite of the tensions that caught her. He seemed the sort of New Man that only American men could be: educated, articulate, kind in a boy-scout sort of way and always masculine. It was like meeting Indiana Jones, *Cosmo* Dream Man and George Clooney all rolled into one. Sometimes, she could hardly believe he was real.

Dean took a swig of his beer. 'So, you been working hard on the Wyndham defence?'

It was public knowledge that the school had filed a statement of claim against the Centre, citing medical negligence as the cause of the children's condition. Fei had spent most of the day working on a counter-claim and a request for further and better particulars and talking at length with the Wyndhams' team of experts. She said, 'We agreed, no work talk.'

'Come on, for a friend.' Dean smiled. 'I haven't been able to get a peep out of anyone these last few days. Give me something to work with. Any little scrap.'

'Look . . .'

'What exactly is this therapy your clients are perfecting? It's not perfect yet, is it? These kids were just guinea pigs, right?'

'Everything you need to know about the therapy has already been reported in the media. There's nothing sinister about that.' Fei pulled out her wallet. 'Here, this is for my part of the meal. Please take me home.'

Dean took her hand. 'No, wait. I'll shut up, I promise. Finish your drink at least.'

She hesitated.

'You can't blame me for trying, can you?' He caught her eye. 'You'd have a go if you were me, I know you would.'

Fei laughed. 'Yeah, I suppose I would.'

'In the best interests of your client, right?'

Dean ordered them more drinks. He watched Qwong thoughtfully. Here was something useful at last. He had not known about the long-term relationship. After months of painstaking work, he knew everything about her family, her education, her career and her friends. But she had never been linked openly with anyone and he knew the talk about town was that she would die an old maid – a rich, successful one but an old maid nonetheless. Dean tasted the fresh glass of beer with satisfaction. So, who was her secret man? If he could find him, he might find a handle on her.

<hr />

Dean hung around the lobby of the National Hospital in KL with the other journalists. The JB medical team had passed on their samples and charts to the forensic pathology team here following the deaths of two of the children. Two weeks had passed since he had last seen Fei. She had avoided him after his probing about the case and was relying on the loan of the Wyndhams' security guards. There had been no sign of the stalker.

But Dean had a damn' good idea who the man was. From Fei's description, he had pegged the goon who had also tailed him a few times. Probably the same one who had broken into his apartment. The clown's search of the rooms would have told him nothing and the bug he had planted Dean had tuned to a local radio station. He had to be after what Dean was after. He was sure that the goon had not given up but had merely faded back into hiding. Fei had seen him because he had wanted her to see him. Why? If he had wanted to harm her, he would have done that by now. The likelihood was that he was trying to force the situation.

More interestingly, Fei's story of a stalker was unconvincing. There had been real fear behind her joking manner. Dean sensed that there had never been a party where she had met a lovesick Romeo. Her voice and body language described some other reality she was hiding from him.

He moved away from the ragtag crowd of newshounds to get a coffee from the machine round the back of the lobby. There was another set of lifts nearby. The journalist front covered his real motives well and usually got him near good sources. But as part of the media pack, he had to sit through these lock-outs like the rest of them. The pathology team were going to the meeting between the Centre and the school board in a couple of days. The health ministry would be represented as would the education department. Normally, the authorities did not involve themselves in civil disputes but there was obviously national significance to what was going on. Fei had scheduled a press conference straight after – she was clearly confident of the outcome. But the Wyndhams had vetoed Dean's pass.

A lift appeared. Doctors and hospital staff straggled out. Dean glanced up without interest.

Then he saw him: a well-built Asian man with angular features. In a suit. Security pass clipped to his breast pocket. Taking off a pair of heavy-framed glasses. His stride was unfurling out of a bureaucrat's shuffle with each step further away from the lift.

And then he saw Dean watching him.

Their eyes locked for a moment. There was recognition and a glimmer of a smile. Without breaking step, the man increased his pace and made for the fire escape.

Dean followed him.

———◆———

Han whipped the visitor's pass from his jacket and pocketed it. It identified him as a health official and had gained him access to the pathology team. They had briefed him on the contents of the official report which they would be submitting to the authorities and on which the Centre would be basing their defence in the civil suit. It was an easy step from there to gaining full access inside the Centre.

Han took the stairs three at a time down to the parking basements. The appearance of the Centre's security staff around Qwong had been significant. It indicated concern for her safety on the Wyndhams' part. And for their own security through her. It made another confrontation with her difficult but his chance would come – or could be created – and then Han would have her. Meanwhile, he had been waiting for the moment to put the pressure on the American. This was it.

There were three levels of parking. As Han reached the first, he heard the fire door above him open. There was a pause. Dean was obviously trying to work out which way he'd gone. Then quick footsteps following him. Han opened the door to the first level but did not go in. He swung down the next flight in four silent leaps, ducking into the second-level door. Flat against the wall, he squatted under cover of a parked car and glanced around. The lot was half-full but there was no one about. Fluorescent lighting cast grey light and shadows across the concrete floor. There was the usual smell of stale air and petrol.

Then movement from behind the fire door, sending it whipping open, Dean coming through in classic police-style, stepping quickly, low and balanced, arms together and close to the body, hiding his weapon. He did not register Han crouching below his line of vision till it was too late.

Han swept upwards. He grabbed Dean's hands on the pistol and kicked his feet out from under him. As Dean stumbled, the weapon spun out of his grip. Han elbowed his windpipe hard then smashed his other fist between the American's eyes. Dean crumpled. Han grabbed the fallen weapon, tucking it into his belt. Dean groaned, tried to move. Han pulled his own Beretta and, hauling Dean one-handed further into the shadows, rammed the muzzle into his cheek. The American's eyes worked to focus, a trickle of blood snaking out of one nostril. He held his hands palms up by his head.

Han said, 'Good, you know the drill. Now, who are you? Who do you work for?'

Dean gasped, 'I might ask the same of you.'

Han pressed the gun harder into his face. 'You know how this works. I've got the gun, I ask the questions.'

Dean's lips twisted into a wry smile. 'Carson Dean, Asia correspondent . . .'

'Who are you really?'

'It was you who bugged my flat, wasn't it?'

Han increased the pressure. Dean winced. He moved his hand to his breast pocket. The barrel of the pistol forced his head back at an awkward angle. Han reached into Dean's jacket and pulled out an ID wallet. Flipping it open, he saw the insignia of the FBI.

'Carson Dean, FBI. Undercover,' the American said.

Han eased back. The Beretta had left a deep impression in Dean's cheek. Han held the pistol level with Dean's chest as he produced his own ID, another alternate persona courtesy of the Family. 'Han Lee-Ren, internal security agent. We have no information on any US operatives acting in this country.'

'Can you put that thing away? Undercover operations don't always go through the usual channels.'

'As a matter of procedural etiquette . . .'

'All right, look, I'm here without all the proper paperwork. Go ahead, turf me out. But we're clearly after the same damn' thing. I could help you. After all, I'm wining and dining Qwong while you're still just sitting out on the pavement. And whatever you got, it'll help me.'

Han said nothing for a beat. Then he hauled Dean to his feet, reholstering his Beretta. He did not hand back Dean's Smith & Wesson 429 semi-automatic, flicking his jacket out to cover its bulk at his belt-line.

They sat in Dean's car in the level three car park, Dean at the wheel, his hands where Han could see them. Dean watched as, in the passenger seat, Han looked through the glove compartment. He would find nothing unusual, Dean had been careful about that.

Han said, 'What did you want from Qwong?'

'Same as you.'

'Why are you after the Wyndhams?'

Dean shrugged. He didn't need to tell Han anything the goon didn't know already.

Han said conversationally, 'We've placed you in Hong Kong and Taiwan as well as Shanghai in the last two years. We know you've tried to contact Red Tiger gang members. Your FBI badge won't protect you if we figure you're a threat to national security or maybe even a spy.'

'Okay.' Dean made a pretence of resignation. His suspicions over the last few weeks had been right. The Asians had been watching the AVA's every move. This was the clown who'd played spies in the bushes outside the Centre, Dean would put money on that. It didn't surprise him that the authorities had clocked his movements. But he was still not sure whether they knew what he knew about the Wyndhams. Judging from the fiasco of this goon's operations, Dean reckoned the Asians had no idea of the dynamite the Wyndhams were hiding up their ass.

He gave Han his official cover story. It would buy him co-operation if the goon thought they were after the same target for different reasons. 'In 1987, a gunman fired off three magazines from a .45 Sig Sauer in a McDonald's in midtown New York. Several bystanders were injured and three were killed. The gunman was pursued to Jersey City where there was a shoot-out in a warehouse by the Hudson. The gunman escaped, leaving two police officers and several others dead.'

'What's this got to do with the Wyndhams?' Han snapped.

'We have reason to believe that Piers Wyndham was the gunman. He is wanted by US authorities on numerous counts of murder and one count of attempted murder, plus charges of aggravated assault.'

Han eyed Dean. 'So why don't you just go up there and arrest him?'

He hesitated. 'We don't have definitive proof that links him to the shooting. Wyndham appears to be of British origin but after ten years in Asia he's got a Malaysian passport. The weapon was never recovered and all we have is circumstantial evidence.

'Given Wyndham's high-profile position in this country, this is a sensitive matter. You're aware of the anti-Western sentiment in Asia – particularly targeted at the US. We can't be seen to be hauling out one of your respected citizens for no reason. To get the extradition order, I need to be sure I have the right man.'

'You got quite a tall story there,' Han said. 'What's your interest in the Red Tiger?'

'We believe they were involved in getting Wyndham out of America.'

'What about the AVA?'

Dean said nothing.

'We know you've tried to contact their top people wherever you've been.'

'I've given you enough to work with. Whaddya got for me?'

Han scrutinised him. Smooth bastard. 'You'll need a friend if you want that extradition pushed through without a hitch.'

He watched Dean chew this over. The American finally said, 'Wyndham worked in Singapore before he came to the US. We can link him to Kei-Win Siew during his time there. The Alliance seems to crop up throughout his story. I'd say they were involved in getting him out of the country after the shooting and hiding him in Asia till now.'

'But why would they help him?'

Dean smiled. 'See, we are working towards the same thing.'

'Why are you so interested in the kids and this therapy?'

'It's a way in, isn't it? Why are *you* so interested? What have you got on the Wyndhams? And the Alliance?'

'For national security reasons, I cannot discuss that with you.'

'Ah, come on – play ball.'

'It's our job to monitor any group or movement, whether political or otherwise, that may be a threat to internal stability. It is a concern of all governments in this region and we work closely with our associate agents in other nations. We believe that an influential movement such as the AVA requires careful monitoring.' Han saw Dean's Western prejudices take this in and swallow it. The Suits would never call in the Family for anything but a serious threat – but Dean did not need to know about the dossier of alleged fraud, corruption, murder and extortion that the Family held on the Alliance. The lie got Dean off his back.

'You think that the disease that's hit the kids is somehow connected to this threat?'

'Maybe.'

'So what now?'

Han handed Dean his S&W. 'I want to know before you make a move on Wyndham.' He gave the American his direct mobile number.

Dean checked the slide action on his pistol. 'What do I get in return for everything I've told you?'

'What more do you want?' Han stepped out of the car. 'You got your freedom.'

Chapter Thirteen

Ben Chang made his way to the monitoring lab. He was jumpy, expecting to be stopped. Ever since Piers had recalled him from JB, he had been unable to sleep, racked with guilt and horror. Piers had kept him on tranquillisers for the last few weeks. He had also made Ben stay out of the labs, confining him to his bungalow to rest. Ben had wanted his wife there too but Piers had stopped him going to Mei-Hong and had prevented him from sending for her. Ben spoke to her every day on the phone but he was convinced that his calls were monitored so he said little, talking only about how busy he was. He was sure that Ong, the security chief, had someone watching Mei-Hong, ready to carry out whatever orders Piers or Siew might issue against her. She was their hostage to ensure his co-operation but in the last twenty-four hours Ben had not taken the sedation. For the first time in days he felt alert, pumped up with adrenaline.

They had killed children. *He* had killed them. And now the Centre was trying to cover it up. That was why Ginny was running around on that legal case, and Piers and his team were working like demons to make ready the next version, gen106. They had no time to think about the children involved, no hearts to pity their innocent victims. Piers could go to hell. Ben needed to see the ones who still lived, do what he could to help them.

He couldn't protect the Centre any more. Could no longer justify the hideous work they did there. He had believed in it all once, believed in a perfect Asia that could be manufactured and controlled like a perfect human being. But all they had done over these long years was kill and damage and torture ordinary people. Behind the façade of the Centre – real patients masking the abused victims, doctors and staff decoys covering the scientists working on the real objectives, the to-ing and fro-ing of legitimate business obscuring the illegal traffic – the murder and evil would go on but he refused to be a part of it any longer. He had to try to heal the horror he had inflicted. He was a doctor. Ben clung to that knowledge as if he hung from a precipice. He had to use every healing skill he possessed to bring life where for so long he had caused only death.

The monitoring lab was where the Centre held all the data on the JB experiment, with live video link-ups to the hospital wards where the kids were being treated. The secure cameras and data transmission equipment had been installed in the rooms by private arrangement with the hospital administration. Money bought everything, Ben reflected bitterly. Piers kept track of the kids' deterioration and worsening symptoms each day, information from the hospital's monitoring equipment relaying to the Centre the condition of each child moment by moment. Ben had to see them. He had to know everything a doctor should know about his patients.

He heard voices through the lab door, barely controlled his blinking. He opened the door. They all had their backs to him: Piers, Ginny, Ricky and the psych team. They were watching the screens. On several, there were shots of the same hospital room taken from different angles. The boy in the bed was Liak. Beside him was a woman – his mother. Pacing the floor was a young man, decked out in gold chains and with a streetfighter's physique – Liak's brother, probably. On other screens were graphs of Liak's heartrate and brain patterns.

Ben stared at the images of Liak. His body was skeletal and still, as if no life whispered through it. It had a frightening insubstantiality, muscles wasted away. He was on a ventilator. His head seemed more like a skull lightly covered in skin. His jaw already sagged like a corpse's. His mother had turned his head so that he could see her face but his eyes remained blank. Only the bleeping of the machines around his bed told them he was still alive.

Isolated in his mind, Liak screamed. He saw shapes and light as in a waking dream. They had no meaning, movements only of colour. Sounds echoed in his mind, disembodied, unrecognisable. He could not move. How long had he been trapped here like this? He was tired and his voice was hoarse. *Help me, someone. Help me.* Could no one hear him? Liak began to cry. At first, he had not been sure that time was passing. Then he had started counting. He had reached five thousand three hundred and forty-eight and then had stopped. Time was real and he was alone, minute after minute, day after day, staring at the moving shapes. Sometimes he would sleep but when he woke again, he would still be here. This was the rest of his life, he thought in terror.

He shouted out into the shadows. *Fuck you, fuck you!* His voice screamed in his head but the silence swallowed it. *I am Foon Wing-Liak! Fuck you all!* His heart hurt in his chest, he felt cold with terror. In his mind, he stood up, balancing on his toes, stretching out to infinity. He spread his arms high and let the emptiness take him, his own name shrieking on his lips.

A single gasp, that was all. And the machines beeped the alarm as the monitor of his pulse deadened to a single monotone.

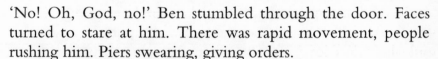

'No! Oh, God, no!' Ben stumbled through the door. Faces turned to stare at him. There was rapid movement, people rushing him. Piers swearing, giving orders.

Strong arms grabbed him.

'Take him to the main ward,' Piers said. 'Increase the dosage . . .'

Then Ginny's voice: 'Go easy on him.'

'We don't have time for this melodrama now. He knew what the risks were.'

'He's young . . .'

'Let's go!'

Ben struggled half-heartedly but despair had drained him of strength. He let them drag him out, sobbing, 'I killed that boy! We murder little children. That's the kind of doctors we are, do you hear? Do what you want with me, kill me too . . .'

Dean stood at the door to the office. Through the glass window he saw the English woman at her computer, shelves of books and files closing in from the walls. Sam Ryder wore a white lab coat over sweatshirt, jeans and suede desert boots. Her hair was cropped short, giving her a girlish appearance even though Dean knew she was in her early-thirties. She was slight, almost elfin in build. She sat with her feet up on the desk, staring at the screen, tapping a pencil on her teeth. Dean whistled soundlessly. So, this was Qwong's 'flatmate'.

He had made further queries about Qwong and his first intuition about her had been confirmed. There had never been a man in her life. But there had been a flatmate who had lived with her for four years and had only recently moved out. Four years was a long-term relationship.

Dean had been trained to pick out the details, see the whole picture in the minutiae. But with Qwong, he had not looked with his usual objectivity. He had found her more attractive than he cared to admit and it had got in the way. Her flirtatious manner and femininity had been the perfect smokescreen. No one would have pegged her as a dyke. Now, seeing Ryder, he felt the veil lift. Qwong's sexuality had always been evident, if only he'd looked properly. There was that distance in her manner he had not been able to pin down, the independence of spirit that had seemed almost too perfect. There was her short hair and trousers; shoes that were stylish but allowed her a long, confident stride.

A combative tension tightened his jaw. Dean stepped into the lab. Ryder looked up, starting out of her seat. 'You can't come in here.'

'Carson Dean, *Global Weekly News*.' He offered his hand, grinned. 'You working on the Johore Baru school case?'

'We can't talk to journalists. Please leave.'

'Pathology told me to come up here. This is Epidemiology, right? They said they'd passed on their results to you.'

'They shouldn't have told you anything.' Ryder was trying to back him out of the lab but Dean did not move. She'd have to push him if she got any closer and he towered over her. 'This is a contamination area, you have to go.'

Dean smiled. 'No, it's not. This isn't a lab, it's an office. Relax.'

'I'm calling security.' Ryder moved to the phone.

'You're Fei-Li Qwong's lover, aren't you?'

She spun around, looking as if he'd accused her of being a Martian. '*What?*'

'You two are an item. Or were. For the last four years. Then a lovers' tiff and you're out on your ear. Am I right?'

'You're disgusting.' Ryder made for the door.

Dean felt his temper rush ahead. He pulled it back. Was it jealousy? The thought surprised him. Or just hurt pride? That it had taken him so long to work it out. So long to get nowhere with Qwong. He said, 'Who's she sleeping with now?'

There it was. A flicker in her face: of pain? Anger? Then she recovered. She wrenched open the door and held it wide. 'I don't know what the hell you're talking about. Now, go.'

Dean moved past her. He offered her his card, bending low to speak into her ear. 'It hurts, doesn't it? Thrown over for another woman. You can get your own back, you know. Give the bitch what she deserves. Call me.'

Sam stared past him. She was shaking inside. People passing in the corridor were a blur. She called out, 'Security! Someone call security!'

She did not take his card. Dean let it fall to the floor as he backed down the passage to the lifts.

A wink and a grin and he swaggered away.

Sam was unable to move. She felt cold with horror. Her emotions were in confusion. Who was this journalist? How had he got the information? She flushed with shame. In spite of all her talk of integrity and pride, she had not been able to own up to the truth. Dean's manner had been aggressive, malicious even. If she had been 'out' with him, he would have used it against her. Against Fei. She had had to protect Fei. Sam felt the fear again that had slithered through her at Dean's machine-gun questions.

She moved inside her office and slammed the door, locking it and drawing the blind over the glass. She had never thought herself afraid of standing up for her sexuality. She had derided Fei for the same terror. She leaned against the door, still trembling.

In spite of herself, Sam thought of Fei with Ginny Wyndham. The way Fei had looked at Ginny that night at the market. A gash of pain whipped across her chest.

⎯⎯➤●◀⎯⎯

Fei's Mercedes sped up the highway towards the Wyndham Centre. She sat in the back seat, one of the security guards driving, the other in the passenger seat. Ginny had changed her mind about using guards after Fei had told her how Dean had pushed for a story. 'I feel safer about you this way,' she had said.

The men had been everywhere with Fei. She had cleared her apartment of tell-tale traces of her sexuality, hiding everything in a suitcase stored on top of the wardrobe. The guards checked the apartment before they let her go in. They waited for her in the office. One would even check out public toilets before she went in. Every six hours, they reported to Ginny. She now knew Fei's every movement, knew who Fei met or spoke to on the phone.

The burly male presences made Fei feel safe against the stalker. But she felt a rising resentment also. She said once to Ginny on the phone, whispering behind closed doors so the guards could not hear, 'Why do they have to check in with you? Why do you need to know what I'm doing all the time?'

'Is that what you think this is all about?' Ginny sounded hurt. 'Doesn't it mean anything to you that I care about your safety?'

Fei flushed with guilt. 'Yes, of course. I'm sorry. But it's just . . . It feels so claustrophobic.'

'Is that how our relationship feels to you?'

'No. Don't twist my words, Ginny. Let's not have this argument again, please.'

'I'm too clingy, isn't that right? And you think that these men who are there to protect you against a stalker – that I'm using them somehow to keep you under my control?'

'Ginny . . .'

'If I didn't care so much about you, I'd recall them and then let's see how you cope . . .'

'Please, don't be like this.'

Ginny had hung up on her.

The next day, she had called back, her voice warm as honeyed milk. 'Come up for the weekend, my darling. We need to relax, spend some time alone together.'

She did not mention their squabble. She never did. It was as if each encounter had no relation to the last. There was always a confidence in her manner in these moments, a certainty that Fei would bend to her seduction. Fei always did and it infuriated her even as she succumbed to Ginny's charm.

The daily newspapers were full of features on the school children – their school careers, photos of their artwork, a poem written by one of them. Class photos of smiling kids milked the poignancy. Friends and parents talked about the uniqueness of each child. There were tributes to Liak. The papers talked of his fighting spirit, the determination that had fuelled his change from trouble-maker to good citizen giving him the will to hang on to the last. His death was a loss to the nation. The suffering of the children moved Fei and after a while she found she couldn't read anymore. Outside her office as she had left for the Centre, a woman had rushed at her, shouting abuse, trailed by TV cameras. The woman had cried, 'You got no heart! How can you defend these evil doctors?'

Fei had struggled to control her emotion. 'I – my clients and I are sorry for the children's suffering but you cannot try them by media. My clients are blameless. This malicious persecution must stop.'

On TV news broadcasts, the first questions were being asked about the Centre's role and the connection with the therapy. The authorities, concerned not to jeopardise the integrity of their official investigation, could not reply but this only seemed to have fired public panic and fury. Supporters of the Centre, including the AVA, countered with accusations of a conspiracy to bring down one of the finest achievements of Asia. They warned of Western media manipulation, aimed at discrediting an innovative Asian institute. It was even hinted that there were CIA agents among the school board who had engineered the poisoning of the children to smear the good results of the therapy. The last bulletin Fei saw reported that regional media were picking up the story as were the international press.

The JB scandal distracted Asia from the financial crisis creeping up, Fei thought as she stared out at the rubber plantations whizzing by. Somehow, the tragedy of a few recognisable individuals was easier to grasp than the horror of the abyss that soon might swallow them all. Japan was being dragged into the whirlpool with the folding of Yamaichi, a hundred-year-old brokerage firm. The yen was at a five-year low, the Nikkei falling steadily. Fei was in the process of extricating her investments from the tangle along with thousands of other small investors. Businesses everywhere were closing, people losing their jobs. Client-account figures in Fei's firm had been decreasing since the start of the year. Everyone talked in circles about the state of the economy and global markets. But there were no certainties and no milestones to mark the way. The mounting crisis was as intangible and as devastating as the Haze, rendering them all powerless. It was easier to focus on a single, recognisable enemy, Fei thought, and the Wyndhams had become the media's scapegoat. Whatever her personal feelings for the children, Fei knew she would have to keep up a dogged fight to protect the Wyndhams from the mob.

Arriving at the Wyndhams' bungalow, Fei was relieved to find Ginny waiting for her alone. Loudly, Ginny talked about the mass of legal work that awaited them that weekend. Then she dismissed the guards and led Fei into the bungalow. The curtains were drawn and the doors locked. In the dim light, the pleasure and desire in Ginny's face were plain.

She folded her arms around Fei, her affectionate words soothing as the caress. 'Piers is buried in his work and the expert team won't arrive till Monday. I've got you for the whole weekend! We'll pretend we're marooned on a desert island where no one can see us and we can't see anyone.'

Somehow, Fei found herself in the bedroom with Ginny. The curtains were drawn but the sea breeze lifted them with a rhythmic motion. Ginny was so close, Fei could feel the burning heat of her skin. She began to caress Fei with her fingers, nibbling at her throat and neck. 'I've missed you.'

'Ginny . . .' Fei began. She always seemed to make every encounter sexual whenever there was the chance. Fei was tired and tense. 'The guards . . .'

'They're off duty while you're here. You'll be safe in the Centre.' Ginny flicked her tongue in Fei's ear.

Fei tried to move away but she could not. It was as if an addiction was holding her. It jammed out everything else with white noise. In spite of herself, Fei buried her face in Ginny's hair, the smell of flowers wrapping itself around her. Ginny's mouth sought out her shoulder, making her gasp. Ginny was undoing her blouse, reaching in to place soft hands on her breasts. Fei's breath caught in her throat.

'It's all right,' Ginny murmured. 'We're alone, I made sure of it. No one will see us.'

'Can't we just talk for a while . . .' Fei's words trailed away. Later there would be time. The drug took hold. There was only the present moment, the simplicity of touch and taste. No time for thought. Her head fell back and she gave in to the breathless pleasure.

Afterwards they lay entangled in the thin sheets. It was late-afternoon. The sea hissed in the distance. A smoky taint hung in the air. Ginny leaned on one elbow, tracing patterns on Fei's stomach. She was smiling as if she couldn't stop, her eyes hungrily taking Fei in.

It all seemed so far away, the clamour and chaos of the world outside. Fei felt languorous with sleep and pleasure. There was something unreal about being with Ginny, she thought, as if they lived out a fantastical passion when they were together. Everything else faded out of focus. As in a dream, there was only each other and the surreal logic of this moment lived outside time. Was this what *folie à deux* meant? she wondered vaguely.

Later, she and Ginny left law books and files spread across the dining table to give the impression of endless working sessions. They made their way down to the beach, the staff they passed, from housekeeper to security guards, greeting Fei by name as if they knew her well. On the shore, she strolled with Ginny to the end of the bay, the thick banks of smog like November fog in England. Only it was stickily hot and acrid on the tongue. Visibility was down to several hundred yards. Barefoot in the shallows, some distance from the main stretch of beach, Ginny held her protectively round the waist. Fei said, 'I've never been to that Orang-Utan Sanctuary down the road, have you?'

'I'm not going again.'

'What's wrong with it?'

'The apes – they're just awful.'

'Do they treat them badly?' Fei couldn't understand Ginny's fierce reaction.

'No. It's one of the best sanctuaries in Asia,' she said bitterly.

'I don't understand.'

'The apes are too human, don't you see? It makes me sick, seeing them.' Ginny pulled away.

'I thought they'd be beautiful?'

'If you want to see them, go by yourself. I'm not going there.'

Fei smiled uncertainly. 'We don't have to go. I was just making a comment.'

'It's the weekend. The place will be packed. We can't be seen out on a trip at a time like this!'

'All right.' Fei's voice rose in response. 'I said, I didn't want to go. Take it easy!'

Ginny glared at her, breathing hard. Her face was closed and pinched, shoulders high with tension. Fei said, 'Why do you always have to turn things into an issue? Sometimes, it's like you're playing a game with me. Flirting then arguing. Clingy then stand-offish. Blowing hot and cold. Why do you do it?'

Ginny stared at Fei with what looked like pure hatred. Fei faltered, shocked. She felt afraid suddenly. Ginny said with a venom that made Fei reel, 'You do everything you can to seduce me but it's so easy to turn your back on me, isn't it? You don't want to know me but I know everything there is to know about you. Don't you love me? Don't you want to know who I am? Isn't that what love is all about – knowing your lover like you know yourself? You sleep with me, mock my passion for you with your easy-come-easy-go flippancy. And you tell *me* I'm playing mindgames?'

Fei was speechless. A wave rocked her.

Ginny pulled out of the shallows and hurried back to the Centre's grounds, fading rapidly into the haze.

Fei had no idea what they had argued about. Ginny's emotion still gored her. But she couldn't let it stand like this. Ginny was always throwing tantrums and then leaving her to a wall of silence. Anger kicked. They had to clear this up once and for all. Fei went after her.

She caught up enough to see Ginny's blurred silhouette hurrying across the lawn. The grass was soft against her bare feet after the roughness of the sand. Fei could not pick up her pace without seeming to be in a panic and now that they were within sight of the staff and patients, albeit hazily through the smog, she could not risk appearing to chase Ginny. She followed her up on to the path leading to the secure unit, the gravel path hurting her feet.

She lost sight of Ginny round a corner. When she came up to the crest of the high ground, the fenced Secure Unit lay ahead of her. Trees and bushes softened the stark edges of the gate and fencing, lined the path to the building beyond. Ginny was nowhere to be seen. The undergrowth was still and there was no sound of movement. There were locks and bolts and a double gate system between Fei and the building. It could not have taken Ginny such a short time to reach the Secure Unit at the far end of the path on the other side of the gates. Fei had heard no sound of their being opened, shut and rebolted.

She stood for a moment straining her ears. The path ended at the gates and all around, undergrowth and trees blocked the way. Where had Ginny gone? Frustrated, Fei turned and headed back down to her bungalow.

In the trance suite, footage of Fei played on the screen in an endless loop. Ginny stood staring at it, the sound off. It soothed her to see the Fei she knew and loved on the screen. It reminded her of the purity of her passion, the perfection she saw in her beautiful lover. The real world was so much more difficult. The real Fei so infuriating and imperfect. Ginny could not control her, not in the way she could control the images on the screen. The world behind the screen was her domain, could be as perfect as she wanted it to be, as beautiful and as rich as the limits of her imagination.

She called up library footage of one of their actors on the sound stage behind the control room. He was doing a traditional Malay dance, hands gracefully curled up, moving with delicate rhythm. Electronic spots marked his body along the limbs, torso and shoulders to form a superimposed dot-marionette of his figure. He wore plain black. The backdrop was a blue screen. Speaking without emotion, Ginny commanded the programme to bring up an image of Fei's face. She enlarged the actor's face – it, too, was marked with electronic dots along the central recognition and movement points of the features. Similar dots appeared on Fei's face. It floated on to the actor's face, the markers lining up with those beneath. At a word from Ginny, the program morphed the two faces, adjusting for size and gradients. In a moment, it was Fei who was performing the dance on the screen. Several adjustments to the body and it shaped itself into the body of a young woman, small breasted, slim-hipped. When the actor smiled, she smiled. *His* emotions were written on *her* face.

Ginny called up a beach scene and there was Fei dancing on the sand. All that was needed was adjustment for shadows and morphing with suitable clothing.

It was so easy. And so pointless. She turned away in frustration and anger. 'Goddamn you!' Her voice exploded into the silent room. She did not know if she cursed Fei or herself.

'Command not recognised,' the electronic tones of the computer stated. 'Please try again.'

Ginny slammed the machine off at the control panel. How could she hope that Fei would ever understand? Asking naive questions, curious about Ginny's unpredictable behaviour, trying to get close – Fei in all her safe ignorance. How would Ginny begin to tell her the truth?

Here in this windowless suite, a tomb beneath the ground, was where Ginny lived her real life. This whole complex of labs was an underground mausoleum to Katie, Piers's work a penance and an act of vengeance on the murderous world. That one terrible day when Katie had been lost embalmed both Ginny and Piers. Her life belonged to him – hers for Katie's: a pitiful exchange but one that helped her live with her remorse. Ginny yearned to open her heart to Fei but how could she tell her about Katie without telling her everything else?

Ginny had a fantasy that she and Fei might disappear – slip away into the smog and never come back. She would be free and unburdened by guilt and self-loathing. Fei might love her then. Ginny felt it like a festering wound that Fei had never been able to tell Ginny that she loved her. But how could she hope that Fei could love her if she hid so much of herself? Ginny

longed to go home again – England with its lush green fields and
a cottage twined with honeysuckle: she and Fei living a life of
suburban ordinariness. It was so banal and so impossible.

She could never abandon Piers. She had seen him on the
edge of sanity after the trial. And then, moving around China in
those first few months, Piers had been a crazed man, lost in a pit
no one else could fathom. Ginny had been there for him, terrified and desperate but always by his side, coaxing him back over
endless months. Siew had been patient but his quiet pressure
had been relentless. If Piers had not recovered, he and Ginny
would have been disposed of, their bodies dumped out at sea
probably. She felt sick at the memory of those months. If she
tried to leave now, there was only one certain outcome: she and
Fei would be found and killed. No one escaped their obligations
to the AVA.

⋯⟫●⟪⋯

Sam dialled Fei's mobile phone. It was switched off. She tried
her office number. A secretary told her that Fei had gone up to
the Wyndham Centre for the weekend. It was Friday afternoon.

Sam clamped down on her unease. Beyond the window, the
smog shifted in the light breeze. Up here in her office, she felt
cut off from the world. With Dean gone and the door locked
there was nothing but her work and the clamouring of her own
thoughts.

She moved restlessly away from her desk.

Fei . . . Sam felt an abyss of regret. They had had a chance
to call a truce that night at the dinner party. By the pool she had
longed to touch Fei but had let the moment pass. And then
they'd had the quarrel. Over nothing. And everything. It hadn't
been about Asian Values or even Ginny Wyndham. It had been
about the two of them, Sam and Fei, shouting across the gulf
they had made between each other. And now this can of worms
with the journalist.

She had to speak to Fei, if only to warn her about Dean.

But Fei was with Ginny Wyndham.

Sam massaged her temples as if kneading away her frustration and hurt.

A knock on the door. 'Sam, are you all right?'

It was Ling, her assistant. Sam let her in. 'Govinda's called a meeting for the Wyndham case report and press conference on Monday,' Ling said. 'His team are convening in five minutes. Aren't you going?'

'I'm not invited.' Sam shifted gear. She had to forget Fei for now. For the whole weekend.

'But why-lah? You've been pushing Pathology on this case . . .'

Sam snorted. Dr Govinda headed the Pathology team. They had been working on the samples of blood and body tissue from the JB school children who had died. Sam had insisted on brain tissue for testing – which Govinda had considered irrelevant initially. Her analysis had shown up the presence of a compound similar to her other Factor Q cases. In this review of her findings, he had reached a conclusion of his own and had refused to allow references to Factor Q in his report. 'You're trying to make your name with this Factor Q business,' he had said. 'I'm not letting you hijack this high-profile and very sensitive investigation we at Pathology are carrying out.'

'But you can see for yourself – this compound . . .'

'I have identified the compound without recourse to your mass epidemic scenario. The explanation is simple. Simplicity is a virtue in science, Dr Ryder.'

Sam turned now to Ling. 'Govinda's conclusion is wrong. But he's staking his claim in medical history with it. I don't have the clout to argue with him publicly.'

'Are you just going to let it drop?' Ling touched Sam's arm in surprise.

She smiled without humour. 'You should know me better than that.'

Ling nodded. 'I'll enter what findings we've got on our database. Oh, and I've checked up on the periods of unaccounted time in the other victims' histories.'

'And?'

'They've been verified by friends and family where the victims had such networks. For those without any contacts, I can't check. A few had employers who noted their non-appearance at work. But for the majority . . .' Ling shrugged.

'No family, no friends, mostly unemployed or in casual work.' Sam gazed out at the swirl of smoke.

'People no-one would notice.' Ling shuddered. 'You think maybe there's more of them that haven't turned up in our records?'

'If they don't make it to a hospital or doctor. If they die alone, with no one to claim the body – the death certificate would probably show natural causes and they'll be buried in paupers' graves.'

'Or cremated. That's more common these days, what with land prices going up.'

Ling bustled through to her own office with a bundle of files. Sam sat on the edge of her desk, swinging her leg absently. A brain degenerative disorder manifesting with differing symptoms across Asia, afflicting mainly those isolated from the usual communal networks. It might almost be a disease of the times, possible only in an Asia of transient, urban populations where the old social cohesiveness had broken down. The JB school children were the exception. Or were they? Sam thought of the boys highlighted in the media hype over the therapy – they were on the margins of the school establishment, trouble-makers facing expulsion and borstal. The therapy appeared to have saved them but something inside, Factor Q in their brains, still worked inexorably to kill them.

But it had not only been those boys who had fallen ill. Star pupils with happy home lives had also been affected. Sam shook her head to clear it. She was being fanciful in trying to find a socio-anthropological link. There was enough of a pattern in her data to suggest an identifiable cause but there was also a random-ness that foxed her. Was it really madness to try to connect these thousands of cases? Perhaps her critics were right. She was chasing a Holy Grail that did not exist. But she did not believe this even as she thought it. Stubbornness refused to allow her to throw in the towel just yet. She would prove them all wrong and it would be a pleasure doing it.

She glanced at her watch. It was late in the afternoon now. What was Fei doing? In spite of herself, Sam could not stop the image of Fei with Ginny from pushing into her thoughts.

Sam stood up and reached for the phone. She dialled Fei's answering machine at home. When Fei's taped voice spoke in Sam's ear, its familiarity was like a shock through her whole body. The machine beeped to record her message. She tried to keep her own voice steady. 'We need to talk. Call me.'

Chapter Fourteen

Han watched Shereen as she dressed. He lay on the bed in his set of rooms above a games arcade off Jalan Tunku Abdul Rahman. She was still in good shape for a woman in her late-thirties. Sex with her always charged him with energy. He could still taste her in his mouth.

'I got to pick up boy-boy from my mum and take him to school.' Shereen brushed her thick hair hurriedly. It was six in the morning. For an all-nighter, it was two hundred *ringgit*. Han had left two fifty in the bathroom for her.

He saw her on and off whenever he was in KL. It suited them both. Her husband was a lorry driver and he was on a two-week stint up through Thailand. Shereen used to have a tailor's shop round the corner but when cheap imported clothes flooded in from China and Taiwan, business slowed. Now she took in small alterations and piecework at home. This sideline whenever her husband was away gave her extra income. Business was clearly good – she had even got herself a pager.

Han got up and pulled on his shorts while she went into the bathroom. He liked this arrangement. He told her – and anyone who wanted to know – that he was in 'import-export', the blanket term that covered a multitude of sins. She never asked him when he would be back, never asked him to tell her anything more about his work. Han thought of his wife – his ex-wife. They had got hitched when they were still in their teens. Pey had got clingy, demanding. Jealous of the secrets he could not share. She hated his disappearing for months at a time, pestered him to tell her what he really did. For all he knew, she was now happily remarried to some guy who came home every day at six and was always at the office when she phoned. Han hoped so. He wondered how his son was turning out. The boy would be about the same age as Shereen's kid. Han hadn't seen him in years.

Shereen came out of the bathroom, beaming. She wrapped herself around Han, playing with his hair and nibbling his ear. 'Thanks, man.'

'You got a photo of your boy?'

'Sure.' Shereen pulled out her purse and showed Han a picture of a cheeky looking seven year old. He was doing well at school, he loved sports. She prattled on proudly. Han still had his arm around her. They might have been a happy family together, he thought.

After she left, he had a shower and put together his alternate persona for that day. He laid out the latex padding and the crumpled bureaucrat's suit on the bed. At the sink, he set out the facial hair and make-up, a pair of square glasses to the side. Few Snakes he knew had your typical domestic set-up. The job just didn't make it easy. The only family Han had had for the last fifteen years had been the Family. The Family had made him – given him an education beyond his imaginings: electronics, weaponry, strategy, five Asian languages, fluency in English, explosives and deception. They had given him a purpose and more than that, they had given him power. He belonged to them as they did now to him. This was his life and it was everything of who he was.

Han strapped on the padding – at the front to give him a gut, round his shoulders to give him the appearance of fat. Over it all, he put on the suit and neat black shoes.

He had downloaded on the computer in his 'insurance office' the details on Wyndham that Dean had given him. That had all been transmitted to the backroom tecchies in the Family's set-up in Jakarta for the story to be checked. Han expected their response within the next week.

He waddled into the bathroom and began transforming his face. False skin patches to give him a double chin and jowliness. A wispy but neat beard over that. A few pockmarks for good measure. On top of that, the nerdy glasses. This was 'Mr Chin', an education department official. He had approached one of the JB parents as Mr Chin and from there it had been easy to get in with the headmaster and school board as an observer to the proceedings against the Wyndham Centre.

Mokhtar had given the go-ahead on this just after that kid Liak died. He was covering his back, Han thought. This thing was getting big and Mokhtar needed to be sure he didn't let the Wyndhams slip out of reach just because the Family was being too cautious. If it turned out that the Wyndhams and the AVA could be implicated in the deaths of these kids, it would be the Family's biggest fucking handle on the bastards. Mokhtar was no fool. But it didn't matter either way to Han – he would have gone in anyway without authorisation. This was not a chance *he* would have let pass, whatever Mokhtar decided.

Han slipped his Beretta into its concealed holster on his left hip. He found the identification card and forged passes for Mr Chin, courtesy of the Family. He was about to pocket them when the thought struck him.

He paused.

Like all Snakes, Han carried various identification papers. Han had posed as an internal security agent to Dean. Had Dean similarly shown him a false FBI badge?

Han pulled out his laptop from under the bed. He connected it via infra-red hook-up to his satellite cellphone and accessed the secure signal to the Family's mainframe in Jakarta. He tapped a message to the tecchies, entering the details he had seen on Dean's badge and referring them to the earlier investigation of Dean from footage of him taken at the Centre. The tecchies would verify through their contacts whether Dean was really who his badge said he was.

⟶➣●⟨⟶

Fei looked round the meeting room. She sat to one side of the table with Ginny. Next to them were their team of scientists, a senior consultant at the National Hospital and food and health experts. Among them was the private investigator Piers had hired.

They faced three lawyers acting for the school. Ranged beside them were their clients: Zainul the headmaster, nominees from the school board and PTA, and parents of the children who had taken part in the therapy. Their team of doctors and specialists sat with them. In chairs against the wall were officials from the health and education ministries with watching briefs. Among their senior representatives was a junior 'bag-carrier', a fat pockmarked man scribbling notes conscientiously. He was sweating although it was a cool day.

A TV crew filmed establishing shots of the meeting for the newscasts that night, following the press conference later. Their lights and equipment prowled the room. And then they were gone, the door clicking shut into stillness.

The meeting was in a conference room in the main building of the Centre, furnished simply with natural wood and carved Indonesian chairs. The windows were open and a cool breeze from the sea rustled the palm trees outside. The lapping sea could be heard, a background to the sounds of the Centre's day – laughter and chatter from the patients in nearby wards and in the grounds below. The smog obscured the view down to the shore.

The atmosphere in the room was tense. Fei opened the meeting and summarised the case. She then presented highlights from a medical report, maintaining a cool, clinical manner. When she finished speaking, the room was in uproar. The school party stared at her in outrage. Some of the parents had started to shout her down but their lawyers were urging them to silence. Fei was aware that beside her Ginny had not moved, eyes lowered to the table although she was sitting very straight. They had not spoken since she had disappeared from the beach. Fei had not seen Ginny till this morning over breakfast.

Fei raised her voice above the others. 'The report I've just given you was prepared as part of the independent investigation carried out by the Pathology team at the National Hospital, headed by Dr Govinda. It was funded by neither of the parties here today. The report, as Dr Govinda will outline for us now, entirely absolves my clients of blame.'

One of the parents cried, 'How can that be?'

Zainul shouted, 'It's lies!'

Fei nodded to Dr Govinda. He was a slim Indian man in his late-forties with hooded eyes and a patrician nose. He said, 'BSE, or bovine spongiform encephalopathy, is a degenerative disease of the brain that affects cattle. The human equivalent is known as Creutzfeld-Jakob disease, or CJD. It is characterised by dementia and gradual weakening of muscles and limbs, leading to paralysis and finally death. It is thought to have originated from BSE, transmitted through eating beef products.'

'How do you know the kids had it?' Wallace Lim said. He was the senior lawyer on the school team.

'The autopsy on the deceased victims showed vacuole and amyloid deposits on the brain. On analysis, these were found to be made up of a substance known as a prion.'

'What's this . . . "prion"?'

'A prion is a protein which is able to pass through the blood-brain barrier, which normally stops foreign bodies from entering the brain. The prion is able to slip through the defence because of its particular molecular weight. It's a one-way transport, leaving no trace in the bloodstream.'

'So it's like a virus?'

'No. It's entirely composed of protein. A virus is made up of a core of nucleic acid – or DNA – encased in a protein shell. A virus needs to use its host body's energy stores in order to reproduce. A prion, however, is self-replicating. Its most disturbing characteristic is that it cannot be destroyed by heat or the standard forms of sterilisation which would usually inactivate a virus.'

'Like cooking or radiation?' Lim looked horrified. The school party had gone pale.

'Correct.'

'But how did the kids get infected?'

Fei spoke up. She turned to the last page of the report. 'I quote, "Known forms of CJD are transmitted through ingestion. After examining and discounting various possible sources of infection in the case of the Johore Baru school children, we would suggest a thorough investigation of the school canteen food – its chain of supply, its transportation and handling – for likely sources of contamination".'

'What do you mean?' The school party were stunned.

'Zainul, did you know that?'

'The school food?'

'I don't believe –'

They moved back and forth in their seats, conferring while at the same time trying to confront Fei and the Centre's team. Fei said calmly, '*Encik* Osman is a private investigator. He has been making enquiries at the school canteen and down the chain of suppliers. Mr Osman?'

The detective stood up, hitching up his trousers. He cleared his throat and waited for the noise to quieten. He read from a notebook. 'The canteen at the school is a private enterprise selling *laksa*, fried noodles and snacks and drinks to the school children. About four months prior to my investigation, the owner, Mr Goh, was told by Mr Zainul to prepare a special menu for the month before the start of the special therapy. The menu was to be high in meat and vegetables, low in starch. This menu would be fed to the whole school who would also take part in the new PE regime. My information is that the menu and PE schedule were requirements of the Wyndham Centre's pre-therapy plan.'

Zainul interjected. 'Yes, yes, the Centre told me that's what they wanted. The school board approved it. They put up the funds for it, it was for the whole school – healthy meals and healthy exercise.'

'My enquiries reveal that Mr Goh did not use his usual supplier for the meat. They were too expensive, he says, compared to the supplier Mr Zainul told him about – Ho Heng-Lap Meat and Poultry.'

'We were looking at costs, you see. To feed the whole school fresh meat, a quarter pound each child every day for one month – that's a lot of money. School funds, you know, we have to use them wisely.' Zainul was sweating. He looked from lawyer to parent to school governor and back again. 'I heard of them through . . . I don't know, someone told me about them, then they called. Mr Ho came to see me. The beef and chicken was all so cheap and the quality was good.'

Osman said, 'The company has since disappeared. The premises it occupied are empty. None of their employees can be traced. I can find no record of anyone going by the name Ho Heng-Lap.'

'What? How can that be-lah?'

'Fortunately,' Osman went on, 'Mr Goh had a few sides of beef in his freezer he had siphoned off for himself. These have been taken for analysis.'

Fei said, 'Dr Govinda?'

Govinda read from his lab report. Through the jargon and statistics, the fact was clear. The beef had been riddled with the Asiatic CJD prion.

——⟫●⟪——

Half an hour later, the press conference was held in the grounds of the Centre. The journalists had waited all morning outside the gates at Fei's invitation. They poured in, scrambling for the best positions near the podium. It was mid-day but it might have been morning or afternoon. Time had no reality in the endless grey. Even the days had come to seem one like the other, each week resembling the next. The haze rolled sluggishly across the landscape like a cloak. From this position, the main building could hardly be seen. Figures in the distance were insubstantial as phantoms.

Fei stood with Ginny on the ground to one side of the podium, out of the spotlight for now. They would make their statement at the end and take questions from the floor. TV cameramen roamed, shooting footage of the key players.

Photographers shifted about, flashing off pictures. Centre-stage, Wallace Lim was reading the statement Fei had drafted for him.

'The school board and PTA and the parents of all the children withdraw unequivocally all claims, charges and statements made against the Wyndham Centre, its founders, directors and staff. They acknowledge that their purported claims against the Centre were spurious and groundless. They also sincerely regret any statements made which may have damaged the good reputation of the Centre and its work and accept that such statements were defamatory and intended to be so.

'They acknowledge and declare that the illness that has affected the students and led to death in some cases is not and never was caused by or connected in any way to the Centre or its therapy on a number of the students. An alternative origin of the illness has been identified, which is unrelated in any way whatsoever to the Centre and its work. An investigation will be carried out immediately into that alternate source and all findings will be placed before the authorities. We are arranging a meeting with the authorities as soon as possible to disclose all that we currently know.'

Fei had made the school party accept the wording by facing them with a worse alternative – a multi-million-*ringgit* damages claim for defamation and costs. The school party had protested at first but their lawyers had realised that their clients would have enough battles on their hands without fighting the Wyndhams too. The health and education authorities were bound to investigate further and the way was open now for parents to bring proceedings against the school board. The horror had not receded, only the culprit had changed.

Fei watched in satisfaction as the media hounds began to bay, firing questions at Lim. There was movement beside her. A tall cameraman, baseball cap pulled low, stubble obscuring his jaw. Wearing sunglasses in spite of the gloom. He wielded the camera on his shoulder like a barrier between them both and the crowd. It was Dean.

Fei started. 'What the hell are you doing here? How did you get in?'

Ginny gasped and stiffened. She made a move to call security.
'I know about you two,' he said. 'You don't want to do anything before you hear me out.'

Ginny froze. Fei could hear her breathing hard beside her. She placed a calming hand on her arm. Dean noticed and smiled. It was almost a leer. He said pleasantly, 'So which one of you fucks the other one?'

'What do you want?' Fei glanced around. Ong and his team ringed the crowd. Her voice sounded hoarse to her own ears.

'A meeting, that's all. Mrs Wyndham' – Dean nodded mockingly – 'and Dr Wyndham and me. Round a table, for a nice talk.'

'We have nothing to say to you!' Ginny's voice rose involuntarily. Fei increased the pressure on her arm.

She turned to Ginny. 'You're due to speak next. Go on up. I'll handle this.'

Ginny hesitated but moved away to the podium. Dean let her pass. He said to Fei, 'Masterful – I like that. I'd rather talk to her but if you want to do the deal, that's fine by me.'

'What do you want?' Fei moved a few steps away from the crowd. He followed.

'Aren't you interested in how I worked it out?'

'There's nothing to work out. Your fragile male ego got hurt because I wouldn't sleep with you. This is the only way you can explain it to yourself.'

'You can believe what you like. But Mrs Wyndham seems to be shitting in her pants. Why is that?'

'She's not interested in what you have to say.'

Dean clucked. 'Too bad she feels that way. It would save her a lot of public embarrassment to talk to me now rather than later. Imagine the headlines . . .'

'All this for a story? Come on.' Fei stopped. She felt a chill. 'You're not a journalist. What do you really want?'

'You're smart, Fei-Li. I've always liked that about you.' Dean managed to sound almost wistful.

Was it an act or did he mean it? Fei felt her hair stand on end. His mixture of tenderness and ruthlessness scared her. She could not square this malicious stranger with the man she had thought of as her friend all these months. What had happened to him? How had it all suddenly changed? Or had he always been this stranger, only she had never known it? Had everything he had meant to her been a lie? Her mind reeled.

He said, 'I have connections who would pay a great deal to save the Wyndhams from themselves. Tell that to Ginny. Tell her they can go back to America – Lovelace will be forgotten. If they play ball.'

'Who's Lovelace?'

'She didn't tell you?' Dean smirked. His face hardened. 'Just tell her what I said.'

Fei sensed suddenly that he was capable of a violence she could barely comprehend. She felt sick. It was all moving so fast. This was not just about her and Ginny, nothing so simple as money and sexual favours. There were other stakes on the table she had not even known were there. Other agendas of which she had been kept ignorant. Her head spun. Her thoughts felt disengaged, skidding out of control. 'Who are you? Who do you work for?'

Dean ignored her. 'A meeting, Fei-Li. Tonight.'

Fei made herself focus. She had to break his hold of the situation. Whoever he was, whatever he really wanted, didn't matter for now. He had only one handle on them all, she thought dimly. She had to wrest control of it from him. Everything else flowed from that one power he thought he had.

'Or else what, Dean?' Fei forced anger into her voice, burning off the deadwood of shame and fear. She suppressed her panic and confusion. She made herself focus only on the one threat he had. She had to turn it around. Somehow.

Fei let her instincts take over. She was speaking fast, her voice hard. She listened to herself as if from far away. 'What the hell are you threatening? That you're going to publish details of our so-called love affair? You're pathetic! What have you got? Nothing but speculation and malice. You try anything like that and I'll hit you with so many law suits, you'll wish you'd put that loud mouth of yours up your arse. I don't care if you're a journalist or the CIA or the bloody Mafia – I'll haul you and whoever you work for through the courts and the goddam' media if I have to!'

'I'm really scared,' Dean said, deadpan. Then, quietly, 'The law won't help you, Fei. The facts don't matter. Not in the court of public opinion. It's all about what things look like and it looks pretty bad for you. Not married at your age. Never had a boyfriend. Lived for years with a woman. Staying over so often with Ginny Wyndham. Short hair, trousers, unfeminine shoes. All I have to do is put a name to you. Lesbian. Dyke. Homo. And I rest my case.

'People think the way we tell them to think. Put it in the papers, or an ad, or a news report: people will believe it. Give it the stamp of authority: people will follow it. Say something often enough and they'll take it for the goddam' truth. People are sheep. Forget justice – appearance is judge and executioner now.'

The clamour of the press conference buzzed around them. Questions were shouted to the school board. Ginny stood frozen behind the podium, darting glances across at Fei and Dean. She was white as death. Fei stared at Dean. Horror and fury battled inside her. Her stomach churned with nausea. She swallowed hard, scrabbling for a response. She worked to keep her voice steady.

'You're right. Appearance is everything. And let's look at how things appear. The Wyndhams are the perfect couple. Every-one who's seen them knows that.' Fei faltered but recovered. She knew about appearances, she had lived with deceit all her life. She suddenly saw the weapon he had handed her. She injected confidence into her voice, pulling herself up straighter. 'The Wyndhams are Malaysian citizens. They gave up their British nationality to become Asian – a sacrifice that shows where their commitment lies in spite of the colour of their skins. They established a visionary mental health sanctuary, the first of its kind in Asia. They have the financial and personal support of Asia's rich and powerful elite, not least of which is the Asian Values Alliance. You're right. With a sex scandal like this, the stakes are very high.'

Fei's voice was hoarse with emotion. She knew how to spin a story as insidiously as he had done. It hung on a lie and it made her sick to do it. But she had to win – she had no choice. 'And how do I appear? A Chinese spinster who has sacrificed love and marriage to support her aging mother, who has put her father-less sisters through school and college and who has funded her brother's business. Why? Because they all helped to put me through university and set me up in my career. To all eyes, here I am the good daughter, the good Asian woman. I am well respected in my profession, as adviser to the leaders of Asian industry and finance with close associations to Asian Values through the Alliance. Yes, the stakes are high, Dean.'

Fei leaned towards him. Her mouth was dry and her gut ached. She loathed herself for what she was doing but she had to go on. She had no other way out. Anger burst through. 'If you so much as insinuate a slur on my good name, I shall scream rape so loud and so long, you'll hear it till your dying day.'

Dean blinked. That was all she needed. She had turned the tables.

She went on, her voice low with threat, 'How do you appear in all this, Dean? A white man. An American. A blackmailer. A coward who tries to ruin a woman's reputation because he cannot have his way with her. A journalist. Or maybe not – even better for my purposes. A man with "connections" who does deals the shady way. A spy, perhaps. Or a gangster. It doesn't matter. The word of a white rapist against that of a good daughter of Asia, in this present climate? You'll be locked up under internal security laws before you can take a breath.'

Fei stared him down. 'You're not in Kansas anymore. This is my country. You play by our rules now.'

She turned suddenly and signalled to Ong.

⸺⸻◈⸻⸺

In the main building, Han wandered through the corridors and terraces, his education department ID clipped to his jacket. In the bustle of moving the negotiation party out to meet the press, he had slipped into the gents and not bothered to catch up. He nodded at nurses and patients in the art therapy room, watched a movement class in progress under the palm trees. Several doctors passed him and they exchanged nods.

He was not sure what to make of the food contamination evidence. So far, it had come from the Centre's hired investigator and not yet been corroborated by other sources. Still, the headmaster's panic did lend the story weight. Han sauntered on, jaw clenched. This was the first chance he had had of getting so close to the Wyndhams. He wasn't sure yet what he was looking for but he would know it when he found it. In the meantime, he was determined to plant a surveillance device in one of the offices.

He found himself in the wards. They were empty, the patients presumably engaged in their daily activities. There was a homely feel with plants and soft furnishings, four beds to a room, decorated with paintings and posters. Nothing of interest. Han began to wander back the way he had come.

Ben Chang looked up from the corner of his ward. He was sitting on his bed, hidden from the door by an armchair. He wore pyjamas and slumped wearily against the wall. Since Piers had hauled him up from the monitoring lab, he had been on constant medication and looked after here where the new patients did not know him. He listened to the footsteps in the corridor. The staff had been painfully kind. They did not make him join in the activities if he didn't want to nor did he have to take part in the group therapies. Piers took on a counselling role, trying to make him see the value of the work that had once excited him. Ben sat through those hours stupidly, the drugs making it easy for him to tune out.

Ben did not recognise the fat pockmarked man who walked the corridor. As his footsteps faded, Ben's sluggish thoughts battled to come together. Perhaps the stranger would listen. The nurses and doctors on this ward indulged him but they did nothing. To them, he was just going through a prolonged psychotic episode. But a stranger: he was not in on the conspiracy, he would see things differently.

Ben pushed himself up from the bed and began to make his way after the man, the corridors listing against his leaden body.

Han headed for one of the many sets of stairs in the complex. Yes, these were the ones. Earlier, as they had emerged from the meeting room, Qwong had hurried up these stairs with her bundle of documents. The security guards that had ringed their group had let her pass. She had returned empty handed. There had to be an office there where she had left her papers.

Ben saw the stranger start up the stairs to the administrative offices. He heaved himself on.

From the bottom of the stairs, he saw the stranger engaged with the security guard on the next floor. The guard was not letting him go any further. The stranger was saying, 'Miss Qwong asked me to fetch her briefcase since I was coming back to use the gents.'

'Sorry, sir, no unauthorised access.'

The guard began to escort the stranger down the stairs.

Ben shrank back against the wall. He felt lost. His chance had been taken from him. What could he do now? As the two men headed down the stairs to the next floor, he glanced up at the empty landing above.

Outside, Fei backed away from Dean, looking as panic-stricken as she could. Ong began to move, speaking into his radio. The nearest security guards headed towards Dean. He started to angle away, the camera falling to the ground.

On the podium, one of the parents rushed to the micro-phones. She was hysterical. 'I want justice! The school poisoned our children . . .'

'Poison!' Excitement raced through the press corps.

'How?'

'What poison?'

Zainul tried to drag Mrs Choo from the podium. The journalists pushed closer. She shoved the headmaster from her. 'You! Don't you touch me! He's the one! He bought contaminated meat to feed our children – to save money, him and the board, they count the cents and kill our children!'

'What meat?'

'What's the contamination?'

'BSE!' She broke down, sobbing. 'Mad Cow disease. All the children ate the canteen food. They'll all die, all die . . .'

In Ginny's office, Ben grabbed her car keys from her desk drawer and staggered down the stairs. He shuffled through the ground-floor dining room, aiming for the kitchen exit. He was breathing hard and sweating. His legs seemed to be dragging through mud. The room swam as he moved. He felt nauseous.

At the front of the main building, Han's guard spoke to his colleague by the door. They appeared unarmed but Han knew that most security companies armed their staff under special licence. Their weapons were probably concealed for the sake of appearances. The second guard, a Malay, said, 'Did you search him-lah, Wong?'

Han laughed. 'You don't need to search me! Look, education authority – my ID, here. I didn't steal anything.' His Beretta lay hard against his hip, below the waistline of his trousers.

'Sorry, sir, we must follow procedure.'

'I just went to the gents, then I came up to . . .'

'Sorry, sir.'

At the press conference, a group of guards circled Dean and began to edge him away from the main crowd. The journalists were shouting like madmen as Mrs Choo was led away. Zainul cowered behind the lawyers. Ginny was making her way tensely to the mikes to close the proceedings. Fei stood her ground now, watching security deal with Dean. It had been a gamble – he might yet call her bluff and shout out his accusations. Her heart was in her throat.

Dean tried to push out from behind his barricade. Journalists near the back turned. He shouted in outrage. A scuffle began. Ong radioed for assistance across the Centre's internal network.

Outside the main building, the alert crackled through the guards' radios. They paused, listening. Han pulled away and strode towards the visitors' car park. Wong called, 'Please stop, sir.'

Han ignored him. What the hell were they going to do, gun him down?

He heard running behind him. Fucking idiots. He pushed into a sprint. Someone tackled him and he fell hard to the ground. A knee jabbed into his back as one guard hauled his arms behind his back. Han's padding slipped. Surprised, the guard began to search him, the disguise disintegrating beneath his hands. The Beretta was hauled out from its holster. The other guard, Wong, crouched by his head, his small pistol held so that it could not be seen. Wong pushed it to Han's temple. 'Please, sir, I don't want to frighten the patients by using this but be assured-lah, we have authority to protect them and the staff of the Centre.'

Han grimaced. He had never been more politely threatened.

At the press gathering, Dean floored several guards. Journalists and parents were caught up in the fight. When the uproar subsided, Dean was held down by three men. He twisted his head and saw Fei. His eyes blazed at her, his face red and taut with rage. She made herself hold his glare without flinching. In the moment's silence, she knew she had won. He had nothing to use against her and he knew it. She turned on her heel and walked away.

In the furore, no one noticed Ginny Wyndham's car surging towards the gates from the staff car park. Through the tinted windows, the driver could not be seen. The guard at the gate, confused by the commotion he could see from his post and listening hard to the radio exchanges, recognised the car and opened the electronic gates. Ben sped past, leaning on the steering wheel. The road down the hill swerved and veered but somehow he made it. The roar of the powerful engine sang in his ears. He blinked as sweat trickled into his eyes. The car plunged down the long road on the delta. He would get Mei-Hong and they would go to the police. He would tell them everything, and then it would end. The horror would end.

PART TWO

Mind

理智

Chapter Fifteen

Ben sat up with a start. He was at home. On the sofa. He looked around wildly. There she was – Mei-Hong – heading for the door. It was dark now. He must have fallen asleep. He had got home somehow, through sheer will and pumped up on adrenaline. He had told Mei-Hong everything, every detail of their experiments, every terrible result. They were not safe, he had told her. He had to tell the police everything while he still could. And the police would protect them, hide them. If anything happened to him, she must go to the police, tell them everything he had told her. She had calmed him, stroking his forehead. She had said she would call the police. He should rest, she had said.

Through the windows, blue lights strobed the living room. The police had come. Ben sank back on to the sofa in relief. Mei-Hong opened the front door. There were voices, then men coming into the room. Police uniforms and others, men in white. Moving swiftly. They came at him. Hauled him from the sofa, strong arms gripping him.

'What . . . Hey! Let me go . . .' Ben began. Then he saw him.

It was Dr Suleiman, one of the psych team from the Centre. He was slight but exuded an air of command. His cold eyes assessed Ben. On his lapel, the AVA logo glinted in the strange light.

Ben struggled against the police officers. Male nurses stood by at the ready.

'Don't hurt him!' Mei-Hong cried. She turned to Dr Suleiman. 'Why are the police here?'

'He caused a number of accidents on the way here. The police want to arrest him . . .'

'Oh, God!'

'I've made an arrangement with them. They'll put him under house arrest at the Centre while we treat him. I'm his guarantor. Be assured we will do everything we can to bring Ben back to health.'

Ben cried out.

Mei-Hong came up to him, wrapped her arms around his neck and shoulders. She caressed his hot face with hers. 'They'll look after you, my darling. Dr Suleiman promised me. He's an AVA man-lah. We all look after each other.'

Ben struggled. He leaned towards the police officers. 'It's them − they are murderers. It's a secret war. A conspiracy to destroy us all. You must stop them. Arrest them. Not me . . .'

The officers stared at him impassively. Dr Suleiman drew Mei-Hong away. He had papers for her to sign. Their voices were low but Ben caught snatches: '. . . committing him to our care . . . safe . . . familiar surroundings . . . you can come up in a few weeks . . . now quiet and rest . . .'

He was shouting but the words were noises he could hardly understand anymore. He fought them as they dragged him out of the house. A sharp sting in his arm, slowly intensifying.

'A sedative to calm him.' Dr Suleiman patted Mei-Hong reassuringly. Ben sagged against the policemen.

Ben felt his wife's lips on his cheek. Smelt her clean soapy smell. Heard her whisper, 'I love you, my darling.'

They bundled him into the back of the ambulance in the driveway, the police officers climbing in with the nurses. Dr Suleiman sat in the front with the driver.

Han was detained at the Centre for several hours after the press conference in the security block. His disguise lay in a heap on the table. He was questioned alternately by the security chief, a man called Ong, and the guy's second in command in a cramped office. As fucking civilians they had no right to hold him and less to quiz him. *Who are you? Why are you in disguise? Why are you carrying a bugging device? Who do you work for? What do you want? Why were you snooping round the Centre?* Han maintained his cover, claiming that his gun was properly licensed. 'Let me see Piers Wyndham. The education minister will haul you through hell for the way you're treating one of his officials.'

But Ong stared back impassively.

'Where's Dean? What does he want from you? I want to talk to him.'

Ong circled him.

'How long are you going to hold me? What's the media going to say about your bully-boy tactics? Get the fucking police! I don't answer to you.'

Han was so close. But he couldn't probe any deeper without blowing his cover. And held by the enemy, his prime objective was to preserve the secrecy of the Family and the job. Unless he could gain the upper hand or worm himself free, he had to sit this one out.

As he had figured, with the press pacing outside, Ong couldn't hold him for long without involving the police. He was handed over to the local police in the late afternoon and held at the station in the nearby town overnight. Dean was transported in a second squad car and put in a cell down the corridor.

'Let me speak to the American, goddamn you!' Han shouted through the peephole but the officers who had escorted him to the cell slid it shut in his face.

———————

In the clamour of the press conference, Fei managed to speak to Ginny.

'That official, Chin – he's the man who's been following me. He was the one that night, in the garage under my building.' Fei felt cold with sweat. 'He was disguised – here – right in the room with us. With a gun.'

'Our security people are questioning him.' Ginny looked gaunt with anxiety. 'Oh, God, what's going to happen? Who is he? What does he want from us? And what about Dean? What's he going to do?'

'He's got nothing on us.' Fei controlled her panic. She hung on to what she knew. There would be time enough to deal with uncertainties.

'What if he says something anyway?'

'He won't.' She tried to sound confident. 'Besides, it's a hostage situation. Our secret is his hostage, and a dead hostage is no good to him. He won't kill it by blabbing it to no good effect.'

'He might use it as a lever later on. What are we going to do then?'

'We'll have to deal with that if and when it ever comes to it.' Fei spoke with more assurance than she felt. She jerked her head in the direction of the media outside. 'For now, that conversation with him never happened.'

Ginny nodded, her eyes wide with fear.

Fei said, 'Who's Lovelace?'

'What?' Ginny paled.

Fei relayed Dean's demands. She took Ginny's hand. It was icy cold. 'What was he talking about?'

'I . . . I don't know. I've never heard of this – who?'

'Lovelace.'

Ginny shook her head vigorously.

A knock on the door. 'Mrs Wyndham, the press are waiting for a statement.'

Ginny stood up and turned to the door. She paused. Fei saw her back straighten, her shoulders go down. Her nervousness seemed to fall away in that instant. She looked poised, gracefully confident. Almost beautiful when she smiled.

Fei was dumbstruck. The transformation was astonishing.

No one seeing her now would ever recognise the fraught woman who had looked to Fei to take charge. It was as if Ginny was two people. Fei felt a veil in her mind shift. But even as she groped towards it, the thought vanished like smoke.

Ginny seemed to sense her confusion. Her tone was both an invitation and a challenge. 'Coming?'

They fielded questions and issued press statements. Later, they met police and security staff. Fei finalised the agreement with the school's lawyers, huddled in a meeting room while the hubbub continued outside. Piers managed the crisis from the Centre's offices, leaving Ginny to be their public front. He spoke to her on her mobile phone throughout the day, sometimes meeting her with Fei and Ong for a war council. He looked as if he was barely suppressing fury. They were all strained and tired.

Fei left the Centre late in the evening. Ginny had wanted the bodyguards to go with her but Fei had refused: 'The police have got that Chin guy in custody. It's over now. I'll be fine.'

She had not offered any information to the police about his intimidation of her.

Ginny said, 'I'll find out through the police what his agenda is.'

Fei needed to believe that she was safe now. That it was all over. She did not want to know about Chin. She did not care what his agenda was. As for Dean, his threats had collapsed and he was out of her sight. She did not care what happened to him either. They were both gone, wiped from her life and her mind. She wanted them never to have existed. She wanted her old life back, its banality and security. This fog of paranoia and the swerving confusion of her emotions had closed in on her since the night she had first come to the Centre. She felt drained. Was it Ginny or the strangeness of the last few months? It was as if all her energy and bearings, her whole construct of reality, had been sucked from her. She could not tell anymore what made sense and what did not.

Fei was exhausted and the drive back to KL would take her four hours in the low visibility. But she had agreed with Ginny that it would be best not to be seen together outside business for a while.

'Don't forget me.' Ginny walked Fei to her car. It was a joke but the tension in her voice gave it a desperate edge.

The ambulance swept through the gates of the Centre and came to a stop by the Secure Unit on the headland. It was almost midnight. The media and visitors had finally moved off in the late-afternoon and the grounds were deserted. The nurses unloaded the stretcher where Ben was strapped. He was beginning to come round, his head lolling as he moaned. Suleiman watched over them as they moved Ben down into the labs through the access hidden in the cover of the wooded scrubland surrounding the Unit.

The ambulance dropped the police officers and nurses at the security block before parking amongst a fleet of other ambulances and vehicles in the concealed underground lot. The men headed for their lockers, stripping out of their uniforms and back into their own casual clothes. Their work done for tonight, they said cheery goodbyes and headed home to their families. On their lapels they wore the AVA logo.

In the morning they would be back in their security guard uniforms.

The next day, Han was taken out of the overnight cells and driven down to KL to the main police headquarters. There, he was held in a cell for two more nights. The police had found no licence for his weapon in the civilian records and their computer search of his identity papers referred them to the foreign ministry. It was clear from the buffoonish way they were handling him that they had never come across anything like this before, he thought. They questioned him several times, mostly in the early hours of the morning, but he always said the same thing: 'Chin Wan-Tai, education ministry. Call this number.' He gave them a number that would patch them through to the Family. There was a standard procedure for situations like this, devised to extract the Snake from the authorities without jeopardising the secrecy of the job or compromising the Family's identity.

Han hurled his own demands back at the officers every time they tried to question him: what had they got on the American, where was he? Han wanted to question him. But all he got was, 'We ask the questions, Chin. What's your interest in the American?' And the whole process would begin again.

Raul turned up late on the fourth day. Han said, 'About fucking time.'

They got into Raul's hired Proton. He said, 'We're going straight back to Jakarta. You're on ice for three months. I've got to take your weapon.'

'Shit.' But Han handed over his gun. He slammed his palm against the side window, working to control his frustration. 'At least they've got the American in custody. Whaddya have on him?'

'He left the country this morning. Back to Washington. Deported.'

'What the fuck . . .'

'He's got some influential friends.' Raul manoeuvred through the rush-hour traffic. 'The authorities here were holding him under internal security legislation. He may be FBI but he didn't have the authorisation for being in this country on official business.'

'Is he FBI or not?'

'No definite answer yet. The tecchies say their US contacts are dragging their feet on this query. They don't know why.'

Han swore.

Raul said, 'The American consul contacted the home affairs

ministry. Orders direct from Washington, apparently, to get Dean out of local custody. At first, the authorities here were gung-ho – they weren't going to let the US interfere with internal affairs, not in this present climate and especially as Dean was here illegally. But the bastard played his ace.'

'Which was?'

'You.'

'What!'

'He figured the media would want to know why an Asian security agent was on the Wyndhams' premises in disguise. Why Asian authorities were so interested in the Centre and the AVA. He claimed to be able to link you with the attempted assassination of Siew at the inauguration ceremony.'

'Lucky fucking guess.'

'Still, it was enough to set home affairs scurrying. They got hold of the foreign ministry. Finally, it went up to the highest level. *Bapa Tua* got an earful from the Suits. He's not happy, especially since Mokhtar authorised all this.'

'So he can't claim "agent gone AWOL" and wash his hands of the whole fucking mess.' Han's laughter was bitter.

He would be confined to the backroom with the techies back in Jakarta fucking number crunching. There was nothing he could do but ride it out. Raul had cleared out his accommodation in KL and destroyed his various false identification papers. The Han Lee-Ren of the last year no longer existed. If he ever got back to Malaysia, it would be with new identity papers. So far as the police officers involved in his arrest knew, Han had been a disgruntled education ministry official out to embarrass the authorities. His release was under the appropriate immunity and the press were fed a short statement to the effect that he had been dismissed and was undergoing care for a nervous breakdown. All enquiries to the education department would bring up the same notice on their files. On the Suits's orders, police records on him would already be lost by the time he arrived back in Jakarta.

Fei sat at the table in the dining area off Sam's kitchen. It was two weeks after the incidents at the Centre.

She had got home at two a.m. and found Sam's message on her answering machine. Nerves still wound tight from the day, Fei had been unable to sleep. She finally called back at four in the morning. Sam came round. She told Fei about Dean's visit to her office. They talked for hours – about Dean, about Ginny, everything they had not been able to talk about for so long. Sam was there, soothing and reassuring, helping Fei contain the turbulence of anxiety and tension. They fell asleep together on the sofa, Fei waking to find herself in Sam's embrace. Breakfast was comfortingly familiar and yet awkward. Over the next week, they found themselves speaking over the phone. They began to meet after work. For drinks. A meal. Nothing special.

Ginny had confirmed the news report about Chin. The police had told her he had been committed to an institution for psychiatric treatment. Fei spoke to her every few days, their conversations shorter than Fei would have liked. Ginny seemed distant again. Fei felt locked out. It made her on edge. It was as if she was reaching out towards Ginny to find nothing but air.

But Dean had been deported from the country. She was safe. They were all safe.

Tonight, she had come over to Sam's house late after work. They sipped cold beers. It was finally over. The shadows that shifted in the smoke were no more than the projections of her fearful imagination. Being here with Sam was like finding a home at last.

Sam said, 'I didn't acknowledge to Dean that we'd been lovers, you know, because I was scared. I even told him he was disgusting. After all my pushing you to be "out" . . . I was so self-righteous, wasn't I?'

'Don't let's go over all that.'

'All my political correctness – it was just a way of getting at you. I blamed you – for making me give up everything for you, to come here to this strange country . . .'

'Sam . . .'

'But I came because I wanted to. I wanted to get away from

staid, safe England. I wanted to be with you. It was harder than I had expected.'

Fei felt the pain of all their misunderstandings. 'I got too involved in my work, in making it big-time. I wanted you to be excited about it the way I was. I forgot how tough it might have been for you.'

'I'm sorry, Fei, for hurting you.'

Tears took her by surprise. She blinked hard. She wanted to take Sam in her arms, to bury herself in the comfort of what they had lost. But she did not move. They couldn't go back, no matter how much she might wish it in this moment. 'You don't have to apologise. I'm the one who should be sorry.'

'No, I said things I wish I hadn't.'

'And me, too. I made it hard for you.'

'I didn't want to understand . . .'

'No. It was me . . .' Fei stopped. Their mutual eagerness to 'give face' seemed suddenly ridiculous. She said, trying to stay serious, '"Love means never having to say you're sorry".'

Sam paused, uncertain. then she rolled her eyes and played an air violin.

'Something like that.' Fei grinned. And suddenly they were both laughing, shaking with the release of their pent-up emotion.

<hr />

News of a CJD epidemic spread panic across the nation and spilled into the rest of Asia. In the drama, most journalists and readers overlooked the education official who had suffered a nervous breakdown. One paper did speculate that perhaps he, too, had eaten beef at the school but the one sentence was lost in the tonnes of newsprint that spewed from the burgeoning crisis. Beef prices were bottoming out. Meat wholesalers and butchers faced ruin. Emergency meetings were held in parliament and local councils, task forces were set up and measures were pushed through for the distribution and sale of beef.

Negotiations went on late into the night over compensation for victims as well as for farmers and those in the meat industry.

There were unconfirmed reports that the butcher supplying the meat to the school had obtained his produce from abroad, probably England. A tabloid news magazine in the Philippines ran investigative pieces that linked various disasters in Asia to sinister motives in the West. The speculation encompassed floods in Bangladesh, famine in Africa, the assassinations of the Gandhis, the death of Marcos and the fires in Indonesia. The theory went that, having lost imperial power in the East, the Western powers – from Spain, Portugal, Germany, the Netherlands and France to the United Kingdom and America – were each working via spies, infiltrators and moles like Dean, to keep Asia, Africa and South America impoverished, unstable and impotent. That edition of the magazine sold out in hours and several reprints had to be run by popular demand and flown to newstands across the region.

A similar epidemic had caught the United Kingdom a few years before and there was new speculation that the British had exported their infected stocks to Asia with falsified health certificates, rather than destroying them. Across Asia, emergency laws were passed to make the importing of beef from the Western nations illegal. Imported steak from Texas were outlawed. Beef products from Australia and New Zealand were barred. British beef was banned from sale but consumers were also boycotting other British products in a mass demonstration of horror. Chat on the internet fed the frenzy and rumours around the global web. Enterprising distributors turned to China, South Africa and South America for alternative meats, marketing horse, alligator, ostrich and wildebeest as the new delicacies for the connoisseur. Lawyers were poised to make a killing, instructions flooding in for claims and counter-claims. The cynical and the poor bought up freezer loads of beef at knock-down prices.

A multi-disciplinary team was appointed in Malaysia to investigate the CJD epidemic. They were to look at long-term strategy to deal with food contamination and advise the health policy-makers on elimination of sources and future prevention. There were doctors, scientists and financial consultants – the latter to work on the economic consequences of any policy. Sam was brought in as a senior epidemiologist, her contract renewed for two years. The Investigative Committee was headed by Dr Govinda and funds were given to his pathology department at the National Hospital to set up a new section devoted to the CJD investigation.

Sam said to Fei, 'I'm in two minds about being on this Committee.'

They were in her office at the hospital. Lunch had become a regular fixture in their diaries. They alternated, with Sam going into town then Fei coming to the hospital.

Fei laughed. 'Typical! You're never happy.'

'It's an honour to have been appointed, I don't deny that,' Sam said. 'But my data does not support an exclusive CJD theory. Govinda hooked into the concept of the prion, and the only known diseases attributable to prion infection are CJD and kuru.'

Fei put down her handbag and car keys. 'Kuru?'

'It was first discovered in 1957 among the tribes of Okapa in the Eastern Highlands of Papua New Guinea. It's a degenerative disorder of the central nervous system, affecting the motor systems and cerebellum, gradually worsening from headaches, to torso instability and finally uncontrollable spasms throughout the whole body. It was transmitted by the local practice of eating human brains.'

Fei made a face.

'The disease was arrested after two generations when the cannibalistic ritual died out.'

'So it can't be kuru.'

Sam looked at Fei. 'You really interested? We're not in a hurry, right?' She pulled up another chair to her computer terminal as she spoke, switching the applications on screen to her data files.

'Sure.' Fei shrugged but Sam had already sat down at the monitor. Fei slid into the chair beside her.

'Look, the prion in the JB school case falls within the category I call Factor Q. This is a range of similar but not identical prions manifesting in a myriad of cases across Asia over decades.' Sam clicked on a data chart, correlated by date and region. 'The incubation period for kuru and CJD is usually fifteen to thirty years but from the evidence, Factor Q incubation is rarely longer than several months and in some cases, only a few weeks. Q is 33–38 kDa . . .'

'KDA?'

'The dalton is a measurement unit used in biochemistry and is equal to one-twelfth the mass of an atom of carbon-12. KDa stands for kilodalton. In effect, Q has a range of different molecular weight from CJD and kuru.' Sam was charged with energy. She was focused, speaking intently.

'A different incubation period and different weight indicate – what? A different entity?'

'Exactly. And here . . .' Sam brought up another screen, a statistical table of some kind. 'The amino acid structure is different from kuru or CJD protein structure.'

Fei was confused.

'Say you have a serial killer and all the victims have got a bullet wound from a .33 revolver. That's like the murder weapon for the kids, and the other cases I've got on my database. But you check the guns licensed to kuru and CJD and they are a different calibre. So they can't be the killer.'

Fei was having to work hard to follow these technical arguments but she was absorbed now. She had never talked in depth with Sam about her work. Seeing Sam so fired up beside her, feeling her excitement – somehow, the science had meaning. She said, 'So the JB case involves the same prion as your other cases?'

'It's not as simple as that. There's a similar protein but there are slight variations in the amino acid chain sequences.' Sam scrolled down the biochemistry breakdown. 'There are 275 amino acids making up the prion in this case – as with all our other Factor Q cases. But here in position 193, and also other positions along the chain, the amino acids are different from the previous cases we've had.'

'So all the cases on your database involve a prion molecular weight within a certain range but each one is slightly different in the way it's made up?'

'Exactly. The different amino acid combinations explain the range of difference in molecular weight. The variants probably account for the variations in how the disease presents in each victim. In the school children, their symptoms are not exactly those of CJD – their spasms and limb rigidity don't manifest in CJD.' Sam went through the chart of case histories and sociological factors for the thousands of victims on her database. 'There's no common factor other than the presence of Factor Q. And until now there were no children affected.'

'The occurrence looks random. But you think it's an epidemic?'

Sam clicked to another statistical chart. 'The oldest case I've been able to trace is nine years ago. Not many more back then. It may be to do with records not being available for earlier cases. But look, over the years, the incidence has increased dramatically. It's like what happened with AIDS – we didn't know people were dying from it because their symptoms were diagnosed as something else, like pneumonia. It was only after the HIV virus was identified that the world realised what was really killing these people. At least with AIDS, they could isolate how the virus was being transmitted and the common factor among the victims: they came into contact with each other, through sexual activity or intravenous drugs use or some other means of exchanging blood or bodily fluids. But here I keep coming up against this blank wall. The victims seem to have no common sociology, no common physical contact, no common behaviour.'

'Food?'

'We've already checked that. Many were Buddhists or Hindus – they don't eat beef. Also there were Muslims who don't eat pork. A percentage were vegetarians . . .'

'No food habits in common then.'

'Right.'

Fei sat back. 'Why didn't this get into the report?'

Sam sighed. She told Fei about her colleagues' views of her

Q theory, especially Govinda's dismissive attitude. 'There are still too many uncertainties in the data – loose ends and un-correlated aspects. I've got nothing but a gut feeling on all this. That doesn't make for good academic science. Besides, from Govinda's point of view, it's easier to get funding and a campaign going for one clear enemy. "Asiatic CJD" has a nice regional ring to it and that helps in this current political climate. I'm just banking that being on this Committee will help flesh out my data and maybe even gain a hearing for my hypothesis.'

'Better to be on the inside than a voice crying in the wilderness.'

'I haven't given up. I'll do whatever I need to do to prove this epidemic exists. Damn it, people are dying from this thing and we're all looking the wrong way, I'm sure of it. Contaminated beef isn't the whole picture but I can't get anyone to hear me out. It's like they've convicted the wrong culprit and the real serial killer is still out there, you know? It makes me mad when I think about it . . .'

'Mad like the cows?' Fei grinned.

Sam couldn't help but laugh.

Fei put her arm round her. 'I know it's frustrating, but you've always been one for lone crusades. You love it, really.'

'You know me too well!' Sam cuddled Fei back. In spite of herself, she felt her heart do a little dance.

The media sold papers and air-time like hotcakes. Everyone wanted to know the latest developments, tuned in for updates, read the special editions for views and horror stories. Cases previously diagnosed as other diseases were now being attrib-uted to Asiatic CJD. Members of the public suffering dramatic ailments – deformities, motor-coordination difficulties – appeared on TV in Japan to be examined by panels of doctors. In Thailand, guests at a dinner destroyed the restaurant when one of the dishes was thought to have contained beef slices masquerading as ostrich – it was later found that the meat had in fact been ostrich. In Malaysia, there were reports of a gunman shooting local herds after rumours spread of cattle being infected by imported feed. A cow herd trying to stop the shooter was gunned down.

Siew Kei-Win appeared weekly on N-Sat appealing for calm and focus. The AVA had kept a low profile during the uncertainties of the JB case but now they swooped to spin the panic to their advantage. He was filmed in light that made him seem to glow with moral rectitude.

'We must unite against outside forces. Calmness of mind and clarity of vision make the warrior effective. A single hand hurts only itself but a thousand hands joined in battle can destroy an enemy by sunset. Be part of the New Asia and we will not be defeated by the vile manipulations of the West. Live by the spirit of Asian Values and evil will fall before our triumphant call. Be proud to be Asian!'

Membership and donations to the Asian Values Alliance went up seventy per cent over the previous year.

The van bumped its way down the unmade track. The sub-tropical air was cool. It was a bright morning in the Guangzhu province in Southern China. The Haze had not reached so far north and the light was glaring. The farm lay in the flatlands in the midst of a cluster of limestone hills, their sharp peaks cupped against the sky.

In the dirt yard of the farm, Dr Suleiman stepped out. The farmer hurried up, his rubber boots splattered with mud. The air stank of poultry and the acrid scent of feed and chicken shit. Low hangars were ranged in rows across the tracts of farmland. There was a whirring, rattling hum all around: the sound of tens of thousands of chickens.

As arranged, Suleiman's men clambered out and pulled several sacks from the back of the van. The farmer beckoned to a worker who stacked the sacks in a barrow. Suleiman handed over the wad of American dollars. The farmer nodded and half-bowed as he counted the bills.

Suleiman said, 'One of these to five sacks of feed. For the G-14-23 chickens only.' The classification number referred to a section of the chicken pens.

'Yes, yes.'

The next day, in Hong Kong, Suleiman met Rocky in a bar. Rocky had no last name. He was lean in the way that a drug habit made a man lean. His tendons and muscles were iron hard against his skin. He wore a jade ring on his little finger, the nail left uncut. His Chinese eyes were impenetrable.

Rocky talked Suleiman through Parkson Chee's daily routine. By the end of ten minutes, Suleiman knew every move Parkson, his wife and his kid made every day of their lives. Rocky handed over a series of photographs of the family and the interior of their apartment.

'Send updates by the usual data transfer every week,' Suleiman said. The internet made meetings such as these redundant but, as Siew liked to say, the old ways of doing business had their advantages. Personal contact forged bonds, secured loyalties, underscored threats in a way that electronic contact could not.

Rocky nodded. 'Surveillance cameras got install' yesterday in all room of apartment. Three angle for each room. Mikes cover space. We link up satellite booster for direc' transmit to your receivers. It set by tonigh'.'

Suleiman allowed himself a smile. He slid a packet of American dollars across the table. He got up from the table, his drink untouched.

Outside, he caught a taxi to the airport. Project Max was under way.

Chapter Sixteen

In the observation cell where Piers had put Ben, Siew tried to talk to his protégé again. Siew had come down here whenever his schedule allowed, rushing to the Centre between his public appearances and business enterprises. It had been over two weeks now and his patience was running out.

The cell was compact, empty but for a bed fixed to the wall. There were no windows. That was standard anywhere in the labyrinth of underground labs. Ben slumped on the mattress in loose pyjamas. On Siew's orders, he had been taken off sedation. Siew wanted him lucid. Ben had been his lodestar for the future, his glorious hope. He had invested in the boy his whole life and the very gift of Asia itself. And Ben had failed him, had dared to doubt the good of his vision. Siew wanted to see him become again the man he had cherished, not by force but through his own will and desire.

'Do what you want with me, I don't care. Do what you want with Mei-Hong. You own her body and soul anyway, she was never mine.' Ben stared at the floor. His tone was listless.

Siew shook him. Ben's head lolled back and he stared at Siew with bitter eyes. His lips curved in a parody of a smile. 'You can't make me do what you want, can you? You can't make me believe what you believe. You can't make me care about Asian Values anymore. It fucking kills you, doesn't it?'

Siew swept his fist, backhanded, across Ben's head. The violent contact was sickening. And satisfying. Ben crashed to the floor. Through blood and thickened lips, he went on, 'And it scares you to hell.'

Ben was suddenly on his feet, his face sheened with sweat. His unshaven jaw gave him a wild look. He was blinking, his head jerking spasmodically. But his eyes blazed. He was jabbering, spraying blood and spittle. 'Go on, make my mind how you want it. Scramble my fucking neurons any way you like. That's the only way you'll ever own me again. No – not so easy. You can fry my brain but you'll never own me. *I'll* know – in my heart, I'll know what you've done. My soul will accuse you through all eternity' – he slammed his hand on his chest – 'here. I will always be in here, whatever you do to my mind and my memory. And any time the Cure falters, any time you forget to top it up, I'll be back. I'll rise up out of the darkness and I will know. I will fight you, and one day I will destroy you.'

Siew could not move. Ben had become a monster. The son he had chosen, the boy he had once loved with all he was, had turned against his creator.

Siew felt revulsion and horror. Ben's words evoked an unnamed fear in the deepest part of him. They seemed like a spell to release chaos and disaster. Icy sweat made him shiver. The terror had to be contained, the evil controlled and brought down. The Cure was meant to remake a man into whatever perfect image they desired, to erase the personality of whoever he might once have been. And here was Ben, who had worked with the flesh and minds of hundreds of subjects, who knew the intricate mechanisms of the Cure – here he was, telling Siew that the Cure had no real power. Threatening him with the ghost of Ben's true self, cursing him with a haunting across the gulf of consciousness. Ben had to be controlled. He was an enemy now.

Siew backed out of the cell. Ben began to scream furiously: 'Do what you want to me. Go on, do your worst. You'll never own me . . .'

The door closed, cutting off his voice, locking it electronically.

Siew found Piers in mission control. The walk through the

maze of corridors had calmed him. He said, 'I want Ben terminated.'

A flicker of surprise crossed Piers's face. Then he nodded.
'Ricky will take care of it from here. We'll use the new version
– gen106. It'll look like an accident.'

'Perfect.' Siew took a long breath. It cleared his head. The
decision was made now. He felt his heart lift. Ben was erased
from his mind. There was only the future. The future was all
that mattered.

———————

Ginny sat cold as stone in the trance suite. Images from her 'fix'
played on the main screen. The directive voice droned over the
speakers. She neither saw nor heard. They were going to eliminate Ben. She had never thought Siew would give such an
order. If Ben was dispensable, none of them would ever be safe.
She did not know how long she had been down here. Ten
hours. Twelve maybe. She had been playing all her 'fixes' over
and over again but without the Cure, they were nothing more
than stupid movies. She did not want to know what was
happening beyond the locked doors of the suite.

Ricky had kept her away from Project Max and at first she
had been humiliated – as she had been over all the other projects
he had begun to run without her involvement. She did not
know anything more about it than its name. Now, she felt
relieved. She did not want to know what further horrors they
were keeping from her. As she did not want to know what
horrors they were preparing for Ben. She flicked a glance at the
closed doors. Out there was their work and all its atrocities.

Piers had finally told her that the American had thrown the
name 'Lovelace' at him as far back as the inauguration ceremony.
They had not been able to get much out of Dean before the
police had taken over. After he was deported, the Alliance had
managed to get unconfirmed information that he might have
been a spy but nothing concrete to say that he was other than a

journalist. The Red Tiger had been ordered to dig up whatever they could on Dean and the psych team was working on updating his file. They would be prepared if he ever came near them again.

She pulled out her cellphone. She had lost count of how many times she had wanted to call Fei these last few hours, wanting desperately to see her. It was madness at a time like this. The plans for Project Max were on full thrust. They were expecting a sea shipment of H cultures. With the therapy deals on the increase, Piers was desperate to produce more vats of the Cure. And there was Phase Four in preparation stage – they would need more of the Cure for that than they had ever handled before. Fei had no place in all of this. If the Alliance ever found out about their affair . . . Ginny felt sick with fear. And what if Fei discovered what their experiments really involved? What the Final Phase was going to be? If she knew Ginny's part in it all, in all the corpses that accused her – Katie's first and always . . . Ginny could not bear to face the disgust and horror and fear she would see in Fei's eyes then.

But her heart ached and every nerve in her body longed for Fei.

She dialled the number. When Fei picked up, Ginny's voice was hoarse with emotion and longing. 'Come, please come. I have to see you. I miss you. I can't go on like this. Tomorrow? Yes, come then, come.'

Siew stood with Piers on a viewing deck at the Orang-Utan Sanctuary. The dawn was bright, the haze a mere smudge in the middle distance. There had been rains last night and strong winds. The worst of it had moved out to sea.

Since the Centre had been exonerated from the JB deaths, there had been renewed interest in the 'therapy' from schools, religious institutions and corporations. Everyone wanted model students, model congregations, model workers and model citizens.

Siew had travelled with Ginny to Bangkok and Jakarta already, arranging for the infrastructure to the 'therapy' to be laid: the health and exercise regimes which fronted the distribution of the Cure, the setting up of cabling and screens, satellite link-ups and access to the personal and sociological details of the subjects. Siew was thriving on the success. It was turning out to be easier than they had thought to prepare Asia for the Final Phase – these manageable segments of society would be transformed step by step, culminating in the final mass sweep.

'You had better have some good news for me on Project Max.' Siew turned to Piers.

Piers made an effort not to sound ingratiating. 'The new version of the compound, gen106, has been distributed. It's full name is HPrp31-gen106.'

'H?'

'We've upped the proportion of H elements to improve stability. The increased supply of H cultures your people are providing has made this possible. The continued presence of SPrp, although in smaller quantities, will ensure effective binding which the H factor might otherwise reduce.'

Siew nodded.

'We've placed gen106 further down the food chain,' Piers said. Gen105 had infected the JB kids through the beef. The cattle had been injected with the compound on the premises of the butcher, a fly-by-night operation run by Red Tiger connections for this one project. The compound had entered the cattle's tissue and within several days had been present throughout their systems. In Project Max, they were now testing the distribution method proposed for use in the Final Phase. For Max, the compound had been mixed into batches of chicken feed at a targeted poultry farm in Guangzhu. The farm supplied chickens to Hong Kong markets and for Max, the farmer would ensure that the gen106-rich chickens would reach a specified butcher in marked consignments. That butcher was where their next subject obtained his meat. 'The first infected feed will have entered the target livestock by now. The subject is currently under surveillance, as you know, and we are sure that he and his family have been consuming the marked chickens. We expect him to be picked up in five weeks.'

'The butcher is in on the deal?'

'No. He doesn't know the consignments are marked. He's selling them to all his customers.'

'The effects on the non-targeted consumers?'

'Expected to be nil. Subjectively, they might feel spaced out twice a day when naturally occurring chronotonin kicks in. They would experience whatever they might be doing at that time more intensely. But otherwise – without our intensive reprogramming at those times – they will be no different from how they ordinarily are. That's the beauty of the Cure. We can target who we want, when we want, so long as it's in the subject's system.'

Siew studied him with cold eyes. Piers stopped himself from running on as if he were doing a sales pitch. Confidence was what he needed to project. In the years he had been in Siew's pay and protection, they had run hundreds of experiments on thousands of subjects. His notes and data on all of them ran to scores of CD-RWs. All those lives sacrificed to the cause – subjects dying in agony or slipping into waking comas, limbs and minds twitching without function, bodies wasting away. They had picked the homeless at first, those without family or friends. Then they had abducted individuals from any walk of life – the wider sampling was needed to hone the effectiveness of the compound. The Red Tiger's net trawled busy markets and malls, lay in wait in lonely streets late at night. The subjects would be deposited back in the same location within a week, remembering nothing of the programming – as instructed. Each would be covertly monitored through discreet surveillance and reports compiled by AVA or Red Tiger contacts.

Different experiments aimed for different changes to the subjects' outlook or personalities – alcoholics were able to give up drink, scroungers were motivated to work hard, ordinary citizens were given happy memories, bookworms suddenly enjoyed sport. These adjustments grew more and more convincing and assured, with only occasional mental disjuncture. But all the subjects invariably exhibited the gruesome symptoms of the compound's instability after a while. The JB kids had been difficult to bear but he had reminded himself of what the demon had done to Katie. Piers had made himself think only of her and the vengeance she deserved. Morgane, too. He could not bear to think of Morgane, how she had died calling his name. He owed it to her and to Katie to make the world perfect, to wipe out the demons that lurked in the human heart. Whatever the cost, whatever lives had to be sacrificed.

Piers said, 'We won't fail this time.'

'*You* failed the last time. The AVA came out of it rather well. Thanks to Miss Qwong. I liked her gloves-off approach to the whole thing – it gave us just the spin we needed. I've had more calls this week – local governments and big business looking for ways to use the "therapy". We're back on track and you'd better deliver this time round.'

Piers said, 'We've got more H cultures coming in. But with this clearing weather, they might have a problem slipping by the coastguards. We may have to wait another few days for the haze to settle back.'

'I don't want to hear your problems, Wyndham.'

'But . . .'

Siew's face hardened. His voice cut like a blade. 'I hope you understand what is at stake. We've been backing you for over ten years now and we still do not have a usable compound. We can't afford any more close calls like JB. These covert investigations on our activities by forces we cannot identify do not bode well. We have to move into Phase Four on time and bring forward the Final Phase.'

'Bring forward? But the production process . . . We need time to get the quantities right. The Cure is not a synthetic compound – we tried to manufacture it once, remember? The synthetic version doesn't fold and bind in the way we need it to. With a natural production process, it takes time . . .'

'We don't *have* time. My people tell me there's a doctor who's making enquiries about some of the deaths linked with the Cure. He's chasing down every lead and collating details of your failures.'

Piers considered this. 'Who the hell is he?'

'My contacts don't know. I've got the Tiger on to it.'

'What's the bastard's interest?'

'You tell me.'

'Shit. We never expected anyone to make a connection between all those cases. We were careful to target different cities and the marginalised to eliminate any pattern being traceable.'

'And now with the CJD Investigation Committee . . .'

'They're barking up the wrong tree.'

'Nonetheless, prions are in the news. The public have seen the Cure now – they just don't know what the hell they're looking at. We need to move before the heat gets any closer.' Siew spoke through bared teeth. 'We'll bring forward the Final Phase by six months. Do it, Wyndham. I don't care how. I'll get you the resources you need but do it.'

Piers nodded, his mouth too dry for him to speak.

They threaded through the overhanging trees along a path. All around them, the dawn chorus roared – the apes calling and whooping to each other through the jungle. Rustling shook branches and undergrowth as orang-utans swung and scurried in their leafy haven. Siew was the mysterious benefactor who had endowed the Sanctuary. He had set it up as soon as he had realised the potential of Piers's research and through the Red Tiger had exported apes to New York for his experiments.

They found Ghuna, the head keeper, by the hidden pens in the heart of the Sanctuary. The pens held the apes chosen for use by the Centre. There were over a hundred pens and in each two to three creatures huddled, fur against fur, spindly limbs poking out of the bars. Ghuna, a thin Indian man, was checking on them. He looked startled when he saw Siew.

Ghuna held an infant orang-utan in his arms, its tiny dark shape curled against his chest. Its long limbs clung to his shoulders, bright round eyes looking up at the two newcomers from under its low brow. Its legs and feet curled into the Indian's waist. Ghuna must have found it on his morning round.

Piers indicated the pens. 'These specimens will be moved tonight?'

'Yes, sir.'

'It's the same number as the last consignment. I told you then: we need more specimens. Double the current rate.'

'That's too many. We can't produce so many in so short a time.'

'We'll take more of the younger animals, then.'

'I can't spare more. That'll deplete the stock. These apes don't breed like rabbits. They mate once every few years, one infant at a time . . .'

Siew spoke up. 'What's the artificial insemination unit doing?'

'We're working to full capacity, Brother-Elder, but there's only so much that is biologically possible . . .'

Siew took a step towards Ghuna, towering over him. 'You're not getting soft on me, are you?'

'I'm a zoologist . . . the welfare of the animals . . .'

'I've come out all this way to see you. It appears you will not take orders from anyone but me.'

'Oh, no, sir. I'm a good AVA member, sir. But . . .'

'I pay you well to supply Dr Wyndham with whatever specimens he needs.' Siew smiled thinly. 'You know what happened to Deng.'

The previous keeper of the Sanctuary . . . Ghuna swallowed hard. There was a sheen of sweat on his dark face although the morning was cool. They had taken him to view Deng's wasted body months ago, before they had closed the coffin and sent it to his family in the shiny hearse.

Ghuna twitched. 'I'll get you what you need.'

<hr />

Fei waited in the reception of the main building for an hour, her briefcase on her knees. The staff knew her and she chatted inconsequentially till conversation petered out. The receptionist buzzed Ginny again but she was still engaged on other business.

Fei tried to talk to her but the line was already dead when she got to the phone. Finally, she went to stretch her legs, stashing the case in the boot of her car.

Fei wandered over to the bungalow but the housekeeper told her that Ginny was not there. Fei had put her work schedule on hold to come because of Ginny's desperate call the night before. There would be calls and problems piling up at the office in her absence. She would have to catch up over late nights for the rest of the week. She decided to take a walk.

This was how Ginny hooked her, Fei thought. Through this jagged flirtation of desire and distance. She had thought once that she could have everything of the passion without the hurt. That after Sam she was free to live how she pleased and love who and when she chose. But Ginny had somehow beguiled her and she had surrendered her independence of mind and spirit to the magic.

Fei found herself up on the headland, facing the Secure Unit. Ginny had once vanished here as if into nothing. Crazily, Fei fancied that hiding somewhere in the mist and trees, Ginny watched her. That this was some kind of lover's test of faith or mean-spirited joke. She moved past the gates. Trees hovered in the haze, gliding by as she walked to reveal an open vista beyond. The land began to slope sharply here on the far side of the head-land, away from the main grounds. She should turn back, Fei thought, but she pushed on obstinately, following the fall of the land. Loose earth and stones clattered down ahead of her. There was no path. She could see a lagoon down below through the haze. It had been hidden from the rest of the grounds by the headland. She paused. The view on a bright day would have been stunning. Today, the Haze had cleared a little and she could see the curve of the cove and the vague shapes of the boulders and headland that encompassed it on the seaward side. Beyond was solid haze. In the stillness, she could hear the waves breaking on the rocks. There was also something else. Splashing. Voices. Clinking as of oars or anchors.

Fei took a few more steps and skidded, scraping several feet down the incline. She grabbed at rocks and grass, her heart pounding. The cove and boulders below careened across her vision. She dug her heels into the soil, stopping short just as the slope disappeared into a sheer drop.

Frozen there, her heart racing, Fei peered down at the lagoon below. There was a boat anchored, a fishing launch. Two sampans were ferrying figures – she imagined to the shore which she could not see. There were other figures in a line in the water, heads and shoulders bobbing along in the deeper parts. As they came up into the shallows, they staggered awkwardly. They looked almost comical, arms unmoving by their sides.

Then she noticed the rifles. Or at least, that was what they looked like. In the hands of a few men in the sampans and held by others on the deck of the launch. Fei leaned back against the slope though she guessed that she could not be seen. She felt dizzy and cold. Had she really seen those weapons? She peered hard into the haze. She couldn't be sure. They might have been oars or fishing rods. But the body language of the men on the launch: in control, strutting almost, weight evenly distributed . . . Fei couldn't think clearly. Get out of there, she told herself. Think later.

Painfully, she inched herself back up the slope, hardly daring to look down. Earth and stones slid away from beneath her feet. Every muscle strained to keep her anchored, pushed her moment by moment upwards to safety.

Breathing hard, drenched in sweat, Fei made it back to the path. She was shaking – whether with the physical strain or from fear, she could not be sure. Her knees gave out suddenly and she leaned against a tree.

Ben slammed the tray out of the nurse's hands. He head-butted the man, hearing the crunch of his nose breaking. The nurse's glasses fell to the ground. Ben dived for the tray as the nurse staggered, swinging it against the man's head.

Ben felt an exhilaration and power as the tray made contact. The nurse fell on to his side. Ben kicked him in the gut, the ball of his bare foot making contact with soft flesh. Quickly, he searched the man's pockets. Found money. The nurse was moaning but did not move. Ben pulled off the man's shoes and uniform.

In moments, he was changed. He stepped over the man and slipped out of the door, checking that its electronic lock clicked shut behind him.

━━━━━⟫●⟪━━━━━

Fei made it back to her car. She was sweaty and dusty, felt weak. She was going home. Damn Ginny. She turned the car towards the gate. The guard there seemed distracted, listening intently to the squawking on his radio, one eye on CCTV screens in his booth. He peered into the car and got her to open the boot. She waited impatiently as he inspected it. What on earth did he think she had stolen? He slammed it shut and waved her on.

The delta cruised by – trees, mangrove, milestones. They were visible today instead of the murky grey of the past few months. Perhaps the turning point had come. Fei couldn't remember the last time she had seen clear skies and sunshine. She felt a strange relief to have left the Centre behind.

Suddenly a figure, stumbling out of the mangrove – coming right at her. Fei hit the brakes. The car screamed to a halt. Her body rammed against the steering wheel. The man slammed up against the bonnet, arms spread. She got out as he staggered to his feet.

'Ben!'

He wore ill-fitting jeans and a sweatshirt. He was splattered in sea water and mud, the clothes were torn and shredded. A shoe hung from one foot. He clutched a shattered pair of spectacles, blood dripping from his hands. 'They want to kill me! Help me!'

'What's happened to you? Come and sit in the car . . .'

'Don't trust the police! They're in on it, too.' He grabbed Fei's shoulders, clutching them till it hurt. 'Siew was like a god to me, why is he doing this terrible thing . . . They kill children . . . There's a conspiracy to – to take your mind and soul . . . I gave them all of me. I didn't know . . . Don't trust them, not the police, ever . . .'

'I don't understand.' Fei tried to shake him off. He frightened her. She glanced round. They were alone on the deserted road. She thought of the men with guns she had seen. The strange figures in the water. 'Ben, what's going on? Who kills children?'

'It's a secret war. They are going to take over your mind. Secret war . . . conspiracy . . . Piers is doing it . . . Siew's dream . . .'

'What are you talking about? Ben, calm down.'

'They want to kill me, help . . .'

'I'll call the police.' Fei dragged herself out of his hold and moved to get her mobile from the car.

'No! Not the police! They know, they're in it! They'll come to get you!' Ben's voice shattered into sobs. He sank to the ground. He couldn't go on anymore. No one would listen to him. Mei-Hong had let Suleiman take him. Mei-Hong, his darling, his wife. She was in on it, too. Her and this lawyer woman. Terror and exhaustion drained everything in him.

He had set fire to a lab. Then he had loosed some of the apes from the holding pens down the corridor. The diversion had been enough to get him out of the complex on to the headland. From there, he had managed to scale the two lines of fencing, scrambling down the slopes into the mangrove swamp. He did not know how long or how far he had managed to make it. But now . . .

Vehicles in the distance. Closing in. Footsteps and voices. Piers. Ben was crying. He felt firm arms drag him up, haul him across to the waiting ambulance. He did not resist. What was the point anymore?

Piers said to Fei, 'Thank God you found him.'

She felt a confusion of relief and fear. What did Piers know about the men with rifles? Why was Ben so hysterical? She did not know where to begin.

Piers took her hand in an uncharacteristic gesture. 'He's had a nervous collapse. It's worse than we first thought. But don't worry, we'll take care of him. Thank you for finding him.'

'Will he be all right?' Fei stared as the ambulance screeched round and wailed off back to the Centre. Piers's car waited, security staff giving them some privacy.

'It's not an easy case. He's like a brother to me.' Piers said the words with his usual coldness. The sentiment sounded odd even as he shook Fei's hand with apparent feeling. 'We'll do what we can.'

Later, as Fei weaved through KL traffic, the bright lights floating above the seething, roaring buzz of the city, she had a sense that everything that had passed that afternoon had been like a dream. Strange, incoherent and seen through a blur, as if only half-remembered.

Chapter Seventeen

The Haze thickened again after its brief easing up. But the fog lacked substance, like a dream fading into consciousness. KL was surfacing, subdued and bleary-eyed. The city seemed to emerge like the walking wounded from the yellow gas of battle. The world it had once known, of wealth and thrusting success, was gone. All that remained to the survivors was smoking ruins and barbed wire amid a muddied battlefield.

Fei's work took all her energy and time. With the deepening financial crisis and the falling *ringgit*, partnership loan repayments had increased alarmingly. More clients were defaulting on bills as they in turn were hit by bad debts, rising interest and decreasing demand for their goods and services. Fei and her partners diverted more resources to client development in the hope of attracting new blue-chip companies to their list. Their litigation department picked up work from broken contracts and defaults but other sectors slowed. The firm had begun to take on work at discount rates to keep goodwill and cashflow healthy – this meant more hours for less money. At least until the economy stabilised, the partners told themselves. So far, they had managed to keep all their staff but there would be no bonus this year nor the usual annual raise.

A banging on the door woke Fei with a start. Her heart thudded in her ears. She felt dizzy. The clock said three in the morning. She had just managed to fall asleep after hours of insomnia.

The banging became more urgent.

She gulped in air and shook herself. What should she do? She looked around the dark room. She had taken to leaving the windows open again when she was at home and now felt exposed.

Bang-bang-bang. 'Fei, it's me!'

Ginny.

Fei unbolted the several locks on the front door. 'What's going on? Are you all right?'

'I had to see you. I couldn't stand it anymore.'

Fei let her in, automatically glancing into the corridor. It was empty. She locked the door again behind Ginny who was saying, 'I'm sorry to come like this. I drove for hours . . . I didn't know if I should come but I couldn't bear it. I've been going crazy thinking about you.'

Fei didn't know if she minded Ginny's being here. She still felt resentment that Ginny had made her wait at the Centre. She wanted to hurl it at Ginny, make her feel the same hurt Fei had felt that afternoon. But even as she took in Ginny's distress, felt the presence of the woman there with her, a fog seemed to fall across her anger. Forgetting was so easy whenever she saw Ginny. She should be annoyed, too, that Ginny had burst into her home like this. Fei had been so scrupulous about this space till now. But, strangely, Ginny's being here did not feel as awkward as she had thought it would. Fei realised how much she had longed to see her.

'I've missed you, too . . .'

Ginny took Fei in her arms, burying her face in her shoulder, pouring kisses on her throat and cheeks, searching out her lips. Fei felt the release of tension like a pure hit. She gave in to her responses. The reality of the other was overwhelming after weeks of separation. Their senses drank each other in, reconfirming, reminding, slaking the thirst.

Afterwards, lying on the sofa, their clothes around them, Fei felt cold although it was a warm night. She pulled on her T-shirt and knickers, remembering how she had lain here on the sofa with Sam the night after the press conference. She could not look at Ginny, sprawled across the cushions, one arm flung behind her head. In the dim light, her skin seemed grey-blue. Her posture was assured, taking up space as if to say: I belong here now.

Fei put a sidelamp on. Ginny screwed up her eyes in the sudden light, pulling herself up. Fei said, 'How about a drink?'

She made them both Chinese tea. When she came back from the kitchen, Ginny had pulled on her blouse but left it unbuttoned. The rest of her clothes were draped neatly over a chair. She obviously planned to stay the rest of the night. Fei had put back all her lesbian books and magazines and hung up the pictures of her friends again. Ginny was looking at a photomontage of Fei's London friends.

'Who's that?' Ginny took a cup of tea but turned back to the photos. She talked about everyone in the frame, drew Fei to her in the embrace of an established couple.

'That's Sam, isn't it?' Ginny smiled.

She was the only woman Fei had not yet mentioned. There were several photos of her and Fei together, arms around each other, heads close. In group pictures they were always next to each other, always touching. 'Yes.'

'She's very attractive.'

Fei took Ginny's hand and led her back to the sofa. 'How's Ben?'

'The treatment's taking time,' Ginny said quickly. She stared at the steam rising from her cup. 'But he's responding. I'll tell him you asked after him.'

Fei hesitated. 'There's something that's been bothering me. I don't know if I was seeing things or . . .'

'What is it?'

Fei told her about the boat and the men she had seen in the lagoon.

Ginny said nothing for a long time. She studied the tea as if looking for the answer in the floating leaves. Her lips were tight. Her head jerked involuntarily.

Finally, she looked up. 'Thank you for telling me. I'll talk to the local police. It's happened before. There's a ring smuggling in illegal immigrants from Indonesia. They take advantage of the smog cover to avoid the coast guards and we don't generally see anything. You haven't mentioned this to anyone else?'

'No. I thought it best to speak to you first.'

'Good. With all the negative publicity already affecting the Centre in these last six months, we can do without immigrant-smuggling added to it.'

'Sure.'

'But why didn't you tell me this earlier? It's been over two weeks.'

'I wasn't really sure about what I saw. It might just have been fishermen. I didn't want to make a big thing out of it.' Fei laughed in relief. She gave in to paranoia too easily, she thought, expected the worst of everything.

⎯⎯⎯⎯⇒●⇐⎯⎯⎯⎯

Piers stood up from the control panel in one of the trance suites. His assistants began to unstrap Ben from the reclining armchair in the centre of the room. They removed the visor and head-phones. His eyes were open but he was staring into the middle distance. They removed the electrodes monitoring his pulse rate, temperature and breathing, then the range of needles from his left arm, dabbing the pinpricks with alcohol and bending his arm back over cotton wool.

It was four weeks after they had brought Ben back from the delta. Christmas Eve.

In Ricky's 'mission control' along the corridor, his team stretched and moved away from their computer terminals. The programme was in standby mode – graphics stripped down to reveal a blue screen against which skinless 'webbed' figures moved. The figures were dot-marionettes of the actors – only instead of human features the three dimensions were represented by webs of lines. The psych team went down on to the sound stage. The actors began to strip off the complex of electronic dots from their faces, each dot corresponding to a dot on the faces of the screen figures. As the actors revealed their own faces again, the heads of the webbed figures crumpled and disappeared. The actors took off their body suits of similar, larger electrodes, each dot connected by wires to sensory and spacial data processing equipment at the back of the stage. The web figures deflated and only puddles of tangled lines remained at the bottom of the screens.

The mood was subdued today, Ricky thought. It was fucking tough working on a guy they all knew personally. Especially as the whole show was always live. Only the backdrops, character features and psych scripts were prepared beforehand. The actors played out the scripts in the electronic guise of the personae projected on to the final screen. Depending on the course of the interactive drama between the personae and the subject, the actors improvised according to the psych team's instructions which were fed to them through radio-link earpieces.

Ben had known the score. He was putting them at risk and no matter how much they all liked the guy, it was time to close down on this application before he crashed the whole system. The best thing for them was to get their minds off the bastard.

Ricky said, 'Back here in fifteen, guys. Now we got this one out of the way, we got to get back on track with Project Max.'

In the trance suite, Piers came over to Ben. The young man looked rested and healthy. His pallor was gone. He wore an expression of calm. Piers said into the light head-mike he wore, 'When you hear me count backwards from three to one, you will begin to wake up.' The voice that emerged from the speakers in the room was Ben's. Piers went on, 'When I reach one, you will be fully awake, remembering all the things that you have experienced. You have done a good job on the JB kids. It's Christmas and you have two weeks off. You're going home to Mei-Hong. Now stand up, Ben.'

Ben stood up. He walked to the door at Piers's command. His eyes were still unfocused and sluggish. He opened the door as Piers instructed him to. Piers talked on. Ben obeyed. He turned and stood with his hand on the door, facing inwards.

'You have come to say good-bye. Three . . . two . . . one.'

Piers pulled off the head-mike and dropped it into the pocket of his lab coat.

A grin spread over Ben's face. He made straight for Piers. 'Merry Christmas! See you in two weeks.' He shook Piers's hand energetically, his eyes focused and alive. Ben moved round the assistants, warmly wishing them well.

'Have a good time! Give my love to Mei-Hong,' Piers told him.

Ben backed out of the room. 'Sure will. That was damn' good work we did in JB, huh? The kids are thriving, I just checked their reports before coming down. It's been three months, a little more – and SPrp-gen105 is stable. We've done it!' He punched the air.

Piers took him by the shoulders. He stared for a long moment into Ben's handsome face and said with feeling, 'We certainly have. Thanks to your hard work and dedication. Goodbye, Ben.'

Ben made his way out of the labs. He had already seen Ginny, Ricky and the others. His bags were in the boot of his car. He made his way across the sunny grounds. It was late-evening, the sun fiery and low in the sky. The heat of day still hung in the air. The Haze had gone. Ben paused. When had it begun to fade? He couldn't remember. It seemed to him as if one day, it had been thick with smog and then, the next, the Haze had vanished as if by magic. He shrugged. It was damn' good to see the sky again! He hurried on and got into his Volvo. It would be dark in half an hour. He had two weeks with Mei-Hong in the Bahamas as Siew had promised. And afterwards they were on track for Project Max and Phase Four, the big build-up to the Final Phase. Ben felt excited and happy. He revved the car and shot off.

The sudden night of the tropics fell as Ben emerged from the road across the delta. He cruised along the trunk road to join the highway to KL, snaked along behind red tail lights, the bright white flashes of oncoming traffic whizzing by on his right. There was a strangely hypnotic quality to the drive. The engine hummed in his head. As he approached the junction to the highway, the traffic was heavier but they sped along at sixty miles an hour, almost nose to tail. There were cars, vans and goods lorries thundering by, motorbikes roaring past, weaving in and out wherever there was space. Their white headlights seemed to strobe his vision. Superimposed on the darkness, he saw flashes of recognisable vehicles but the kaleidoscope of lights began to swamp him.

Mei-Hong was suddenly beside him. They were on holiday, driving along country roads. As white lights dazzled him, vistas of an empty highway opened up through the dark. It was a sunny day. Beautiful fields to either side. Mountains in the distance. 'Let's take that road,' she said. The view was inviting and, after all, why not? They were on holiday for two weeks, they could do as they pleased, go where they wanted. But a residual sense of unease made Ben hesitate. He wasn't sure why. Just a feeling that it wasn't right. 'Please, go down that road. It's an adventure.' Mei-Hong pouted prettily.

In the rear-view mirror, the car behind them had its head-lights on high beam. The glare hurt Ben's eyes. The sunny country road was tempting – empty, fresh and romantic. 'Go on, darling,' Mei-Hong pleaded. Ben looked up at two sun-slashes of light shooting towards him, straight into his eyes. The country road curved right, opening out into a vista of poppy fields and lush grass. Ben smiled and yanked the wheel round to the right, stepping on the gas.

The driver of the timber lorry slammed on the brakes as the Volvo skidded out of the oncoming lane and straight into his path. The truck's fender crumpled the car's bonnet, knocking the vehicle sideways like a matchbox. Metal crashed and squealed. The momentum of the lorry rammed the car several yards along the road before scraping to a halt. A pile-up behind shunted the lorry and the crushed remains of the Volvo a few feet more. Ahead, cars skidded and crashed as they tried to avoid the debris coming at them. Other cars distracted by the accident careened out of control, smashing into oncoming traffic. The lorry driver tumbled out of his cab, shaking. The Volvo was a twisted, crumpled tangle of metal, hardly recognisable as a car.

There was only one body. It was a mess of flesh and blood in what was left of the driver's seat. The lorry driver could not tell whether the mangled corpse had been a man or a woman. He doubled up, retching.

⸺⸺➤●◄⸺⸺

The immigration officer at KL International Airport eyed the Australian. It was January. The white man was well-built and tall, his face hidden behind a dark beard and thick glasses. His hair was lank. The passport said, 'Kyle Laddman, ornithologist'. The officer checked the computerised records. Clear. He said, 'What is your business here?'

'Holiday, mainly. And professional.' Laddman's accent was strong, flattening the 'a' sounds hideously. 'Bird-watching in your *Taman Negara.*'

The officer took in the metal camera cases at Laddman's feet and his khaki photographer's vest bulging with lenses and film cartridges. His landing card gave a hotel in KL and the National Park details. The officer stamped the passport and let him through.

Laddman made his way across the vast marble floor, steel and glass soaring high above him. He picked up his tote bag from baggage claim. Outside, the air was hot and sticky after the artificial cool of the gleaming complex. Laddman stowed his cases in the boot of an old Mazda waiting in one of the bays. He got into the passenger seat. The windows were tinted. Hsien, at the wheel, pulled the car out into the sweeping one-way system of the airport grounds. He said, 'You're staying in graduate flats near the university. The equipment's set up and running. Keys in the glove compartment.'

Carson Dean took off the heavy glasses and reached for the keys. Also in the glove compartment were a 9mm P228 SIG-Sauer automatic pistol and several magazines. He grinned. 'I like your taste.'

He shoved the weapon into the shoulder holster hidden

under his jacket, dropping the spare clips into his pockets. He had come from New York via Hawaii and Perth, his contacts in Australia providing the new identity.

His employers in New York had bawled him out for getting them involved in extricating him. They had had to pull in favours with Washington to do it. But the bottom line was that they needed him. The other bidder had laid on Hsien to back Dean up. Freelancing gave Dean this flexibility – and double the sources of income.

The journalist/FBI cover had been useful. But now he couldn't use them again. It left him more exposed in any encounters with the authorities. And he would have to approach the target even more tangentially than before. But two months of sitting around back in New York had given him a new look at an old problem. He had kept what he knew about Fei-Li and Ginny Wyndham from the authorities. Fei had been right: he had had nothing of substance against her. Unproven accusations would only have tied him up in the local legal system to no avail. Besides, blackmail only worked while the threat continued – once the secret came out, the women would no longer be vulnerable to his designs. A quick extraction had been the only practical option.

Hsien had been keeping him updated. It had been Hsien who had cleared out his apartment after Dean had left the country. The authorities had not found the transmission and communications equipment hidden behind a false wall. The electronic signals from the hi-fi, TV and PC fronting the wall would have jammed any sweep they might have done, although Dean doubted if they had thought to do one. Hsien had now set up the new place with all Dean needed to get on with the job.

Dean had hiked up his price with his bidders. They had both agreed to it in spite of their anger over the deportation. As a free-lancer, he could work in ways they did not need to know about. That was why he had left the Service in the first place. Better money and he was his own boss. Dean laughed. The American dream! He took out a wad of dollars from his wallet and handed them over to Hsien. 'A new year bonus.'

Hsien did not take his eyes off the road as he slipped the packet into his jacket pocket.

'How much?'

'Another three.' Thousand American dollars.

Hsien pulled a face. 'Not bad.' But Dean caught a creasing round his eye. The bastard was happy.

'Qwong?' Dean said.

Impatience had charged him into the Centre in a disguise that had failed and set him back several levels in the game. If he had hung on, followed up on the dyke lead and got some hard facts, he might have had the lever he needed by now.

Hsien had done the waiting for him in the last months. He said, 'You got a full house this deal. Ginny Wyndham went up to Qwong's condo before Christmas.'

'That's a first.'

'They've spent more time there since. They still use the Wyndham place, too. They must be going at it like fucking rabbits.' Hsien sniggered. 'You picturing it like I'm picturing it?'

Dean said nothing. The day was glaring bright. The sun through the tinted windows burnt his shoulder and arm. He wanted to see Fei again. He wanted her. Like some goddam' lovesick bastard. After all this time, he hadn't fucking shaken her hold on him. It wasn't meant to be like this – *he* was supposed to have the hold on *her*. He had allowed his personal feelings to distract him the last time. He could not let it happen again, he told himself even as Hsien's obscenity riled him. But the thought of Fei gave him an ache he could not break free from.

He said to Hsien, 'Just fucking drive.'

⋙●⋘

In Hong Kong the following week, Parkson Chee kissed his wife goodbye. It was a crisp, cool day. He knelt on the pavement outside their apartment block and hugged his seven-year-old son, Maxwell. 'Be a good boy, Max.'

'Bring me a present, Daddy.'

Parkson got into the waiting taxi and waved to Ah Fa and Max. The cab headed for the airport. He would be away for just over a week. He would be meeting his friend, Alfred Wong at KL airport. Parkson was an accountant, salaried in a middle-ranking firm servicing small businesses. He was doing okay but he was in his late-thirties and by now should have been a senior partner in one of the international firms, earning megabucks. But somehow he had never made it into the big time. He worked hard, he was honest and meticulous. Where had he gone wrong? He had a few investments, nothing too risky. He dabbled a bit in business but nothing had ever taken off as he had dreamed it would. He was doing okay while his former class-mates now owned their own companies or headed multi-nationals. They lived in big houses, some even had their own yachts. All their children were educated overseas. He wanted all these things, too – not for himself but for Max, so the boy could have the best in life.

Alfred would tell him, 'You play it too safe, Parksy. You're too sensible. You follow the rules too much. Live a little, man. To get to the top, you got to cheat a bit.'

They played golf at the same club every Saturday. No one had ever called him Parksy before. Alfred was full of confidence, always ready for a joke, a real man's man. He was a property dealer, jetting about Asia buying and selling land and develop-ments. He had to have millions to his name, Parkson thought, but no one would ever know it from Alfred's down-to-earth manner. Alfred had invited him into a consortium purchasing an island off the coast of Malaysia. 'It's worth peanuts now, nothing but coconut trees. But my people' – a wink – 'tell me that the government are planning to designate it for tourism. Next year. Boom! We sell it, we make money. We keep it and run our own hotel, we make money. Win, win situation, man.'

It was about time he became a winner, Parkson thought. He was going to meet the other partners in the venture. They would view the land, stay in a resort in Penang, play some golf, get to know each other. All the way to KL, sipping champagne in busi-ness class, he dreamt of the life that might yet be his.

At KL airport, Alfred was waiting in a black Mercedes limousine. They drove into the tropical landscape. It looked hot out there but the aircon kept the temperature comfortable inside the tinted enclosure. Parkson laughed and chatted with Alfred, not noticing the time. After a while, he looked out of the window. Rubber plantations whizzed by. He wasn't familiar with Malaysia but they seemed to have been driving for hours. 'When are we getting to the hotel in KL?'

'Change of plan. You don't mind, Parksy? We're going to pick up one of the other investors. Not long now.'

They drove through a long stretch of jungle and mangrove. Parkson squinted out of the window. Where were they? They began to wheel up a hill. When he saw the sign – 'Wyndham Centre for Mental Health and Excellence' – he was confused. Why were they going to a mental asylum?

He turned to ask Alfred and stared down the barrel of a pistol.

⸺⸺⟫◆⟪⸺⸺

Piers studied the weak, flabby features of the subject strapped to the trolleyed stretcher. Beneath the bright surgical theatre lights, Parkson Chee looked even more insubstantial than his video-ed image. His eyes darted about in a frenzy of panic, sweat drenching his pasty face. Thick tape over his mouth kept him silent. He was naked under the sheet. The medical team, masked and robed in white, were checking his physiological condition – heart rate, blood pressure, brain activity status – and running the pre-induction blood and hormonal tests and cell counts. Piers glanced up at the video camera recording their activity for Siew. His voice was ironic through his mask, 'This is your assassin.'

A muffled croak escaped the subject.

Piers had deliberately targeted unpromising material. The subject was slow in making decisions, lacked incisive thought and had a tendency to anxiety and fearfulness. He might have been any of hundreds of thousands of ordinary people one might pass on the street any day. For people like these, cowardice and self-preservation rather than principle prevented them from breaking the law or giving in to their primeval reservoir of violence. If Project Max could turn him into a ruthless assassin, then the Final Phase was only a breath away.

Piers reflected that he felt no emotion in considering Parkson Chee. He had been reluctant at first to take on this aspect of Siew's vision for Asia. His work had been meant for the creation of a perfect society, free from human violence and destruction. But in the battle for the Final Phase, they would need an uncompromising force who would carry out any order, fight any opponent and take any risk. And it was these assassins' expendability and unquestioning obedience that would make them the Alliance's ultimate enforcers. Such men – and women, if need be – would protect the perfect Asia about to be born. Their actions would be merciful and justified for they would be destroying true evil and safeguarding the purity of the Alliance's will. True evil had murdered Katie. True evil stalked them all now, waiting to bring down the one perfect hope for the future. It was in those who opposed Asian Values, who carried on with their hideous, tortured lives even in the face of a glorious chance for happiness. Real, untarnished, innocent happiness. True evil had been Ben's rejection of all they had offered him. Siew had sacrificed his adoptive son to the cause. Piers felt an overwhelming admiration for such a man. It was right that Siew should lead them into the new dawn. He was a godhead to them all.

Piers knew that in the shadow of such passion, he himself could not falter from any weakness or misgiving over this target out of all the thousands they had treated, nor out of pity for the subject's wife and child. He did not allow himself to think of Katie, a child like Max. He closed his mind to Morgane who had died as the subject's wife would die. He was doing this for them – as everything he had done since the day Katie had disappeared had been for them both. Piers would have killed *him* in the McDonald's that day but he had failed. Piers realised now that there had been a reason for that failure. If he had succeeded in killing *him*, he would not be here today and Asia – and ultimately the world – would not have the chance it had now to rid itself of all the demons and all the evil that stained it. Project Max was his greater weapon than all the semi-automatics and grenades he might have amassed for that day long ago.

Siew had saved him for a bigger purpose. He owed to him, to Katie and Morgane, to Ginny and to himself, to do what needed to be done, without fear or hesitation.

He said, 'Take the subject to the trance suite.'

Chapter Eighteen

Sam stood beside Dr Govinda at the computer in her office. A warm breeze clattered the venetian blinds at the window. Outside, the sky was bright with puff-ball clouds. They were reviewing the analysis of the brain sample that her assistant Ling had double-checked. No doubt about it. Another Factor Q case. Govinda had to realise that, surely?

On the desk beside them Ben Chang's file lay open. In it were the post-mortem report and details of the coroner's verdict following the inquest that had taken place two weeks before. The post-mortem had been carried out by the Pathology department of the hospital in Ipoh where Ben's body had been taken after the accident. It had reported traces of sedatives which might have impaired his judgement while driving. Cause of death had been attributed to severe injuries to the head and multiple trauma to the rest of the body. No mention had been made of brain tissue investigations. At the inquest, Dr Wyndham had confirmed that Ben had been prescribed sedatives as part of the treatment for his nervous collapse although he had been taken off them two days before the accident. The coroner had recorded death by misadventure.

In the wake of the JB school deaths, the CJD Investigation Committee had issued notification requests to all hospitals in Malaysia and Singapore. The investigation team was to be alerted in the case of the death or illness of anyone connected to the JB School where Asiatic CJD had first been identified.

Chang was the first adult who had died. The Ipoh Pathology department had sent a sample of brain tissue to the National Hospital in KL as part of the administrative procedure the Committee had set up. The sample had been analysed by a lab technician in Dr Govinda's Path team and the results filed as not relevant. It was only because Sam had personally double-checked the results that she had spotted the startling evidence Chang's case presented.

'How did these results get overlooked?' she said now, indicating the data on screen.

Swinging round slowly, Govinda pressed his artist's hands together in an arch. He said, 'They weren't overlooked, they were considered irrelevant.'

'But it's a prion protein of similar composition to what you've called Asiatic CJD.'

'The molecular weight is different. And there are variations in the amino acid sequence.'

Sam said, 'Such anomalies are common in all Factor Q cases. My view is that they are all mutations which can be linked to one patent prion, if only we can pinpoint what's causing the changes in structure.'

Govinda spoke as if he had not heard her. 'Chang must have eaten at the school, the same as the kids.'

'The compound in his brain is *similar* to the one found in the kids. If he had eaten the same food, we'd expect it to be *exactly the same.* It's not. Doesn't the difference interest you?'

'The Committee was set up to investigate Asiatic CJD. We're here to find out and record the relevant facts. I'm not going to let you start a panic with sensationalist views and theories of mutating compounds. The facts are clear. The protein in this victim is not that of Asiatic CJD. He exhibited none of the symptoms associated with CJD in his last weeks of life and he died in a traffic accident. You can't twist them into your grand unified theory of a prion epidemic.' Govinda stood up. 'These results are not relevant. My technician acted correctly.'

'But . . .'

'Dr Ryder, let my staff do their job. You are to stop the practice of reviewing their data and analyses. We're no longer a colony of the British and we don't need you to supervise our work.'

Sam flushed with anger. 'I thought we were trying to conduct a scientific enquiry? By limiting the scope of the investigations, your team isn't getting the full picture.'

'You mean "your" picture?'

'This isn't about me against you. As a scientist, surely you can't ignore questions merely because they can't currently be answered? The questions still remain.'

'Legitimate questions, yes. But not those imposed on me out of your own private agenda . . .'

'I'm not working towards any agenda. I just want to find out the truth.'

Dr Govinda snapped, 'This is an investigation of national importance and I will not let you manipulate the committee's work and reputation just because you want to score points by discovering a disease that does not exist.'

Sam locked her glare into his. For her theory to be taken seriously, she would have to find the missing pieces of the puzzle and prove the damn' thing point by point. Till then, she would lose every argument and every politicking manoeuvre.

Govinda gathered the bundle of papers and disks that comprised Ben's file. He turned and strode out of the room.

He did not know that she had scanned and copied everything on the file into her personal encrypted database. Sam smiled thinly.

On a notepad, she jotted a list of names. People she might follow up who had known Ben or who had had contact with him in his last weeks. Mei-Hong – wife. Dr Wyndham – treating doctor. Ginny Wyndham . . . Sam paused, her heartbeat in her ears. She thought of Ginny Wyndham as she had seen her that night in Petaling Street, glowing with the heat of love. A knot twisted in Sam's gut but she clenched it into defiance. She wanted to meet this woman. She underscored the name twice.

Sam wrote a final name on the list: Fei.

Dean slouched down in the car. He had not been able to get close enough to the coffee-shop without being noticed and was parked across the street. It was midday. The air-conditioning hummed out tepid air. The heat with the tinted windows wound up was stifling. Through the passing traffic and a gap between vehicles in front of the shop, he could see Fei and Ginny. He could not use the zoom mike inconspicuously in this setting and had to make do with visual surveillance.

He had seen them at Ben Chang's funeral. He had seen them meet for business at Fei's office and in the evenings mostly at the Wyndham apartment and once at Fei's condo. He had never managed to get closer than the street outside and it gored him.

He had also noted Ginny's various overseas trips with Siew. It was well-known by now that the Wyndhams were working with the AVA in implementing their community-based social therapy with all who might want the service. Dean's journalist contacts told him of the most recent press release from the Centre. Ginny's next trip would be to Osaka to meet family-concerned organisations there. The contract would be to create a therapy to address falling marriage rates, increased divorce and the rising number of children born out of wedlock. The rest of Asia was watching this development with interest. The aim was to implement the therapy in schools for fifteen to eighteen year olds, teaching them the value of commitment, parenting skills, respect for the institution of marriage and the social shame of divorce. Siew's personal presence underlined the importance of the mission. It was more crucial than ever that Dean gain the access he needed to the Wyndhams' work.

He glared out at the hot day. The coffee-shop's specialities were spelled out in red lettering across the windowed chopping counter at the front – 'Roasted duck: best in all KL' and 'Char Siew: like your mother's one'. The Sunday crowds were full of families and young couples with mobile phones. He had followed Fei in her gleaming Mercedes from her condominium. She had arrived first. The only table available had been out on the 'five-foot walkway' fronting the shop. Ginny had come in a taxi ten minutes later.

Fei leaned on her elbows, clasped hands by her cheek. Ginny had moved her plastic stool to sit adjacent to rather than opposite Fei. Their torsos were inclined towards each other, Fei tucking her chin into her shoulder to glance at Ginny. Ginny was in a loose shirt and khakis. Her hair was unstyled. Without make-up, and with her sporty build, she might have been mistaken for a feminine boy at first glance. Fei was sleek even in jeans and crop top, a touch of lipstick adding to her allure. Dean found himself watching only Fei, taking in every movement of her body, every change of her expression.

Ginny looked at Fei askance, shifting her body coyly, as Dean had often seen women do when flirting with men. She was teasing Fei, Dean guessed, and then a burst of laughter from Fei, her Oriental eyes disappearing, her nose wrinkling. An open-mouthed, easy laugh. She shook her head as if to say Ginny had won, looking down. Then up again from beneath her lashes, with a smile that caught Dean's heart.

He lifted the camera from his lap and fired off a couple of shots.

After the meal, the women walked to Fei's car, crossing the road in front of him. Ginny's hand was on Fei's back, in the patch of caramel skin where Fei's short top pulled away from her jeans. Fei did not move away from the touch. Dean took more shots.

His mouth felt dry. He forgot the stifling heat. The women were very close, heads bent towards each other. As he had first seen them together at the inauguration ceremony all those months ago. Fei was smiling as if she couldn't stop.

He followed her Mercedes through the traffic. They were heading for Fei's apartment. He pulled up some distance behind as Fei's car swept into the basement car park.

Dean parked round the corner under some frangipani trees. He stood in the shade, the fresh air a relief after the closeness of the car. Even though it was Sunday, the whirr of machinery sliced into the afternoon. Fei's block was one of several that had been completed over the last few years. New towers had sprung up around the area, some breaking the view down the slope towards the centre of town. Work was continuing apace in most of them, in spite of the economic downturn.

Dean's options were slightly wider here than when the women went to the Wyndhams' apartment. Tight security in that exclusive block meant he could never get internal access. He had tried the high-rises neighbouring the Wyndhams' suite but in that upmarket part of town they did not tolerate un-authorised persons trying to gain entry. Besides, the privacy of the Wyndhams' block was protected by mirrored glass that gave no view into the apartments.

But here . . . Dean waved a fly from his face. Sweat trickled down his back where his shirt did not cling to his skin. He squinted into the light. These last weeks, he had come to read every nuance between Fei and her lover. He scowled. He had never looked properly before, had arrogantly thought them just friends. His ego had got in the way and he had seen only what he had wanted to see. He shook his head in irritation. The photos he had so far proved nothing more than close friendship between two women. He had to see more if he was going to get the lever he needed.

Dean looked down the slope at the sprawl of KL in the distance. In front of Fei's block was an unfinished tower block, its twenty or twenty-five storeys half-dressed. The top floors were still open to the elements, the bottom two-thirds encased with glass and walls. At the foot of the development, the gates and fencing were sealed. Dean had not seen work progressing there for some time now – one of the first casualties of the economic crisis, poor bastards. Then he looked up at Fei's block. Her apartment was on the tenth floor. He grinned suddenly. He calculated that, allowing for the slope of the ground, the eight-eenth floor of the unfinished block would give him the best view into her rooms.

He grabbed his camera and hurried down the street. At the

perimeter of the abandoned works site, the high chain-link fence was interlaced with barbed wire. Climbing it would be to risk being shredded. Dean worked his way round the whole site. The fencing was additionally wired with alarms. The only course would be to cut his way in without disturbing the alarm settings. That would take time and tools he did not have with him. Dean swore. He would have to come back under cover of darkness, work to gain access, cover it up again for when he next needed it. And hope to hell there would be a next time.

<hr />

The vast open-plan floor was sealed from the heat of Indonesia and climate-controlled to a more temperate level. Han sat at his bank of computers, one terminal among the hundreds stretching out in white rows for as far as the eye could see. This was the tecchies' base at the Family's secret headquarters several hundred miles out of Jakarta. He had been here for almost three months and every day was a day in air-conditioned hell. He fidgeted as he number-crunched, sliding back and forth on his wheeled chair, cracking his knuckles, tapping the desk furiously with a pen. The regular research tecchies to either side of him could purse their lips as much as they wanted but by now they knew better than to confront him.

Raul and other Snakes had been called in to Indonesia since the rioting and looting had overtaken the city following the collapse of the *rupiah*. Unemployment had worsened, businesses collapsed, thousands were left destitute and starving. Protests against the government had turned into full-scale confrontations with riot police. Over the months, the riots had escalated into violence between ethnic groups. Chinese shops were burnt to the ground or looted, the owners hacked to death. Christians and Muslims battled each other with illegally obtained weapons. There were rumours of ritual cannibalism reviving, tribal groups in provincial villages gnawing at the body parts of their enemies. Out there in the heat was where the action was. It was where a

Snake should be, Han had stormed at Mokhtar: if Han was stuck in the Family's backyard, then at least he should be used at a time like this. But, no, *Bapa Tua* had been adamant. Han was to sit this one out.

The AVA spoke in the press of Western conspiracies to destabilise Asia and incitement of the rioters by the CIA and other foreign elements.

Han let out a string of obscenities. He slammed back in his chair and stretched. His screen flashed a message. Incoming data. Without enthusiasm, he clicked on to the relevant screen. The stuff was from the Snake in Washington. The first legible words were being de-encrypted.

'Re: Dean, Carson.'

Han was alert now. He rolled closer to the screen, still and silent. The tecchies around him looked up in surprise but he ignored them. He had been waiting months for this feedback.

There had been no response through the tecchies' normal routes of enquiry. He had had to ask the Snake in Washington to do some digging informally. This message was the result at last.

Han slammed a fist on the table. His keyboard jumped. Heads turned.

There was no record of Dean in the FBI personnel files. The details on the badge he had flashed did not correlate to any issued to their bona fide agents. The Snake in Washington had learnt that an unnamed third party had taken Han's query out of the Bureau's hands and referred it elsewhere, apparently for authorisation to respond. None was given. The Snake had pulled in a series of favours to get this much on Dean.

Han scowled. Who the hell was the third party? Obviously somebody with higher authority or jurisdiction than the Bureau. What was their interest in Dean? Were they protecting him? Hiding something?

The Snake had also double-checked Dean's story about Wyndham. There was no Piers Wyndham on either police or FBI files. But there was information on a shooting in McDonald's at about the time Dean had indicated. It was attributed to one Justin Lovelace. But FBI and police files had subsequently been closed when Lovelace was located a few years after the shooting. He'd resisted arrest and been killed in a shoot-out with the FBI.

Han frowned. What the fuck was going on?

'We're all still shaken by what happened,' Ginny looked up. It was two days after her return from the trip to Osaka with Siew.

Sam met her gaze. Ginny was sitting behind her desk, a view of sea and palm trees behind her. She clasped her hands like a priest, her face shadowed against the light. Her voice was carefully modulated. It was the voice that all mental health professionals used, Sam thought. 'Ben was a brilliant young doctor. The patients loved him.'

Sam nodded. She made herself sit back in her chair, posture relaxed. She glanced casually round the office. It was neat and efficient, cosy in a professional sort of way. Nothing out of place. Exactly how you might expect Ginny Wyndham's office to look. Sam could hear the buzz of the Centre beyond the open windows. They were happy sounds – voices, music, laughter, birdsong. It felt strange being here. This was a room that Fei knew, had spent time in. But it struck Sam that this was not a room where Fei would have known the real Ginny.

The woman sitting in front of her was polished and charming, elegant in a well-cut suit. She had the distant friendliness of someone well versed in dealing with the public. Sam remembered the Ginny she had seen in Petaling Street. That woman had worn little make-up and her manner had radiated nervy energy. That Ginny had seemed awkwardly happy, like a teenage boy on a first date. Sam watched her with a steady gaze as if to catch a glimpse of that other woman but found only cool amiability. She could not see what attracted Fei to Ginny Wyndham. There was a reserve about her, a propriety and respectability that left Sam cold. She was too different. But maybe that was it. Ginny was the opposite of Sam and that was what drew Fei to her. Sam felt an ache in her gut.

She made herself concentrate. 'Can you tell me anything about Ben's condition that might have contributed to the accident?'

'It was all gone through at the inquest. You have the report, don't you?'

'These enquiries form part of the CJD investigation . . .'

Ginny looked surprised. 'But it was a traffic accident.'

'Because of his connection with the school in JB affected by the outbreak, we have to tie up some loose ends. I've already spoken with Mrs Chang . . .'

'Mei-Hong?'

Sam remembered Mei-Hong the night before, puffy-eyed and drawn, becoming more and more agitated. She had not made much sense, crying hysterically at the end of the interview. It had been a disaster, her parents rushing in, her father bustling Sam out. She would not have much longer before a complaint reached Govinda. She had to get what she could out of Ginny before he or anyone else put a spanner in the works.

'What did Mei-Hong say?'

'It would be a great help if I could hear your professional opinion of Ben's condition?'

Ginny seemed to assess her for a beat. Then she nodded, her voice taking on its careful tone again. 'He was ill. He had a nervous breakdown. We thought he was better, so we let him go home for Christmas.'

He was ill, he had a nervous breakdown. The words in Mei-Hong's voice had had an edge of distress. *They thought he was better so they released him for Christmas.* Her face had crumpled, tears welling.

Sam studied Ginny. Had they both used the same words or was her memory telescoping the two encounters? She said, 'Had Ben eaten at the school?'

Mei-Hong's hysteria had risen at that question. *I don't know anything, why do you ask me all these questions? He didn't know anything, he was just under a lot of stress.* What had she meant: he hadn't known anything?

Ginny said, 'He may have had meals at the canteen. He was there in the month leading up to the therapy, supervising the physical education schedule and the diet preparations.'

'Mei-Hong said to me that Ben was a kind man, that he wanted to do his best for his patients and for the kids.'

'That's very true.'

Sam watched Ginny. She said, 'Mei-Hong said he didn't know anything. She said *she* didn't know anything. What do you think she meant? What is there to know?'

With the light behind her, Ginny's face was difficult to read. After a pause, she said, 'Mei-Hong has been terribly upset by this tragedy, the poor thing. She had to live through it all again at the inquest and now with your questions. I will not indulge in speculation as to what she may or may not have meant. I want to help you, Dr Ryder, but keep your enquiries to the point.' She smiled again to soften the harshness of the words.

Ginny felt rattled. There was an ease about Sam that unnerved her. Her manner was direct and confident, gaze unswerving. Her complexion had the tanned healthiness of a sportswoman and she moved with an unconscious sexuality. Ginny could not take her eyes off her. All she could think of was Sam with Fei. Ginny felt an abyss open inside her. Had Fei really not seen Sam since their relationship had ended? How could she not have? Had she really given up Sam for Ginny? Absolutely? Completely?

Sam said, 'Tell me about the treatment prescribed for Ben?'

'I'm not medically qualified. You'll have to ask my husband – he was Ben's supervising physician. I'm afraid he's very busy and can't be disturbed, though I'll suggest to him that he telephones you.'

'Please do. I need to know if he was aware of any symptoms associated with motor-neuron degeneration or brain dysfunction.'

Ginny felt her heart stumble. 'What do you mean?'

Sam described the motor-coordination problems and dementia that had affected the school children. She listed symptoms that accurately described Deng, the keeper at the Sanctuary. She gave the symptoms presented by the two subjects in New Delhi. She could not have known the adults and yet she knew what they had suffered. Ginny kept her voice steady only with an effort. 'Ben didn't have any of those problems.'

'In his state of mental collapse, could some of these symptoms have been misdiagnosed or overlooked?'

'Are you trying to say that Ben had what the kids had? CJD?'

'Or something similar.'

'But why? What makes you so sure?'

'A sample of brain tissue revealed deposits of an unidentified protein . . .'

'Brain tissue?' Ginny fought a tightening in her throat. 'But I don't understand. The inquest . . .'

Sam began to explain an administrative procedure the CJD Investigation Committee had set up but Ginny was hardly listening. All she could think was: Sam knew.

And yet she did not know. No one had tracked the trail of biochemical evidence so close to the truth before. The facts stared Sam straight in the face. Her conclusion that would determine all their futures. She might not make the connection to the overall picture – after all, how could she? She knew nothing about the Centre beyond what Ginny and Piers presented to the world. Ginny could let her leave, never tell Piers or Siew exactly what they had talked about. It was not for her to make the judgement, her hands would be clean then, whatever happened to Sam. And, possibly nothing would happen. She might make no headway with her enquiries, cause no more than a momentary ripple in the whole scheme of things and then what she knew would no longer matter. But she knew and that was enough.

Ginny stared at Sam, cold certainty seeping through her. What she knew made her a threat to the Centre's work and to the success of the Cure. It made her an enemy to Siew's Final Phase and the Alliance tolerated no one who stood in their way. It might as well be settled now as later, Ginny thought suddenly. And it might as well be she who did it. Settled it for her and Fei.

Ginny interrupted Sam with a gentle movement of her hand. She picked up the phone, overriding the video link.

Piers answered, brusquely as usual. She said, 'Darling, there's someone here I think you'll want to meet.'

Her public voice was a signal to grab his attention. 'Go on.'

'It's Dr Sam Ryder. She's asking about Ben.'

'Stick to the story . . .'

'I know you'll want to talk to her.' Ginny spoke it like a command. 'Right now.'

Chapter Nineteen

Piers pored over Sam's papers and data, probing her on her wider research. She seemed reluctant to give away her methodology but spoke in general terms about her theory of a prion epidemic across Asia. His knowledgeable responses drew her out as they hunched over the file she had brought with her. Much of the medical jargon meant little to Ginny who stared unseeing out of the window. Sam seemed excited to speak with another doctor who was taking her hypothesis seriously, especially when she'd learnt of Piers's expertise in neurology. He played his part perfectly. He always did. Sam would never know he had just come from supervising Project Max. Ginny did not know the details but the tension of the team as they shuttled back and forth between mission control and the trance suite told her all she wanted to know. Whatever Project Max was, it was safer to be out here in the real world.

Piers showed no anger or stress, only the passionate interest of a scientist. He allowed a few softer touches when speaking of Ben. 'He was like a brother to me.' It was his usual line.

'Thank you for coming to us with this information.' He held Sam's hand in both of his. 'The discrepancy in the amino acid sequence is a wild card but I can only think that Ben must have eaten at the school canteen. We will be taking legal advice as to what compensation Mrs Chang might obtain from the governors. Money will not bring him back but it may be of some help to her.'

By the time Ginny walked Sam to her car, it was one-thirty.

After the cool of the office, the day was blistering hot even with the sea breeze. Ginny felt the sun on her skin but it did not warm the ice in her veins. She was aware of Piers watching them from the first-floor verandah. Sam did not look at her as they walked.

Ginny said casually, 'I gather you know the Centre's lawyer?'

Sam said nothing.

'Fei-Li Qwong.'

Sam unlocked her car then turned to face Ginny. She smiled as if to say: I wondered when you would bring that up. 'You know very well that I do.'

Ginny flushed and looked out to sea. Sam knew of her relationship with Fei. How? Had Fei told her? But she had not seen Sam since the break-up – or so she had assured Ginny. The warmth in her face increased with anger and the shock of betrayal.

Sam said mildly, 'What do you want to know?'

Ginny tried to gather herself. There were so many questions she wanted to fire at Sam. But she was afraid of the answer to the one question that gnawed at her. She had settled her jealousy by offering Sam up to Piers, like Salome's gift to Herod. Piers waited now to tell her what would be done. She felt loathing and anger, not the satisfaction she had expected. She had betrayed Fei. And Fei had betrayed her. Unless . . . unless Sam had found out some other way? If that was the case, Ginny would need to know how, plug the source before anyone else found out. But even as Ginny grasped at that one hope of Fei's innocence, she knew it did not save her.

Ginny had thought once that she loved Fei with all her being. But the love she had was shrivelled and decayed. It had fed till it was glutted on Fei's energy but its vigour could not be sustained, shrinking and dying even as she longed for more. And how she longed for more! More of the passion Fei gave her, more of their lovemaking, more of being alive, more of Fei, her life, her thoughts, her laughter, her confidence. More until she owned Fei's mind and body and soul. After a pause, she said to Sam, 'Do you still see her?'

'Sure, occasionally.'

Ginny felt the truth like a barbed wire in her heart. 'Do you still get on?'

'Sort of.'

Ginny took a breath. 'Did you love her?'

Sam said quietly, 'Yes.'

Finally. She had come to it. 'Before this' – a gesture that encompassed their present lives – 'before this, did she love you?'

'Yes. Once.'

'Does she still love you?' Ginny could hardly say the words out loud.

Sam stared at Ginny curiously. She thought of all the times she had seen Fei since she had moved out. Their arguments had eased off and they were – amazingly – getting on well again. There was something there still, beyond mere friendship. So many times she had almost kissed Fei. If she had, Sam had a sense that Fei would have responded. But a foolish notion of honour and doing the right thing always stopped her. Sam made a face and looked away. There was no going back. But it cheered her that Ginny had had to ask. If she didn't know who Fei loved then maybe there was still a hope for Sam. She couldn't stop a smile from tugging at her mouth. It would be so easy to squash Ginny. *Yes, she adores me, didn't you know?* And watch her fall apart. But what would be the point?

Sam said, 'She's crazy about you.' It was the truth after all.

———➤●◄———

Back in Ginny's office, Piers was waiting at her desk. He sat straight-backed, arms on the rests, both feet on the ground. 'Ryder's in the medical wilderness with her theories, otherwise she would have got closer to the truth before now. That gives us a little time. But not long. I want your file on her.'

Ginny gave him the access codes through the several levels of security clearance.

'Ricky will work on her Double Alpha reprogramming

schedule and scripts with the psych team after Project Max is completed. We'll have the bitch on a leash then. It'll be good groundwork for Phase Four – we'll need to have mastered all the personality types by then. P-Four needs to be perfect.'

Phase Four was six months away, the small-scale try out before the Final Phase. After that, they would have two years to go. Siew had kept bringing forward the deadline for the Final Phase from the initial five-year lead time. More than ever, he needed progress before there were other security incursions. He had received death threats from Westerners and pro-Western Asians for his outspoken derision of their ideals. The Alliance had chosen its moment to lure Asia into the den. The economic slide was avalanching. One of Asia's largest investment banks had collapsed. The *rupiah* was in free fall, Indonesia riot-torn. Asia was in shock and amid the wide-scale panic the Alliance tapped people's fears and sense of impotence with their pronouncements on Western conspiracies, foreign agents and enemies within. The only salvation was through the path of Asian Values. Friends, colleagues, families and lovers found themselves taking sides in the controversy. Asia was being divided into those who were followers of Asian Values and those who were not.

'The time is ripening,' Siew would almost croon, his eyes bright with excitement. Since Ben's death, his obsession with the Final Phase had intensified. His language, especially to his ardent flock, was taking on a prophet's cadences. 'At the day of reckoning, the wheat will be separated from the chaff. But all will be saved. All will be Cured. None shall be left to the enslavement of their own will. For the Alliance is compassionate and we will be the saviours of those who cannot – or will not – save themselves.' He spoke of little else, goading Piers and his teams to the limit. He had sacrificed Ben for his vision and now he would let nothing more stand in his way.

Piers's eyes roamed the room. He had had little sleep in the last weeks, working like a man possessed. Now, with Project Max in hand, he seemed even more assured, more dangerous. His lips were tight with fury and satisfaction. 'Ryder was under our noses all the time. All her hard work – and the only thing it's got her is the promise of a new life.' He smiled thinly at the joke.

Ginny said nothing. She could not speak. Her chest was tight and her pulse raced. Fei loved her and Sam had acknowledged it. Ginny had got what she wanted. She had won. And yet the abyss cracked wider.

'What about Fei-li? What does she know?'

'Nothing.' Ginny met his gaze, startled. It was as if he had read her mind. Panic made her dizzy. He was going to ask her about her file on Fei. She had dreaded this moment for so long. She had to protect her lover. And herself. But how? Her thoughts spun. Ginny closed her eyes as if to close her mind. She felt herself steady, sensed the still floor beneath her feet.

When she opened her eyes, Piers was watching her. He came up very close. His features seemed softer. The zealous mood appeared to have fallen from him. He put one hand to her cheek. 'How's Fei-Li's file coming along?'

Ginny felt the floor fall away again. She managed to say, 'It still needs work.'

'Yes, of course it does.'

They stared at each other. Ginny saw the pain and the love in his eyes. He knew. She felt the bottoming out of terror. But then, he had known for a long time, she realised suddenly. And had said nothing. Done nothing. He was bound to her as she was to him. Even after all this time. Even in spite of his all-consuming devotion to Asian Values and his loyalty to Siew. In spite of the ruthlessness that edged him like armour. She mastered her breathing, swallowed against the dryness of her mouth. For a moment, she saw the old Piers beneath the man he had become. He seemed to look out at her from a long way away, like a hostage from his cell. He began to say something. But the moment was passing and even as the words formed, the old Piers was gone. He said, 'You're not involved, are you?'

'Involved?'

'In anything we might regret?'

Ginny reached for his hand. 'No, don't worry.' It was what they both wanted to hear.

'How dare you harass my client!' Fei stood combatively in Sam's office. In spite of her anger, her voice was low. Sam had locked the door and pulled down the blind for privacy.

'I was following up on some unresolved medical question marks.' Sam kept her voice mild. She had wondered if Fei would show up. 'Did Ginny ask you to come and fight this battle for her?'

'No. She didn't need to. She told me you'd been to the Centre. What did you want? To make a scene with her?'

Sam smiled. 'Is that what this is all about? Not "your client" but Ginny.'

Fei said nothing but Sam saw her flush.

Sam said calmly, 'We had a very civil discussion. Piers joined us and did what he could to answer my questions. But there are still some gaps in the picture. You knew Ben Chang, didn't you? I'd like to ask you . . .'

'What questions are there left?' Fei interrupted. 'The coroner's verdict on poor Ben was clear. What the hell are you playing at? You just wanted to take a look at Ginny, didn't you? See for yourself. Put her on the spot. And I thought that you were being so mature about it. That was just a front, all that cool "who you sleep with is not my business" act you put on the other day!'

'Fei, it was a business visit. Why are you flying off the handle?' Sam shook her head in exasperation. She outlined for Fei the queries she still had on the brain tissue analysis and held out her hands, palms up. 'I promise you, that's all I wanted.'

Fei sat down. She avoided looking at Sam. The explanation sounded logical, but it wasn't just that which reassured her. As Sam had set out each step of her encounter with the Wyndhams, there had been an energy in her words, a spirit of pure enquiry, that was beyond pettiness. Fei had found herself not really listening, tuning in only to that . . . that what? That response that was just so Sam – so earnest and so guileless. It had infuriated Fei before but suddenly she remembered how, long ago, it had once been everything she had loved about her. She hung her head. Sam knew that look. She said, 'So you should be embarrassed. Quite right that you're sorry.'

Fei glared at her but a grin was already breaking through. She rolled her eyes. 'God, I hate you sometimes.'

'The feeling's mutual, I assure you,' Sam laughed.

Fei shifted. 'What did Piers say about Ben?'

Sam told her. 'I just don't buy this food explanation.'

Fei hesitated. She had come to fight Sam for the sake of Ginny. She had wanted clear boundaries between them. She had wanted the past definitely separated from her present. And now, here they were getting on again. What had happened to their confrontation? In confusion, Fei found her fighting reserves empty. This sudden ease together was just like the best times, and was the last thing she wanted now. Fei asked herself what she had really wanted in coming here? The answer was blindingly clear. To see Sam again. That was all. The urgency and determination that had propelled her here as soon as she had left Ginny had been just an excuse. She blinked. She should leave. This was getting too confusing. But she couldn't make herself go. All right, she thought, she would hear Sam out, that was only fair. But she would keep the conversation neutral. 'What do you think of the Centre?'

'Impressive.'

'They do wonderful work there.' Fei started to tell her about the therapies and facilities. It felt strange, making conversation like this.

'You sound like a brochure.' Sam grinned. But she was obviously trying to follow Fei's cue. 'The grounds look vast.'

'There's this ridge, did you see it? There are the most spectacular views from there. If you get a clear day which you can now the Haze is gone . . .' Fei paused. Should she tell Sam what she had seen from the ridge? Ginny had instructed her not to tell anyone.

'What is it?' Sam was gazing curiously at her.

'Well – um – nothing . . .'

'You looked worried suddenly. Like something scared you.'

Fei hesitated. Then she told Sam about the boat and men she had seen from the headland. And about her conversation with Ginny afterwards.

Sam said, 'But why would they have guns as if the immigrants were captives?'

'I don't know. Maybe it was to protect themselves in case they were discovered.' Fei frowned. Her answer did not sound convincing to herself. She thought hard about what she had seen. The men with rifles had been guarding the men in the water, she was sure of it.

'The Haze plays tricks on your eyes, you know?' Fei said, almost to herself. She told Sam about chasing Ginny across the grounds in the fog and losing her suddenly up on the headland. 'Just like that. No sound of a gate or anything.'

And then Fei was talking as if she could not stop. She told Sam about Ginny's erratic behaviour, her swings of mood, the games she seemed to like to play. It was a relief to voice it all at last, to give a name to the nebulous conflict that had hovered all these months. She talked on and on. Went over the strange incidents of stalking, the unknown man who had been asking her family and friends about her, the charade that Dean had played with her, his transformation at the press conference. What had he been after? And the stalker . . . And Deng, grabbing her and spouting about Armageddon . . . And Ben running up to her car out of the swamp, his eyes wild, his clothes torn.

'He was shouting about conspiracies and warning me not to go to the police. He must have really felt guilty about the kids who died. It broke him. Maybe I'm going crazy, too. None of this makes sense. Maybe I'm being ridiculous trying to make any sense of it. All these things – they're all so random, you know, unconnected but at the same time, I feel as if I should be able to find a connection.'

'What?' Sam jerked forward, taking Fei's hands.

She had been listening intently, sitting close. Fei had not spoken about these doubts to anyone before and it felt right that it was Sam who heard her out. Sam's hand had crept on to Fei's shoulder and she had not shrugged it off. It had felt comforting there. Sam's sudden movement startled her.

'What did you say?'

'Sorry?'

'You said it before: "random". *I've* said it before. "Random but not random". That's it!'

Fei stared at her, confused. 'What on earth are you talking about?'

'Factor Q. Its occurrence appears random.' Sam was talking excitedly. 'Apart from the JB kids – and now Chang – most victims were isolated samples here and there. As if picked at random. It's the randomness that's so strange and that's what hooked me.'

Fei could not believe it. She had been pouring out all her anxiety and confusion to Sam and all *she* could think about was bloody Factor Q! 'What's this got to do with anything?'

'The fact that there was no obvious pattern, no immediate scientific explanation. The only thing we had was prion Q. But science is orderly, nature is logical as mathematics. Here randomness is the only consistent thread.'

'I don't believe you. Goddamn you, Sam! I'm telling you things I've never told anyone and all you're focusing on is Q, Q, Q!'

'I *was* listening to you, just not . . . Oh, God.' Sam closed her eyes. She took a breath and looked Fei in the eyes. 'I'm sorry. I'm a complete idiot. I *was* insensitive and I'm so sorry.'

But Fei's hurt was like a gash that could not stop bleeding. Her anger and anxiety poured out. 'You've always been like this. You're like a dog with a bone. You get an idea into your head – whether it's about "coming out and being true to yourself", or "money is the root of all evil", or your wretched *sepak tekraw*, or this Factor Q nonsense. And you just nag and nag and dribble away with that rattan ball and snap at everyone's heels until you exhaust them – and yourself – or they turn on you, whichever come first.'

Sam stood there squirming. Fei's words made no sense to her

own ears but she had to keep going. It all had to come out. She raged, 'You always have to be bloody right, don't you? Give Q a rest! Your colleagues have told you you're wrong, but no, you can't accept it. You have to be right. You have to be the one with all the answers. Why do you always have to be the lone goddam' crusader? What about me? What about us? Why do you always have to cut me out just when we're getting close? It's always been like that. All those years we tried and tried and asked ourselves endlessly what was going wrong. Every time we're really talking again – or so it seems – you go and do something and then we're back to principles and truth and integrity and concepts and everything but what really matters, everything but *us* . . .'

Fei trailed off. She felt as if her mind had short-circuited. She was acting as if she and Sam were still together, as if they had never really parted. As if all the time she had spent with Ginny had not changed anything. Had not changed how she really felt about Sam. In the last weeks, it was as if they had gone back to a time when they had been in love – before arguments and complexities had got in the way. So much for keeping the conversation neutral.

Sam stared at Fei but she was seeing all the times they had argued before, Fei was right. Sam had always escaped into intangibles at the crucial moment. Somehow, they had always felt safer to her. They gave her her swagger and her armour. Just as Fei hardened into her persona of lawyer and businesswoman. Sam hid in the equations of science. She slumped, saw Fei blinking back tears, trying to control her breath. Sam tried to speak but couldn't. She had felt too intensely all her old longing and desire and love for Fei as she had sat there so close, listening to her voice, taking in her distress. She had wanted to rescue her, make it all right for her. She had longed to gather her up in her arms, tell her how much she missed her, how much she loved her. Give them both a chance to do it right this time. But the Pavlovian reaction had kicked in, her mind had hooked on a word, a concept, an idea in all its irrelevance – and out of her mouth had come everything and anything but what she had really wanted to say.

Sam reached out to Fei but she backed off. Cringed away from Sam. Refused to meet her gaze. No, not this, don't go. But Sam found herself without a voice.

Fei shook her head. 'I can't do this. I should never have come.'

And she was out of the door.

Fei drew Ginny down on to the bed. It was the next day, a dull afternoon. She had called Ginny that morning, unable to shake off the memory of the scene with Sam. Ginny had been over-whelmed by the neediness in Fei's voice, had dropped everything and come immediately. Fei had wanted her at her condo. Somehow, it seemed right. Ginny's rage and jealousy over Sam were gone. She seemed happy. It was almost like one of their first nights together. Fei felt relieved. It told her that she had moved on, that Sam was no longer significant in her life. This was a clean start. She had been crazy to think that she and Sam might have any relationship – any friendship – without the arguments starting up again. Things might yet work with Ginny, Fei told herself.

She nuzzled Ginny, peeling off her clothes. There was a glow and excitement in her, shorting her breath, making her tremble. It was as if being here at last, invited here with such urgency, had somehow given her what she craved. She was hasty with desperation, devouring Fei with her mouth, moving like fire against Fei's body.

'Slow down,' Fei whispered.

Through the open windows, the sky was grey. There would be a storm tonight. The breeze lifting the curtains was damp with the smell of rain. Fei opened herself out to Ginny's caress. She loved the freedom of the open vista through the windows. Up here, no one could see them. They did not need to hide behind drawn curtains and shaded blinds. There was only the sky and the flowing air. She thought of afternoons here with

Sam, weekends spent in bed, drinking wine and munching on junk food.

Sam.

Fei leaned up and buried her face in Ginny's hair, licking her ear, nibbling her throat and shoulders. There was only Ginny now, their limbs entangled, Ginny's soft body arching and snaking against Fei's. Fei needed the drug of their passion, longed for it to wash over her. But her mind was clear. The bliss did not kick in. She felt herself going through the motions, playing out the ecstasy like an actor. And all the time her heart was cold and still. In spite of all she did, all the energy she poured into Ginny, she could not lose this strange detachment.

Afterwards she lay with Ginny curled up against her, listening to her lover's breathing. She glanced at Ginny's sleeping face. The mouth was parted. The features relaxed. Curiously, she noted that there was no charm in them now. She had looked into this face so many times before, in a wonder of infatuation. But she felt nothing. This moment had been bound to come one day, she thought without surprise. Today was obviously the day.

Fei stared up at the ceiling. All she could think was: She's not Sam.

⟶➤●◄⟵

In the abandoned tower block across the way, several storeys above the banner that said 'Happy View Luxury Con-dominiums', Dean shot off the last frame. The digital camera could take hundreds more in its memory but he had all the pictures he needed. He had followed Fei home from work after lunch. It was a weekday and this sudden return was unusual for her. When Ginny's car had pulled into the premises, Dean could hardly believe his luck.

He had crossed the street as casually as he could, ducked down through the empty lot beside the works site to a part of the fencing obscured by trees and tall grass. In a moment, he was through the opening he had cut, swiftly replacing the wire. As he had calculated, the alarm remained undisturbed. Then it was up the rough concrete steps, hauling himself over scaffolding the last few storeys where the stairs had not been finished. The next forty minutes had passed in a blur, the clicking and whirrings of the camera filling his head. In the viewfinder, the electronically conveyed images of the two women loomed in his vision. The intimate way they moved about the apartment, their true selves emerging in this apparent seclusion. Their first sexually charged touches. The way their bodies seemed to entwine in a secret dance, slow and mesmerising. Their nakedness and then the sex. At last.

Dean had caught it all. Afterwards he slung the camera over his shoulder. Without the zoom lens and digital light enhancement, Fei's windows were small squares of darkness. He was trembling and his breathing was uneven and shallow. His erection ached. He swallowed against the dryness in his mouth.

He turned and made his way down eighteen floors. As he crossed the works site, the first fat drops of rain began to fall.

Chapter Twenty

Some days before, the re-programming of Parkson Chee had begun.

In the trance suite, Piers supervised the assistants strapping Chee into the chair. The subject had consumed chicken from the infected stock for over a month. The Cure had permeated through the cerebral cortex and diencephalon. A small dose of the chronotonin trigger had put him into a light hypnotic state and he was now docile. The assistants fastened the visor on to his head. It was the refined model with 3-D visuals and stereo sound. A screen on the wall in the trance suite and in Ricky's 'mission control' showed what Chee would see. At present, the screen was blank. They hooked him up to the syringes of chemicals and hormones intended to heighten his experience of the trace, dosage to be synchronised remotely by Piers at the control panel. Electrodes were attached to his limbs and torso. In addition to the passive monitoring equipment, these attachments would pass electric currents in varying degrees to his muscles and heart to stimulate contractions.

This suite was clear of furniture apart from the chair which would later be moved aside. On one wall, a panel of props was secured, to be released in the sessions to come by remote control. There were various models of sub-machine guns, life-like dummies of a female and a young boy, machetes and axes. The room was sound-proofed and reinforced with steel plates behind the white plasterwork. The control panel was protected behind bullet-proof glass. At the bank of equipment were screens linking the operator to Ricky and the sound stage in 'mission control'.

Piers took his seat at the panel. The assistants took their places beside him, monitoring blood pressure, pulse rate and brain activity. The dose of chronotonin was increased and the programming began.

On the first day, Chee was confined to the chair. His limbs twitched and worked against the straps. The monitors recorded tension and movements in the muscles. Piers spoke a continuous narrative into Chee's mind through a mike link to tiny receivers they had placed in the subject's ears. Chee would hear his own voice talking him through the events, telling him how he felt, what he wanted to do, telling him all his thoughts and sensations. He cried out in disbelief and horror at what he saw on the screen. He shook his head, trying to close his ears to the voices. His pulse rate went up, breathing quickened. He was sweating.

As the day progressed, Piers helped the symptoms along with doses of adrenaline and light electrical stimulus to increase tension in the muscles. Insulin was injected to raise blood sugar and corticosteroids to increase heart rate and blood pressure. The reactions of stress were thus mimicked and then intensified and sustained. Chee's subjective experience of what he was watching and hearing became more horrific and emotionally involving. The program being re-written into his brain was etched more deeply, invading the neural networks through the triggered HPrp-gen106. His own memories and thoughts were arrested, then chemically over-recorded by what he was experiencing now.

By the second day, horror began to turn to anger and disgust.

On the sound stage, an actor in her body suit played Ah Fa, Chee's 'little flower'. Another played Max, his image adjusted on screen to the relative size appropriate to a young boy. The psych team communicated with the actors through head-mikes, working from a score of alternate scripts, improvising where necessary in the face of Chee's reactions. The scripts were designed for maximum psychological impact, derived from the research gathered over months of surveillance and investigation into Chee's personality, values and lifestyle. The actors spoke the words and acted the sentiments fed to them even as they listened to instructions over the headphones for the next move. Others joined in as required, one playing Chee himself, another his best friend, another Alfred.

On the screens, Ah Fa and Max interacted with Chee as if they were really there in the flesh. Ricky and his graphics team pasted the background on to the blue screen: roving angles of the Chee's flat. Rocky, the Red Tiger contact in Hong Kong, had broken in one morning and shot off hundreds of digital photos, transmitting them to Ricky by e-mail. Concealed CCTV cameras in each room had been sending every domestic interaction back to the Centre. As the re-programming scenes unfolded, Ricky played up colour, intensity and sound, working in synch with the psych team and Piers. He added music and sound evocations. Adjusted facial expressions to intensify the effect, controlled the voice tones for deeper psychological resonance.

By the third day, they let Chee loose. He moved around the empty suite as if about his own home, detouring empty spaces on the floor where furniture he saw would be. The same version of events was played over again as it had been throughout the last few days. Each repetition had modified the same scenario, made it more horrific to his subjective mind. The external controls of his physiological reactions were underpinned by the constant narration. By now, he was ranting and shouting at the phantoms he believed to be real.

Ah Fa laughed on the screen, kissing Alfred as they rolled naked on Chee's bed. She let Alfred take her from behind. Piers added a small dose of amphetamine sulphate or speed. Chee careened around the room, punching at the air repeatedly. He was manic now, his movements jerky. Poor bastard, Piers thought, he had been completely taken in by Alfred, a Red Tiger conman who had played his part to perfection.

Later, Max made seductive, obscene gestures to Chee, his seven-year-old body enhanced to sunlit beauty by Ricky. Piers administered a powerful shot of freebase cocaine – cocaine without hydrochloride salt, prepared by alkalinisation and chemical extraction. Chee suddenly stood still, taken by the rush of intense euphoria the drug would be giving him. Piers's assistants monitored an erection. He directed Chee to jerk himself off. Chee struggled a moment and then obeyed. Max on the screen did the same. Ricky tuned up the glow. When Chee came, Ricky gave the boy's image a simultaneous climax.

The down-swing of the freebase, or crack, came within a few moments. The monitors showed increased body temperature, sweating, trembling. Chee would be feeling panic, anxiety, anger and stress. As expected, he began to cry and scream. Piers's narration through the electronically engineered voice was no longer needed. Chee knew what he felt and it was all going to plan. He shouted abuse at the boy on the screen. 'disgusting . . . evil . . . the devil . . . who taught you such evil? . . . monster . . .' Max only laughed and Ah Fa joined him, both laughing at Chee. 'Don't be such a prude, my darling,' Ah Fa said.

The next day, Piers hardly needed to speak into the narrative mike. At the point of the downswing, he told Chee about the weapons and the subject saw them. Chee grabbed them in turn. The dummies came into play here. The axe and machete were simple. He swung them with wild rage, splitting the dummies till there was nothing left but debris. The impact of each blow gave him what would be described as satisfaction. Piers noted only a decreased heart rate, slowing breath. The release of endorphins, marking an easing of the stress. Later, they directed him to the machine guns. He sprayed the room with blanks, screaming with frenzy, the noise ear-splitting. On the screen, Ah Fa and Max exploded in red pulp and gushing blood but stayed upright, laughing in his face. Chee pumped magazine upon magazine at them and only after several rounds did they fall to the ground unmoving.

Project Max was going perfectly. Piers thought. And the Red Tiger bugs of the apartment had revealed a trigger phrase he could use for the final sequence. 'Your little flower missed her big busy bee today,' Ah Fa would say. 'Buzz, buzz,' Chee would go, showering her with kisses. Piers worked it into all the sessions from then on.

———◦◦◦———

Fei looked out of the window of her cramped office. The Twin Towers gleamed like knights in armour against the brilliant sky. The day looked searing hot beyond the cool of the air-conditioning. She sighed and turned back to her desk. Work had been tailing off recently, the economic decline strangling new developments and projects in the commercial sector that her firm relied on for business. She and her partners had tried to be up-beat about the slowing down but there was no doubt about it, they were all a lot less busy than they had been for a long while.

She had not seen Ginny since the afternoon at her condo. They had spoken on their cellphones but Fei had kept the calls short and superficial, pleading a heavy workload. Ginny was about to go on another trip, this time with Siew's vice-president, Ibrahim. They were due to take the morning flight tomorrow to Manila to meet community leaders there. She would be in her apartment tonight. Fei was not sure if she wanted to see her but could not yet bring herself to break off the affair. Perhaps she had merely been tired and confused that afternoon, especially after the stupid confrontation with Sam. All lovers had off-days, she told herself, and maybe, if she saw Ginny again, they might manage to recapture the heady madness that she remembered.

There was an e-mail, the screen on her computer told her. Beyond the open door of her room, secretaries lounged at their terminals chatting. Lawyers walked around with papers, calling into each other's rooms ostensibly to talk about work but really to chat and look busy. Fei went into her e-mail screen. The mail was from an address she did not recognise and the page was blank. But there was a data file with it. She opened it.

The screen went blank and slowly began to re-form with

coloured pixels. The photograph began to appear in patchy segments from the top down. Fei frowned. She rarely got pictorial mail. Photos were something Sam usually used for encrypting sensitive information but Fei thought it all too cloak-and-dagger to be taken seriously.

As a lawyer, she still put her faith in paper and would send anything important or sensitive in a physical bundle by courier. The picture on the screen was forming. Walls, pictures, a lamp, part of a wardrobe. They looked curiously familiar. Another jagged band of colour appeared, filling in more detail. It was her own flat.

'What . . .' Fei was confused. Was it Sam playing a joke? She scanned the sender's address. No one she knew, she was sure of it.

Bodies began to emerge. Naked skin, pale limbs, caramel limbs, buttock, dark hair. Breasts. Part of a woman's face. In profile. More. Ginny.

Fei felt a shard of ice pierce her gut. The room seemed to spin. A crevasse cracked open beneath her.

Her own face, sideways on.

Fei couldn't breathe. Her heart felt as if it would explode. Chill sweat drenched her.

'Hey, Qwong, you okay?' Stanley Siap poked his head round the door in mid-stride.

'What?' Fei started up. She blinked. 'Sure. No problem.'

She was at the door and closing it in his face. She locked it. Leaned against it. As if in a dream, she made her way back to the other side of her desk. The photo was still on the computer screen. It was fully downloaded now. It was a shot of her bedroom, taken through the open windows. Ginny hovered above her, her face close to Fei's breasts, her tongue flicking at a nipple. Fei was looking at Ginny, caressing her hair. Their faces were clear and recognisable.

Her legs seemed to give out. She sat down in her chair. A text box began to appear in the bottom corner of the screen, placed so as not to obscure any body parts. The message came up.

'I think we should talk, don't you? Cass.'

His voice came out of the screen suddenly. There was a smug, teasing tone to it as it repeated the typed message. It played over and over again.

Fei grabbed the mouse. She was shaking so much she could hardly manoeuvre it but somehow she managed to shut off the sound. She closed down the file. But it was there, an innocuous line in her e-mail application, a disaster about to explode on her hard drive. On the office networked system.

She would delete it. She grabbed the mouse again. But no. She had to talk to Ginny. Dean had got the photo somehow. Was he back in the country or was there someone else working with him? The stalker? How had they taken that photo? But none of this mattered. The fact was that he had the picture. He had had nothing before and now he had his weapon. Fei felt sick with fear and panic. She had to show this to Ginny. Together, they would work out what to do.

Get the picture out of the system, that was the first thing. Fei made herself think. The file was too large to fit on a floppy disk. She scrabbled in her drawers and found the stand-alone Zip drive and a set of 100MB disks. She often used these for storing backups of the documents on her hard drive. She connected the Zip drive to a peripheral port and loaded a disk. She had to get this right. She made herself stop. Took deep breaths. Started again, taking each step slowly. She clicked the mouse with care, read and re-read the prompts. In ten minutes, she had moved the photo and message off the computer on to the Zip disk.

She got out her cellphone and called Ginny.

———— >●<‹ ————

Han dialled up the remote link to the computers in the 'insurance' office he still kept on in KL. He did this every few days to check his tap on Qwong's electronic exchanges. He leaned back and stared down the grids of computers in the R&A suite, the techies' heads like dark moons rising behind the screens. The tap had produced legal discussions, drafts of agreements, chatty personal messages, subscription-only articles from on-line journals – and nothing useful. Han still plugged on with it anyway. It was the only thing he had to work with now.

He had talked to Mokhtar again that week. *Bapa Tua* had never clarified how long Han was to be here in the tecchie doghouse. 'Three months and I've learnt my lesson, I tell you,' Han had said to Mokhtar.

'I'll see what I can do.' It was what he had said the last time Han had asked. And all the times before that.

Han swore. He sat forward, the connection was complete. He keyed into the application that got him the duplicates of whatever turned up in Qwong's e-mail in- and out-trays.

Han opened the list of files and messages methodically, hardly paying attention. The usual boring lawyer's stuff.

Until he got to the photo.

He paged Mokhtar, who was by his side within the hour. At last the bastard was impressed. *Bapa Tua* would have to give Han clearance now – particularly as Dean was back in the game.

By evening, Han was collecting the papers and identities he needed to get back into KL.

Fei sat in the window seat in the study of Ginny's apartment. Beyond the cold glass, the lights of KL glittered like sequins, the Twin Towers and Telecommunications Tower torches against the dark sky. It was almost midnight. Ginny had set off as soon as they had spoken and Fei had met her here in the early-evening.

Dean had called Fei at her office just as she was about to leave. She felt sick with anger and horror at the sound of his voice. It was hard and brutal. He wanted her and Ginny to meet him. She had refused at first but then realised she had no choice. 'Tomorrow morning. Eleven-thirty.' And he named a fast food outlet in a shopping mall in the Bukit Bintang area.

Fei glanced over at Ginny. She had never seen this study

before. It was lined with computer paraphernalia, manuals, files, disks and boxes of software programs. Ginny sat at the monitor, a state-of-the-art black-bodied terminal with a large flat screen. A bank of what Fei assumed were hard-drive processors took up the wall nearest the monitor. The room was dark except for the glow from the screen and the light from a desklamp. Ginny was engrossed, keying in figures and commands, switching between the photo on the screen and different windows showing statistical data and graphs of varying colours.

At first, they had both been frantic, Ginny rushing them in here to play the disk. They had paced the room, turning on each other, turning on the phantom of Dean beyond the silent walls, their voices jagged and merging into a manic chorus. *How could you have let this happen? Why didn't you close the curtains? I didn't want you in my flat in the first place. You called me to come there. You said Dean was gone. What does Dean want? Why is he so bent on destroying us?*

But they had had no time for such queries, they had known that. They had made themselves talk. Go through everything they knew about Dean, analyse every memory they had. Trying to find a handle on him, a loophole to work with.

'His camera's digital,' Fei had recalled. 'He showed me the photo he had taken of me at the ceremony. I asked him. He said it was digital, I'm sure of it.'

Ginny had set to work then. She spoke in jargon, curt with tension. Fei had watched her at first but could not understand what she was doing, each step seemingly so laborious, each spread of figures and names in the tables she pulled up so meaningless.

'I'm analysing the photo for its colour response characteristics,' Ginny had explained. 'Different films have very particular responses to the different wavelengths of light – like how well they pick up reds relative to blues. Such responses are different from the responses of a digital camera where the image results from photons striking the charge couple device, or CCD, a silicon chip at the heart of the camera. If the picture is a digital image, Dean would have no negative. If he has no negative, he has nothing on us.'

'What do you mean?'

'A digital image is nothing but electrical charges stored in a chip. I can create any image I want out of here' – Ginny tapped the bank of processors – 'and I can manipulate it any way I want. I'm going to show that Dean might easily have done the same.'

'But he saw us! That picture is real.'

'So he says. But you and I might say otherwise. And who's to know which of us is telling the truth?'

'But the picture . . .'

'*Is* it real? By the time I finish, no one will know what is real and what is not.'

Ginny had been working for hours now. Fei dropped the venetian blinds so that they were closed off from the world.

Ginny suddenly swivelled round, triumphant. Her eyes were bright, her manner energised. 'You were right! It was digitally produced. Look – I abstracted data-points from different parts of the picture and compared them with known light response calibrations from five of the major makes of camera film. None of them match. So I made comparisons with the photon-CCD colour ratios for digital image production and there's a very close match with one high-end professional brand.'

Fei stared at the statistical chart on the screen but it made no sense to her. Ginny put an arm around her waist. They had not touched all evening. Fei felt a sense of claustrophobia but managed to stop herself from moving away. They were in this together. She needed Ginny to get through it. To get them both out the other side. For now, she had no choice but to focus her energy on the problem. She had time enough after that to work out what to do.

'How does that help us?' She placed her hand on Ginny's shoulder.

Ginny changed windows. The photo came up. But it had changed. 'This is a copy. I've put on different faces.'

They were the faces of women Fei had never seen before.

Ginny went on, 'I got the images from a photo library. They're models.'

The heads were askew and it was clearly a cut-and-paste job. She said, 'I'm going to show that Dean could have put our faces on the bodies of any soft-porn picture he might have got off the Internet. With some work, I can smooth out the image, add shadows. I can correlate the colours not just visually but to the statistical proximity of the original so that no one doing a colour response analysis would know the difference. The whole picture will look so real, Dean could even believe he took it.'

'And without a negative, he can't prove otherwise?'

'Exactly.' Ginny nuzzled Fei's belly. 'We'll get out of this, don't worry.'

Fei embraced her, kissing her brow. Ginny was strong, in control. Fei needed that right now. Ginny looked up at her with glowing eyes. Her face was alive with confidence. Fei had expected her to go into a spiral of panic, coil into frantic tension. But this vigour and certainty – Ginny was a hero saving the day.

She said, 'You go to the meet with Dean tomorrow. Piers is away in Hong Hong – that's good: he's out of the way. He doesn't have to find out about this. I have to keep that engagement in Manila with Ibrahim. I can't cancel – the Alliance must never suspect.'

'But what shall I tell Dean?' Fei sounded weak and frightened to her own ears.

'You're meeting him to find out what he wants, that's all. It'll show we're not fazed by him. Don't let any of this out of the bag.' Ginny indicated the computer. Fei thought how strange it was that their roles seemed to have been reversed. Ginny evidently relished it.

Fei nodded.

Ginny said, 'Tell him you'll relay to me what he says and we'll come back to him. Just hold him off for the next few days. I'll transfer this on to my laptop and work on it in the meantime. When I get back, we'll have what we need to cut his balls off.'

The words sounded incongruous in her crisp English voice.

Ginny went on, tapping Fei lightly on her bottom, 'You'd better get home. We have to keep up appearances while this is going on.'

Fei hesitated. Ginny stood up as if dismissing her. Fei let her kiss and fold strong protective arms around her. Ginny's voice was husky in her ear. 'Go on. We'll be fine. Trust me.'

Chapter Twenty-One

Earlier that evening, just after seven Hong Kong time, Parkson Chee stopped his taxi down an alleyway off Shanghai Street. A man emerged from the back of a wedding outfitters carrying a heavy-duty black briefcase. He passed the length of the cab and then opened the boot, tossing the case inside. The boot slammed down and the man continued on his way. Parkson nodded to the driver and the cab drove on.

Outside his apartment building, Parkson unloaded his luggage and the extra case. As the cab pulled away, he turned to go in and felt as if he'd awakened from a dream. The last six hours were a blur, the trip from the airport vanishing like smoke even as he tried to catch it. All he knew was that he was home and what a pleasure that was.

Ah Fa was laying the table for dinner as he came through the door. He smelt *won ton* soup and ginger chicken, his favourites. The apartment was warm and bright after the cold night outside. The TV was on but Max was already up off the floor and running into his arms. 'Daddy! They're going to trick Superman, come, look . . . I beat Anson on his GameBoy today . . . You wanna see my scar? Football yesterday. Jimmy tripped me . . .'

Parkson laughed, burying his face in the boy's sour-sweet smell. 'Hey, son-son, take it easy, we got all the time in the world, *Ah Ba*'s home now!'

'You got me a present?' Max began to scrabble at the

luggage. Ah Fa came up and Parkson smiled up at her. They did not touch but her eyes, beaming at him, told him all he needed to know. Max reached for the black case.

'No!' Parkson shouted, startling them all. He blinked. His heart was racing. He didn't know why. Only that the case was special. Not to be touched by anyone but him. More gently, he said, 'That's not for playing with. Here, look in this one . . .'

Max shrieked with joy at the gadgetry Parkson had got him – a Lego robot, a set of talking, sneezing Furbies and a computer game. Ah Fa said mildly, 'You spoil him.'

Parkson shrugged. 'The deal is going to make us rich, honey sweet.' He spun her round and pulled her into the kitchen for a hug. He was a traditional man and did not like to embrace his wife in front of the boy. Ah Fa giggled like a young girl and kissed him back. He began to tell her about the trip. In the cramped, steamy kitchen it was hard to believe that he'd spent the week in five-star luxury. He remembered the pristine golf course, the lavish meals they had had at the best Chinese restaurants in KL. He saw Alfred at the centre of it all, making them all laugh, talking straight with them on the business side. For the first time in years, Parkson felt as if he had really lived as he deserved during that short week. What memories he had to share with Ah Fa and what inadequate words. 'If only you'd been there, Ah Fa. The island . . . I can't describe it, it was so great. It's small . . . and – and beautiful. Like you, my little flower . . .'

Ah Fa blushed and turned her head coyly. She leant against him, whispering, 'Your little flower missed her big busy bee so much.'

Parkson did not move. Rage sprang up inside him. The hideous images flashed into his mind. Even when he shut his eyes, they were there. He knew her filthy secret. He had seen them together, her and Alfred. He had seen her with other men. When he was out at work, when he was working hard to provide for her and their family, she was fucking her brains out. It wasn't suspicion or fear – he *knew*. He knew because he had been there and seen them, heard them, smelt the stench of sweat and sex.

Parkson stared at Ah Fa. She looked frightened. 'Why are you looking at me so strangely, darling?'

He slapped her. 'Slut!' The impact stung his palm. But he felt a sense of release inside. She would pay for what she had done. Her cry goaded his fury. He began to pummel his fists into her, each blow giving him increased satisfaction. She was gagging, half-sobbing, trying to scream. Her arms flailed to protect herself but they were pathetic against his onslaught.

Max stood at the door, wide-eyed, face crumpling into tears. He looked terrified, bewildered. Parkson felt revolted at the sight of him. He screamed at the boy, 'You're evil, you scum! Fucking filth, you and your whore mother!'

Parkson flung Ah Fa aside, the thud of her fall shaking the floor. With a yell tearing his throat, he swept the pots and wok off the stove, not feeling the scalding juices and flames. The clatter rang in his ears. He headed for the door, picking up the slight boy and throwing him against the living-room wall as he moved. Skull cracking. Thump of flesh against brick. Parkson did not break stride, grabbing at the black case. He knew what he would find in there.

He flicked it open and pulled out the body of the submachine gun. He hardly heard the wailing behind him. He screwed on the muzzle, rammed in the magazine, flipped out the folded butt. They deserved to die. They were sick, evil demons.

Turning round, he squeezed off a round as Ah Fa staggered through the door. She was dragging herself towards Max as the bullets ripped into her torso. Relief surged inside him. She deserved it. She deserved to suffer. He swung round to Max, the boy writhing and groaning on the floor. A second round of fire burst from the weapon, juddering the butt against Parkson's body. Smears of red and explosions of flesh. Parkson swung back and forth like a madman, squeezing off round after round, glass shattering, plaster shooting off, lamps and china and the TV exploding. The bodies jerking and jumping grotesquely as flesh was ripped away and bone splintered. Blood splattered everything.

Silence. A ringing in his ears. Parkson pulling the trigger

desperately. Nothing but gunsmoke. But there was another smell that frightened him. A smell that was permeating his insane rage. It was sickly sweet and thick in his nostrils. He had never smelt that before. Trembling, feeling the rush of euphoria at the justice he had executed, Parkson stood still, breathing hard. The smell reached into his belly, filled his lungs, spun his head. It was the smell of blood.

He stared at the mangled corpses of Ah Fa and little Max. They were hardly recognisable. What had he done? This was a dream, it had to be. But he knew it was not. He had been possessed like a maniac, hardly remembered what had happened, how it had all started. The smell made him gag. He stared at the weapon in his hands. How had he got it? How had he known how to use it? He threw it down with a cry and stepped towards the carcasses. They were hardly human anymore, just entrails and bones and flesh. Even as he gagged, he was already retreating, stumbling backwards out of the apartment, running out of the door.

He hardly saw the neighbours crowding their doors, diving away from him as he passed. He tumbled down the stairs, two, three at a time, falling, getting back up, running from the terror that was himself. Out in the street, he pushed through the crowds. Above the noise in his ears, he could hear sirens shrieking in the distance. He stumbled on, not knowing where he was going. Only – his feet seemed to follow a route he had somehow chosen in another lifetime. They ran for him, sure and swift, even as his conscious mind darted madly between memory and reality.

Parkson turned down an alley between two high-rise blocks. It was dark and stank of urine. He pushed on. And then stopped.

A face hovered at him out of the darkness, wavering in the glow of a lighter. It was a pale, cold face. Parkson hesitated but spurred himself forward. It was a face he had seen before but he did not know where. It was an evil man, he knew, but he did not know why or how he knew this. He should fear this man but he did not. He loathed him with all his being. He screamed, 'You! You did this to me! I'll kill you! You did this!'

The man stared at him with dead eyes. A movement. Looking down, Parkson made out a pistol in the man's outstretched hand. The butt was facing Parkson. He grabbed it and the man let him take it. Parkson eased the safety catch off, aiming the pistol at the man.

He opened his mouth and spoke. Parkson's own voice came out of the darkness. 'Do what you have to do.'

Piers watched Chee struggling against the trigger words he had implanted in the last stage of the programming. The subject was sweating, eyes blinking. He was breathing hard, his whole being fighting the power of the Cure. He had been meant to turn the weapon on himself in the apartment but something had flipped him into his real consciousness. Fortunately, Piers had implanted alternate instructions that had kicked in, sending him to this alley, even as the subject had thought himself to be acting of his own free will. Piers stared into Chee's true self through his tortured eyes for one last moment. It upset him that Chee had awakened just when he had – that he had comprehended what he had done. Piers had not wanted him to suffer like this. Still, knowing what he now did, Chee would thank Piers for this final *coup de grâce*.

'Do what you have to do,' he said again into the head-mike. Chee's voice spoke the words out of the speaker in his breast pocket.

Chee's eyes glazed over and he turned the gun towards himself. He shoved it into his mouth, barrel pointed up as he had been instructed to do in the lab. As he pulled the trigger, Piers turned his face away. The subject was dead before the sound of the shot faded.

Piers skirted the body and snapped the lighter shut. He slipped the head-mike off. In the confusion of noise and sirens, he was across the street before anyone reached the alley.

In a secret location in the backstreets of Bangkok, Siew flicked off the giant TV screen and turned to the assembled men. The room was darkened, blinds drawn. It was luxuriously decorated with thick-pile carpet, mahogany furniture and Asian antiquities in contrast to the seedy decay in the streets outside. Siew's hand-picked aides lined the walls. The setting said to the Alliance's guests: We have the means to make a Shangri-la amidst chaos – just for you, just for tonight.

The six guests were still in a state of shock. The live transmission of Chee's rampage, from the point when he had arrived home, had been relayed to them via the CCTV cameras in the subject's flat and 'specially installed cameras in the alleyway. Siew was impressed. Piers had thought of every last detail, down to that nice dramatic touch with the handgun. It showed the guests who controlled Chee, even in the subject's desperate attempt to break from his programmed behaviour.

Siew said, 'You saw the clips of what he was like before we gave him the Cure.'

The men turned to him, still processing what they had seen. They were hard men, thickening with the ease of success. They had seen men killed in war and civil unrest. It was little to them to give the command for bombings, military raids, fatal missions and shoot-to-kill tactics. Among them were five-star generals and the heads of special forces from several Asian nations. But they had never encountered anything like Siew had shown them.

He went on, 'This is what we can make out of ordinary fodder. Think what we can do with a well-trained soldier. A secret force of unquestioning assassins ready to take on suicide missions at your command. Who will stop at nothing. Without fear, without conscience and without independent thought.'

Siew paused to let them take this in. He could tell from their faces that they liked what they were hearing. A few nodded. Some exchanged comments. He said, 'Chee was the prototype to demonstrate to you the basic principles and the possible scenarios.' Siew did not tell them about the compound. That was the Alliance's prime weapon and knowledge of it was on a need-to-know basis. And no one beyond Piers's hands-on teams and Siew's inner sanctum needed to know.

He continued, 'These techniques will be adapted for mass programming within whatever context you choose. Once the infrastructure is set up and the process initiated and maintained, groups of any number can be worked on with relative ease. We can offer different levels of programming from light control through to full personality transformation as you have just seen.

'Costing, phasing and such details I am sure we can finalise in due course for whatever program you might require. Tonight you have witnessed a world first. This is the moment of Asia's re-birth. We shall be powerful again and all our enemies shall be vanquished. In partnership, your forces and the Alliance will create a secure, stable region where only our worthiest citizens will thrive and prosper.'

The aides served champagne. The guests stood and, with Siew, toasted the future.

Later, when the guests had slipped away under escort to their waiting vehicles, Siew linked to Piers in Hong Kong through the interactive module attached to the TV set. Piers looked drawn but upbeat on the screen. Siew said, 'What the hell happened? Why did he snap out of it?'

'We've been reviewing the tapes. My guess is he smelt the blood. It disturbed his consciousness so he flipped out of trance. We'll factor in this aspect to immunise future subjects. I'm pleased nonetheless that the alternate scenario kicked in.'

'Good work.' Siew was already on to the next project. Time was the only external he could not control and it goaded him. They had no margin in which to rest on their success with Project Max. The goal, always the ultimate goal, was yet to come. Move on, forge through to the next phase and they would be one step closer. He said, 'We're on course for Phase Four, then?'

'Absolutely.'

'Enlightenment Utilities has just finalised the water deal with the public sector. We came through with the best bid. We'll be up and running within this quarter.'

Piers nodded. 'You'll have the quantities of the Cure you need by then.'

Enlightenment Utilities was a company within the Enlightenment Industries group. They had just won the bid for the privatisation of the water utilities in the state of Kilming on the west coast of Malaysia. The purification station supplying the town's drinking water would now come under Siew's control.

———⟫●⟪———

Fei got into the taxi that pulled up at the busy bus depot at the edge of KL's Chinatown as Dean had told her to on the phone the day before. The driver said nothing and ignored all her questions. He took a convoluted route, doubling back and taking sudden turns across several lanes of traffic. It was mid-morning and the day outside was already glaring white.

Fei did not know how long she could stand this state of screaming tension. Her head ached. She had hardly slept after returning home from Ginny's apartment. There had been a message from her brother – three of his construction contracts had been cancelled, sending his financial projections into tailspin. She did not have the strength to call him back. Surfing the satellite news channels, she had stayed up till dawn watching news breaking of Asia's economic meltdown. Currencies had been diving for weeks, corporations had been failing and there had been runs on banks. There had been another Asiatic CJD death in JB. Violence was escalating in Indonesia. An accountant in Hong Kong had killed his family and then turned the gun on himself. Several children and elderly people had died from a 'flu outbreak in Hong Kong and southern China. Queues lined up in hospitals for inoculations but doctors could not identify the new strain of the virus. Fei's head spun with images of street battles in Jakarta, bloodied bodies in a Hong Kong apartment, weeping crowds clamouring at a bank in Korea, investors shellshocked outside stock exchanges, anxious mothers with sick children crowding hospital corridors, dealers in bright jackets deflated on the stockroom floor.

In the back of the cab, staring out at the city rushing by outside, she noticed how quiet the roads were. It was as if its populace were numb with shock, unable to move beyond their front doors. She felt as if she travelled through a nightmare, the landscape of Armageddon just beyond her vision. Asia in turmoil, everything they had worked for in ruins. And, unrelentingly, the reality of her own present: Dean's harsh voice echoing in her mind, her whole life on the knife edge between his will and Ginny's bluff. The digital photograph seemed pasted on to everything Fei saw, horrifying in its beauty and terrible fragility. They were bound together now for as long as this threat endured, she and Ginny. There would be no end, no breaking free.

The taxi stopped. They were at a red light at a busy junction. Fei did not know where she was. The driver indicated the battered Ford in the lane to their right. The passenger door of the Ford swung open. She glimpsed Dean's face in the interior and then he was getting into the driver's seat. Fei got out and slid into the Ford. The lights changed and the taxi pulled away to the left. Dean's car headed straight on.

'Where's your girlfriend?' Dean shot at her. He wore dark glasses.

Sam? And then Fei realised he must mean Ginny. 'She's not interested in what you have to say.'

'We'll see about that.'

They drove in silence.

'Where are you taking me?' Fei said with as much authority as she could muster. Dean frightened her. He was not the same man she had trusted months ago. It chilled her to think how easily she had been taken in by him. She felt disoriented, not sure whether this was the nightmare or whether the past was the dream. They were heading out of town.

Dean did not answer.

'What do you want? Money? What have you got against the Wyndhams?'

He ignored her.

Forty minutes later, they bumped off the highway down an

unmade road. The oil palm plantations that had formerly been here had been razed. The land was an endless scar of red earth. Behind them, the motorway receded. All around was emptiness. In the distance abandoned construction machinery stood near the beginnings of a housing development – another fallout from the economic crisis. There was no one to be seen.

Dean stopped the car and they got out. The day was eerily silent. The midday sun scorched Fei's skin. She screwed up her eyes against the glare. Dean came round to her side. She backed away. He said, 'I won't hurt you. You know I couldn't, even if I wanted to.'

His sudden tenderness unnerved Fei. She felt her hair stand on end. She burst out, 'Will you just tell me what the hell this is all about? Please?'

'I need you to help me. I . . . I went about it all wrong. You were different from the rest but I never saw it till it was too late. By then, I'd screwed up. I'm sorry. I didn't want to scare or hurt you. But you're my only hope.' He showed her his ID in a black leather wallet. 'I work for the CIA.'

Fei felt numb with shock. 'What . . .'

'Undercover.'

'What . . . what do you want from me?'

Dean shifted as if trying to shake off his personal feelings. His voice was professional now. 'We have reason to believe that Piers Wyndham – aka Justin Lovelace – is working on secret experiments which are a threat to international security. We have linked numerous deaths, intimidations, abductions and torture to him, both in the United States and here in Asia. My job is to obtain details of his work and bring him back to the United States to face justice.'

Fei's mind reeled.

Dean talked on. She barely heard him. His voice threw words at her which she struggled to comprehend. 'We believe that the experiments are part of a biological warfare programme. He worked on animals illegally and also some human subjects. Our sources tell us he picked up vagrants and abducted loners to use for his experiments – they were kept in cages like animals and tortured in the name of science. Wyndham is also wanted for the murder of police officers and a string of other homicides.'

'Piers?' Fei gasped. 'Are you sure you have the right man? He's distant and aloof and obsessed with his work – but torture? Biological warfare? I can't believe this!'

Dean did not reply. His look said: Believe what you want – this is the truth.

Fei looked out across the surreal landscape. After a long moment, she rounded on him. 'What does this all have to do with me? Why blackmail me now? Go in there and arrest them. Or is this all just bullshit and you really have no case?'

Dean smiled. The old smile. 'Even when you have every-thing to lose . . . you're quite a woman.'

Fei shuddered and stepped back. She tried to bluster on. 'Well?'

'You put the finger on it yourself: I don't know I've got the right man. All we've got is circumstantial evidence. The situ-ation is delicate. What with anti-Western sentiments as high as they are . . . Besides, we're talking international security issues. Not matters we want dragged through the open courts here. This is something for Washington and NATO, to be dealt with under appropriate official secrets legislation.'

'So you wormed your way into my life to get to the Wyndhams!'

'In a nutshell. But you wouldn't kiss and tell. You wouldn't even fucking kiss. So I had to try another approach.' Dean shrugged and took off his sunglasses. He gave her his old 'little boy lost' look. 'I'm sorry, Fei-Li. I don't want to hurt you, believe me. But I have no other choice.'

Fei said nothing. She remembered what Ginny had told her to do. It galled her but she had to stick to the plan. Buy them a few days. 'What do you want?'

'Tell me about the Wyndhams' work?'

'It's community-based therapy. Look in all their brochures – they tell you clearly what it's all about.'

'*You* tell me.'

Fei took a deep breath. She stared to describe everything she knew about the Centre – information she remembered from their publicity material, what she had read in the papers, what Ginny had told TV interviewers, what Ginny and Piers had told her.

Dean was studying her. He was working out whether to believe her or not. She said, 'That's what they do. This biological warfare stuff is crazy! It's libellous . . .'

Dean cut across her. 'Get me details of Wyndham's scientific notes and documents – disks, whatever. What experiments they're working on. What they're planning. What the AVA's involvement is in it.'

'And if I don't?'

'Then I give the photos to the media and authorities.' Dean snapped his fingers. 'And you're both finished.'

'There's more than one?'

'The one you saw was just a taster. There's a whole series. Every little move you two made. Mmmm-mmm.' He licked his lips mockingly.

Fei turned away. The sky was white. Sweat soaked her. The air was thick and heavy in her lungs. What if Ginny's bluff failed? What if this hit the news and got to the police in spite of everything? Her head spun. What about these experiments? And that name again – Lovelace. Dean was CIA! There had to be some truth in what he was saying. If there was . . . what then? Fei's mind seemed to split into two with a piercing pain. Who could she trust? Dean? Ginny? She couldn't think. Work it out later.

She turned back to Dean. Took a breath. 'All right. I'll get you what you want. Whatever it takes. Just keep those pictures out of circulation.'

Dean grinned. 'That's my girl.'

Fei talked fast, giving him what she knew he'd expect to hear. No one went down without a fight and she needed him to believe that she was sincere. 'Ginny will do it. She can get access to everything. Piers need never know till it's too late. I'll make sure of it. We'll get you what you want. She'll want a deal, though. Piers for her. Guarantee amnesty for her and we'll do the deal.'

Dean was impressed. 'You're good, very good. I have no authority but . . .'

'Amnesty. Or I won't be able to get her to deliver. I need her, don't you get it? Piers won't trust me . . .'

Dean seemed to undress her with his eyes. He grinned. 'You and me, we could be good together, you know. I'll get the authority. Gimme Piers and I'll give you Ginny. More's the pity. We got a deal?'

Fei nodded.

'I'll contact you in two days. If anything changes, you can find me here.' He gave her a slip of paper. 'Let's go.'

Dean held the door for her. Fei moved to get in.

He scooped her up suddenly, thick arms pinning her to him. His huge body was hot and suffocating. His mouth engulfed hers, hard tongue thrusting. She felt his erection stiff against her. Nausea rose. She couldn't breathe. She struggled but he held her like a vice. He arched her back, off-balance, his bulk looming over her.

She bit down on his tongue. Hard. Till she could taste blood.

He roared, his arms loosening, and pulled away. In that moment, she jabbed her bunched fingers into his erection, nails digging in, then let him loose. Dean stumbled back, clutching his groin and mouth. Fei stood breathing hard, weight on both feet, coiled with fury. Blood with saliva trickled down her chin. She spat out the taste of rust.

He gasped for breath and pulled out a gun. Wavering on his feet, he aimed it at her head. His eyes were wild with rage and agony.

Fei said, 'Put that thing away. Don't let your ego get in the way of business.'

He blinked.

'Get in the car and take me home.' She climbed into the passenger seat and closed the door. She was trembling.

Piers met Rocky at the designated noodle-hawker's stall near the safe house where the Max team had been based during the shooting. The rest of the team were now on their way back to Malaysia. Rocky had paged Piers as he had been leaving for the airport.

'The farmer mix all your sack stuff inside feed for other chickens also, not jus' for Max ones. Half his chickens go' the mix-up feed.' Rocky moved away from the stall. Piers followed. The crowds on the busy shopping street jostled them.

'Not a problem. The compound's stable.'

'Two his labourers now go' sick.'

'What do you mean? What kind of sick?'

Rocky shrugged. ''Flu. Fever. Vomit. Like the one kill the ol' people and ki's in news las' few day. Chickens also.'

Piers snorted. 'You drag me here to tell me that?'

Rocky bristled. 'You sai' you wanna hear all sickness whoever go' contac' with stuff in sack.'

'You were right to tell me.' Piers made a placating gesture. 'Keep me posted on any others.'

Rocky grunted and disappeared into the crowd. Piers walked on. He felt rising panic. Could it be possible? That somehow the 'flu was related to the chicken feed that had been misdistributed? But gen106 was stable, he was sure of it. Besides, this fucking outbreak was 'flu, for God's sake: there were none of the usual signs of brain and motor degeneration. Piers tried to put it from his mind. But could not.

He took out his cellphone and called Dr Hiew at the main hospital in Hong Kong. Hiew was their AVA medical contact here who had been monitoring the levels of the compound in the chickens sold by Chee's butcher.

'See what you can get on any of those 'flu cases, especially the labourers from the farm,' Piers said.

Chapter Twenty-Two

Fei hung up before the line connected. It was the seventh time she had dialled Ginny's number only to cancel the transmission. She tossed the cellphone on to her bed and stalked the floor. She wanted to talk to Ginny, go over with her what had happened with Dean. But the things that he had told her whirled in her mind. Was any of it true? He had shown her his ID. He was legit, and yet how could she believe that Ginny was involved in sinister experiments and criminal activities? Her mind could not encompass it. Those things only happened to other people. Her mind oscillated between what she herself knew of Ginny and the verbal construct of her lover that Dean had given her. Which one was real?

But the truth was she did not trust Ginny now. No matter how often she told herself that Dean might be wrong or mistaken, his version of things had infected her mind and there was no ignoring it. Everything had changed. She looked out at the world through different eyes and there was no cure. She recalled Ginny's inexplicable changes of mood, her sudden distances after the most intimate times together. She had denied knowing who Lovelace was – had that been truth or pretence? Fei had not pressed her, taking her at face value at the time. But had that been right? Fei massaged her temples. More truth-fully: had Fei been uneasy then, but fobbed it off because believing Ginny was safer than not believing her? There had been untruths not only in Ginny's façade before the public but in her behaviour to Fei herself – she had always sensed them there but had preferred to ignore them. Ginny had never talked much about herself. Fei realised suddenly that she knew hardly anything about her and only the barest outline of her life before the Centre. She thought of all Ginny's emotional explosions – terrible and disturbing flashes of despair or anguish or hatred. She had not asked what lay behind them – she had never wanted to know.

Fei went out on to the balcony. The night was warm but she felt chilly. She had never wanted to know Ginny. Really know her. Because to know the other, deeply and intimately, was to have them live inside you, to draw them into you like a transfusion of life's blood, to be bound to them and them to you. It was to love them. And Fei did not love Ginny. She never had.

Fei went back inside, closing the terrace door against the chill she felt. She did not shut it on the latch. She found the phone and dialled Sam's number. The answer machine beeped on. Fei hung up. Where was Sam? She needed to hear her voice, talk to her. Sam would know what to do. Fei tried Sam's office – the voicemail came on. Damn! She could not let it rest. She scrabbled for her address book and began to call all their mutual friends and contacts. It was as if she were driven by something she could not control. This was crazy, what she was doing, but she could not stop herself. Sleepy, surprised, annoyed voices on the other end – and finally she got the answer. Sam had flown to Hong Kong that night following a call from an epidemiologist at the main hospital there.

She fell asleep at last, fully dressed and half out of the covers of her bed.

Fei woke suddenly. The light was on as she had left it. But there was something wrong. A breeze. She shifted.

A man sat in the chair looking at her.

Fei sat up. Her rapid heartbeat choked her. She scrambled backwards, caught up in the sheets, slamming into the wall and headboard.

'Don't be afraid.' The man spoke it like a command.

She scrabbled for the phone.

He held up her cellphone. 'And the land line's disconnected.' He saw her glance at the door. 'Locked.'

She stared at him, struggling to control her breathing. It was the man who had stalked her. The same angular face, the hard gash of a mouth. Eyes dark and penetrating. His muscular bulk filled the whole chair but he sat poised lightly, as if about to spring. The door to the balcony behind him was open. He must have come in that way – via another apartment's terrace or somehow crossing the void from the fire escape. Fei said, 'Wh— who are you? What do you want?'

'Call me Han. What did Dean want from you?'

'Dean?' Fei's mind spun. 'Who . . . what . . . What's going on?'

Han pulled out a picture. It was a duplicate of the one Dean had e-mailed her. He said, 'It doesn't matter who I am. All you need to know is that this is a matter of regional security. I know Dean is trying to blackmail you.'

Fei opened her mouth but shut it suddenly.

Han said, 'Look, I don't care about you. I don't care who you sleep with. We want Dean. You can either help me and we'll take care of Dean and let you get on with your life. Or you don't and we take him anyway and you, too, just for the hell of it.'

'Who's "we"?' Fei remembered his menacing figure waiting for her in the basement car park. His car ramming her in the dark night. The security guards hauling him away at the Centre.

'This is a matter of regional security. I can tell you no more.' Han held up an ID but so quickly Fei could hardly catch it. She saw the government crest and the words 'Security Special Forces'. He said, 'What does Dean want from you?'

Fei could barely think. Han was a stalker. He'd had a nervous breakdown, the papers had said. Was out to discredit the government. And now he was telling her he was a special agent of some kind?

'He works for the CIA,' she said, as if somehow she might use that as a weapon.

Han snorted. 'Or FBI or whatever. He's not CIA. Don't trust him.'

'And I should trust *you*?' Fei jerked her head up in a show of defiance she did not feel.

'You have no choice. If you continue to be uncooperative, we'll arrest you on charges of indecency, conspiracy to de-stabilise internal and regional security, aiding a foreign spy – which by the way amounts to treachery – the penalties range from imprisonment to death. On the other hand, if you work with us, I promise you the photos will never be released and you will secure immunity and state protection.'

Fei felt dizzy. Could she believe him? She said weakly, 'You chased me. Then at the Centre . . . you want the Wyndhams, too.'

Han was silent.

'Oh, God.' Fei slumped against the wall. She felt powerless. 'What's Dean after?'

Fei hesitated. She did not know if this was the right thing to do, going along with Han. But she did not know what else to do. Dean had an arm-lock on her for now, and Han had the same weapon against her and worse. Ginny's bluff might diffuse Dean's hold on them but Han – he had a more frightening arsenal. He probably knew more than he was letting on. It didn't matter either way whom she helped so long as it got her out of the cage they'd shut her in. She took a breath and told him what Dean had wanted her to do.

'Where is he?'

'I don't know.'

Han studied her. Would he believe her? She didn't know why she did not want to give him this last piece of information. Perhaps it was a last vestige of trust she still had in Dean. Or a hope that this stand might somehow give her an advantage over Han, no matter how small. She said, 'He told me he would contact me again.'

'I want you to pass on to me everything you pass to him.'

'Why don't you just haul him in and arrest him and be done with it?'

'I need him where he is. He's not the goal.'

'And the Wyndhams are?'

Han did not acknowledge her question. Fei closed her eyes. The Wyndhams were her clients. Her major clients. As their lawyer she should be protecting them, standing by lawyer–client privilege. But she had compromised herself in the affair with Ginny and now, in her cowardice, she was saving her own skin. Dean was using her. Han was using both of them. When she opened her eyes, Han was watching her. She nodded, 'All right. I'll do what you want.'

He drilled his gaze into her, spearing her like prey. She could only stare back, the bile of fear rising.

'You'll hear from me in a few days.' Han stood up and slipped out on to the terrace. A swift movement and he was over the balustrade. Fei moved to the door in time to see him reach the fire escape and reel in the wire that had been his route across the void. And then his dark figure faded into the night as he seemed to glide down the iron steps.

Sam walked through the corridors of the hospital with Dr David Grossman. He showed his pass at the door to the morgue in the basement and signed her in. The air was chill and smelt of formaldehyde. Outsize steel filing cabinets lined the walls. Grossman led her to one of the drawers.

He was a good-looking Canadian in his thirties, on second-ment from Toronto, a physician and also an epidemiologist like Sam. He had short peroxided blond hair and a single eyebrow ring. They had met at a conference a few years before and she had been immediately drawn to his soft-spoken maverick approach to medical tradition. He was one of the international connections who helped keep her Factor Q database updated. He pulled open the drawer.

Inside was a middle-aged Chinese male. The entire top of his skull had been cut circumferentially to enable the removal of the brain for analysis. Grossman opened his electronic palmtop and called up his notes using a stylus on the touchpad. 'Ping Ren-Hwa, 51, labourer on a chicken farm in Quangzhu. Collapsed with influenza symptoms – fever, chills, headaches, coughing – while delivering a consignment of chickens to a market here. The farm has since been quarantined. Half the chickens have a viral infection and several more workers have come down with similar symptoms. Ping slipped into a coma and died twelve hours later. That's all consistent with severe influenza but there were a few other symptoms that didn't make sense to me.'

'Like what?'

'Before he became comatose, he developed some very bizarre neurological findings: rhythmic cyoclonic jerks in his limbs, persistent nystagmus on eye exam, and re-emergence of primitive reflexes – you know, positive Babinski and the like. So that made me suspicious that maybe something else was going on that was neurological. That's why I sent a brain tissue sample to Pathology.'

Grossman tapped in another command and an image of the tissue sample seen under the electron microscope appeared. He gave the palmtop to Sam. She saw it at once, the same pattern, the same molecular conformation: it was Factor Q. Grossman said, 'I'll download it to your e-mail account – encrypted as usual. It'll be there when you get back to KL.'

Sam's mind was scanning the possible connections. She said, 'The chicken farm. Anyone checking it out?'

'Dr Hiew – he went out there a few days ago. But he's been slow in disseminating the results of his analysis. He's being very cagey about it, God knows why. I'll follow up. We've got new cases of this 'flu coming in every hour. Other hospitals, too – and on the mainland. Primarily kids and old folks but some otherwise healthy adults. There've been a few more deaths. I've got them checking brain tissue.'

Sam nodded.

Grossman closed the drawer. 'The virus found in these victims matches a virus that infects livestock, in this case fowl.

Normally this virus isn't zoonosic – it usually infects only chickens and not humans. In this case, for reasons we do not yet understand, the virus has crossed over into the human population and we do not have a vaccine.'

Sam walked with Grossman back up to the main hospital. 'Q is the unaccounted for factor.'

'You're thinking it's the cause of the 'flu?'

'No, more that its presence in the victim's body could have affected his immune system – to such an extent that he became susceptible to this zoonosis. The other finding that didn't make sense initially was a profound leukopenia. Normally with influenza you would expect an elevated white count, but this man had no lymphocytes. At first I thought it was HIV, but the ELISA was negative. Q must be the culprit.'

'So ordinarily he'd walk past an infected chicken and be fine. But because Q in his system has turned off his immunity, he walks past the same chicken and catches the virus?'

'Put simplistically, yes.'

'But how did Q get there? Who else has it?'

'Q deposits in the brain. There's no way of telling who has it and who hasn't. It doesn't show up on blood tests or through other diagnostic methods. You have to look at the brain tissue and we can only do that after the victim's dead. At each manifestation, it's apparently in altered form, with varying symptoms. This is the first time that the immune system appears to have been affected – or rather, the first time that I'm aware of. There may be other cases of death from 'flu, pneumonia or whatever where no one made the connection to Q.'

Grossman stared at her in horror. 'This could be a timebomb.'

———◆———

Fei hardly dared to breathe. She sat frozen in the study at the Wyndhams' apartment. In the living room, Ginny was talking to Siew. Fei had met her an hour before when Ginny had arrived

339

from the airport after her trip to Manila. Siew had called by shortly afterwards for a de-briefing. Fei heard the rumble of his voice interspersed with Ginny's upbeat, higher tones.

After he left, Ginny came back in. She said tersely 'His second-in-command could have told him how the deal went. He was checking up on me. He does that sometimes. Needs to show me who's boss.'

Fei had been telling Ginny about her meeting with Dean. She resumed, tension making her speak fast. She left out his sexual advances. 'So I have to meet him again, the day after tomorrow.'

Ginny seemed full of nervous energy, unable to stop moving about the room.

'Are they true – all the things he told me?' But even as Fei spoke, she knew she did not want to know the truth.

'No!' Ginny turned on her with anguished eyes. 'I don't know who the Lovelaces are. I don't know why Dean's linked us to them. They're monsters! The work we do – you've seen the work we do: it helps people, it gives hope, comfort . . . You know me, you know I couldn't do any of the things Dean's accused us of! Don't you? Don't you!'

Ginny gripped Fei, her face taut, her voice pitching high. Her gaze burnt into Fei. Her grasp was rigid and frighteningly strong. Fei wanted to believe her, was afraid not to. She nodded. 'Of course I believe you . . . Ginny, you're hurting me.'

Ginny stared at Fei and saw her fear. She wanted to hurt Fei. For her lies about her friendship with Dean. Her lies about Sam. Why was it that it was Ginny who was pleading for Fei to believe her? Fei had been seeing Sam all these months and she had kept it a secret. The knowledge poisoned Ginny's mind. She had confronted Fei and Fei had talked her way out of it, as she always seemed to do. Ginny had let herself believe Fei's justifications. She had forgiven Fei. Now she had a right to expect the same trust and love.

Ginny let Fei go. With a visible effort, she controlled her emotions. 'We've got to disarm him, that's the thing to focus on. Yes, focus.' She opened up her laptop. Narrated each step, talking herself down. 'Password, processing – OK, we're through. Call up directory . . .'

She opened the photograph and new versions of the file. 'I worked on these whenever I got the chance to be alone in my room. It's almost done. Just some fine tuning.'

She switched between windows so that Fei could see the contrast. The first picture was the original. The second showed the two substitute faces welded on to the original bodies. The third was the same as the second but the postures had changed slightly.

'That's amazing!'

'The two modified versions look real enough at first glance,' Ginny said. Her energy now was channelled into nothing but the present task. 'Some shadowing's crude and there's still a two-dimensional flatness to the faces. I need some additional software tools but when I finish, we'll have the counter-weapon we need. I'll show Dean and whoever he brings in on this that you can do anything to digital images, prove anything you want. Given enough time, I could even collate enough different postures to run you a home movie, complete with juddering camera and white spots. Dean has nothing but phantoms in his head.'

Ginny transferred the files from the laptop to her main computer by infra-red link. She keyed in commands and went through a series of decodings and security clearance steps. She said, 'I need to access the mainframe at the Centre for the tools. This terminal has a secure link with it so there's no chance of anyone else intercepting the download.'

Fei took up her place on the window seat again. She felt afraid of the woman across the room. She had not told her about the encounter with Han.

Fei didn't know anymore who she believed or trusted. If the stories Han and Dean had told her were true, Ginny was more dangerous than either of them. But if they weren't . . . She couldn't think. Couldn't make the right choice. She had wanted to call the police after Han had disappeared. But a memory had stopped her. Ben covered in mud, sobbing: *'Don't trust the police.'* She had thought him mad, suffering from a nervous breakdown.

But was there truth after all in his outburst? She thought of Han's mean, cruel face. He was a security forces agent, overriding anything the police could do. They would turn her over to him again. Fei bit her lip. Her only hope of sidestepping Dean and Han lay with Ginny for now. Fei had to get through these next few days bound to her. After that . . . After that, she did not know.

The computer suddenly emitted a series of mocking laughs. *Nyah-nyah-nyah-nyah.* 'Damn him!' Ginny cried.

'What . . .'

'Ricky's locked me out. He's got a firewall up and several levels of restricted access zones between here and the mainframe. I can't get through any of them.'

Fei came towards her. A sneering joker face bounced about the screen. Ginny hit 'Esc' on the keyboard and the face disappeared.

Ginny bit down on the panic inside her. She had to be strong. For both of them. When Fei had first shown her the photo, Ginny had felt strangely relieved even in spite of the horror that had gripped her. It was as if what she had been dreading for so long had at last happened and somehow it was not as devastating as she had always feared. This photo bound Fei to her. It was proof that their love was real even as they needed to deny its truth to the world. It was Ginny's evidence against Fei and any denial she might one day seek to make. It was the catalyst that changed the balance of their relationship. For the first time, Fei needed her. Fei looked to her to save them from disaster. Ginny was in control now. She owned Fei at last.

This knowledge had made her strong. She had taken charge. It was she who could reassure Fei, she who had the answer, she who fought the battle. For so long, she had been passive and obedient to Piers and Siew and even Ricky. Now she was the one who took action and controlled the scenario. Exhilaration and passion had welled inside her. She had wanted Fei more than ever, desired her with a new intensity. That first night in the study, she had wanted to make love to Fei as Fei had come up to her, scared and needy. But she had sent her home. The erotic

342

cocktail of fear and strength and desire had been like a drugged high she did not want to lose. Over these last few days, cut off from the reality of Fei, working on the photo-images, that passion had endured.

Ginny worked feverishly to break through Ricky's firewall. She tried sequences of instructions and security overrides, approached tangentially via other access routes. She searched the reams of programming code underlying the applications. Mocking electronic laughter was all she got. And the bouncing joker's head. She was hardly aware of the hours passing. The screen blazed and swayed, blurred and eased back into focus. Her head and eyes throbbed. Her fingers and arms ached from frantic typing and mouse-work. Her back seemed locked into rigid tension.

The laughter again. The face bouncing across the screen. Ginny slammed on the desk and skidded back on the chair. Damn Ricky! She stared at the screen. Ricky. The little twerp with his gangly limbs and mocking laughter. The names he called her, his swagger and his noise. The damn' music he played at full volume, singing along as he wrote strings of code.

Music.

Was that it? Ginny sat forward on her chair. His favourite band – who were they? Juicer! Ginny exited from the secure link to the Centre and dialled up the World Wide Web. She encrypted her own private files using a photograph of Fei, her favourite from a freeze-framed video image taken at the inauguration ceremony. It was a typical and simple method of security used by a number of programmers she knew. It was impenetrable unless you knew the exact match of the billion pieces of digital information that made up the picture. She hit on the Juicer web site, full of garish photos of the pop group and sub-colloquial text in a mixture of Americanese and English street dialect. She found their music samplers. There were ten buttons to choose from. Ginny stared at the titles. None made any sense to her: 'I want you (like a Nike)', 'Hairy green love', 'Prozac Love'. She massaged the bridge of her nose. What did Ricky sing all the bloody time? Jarring guitars and clashing drums reformed in her mind. The melody was a repetitive chant, eight notes, words croaked unintelligibly. She hummed the tune. The words, what were they? Ginny opened her eyes and looked through the buttons on the screen – there! 'Gimme all your fucking love.'

She clicked on the button and downloaded the sample. Back to the secure applications. She went to the gateway and at the security prompt, played the sample, a wall of noise bursting from the speakers into the silent room.

And she was through.

———————

Ginny stared in horror at the images. She was vaguely aware of Fei beside her. They both watched the screen with rising disgust and fear.

Ginny had easily located the graphics software tools on the other side of Ricky's firewall. She had been about to exit again when she began to browse through Ricky's files. The triumph of getting the better of the little shit had made her bold. She would find out what secrets he was keeping from her. She would know at last what Project Max involved.

Now she knew and wished she did not.

She watched the tape of Chee's programming, edited for Siew. She saw the images that Chee had seen, the wife and child and other man in sexual ecstasy, Chee jerking off before the image of his son. Then she saw the CCTV recordings of Chee's return home, the shooting, the cameras zooming in on the dead bodies after he had run from the room.

A movement beside her. Fei turning away, gagging, her hand to her mouth. Sweating and sobbing. 'Turn it off! For God's sake!'

Ginny keyed in the exit commands. Her fingers could hardly hit the right keys. She was trembling. She stood up but her legs felt weak.

She moved to touch Fei.

Fei backed away, shaking with fear and disgust and rage. 'What the hell's going on? Tell me the truth, Ginny! Goddamn you, tell me the fucking truth!'

———————

At mission control, Ricky sat alone at a bank of computers. He had been working on Sam Ryder's file on the mainframe. She was the next target now that Project Max was done. He had to fit her in before Phase Four and these late-night sessions were as good a time as any.

The intruder alert he had set on the restricted access directories of the mainframe had gone off as he had been working. It was set to run as a police siren and the noise had made him jump in the silent control room.

Ricky had switched on a neighbouring screen and typed in commands to show him where the intruder was in the mainframe. The screen showed a duplicate of what the intruder was seeing on their screen. Over the top of it, he ran the tracer program and after a moment, it showed the identity of the external computer that had penetrated his firewall. It was Gin-Jeanie.

He watched as she ran the Project Max files.

He picked up the phone and called Piers.

Chapter Twenty-Three

Ginny paced the living room, unable to escape from Fei's gaze. She had run out here and stopped. Through the open door, the computer screen flickered in the darkened study beyond, a reminder of the world on the other side of this reality. This was the moment she had feared. And longed for. Fei stared at her, confused, afraid, angry. She had a right to know. But afterwards, after she knew – what would happen to them then? She imagined Fei's horror, her accusations and disgust, judging Ginny, loathing her. Turning from her and their love to betray them all to Dean. Ginny could not bear that. She could not live then. She knew it with a terrible certainty. Without Fei, she could not live.

She stared at Fei's beautiful face. How would she ever be able to hold on to her? If Fei panicked, Ginny would have to stop her. No matter what it took, she needed Fei to stay with her through this. Through into their new lives together. The secrets that Ginny kept from her were like an abyss between them. If she shared them Fei might yet be able to pass over into the void, – give herself entirely to Ginny as Ginny would be doing to her. Ginny longed for release from this fear. Longed to succumb to Fei's embrace. To say: This is who I am, the whole of me, and yet you love me.

Ginny sat on the floor. Fei had slid down into an armchair and Ginny had curled against her legs, one arm across Fei's knee. She felt trapped, sucked into Ginny's relentless gaze. There was such longing in her look – for understanding, acceptance, Fei could not be sure – and such hope. Hope that in telling all this to Fei, she might at last belong to her.

Ginny said, 'I'm Piers's sister.'

'I . . . I don't understand.'

'His name is Justin Lovelace.' Ginny did not seem to hear Fei. It was as if now that she had resolved to tell the truth, nothing was going to get in the way. 'My name is Susan. It was madness to think we could escape who we are. The past caught up with us in Carson Dean. Whoever he is, whatever he wants, doesn't matter anymore. It's survival now. Like it always was.'

'So what he told me was true?' Fei went rigid with horror. But she dared not move. She tried to relax her muscles. Ginny sat entwined against her like a snake.

'There was a time when we were all free. I remember it like an eternal springtime, you know?' Ginny shifted. Her voice held a deeper resonance, as if someone else spoke. She seemed to drift away into a past Fei could not share. As she spoke, it was as if Fei no longer existed for her. 'Piers and I had always been close, even when he was in Europe and America and Singapore doing his research, getting his double doctorates. He married Morgane and went out to New York where she worked as a zoologist. He got a position as a neuropyschologist at the Carl Heinsmann Hospital. I was back in London with a small software programming company – computers were really taking off then and I was in the thick of it.

'Piers couldn't get any interest in his neuro-restructuring hypothesis nor any funding for his research into that area. The medical establishment laughed at him and those who didn't accused him of trying to play God, threw the Nazis' eugenics experiments into his face. Piers was determined to prove them wrong. He set up labs in an old warehouse outside Jersey City, on the edge of the Hudson. He got tramps at first and paid them – twenty dollars and meals – or anyone he could find who needed the money: junkies, prostitutes. You know, people who didn't matter. But there were bad side-effects. Word got out on the street. A few of the subjects died and Piers had to dump the bodies. Luckily, no one traced them back to him. After a while, he used whoever he could find – usually those living alone, the ones no one would miss for a while. He didn't have to pay them then. Just took them as he needed them.

'I didn't know all this then, I promise you, Fei, don't judge me for those times. Piers told me about them a lot later, that's how I know, you have to believe me.'

Ginny fixed Fei with a desperate gaze. A horrible fascination gripped her and all she could do was nod.

Ginny went on. 'It was 1985. The summer. I went out to stay with Piers and Morgane. A two-week holiday – that was all it was supposed to be. I was going to help him set up some visual aid programs for his research. Just on one old computer, wired up with more memory and a faster processor. But I spent more time playing with Katie than at the warehouse. A few days later, Morgane let me take Katie on the train to Manhattan to see the sights. Katie was the most adorable child – blonde, a perfect, happy little girl. Everybody loved her. She was everything to Piers. I took her to Battery Park. We watched the boats, played on the swings. I let go of Katie's hand to buy ice-creams.' Ginny was pale. She could barely speak. She watched the ghosts flicker across her mind. 'When I turned back . . .

'I saw them for a moment in the crowd. His face stared back at me. And then they were gone. Lost in all the bodies and faces and movement and noise.'

Katie's body was in the water for almost a month before they found her, wedged by the current in the struts of an old pier. The police arrested Logan Connelly, an unemployed construction worker. There was no forensic evidence linking him to Katie. The prosecution case relied on Ginny's identification of him. The defence case turned on discrediting her testimony. They questioned her about her single status, whether she had ever had any boyfriends, whether she was in a current relationship, as if trying to probe her character. 'No, I'm not in a relationship,' she repeated twice at defence counsel's prodding.

Ginny looked up at Fei. 'We didn't know then that the defence had hired a private investigator. He'd tracked down Alison in London. Alison . . . there's only ever been Alison and you. She was my passion, my life. The defence had got a tip-off from the handyman who worked for Piers. He'd listened in on the kitchen phone to a conversation I'd had with her. Alison was called to testify, flown in at the expense of the defence. She told the truth. My darling told the truth.'

It destroyed Ginny's testimony. And their relationship. Ginny had lied in court and she was a degenerate, the defence claimed: how could the jury convict on the testimony of someone like that? There had been a recent spate of child abuse cases in the headlines in the months before the trial. A baby had been shaken to death by an au pair. A mother suffering from Munchausen's by proxy had tortured her child and finally killed him. A girl staying with her aunt for the holidays had been found dead. All the accused had been women. Connelly's defence team entangled Ginny's sexuality and lies in the hysteria of those times and Connelly was acquitted. The media tore Ginny apart.

'Afterwards Piers threw himself into his work. He wanted to create a programming technique that would wipe out the likes of Connelly. He wanted something good to come out of what happened to Katie. But he couldn't bear the pain. And he couldn't forget Connelly.

'It was two years after that day in Battery Park. Piers had been stockpiling weapons and explosives ever since he had started his experiments. "No one's going to get their hands on my work," he would say. "If they come for me, they'll find nothing but blood and ashes. They shove me out into the cold, they'll not benefit from the risks I took." He booby-trapped the whole place, ready to wipe it all out if the authorities ever chased him down. He'd been following Connelly for months, charting his routine. He confronted him a few times, shouted at him and tried to beat him up. But Connelly always got away.

'Piers decided to kill him. Morgane and I knew what Piers was going to do and we wanted him to do it. God forgive us, but that was how it started. After Katie died the way she did, no one could know our pain. No amount of sanctimonious mouthings could ever stop it. We felt no mercy, no forgiveness for anyone.

'Piers got a semi-automatic rifle and went for Connelly in a McDonald's in midtown New York. Connelly was hit but he survived. He's like a demon who can never be destroyed, don't you see? Bystanders were injured, some were killed. But not him! Piers escaped, somehow got back to the labs.

'Morgane and I were waiting for him there. We thought that we would be safe. No one knew about the warehouse. But the police followed him back. Two cops came in like Rambo. They didn't have back-up, like they wanted to be heroes. Morgane got hit trying to cover Piers. She screamed his name in warning and the shooting went mad. Piers killed one cop and the other was wounded. Afterwards Piers started going round the place, shooting the apes he used in experiments execution-style. One bullet to the head. Blam. Pause. Blam.'

Ginny stopped suddenly, choking with tears. She ground at her eyes with her hands as if to scrub out what she was seeing. 'I didn't know what to do. All I could see was Morgane, her head at an awful angle, the gaping wound in her chest. Katie looked so much like her, you know?

'He got to the human subjects. Blam. Blam. One after the other. The gun he was using – it splattered their brains everywhere. The heads just . . . exploded. I couldn't bear to watch. I was screaming, going crazy.' Fei started. Dean had not told her about these subjects. Now she thought about it, he had revealed very few details. She wondered what else lay behind any of the stories she had been told in the last weeks. By Dean. By Han. Even more, by Ginny.

Ginny talked on. 'Then Piers got to a woman, about my age, my build, a drug addict he had picked up.

'He left her to last. Then dragged her out of the cage. He tied the grenades to her. She was wailing. Shat in her pants. She tried to run. Struggled like crazy. She was strong. Piers pushed her up against the dead policeman. One shove. Then he tossed the one grenade he had left and dragged me away. She was still screaming when the explosion came.'

Ginny glanced up. 'The police thought that woman was me. It helped us get away. They were looking for a lone man and we were a couple. Siew got us out. Hid us around Asia and in China. He got us new identities, had everything forged – he even got the loose ends tied up in the UK so everything looked right if anyone ever double-checked. We owe him our lives.

'In China, Piers started the experiments again. This time with Siew's money and connections, he had everything he needed and more. But the authorities got wind of it, wanted to do a deal, get the findings for themselves. Siew got us out again. Piers destroyed everything just like the last time. We had to start over again from nothing over here.'

A burst of revulsion propelled Fei from the chair. She stepped over Ginny, feeling sick with horror and outrage. She couldn't stand to be touched by Ginny anymore. She remembered her first meeting with Ginny, all the lies she had believed about the Centre and its therapies. All the lies the whole country and region believed. Everything had seemed so normal. So real. The legal work she had done for them – the applications and dry legal processes – had been all based in the dullness of ordinary life. Her mind reeled now with images of animals and people tortured, shootings and violence, a woman exploding in a grenade attack. She remembered TV images of Liak's terrible, slow death. The video she had just seen of a man made mad, his wife and child dying by his hand.

Ginny told her about Teck, the previous lawyer. He had been an AVA insider, close to Siew, but could not take the strain. He had been going to betray them to the authorities so Siew had had him terminated and it had been made to look like suicide.

Fei cried, 'How can you be a part of all this? How can you have done those things?' She trailed off. Was Ginny threatening her with that reference to Teck? Fei felt sick.

'Can't you see? We believed that this therapy would be used only for good. It was Piers's dream to create a better society.

Can't you picture it? A society without crime or violence, criminal behaviour curbed through the curbing of undesirable thoughts.'

'But what you have done . . . the killings, the torture . . .'

'The sick are everywhere. We're all sick. I'm sick, you too. We have to save the sick from themselves. It's the only way. That's what Piers always says. While we live in this world with all its evil, we have to fight like with like. Sacrifices have to be made now for the perfect world to come, don't you see? All this is just a means to an end.' Ginny raised her arms in entreaty. 'It's the price we have to pay. I don't want people to be hurt, nor does Piers. But in a world where there is no pity nor justice for a child like Katie, why should you or I show mercy? It's just survival, my Fei, can't you understand?'

She shivered violently, feeling cold to the core of her. 'What are you saying? This is . . . it's madness!'

Ginny hardly heard her. 'That's why I had to wait. Ten, eleven years now I've waited for the experiments to be perfected. So that there'd be no side-effects. I had to be cured. I started all this. If it weren't for me, Piers would be happy now. Katie and Morgane would still be alive. We would have no need for the Cure.'

'What are you talking about?'

'Then you came along. You with your beautiful eyes and glorious smile. You made me live again. I was yours the moment I first saw you. I wanted you for so long. It kept me going, through all the horrors. I didn't know it all, I swear to you. Those murders and that evil in there' – she indicated the study – 'I had no part in. I wanted to escape so often but I owed it to Piers to stay. I did this to him and so I owe him my life. I owed him my love. My love destroyed us all in New York. I swore I would never let it happen again. And then you came along.'

Ginny got to her feet and cupped Fei's face, kissing her with a shudder of passion and suppressed violence. Fei panicked, suffocating, revolted. But she dared not resist or move. She was drenched in icy sweat. Her mind was racing, trying to assimilate the madness Ginny was revealing. There was something missing, something vital that Ginny wasn't telling her. What was it? Where did it fit in?

Ginny went on, 'I couldn't give myself up now. To be cured after this is to die again and I don't know if I would want to go on if I couldn't love you. But what we do is disgusting and hideous, don't you see? It's unnatural. I've been punished for it over and over again – at the trial, in the papers, in my heart and every day I live. You made me love you. I should hate you for that. You made me see I had a choice. You made me want to choose you above all else. But I can't make the choice – I can't! I'm sick and I must be cured. There is no choice.'

Fei was horrified by the intensity of Ginny's self-loathing even as she proclaimed her love 'This is like a nightmare. What you've told me – they're either crazy lies or . . .' Fei stared at Ginny '. . . or the crazy truth.'

Ginny clung to Fei, searching her face. 'Do I look crazy to you? Don't leave, you can't. I've told you the truth. I'm trusting you with my life. I was so afraid before. I thought you would never understand. But you do, don't you? You see how it is. How it was. How we couldn't help the things we did. That it was all for the good. I didn't know how far Siew wanted to take it but even for Project Max, there must be a reason – it's just we don't know it yet.'

Ginny's grip was gouging into Fei. She did not dare to move or struggle. Suddenly Ginny burst into tears, racking sobs shaking her. She drew Fei into a tight embrace. 'We're bound together now. You know the whole of me. You know the truth. You know what I've done. You still love me, don't you? You're one of us now, a part of Piers and me and the Alliance. I belong to you and you belong to me. You'll always be mine, whatever happens to either of us.'

Fei put her arm tentatively around Ginny. Her legs felt weak and she could hardly breathe. But she had to maintain the pretence. Ginny was right. They were bound together now and Ginny held Fei's life in her hands. The realisation struck her with a sickening impact. Ginny would never let her leave unharmed if she thought Fei would betray her. She had to buy herself time.

Think. Work out what to do. Swallowing against her fear, Fei soothed Ginny, led her to the sofa.

Ginny sank down, pulling Fei with her. She sprawled against Fei, covering her in kisses, seeking out her mouth. Even as Ginny sobbed and cried, she touched Fei under her shirt, her hands desperate with desire. The explosion of emotion was terrifying, rising to a mad pitch. As if, now released, it would never be contained. Fei did not know the woman who howled and wept and clung to her, her relief and despair and grief like the death throes of a monster. Fei made herself lie still through it all, rocking Ginny, crooning to her till she began to quiet, Ginny's weight half on her, her breath hot against her cheek.

<hr />

Fei woke suddenly. It took her a moment to remember where she was. Ginny was half on top of her in exhausted sleep. From the clock on the wall, Fei saw that it was just after five in the morning. Her arm had gone numb. Carefully, she eased herself out from under Ginny, her whole body stiff. Ginny mumbled and shifted but did not wake up.

Fei massaged her neck. It hadn't been a dream. She was still here and everything Ginny had told her was clear in her mind. She looked around her at the apartment. What was she going to do?

The VDU glow from the study caught her eye. She hesitated then went through, glancing back to see that Ginny still slept. The screen-saver circled on the monitor, the single lamp by the terminal encircling the keyboard in mustard light.

Fei sat down at the computer. The touch of a key and the screen-saver gave way to columns of words and figures. Fei glanced at the door. If Ginny found her at the computer . . . She remembered Ginny's grip digging into her arms, those furious and desperate eyes. Fei felt afraid again. But there was only stillness in the other room.

She scrolled up and down and across the screen. It was the

main directory within the mainframe computer at the Centre. The sub-trees with the words 'max' within their reference had been highlighted from Ginny's session at the terminal. There were other paths with recognisable names amongst numerals and other letters – 'johor', 'liak', 'kilming'. Fei began to open directories and follow branches.

She saw her own name.

Fei opened the file. Her vitalstats came up: passport details, address, identity card number, description. Then a series of photographs – from the inauguration ceremony, at public events with the Wyndhams, some outside her office and condo taken by a long-range lens. Fei's mouth felt dry. She moved through the file. A report to Ginny by an unnamed source about Fei's movements – 'as you instructed' – and the times when the photos had been taken. Ginny had had her followed! From the dates, it looked like it was just before she had pressed the bodyguards on to Fei. A chill shivered through her.

She read on. The body of the file was a document of over a hundred pages. It contained details of her habits, opinions, thoughts, values, friends and family, all the minutiae of her life and emotions. It listed her favourite foods, the books and movies she liked, how she curled up on her side when she slept, every throw-away line she had spoken. Fei felt a creeping horror as she read and yet could not stop. She paged down the file, scanning each paragraph, transfixed. It could only have been written by Ginny.

Fei flicked a glance at the door. She could not see the sofa from here. Images of Ginny lying there, of Ginny holding her, watching her, asking her so much about herself, touching her, snaring her in kisses – the kaleidoscope spun in her head. Her instinct was to run, get away as fast as she could, hide, out of Ginny's grasp. But she stayed rooted in the chair.

Fei clicked out of her file and scrolled through the directory. Sam's name. Dean's. Ben Chang's. She opened each in frantic succession. They all held similar details on each of their subjects, each life transformed into digital text and psychological analysis. From the varying styles of the reports, Fei guessed that Sam's also had been prepared by Ginny but not the others. That was why Ginny had wanted to know so much about her. Fei felt a twist of horror and disgust. Ginny's obsessive jealousy had transformed all the information she had wormed out into – into what? What were these files? Why was the Centre collecting such data on her and Sam and all these other people?

Fei's mind blocked the terrifying thought. Its hideous head nudged at the edge of her consciousness. To let it in would be to lock herself into paralysing horror.

A movement from outside. Fei stared at the empty doorway, listening. A moan. Shifting. Then silence.

Her heart drumming in her ears, Fei exited out of Sam's file. She stared at the web of names and figures on the screen. Her breath came in shallow gasps. She felt sick.

Suddenly, she knew what to do. She rolled the chair back from the desk, scanned the shelves and table tops. Quickly! Come on! The clock at the bottom of the screen said 6:10. Ginny might wake at any moment.

There. Fei saw the box of rewritable CD-RWs and reached for them. A pile of floppies next to them tipped off the shelf as she nudged against them. She tried to catch them. They slid from her fingers, tumbling through the air.

Hit the floor with a clatter.

Fei froze. Noise from the living room. She was at the door in two steps. Ginny was muttering, shaking her head, shifting. Fei swallowed. Ginny turned away from her and settled into sleep.

Fei went back to the terminal. Slotted a CD into the rewrite drive. Her hand was trembling as she tried to guide the mouse. She closed her eyes and took a steadying breath. Then she moved through the directory, selecting the files she had opened, the 'max' files, those with names she recognised, others with scientific names that meant nothing to her, then as many as she could click on at random. She hit the 'copy' command and let the mouse go.

The computer and CD drives whirred. To Fei's ears, the noise was as loud as sirens. She sat unmoving in the chair, listening to the computer, straining to hear the silence in the living room. The minutes dragged by. And the stillness.

Fei extracted the CD, moved the cursor back to where it had been when she and Ginny had left the study. Her head ached with tension. She put the box of CDs back on the shelf, arranged the floppies against them as best she could.

She was back in the living room, the CD down the front of her jeans, its metallic cold warming against her skin. Ginny stirred and looked up as Fei knelt to kiss her. Fei said gently, 'I should go.'

Chapter Twenty-Four

Fei was alone in her office. It was seven a.m. She had come straight from Ginny's apartment. Ginny would have the modified photos ready by tonight. Then it was a matter of meeting Dean again. And Han. Fei stalked the cramped cubicle, crazy with pent-up energy, going over and over everything Ginny had told her. The Cure, Ginny had kept talking about the Cure. The side-effects she had talked about – how had they been caused? How could televised images have had such a hideous and murderous effect on the man called Chee? That was what had been missing from Ginny's disjointed ravings. She had never given Fei an intelligible explanation of how the Cure really worked.

Fei picked up the CD-RW she had placed on her desk. Now that she had copies of the Centre's files, what was she going to do with them? Frustration and fury cut through her panic. She had been Ginny's plaything, despised and condemned for her sexuality even as Ginny had fawned over her. She was a pawn for Dean, had always been, even while she had thought herself to be controlling him. And Han had always been there in the background, watching her, playing with her paranoia and fear, entwining her in his obscure manipulations. It was as if everything she had thought real had been nothing but shadows cast against fog.

Fei picked up the phone and dialled Sam's number. The answer machine again. She tried the hospital. For an hour, cajoling, pleading, bullying, she made the rounds of the hospital network and Sam's friends till she got the home number of Ling, Sam's assistant. From Ling, she wheedled a contact number in Hong Kong.

Sam's voice on the line was strong and clear. 'Fei, how on earth . . .'

'I need to see you.' She heard her own desperation. 'Please. Come back now.'

'What's happened?'

'I can't tell you on the phone.'

'I'm in the midst of something huge here. The chicken 'flu – it's a major lead on Q. I can't leave now.'

'I don't know who else to turn to.' Fei felt trapped. How could she convey the monstrous things she knew? 'I'm scared.'

'What's going on?' Sam sounded alarmed. There was silence. Then: 'There's a flight to KL in a couple of hours. With the time difference I'll get into KLIA by one in the afternoon.'

'I'll meet you at your office.'

———◆———

Ginny was hunched over the computer when Piers arrived.

It was mid-morning, the sun bleaching the cityscape beyond the windows. She tried to close out of the photo applications but he already knew. Ricky had probed her hard drive remotely while she had been on-line to the Centre mainframe. They had seen the photos, the original with Dean's message and her modifications. Piers stood in the middle of the study, rigid with anger and strain. Stammering, panicking, Ginny told him every-thing – about Fei and what had passed between them the night before.

'Fei can be trusted, I swear it,' she cried. It was a plea and a cry of defiance. She had lived in fear of this moment and now she felt a curious exhilaration. 'We're bound together, she's in it like we are and with everything to lose.'

Piers swore. 'Months ago I saw how happy you were, that's

how I knew. But I hoped you'd wake from this infatuation before it brought us to something like this. That I wouldn't have to . . .' He couldn't finish the threat but turned away.

'She loves me – that counts for more than any threat, believe me. Like the love you and I have. Love holds us here, doesn't it?' Ginny felt strangely triumphant. It was as if she had used up her last reserves of fear in her night with Fei. What had terrified her most had been the thought of Fei's possible rejection and disgust. Panic and a flight to the police or the authorities would have forced Ginny to act against her lover. But Fei had embraced her, taken her into her arms, stayed with her through the night.

'The Cure is still unstable but if I have to choose between you and our cause . . .' Piers said quietly. 'I can't let you ruin it all again like you ruined it for Katie.'

'I know.' Even if Ginny were to lose this self, even if her memory and passion and knowledge of Fei were to be wiped clean by the Cure, Ginny suddenly knew that she would not fight it as she had once thought she would. Fei had accepted her, willingly bound herself to Ginny. It was Ginny's most precious treasure and to have owned it even fleetingly was everything to her. There was nothing more that she desired. Nothing he could do to her that she feared.

Piers sat down suddenly on the window seat. His unyielding determination seemed to drain from him. Ginny went up to him. His blond head was bright in the sunlight. For a heartbeat, she saw him with Katie, their golden heads close together, laughing at a secret joke. But that was another lifetime ago. She saw Chee screaming at his wife and child, shooting them in a mad rage. What had Piers become? And she herself? Disgust and bitterness spiked her words. 'Why Project Max? We were doing this for good. To destroy men like Connelly, not create them!'

A cry escaped Piers at the mention of *his* name. He turned on Ginny, his face twisted with anguish. 'Because we need ruthless hands to do our will. The Final Phase will be the Armageddon the world has been waiting for. There will be those who will rise up against us. We must be ready.'

Ginny backed away. The Final Phase was to have been a peaceful solution, a tranquil shift towards happiness for all. In his phrasing and intensity, it was as if Piers had become Siew. She stared at her brother as if seeing him for the first time. In the beginning, he had clutched at Asian Values as his salvation. Siew had been his anchor in the dark years after Morgane was killed. The values Siew preached had given Piers new hope, brought him back his will and determination. But this religiosity, this frightening acceptance of violence and murder, how had he made this shift?

Ginny stood very still. She saw herself giving the command for Dean's beating. She saw the bodies they'd disposed of week after week for more than ten years. The animals in their cages, dissected, implanted, tortured in the name of their work. The JB children wasting away. The thousands across Asia plucked out and then thrown back into their lives, to die in bewilderment and terror. She had stood by throughout all these killings and pretended to herself they could be justified for the sake of a better future. She had created the means by which the programming would succeed. She waited like a coward for the perfection of the Cure, sacrificed these others so she herself might be safe. Because she didn't know them, didn't feel their hopes and loves and fears, it had been all right to let them suffer and die. And it had been so easy.

Ginny felt a part of her fragment away, as if she viewed herself and Piers from a distance. They were captured there in time, he on the window seat and she standing close by. She had said to Fei that the Lovelaces were monsters, a smokescreen of words to cloak her own guilt. It had been so easy with Fei to disassociate her consciousness from who she really was. She was Ginny Wyndham. The other, the one who did the hideous acts – she was Susan Lovelace. Together, she and Piers had made Connelly their justification. His evil had made them righteous. His violence against Katie had given them permission to indulge their dark ambitions. Ginny saw it clearly now. Piers had worked on these experiments in New York even while Katie had lived and thrived. She had helped him: sending him programs, trying different strategies, willingly setting up his computer systems. What had happened to Katie had been just the excuse.

Ginny felt her whole mind collapse. Her construct of reality was imploding, breaking into shards. At some unfathomable level, had they both hoped for something hideous to happen so that they might at last have the right to inflict their own violence on others? She was shaking, dry yelping sobs tearing from her breast. In the reforming fragments, a kaleidoscope settling into a new reality, Ginny knew them at last for what they were, Piers and she, monsters of their own creation.

Piers was watching her. His face was masked again, his eyes narrow. 'I will deal with Dean. You have one chance only left. Control Fei.'

Ginny nodded, trying to connect a meaning to the sounds she heard.

Piers said again, 'Control Fei. Or I will.'

This time the threat sank in. Ginny felt her heart stop. She rasped, 'I'll do anything. Just don't hurt her.'

—————◆—————

'All right, Dean, let's talk.' Piers spoke into his cellphone as he drove back to the coast. 'My people will pick you up. I'll make a deal with you.' He gave a time and a meeting place. Hung up before Dean could reply.

The phone rang. It was Dr Hiew from Hong Kong. Piers turned on to the highway out of KL, climbing out of the Klang valley through a hilly landscape. Hiew said, 'The chicken 'flu is turning into an epidemic. Government health officials are all over the city and southern China. They're going to slaughter thousands of birds.'

'They haven't identified the so-called "virus"?'

'Not yet. But we've got a problem.'

Piers was alert.

Hiew went on, 'There's a doctor from KL here: Sam Ryder. She's been asking a load of questions, wanting brain tissue samples from the deceased. She's got one of our doctors on to her theory – she calls it Factor Q.'

'Shit! We've been working on her file. I expected to have a little more time.' Piers scowled. 'We'll take care of her.'

'I'll handle Grossman. Without her, he's got no clout here. He'll keep quiet unless he wants to be back in Toronto on the next flight.'

Piers was taut with tension. He had not notified Siew yet about the Hong Kong problems, and Siew had obviously not yet made the connection between the 'flu and Project Max. But it was only a matter of time. Piers had promised Siew a stable compound this time, and he had failed again. And the new failure was inexplicable in its manifestation. How had the compound affected the immune system? Frustration seethed in his gut. He had believed himself to be in control, master of the materials and the people he worked with. But the compound would not be subverted to his will. And people would not obey without question or error: the farmer distributing the mixed feed as he pleased; Ben giving in to his conscience; Ginny taken in by love. He floundered in the dark, each step a guess that might take him closer to the goal or plunge him further into chaos.

He called Ricky. 'Activate the Dean file. We take him tonight. And we need the Ryder file on standby. We're bringing her in.'

He called his Red Tiger contact and gave him the order to find Ryder.

He had no choice but to go on, impose control, whatever it took.

Sam still felt raw from her last encounter with Fei. It had been crazy to drop everything and rush back to KL just because she had called. But there had been a tone in Fei's voice that had cut through her defence mechanisms. Fei was not playing games. Something was wrong.

In Sam's office, Fei rushed headlong into disjointed detail, her face pale, her manner fraught. Sam had to make her stop and start in sequence, piecing it all together. Mind-control experiments in New York and China, and now here in Asia. Ginny and Piers and the Alliance in a conspiracy to transform Asia.

Fei cried, 'You don't believe me, do you? Maybe I *am* crazy. I don't know what makes sense and what doesn't anymore. Sam, you're the only one who's real to me. You've got to help me.'

'But how? What can we do?'

'I . . . I don't know.' Fei looked around as if the shadows might swallow her. She dug in her pocket. 'I copied this from Ginny's computer.'

The CD glinted in the light. Sam slid it into the CD drive of her computer. Fei talked over the information that came up on the screen, psychological reports on both of them and data and analyses of the JB therapy. There were files on her, Fei and Dean. Fei told her about the psychological profiles, her voice shaking. Sam ran the 'max' files, staring in horror at the images that sprang up from the screen, Fei turning away. She scanned the individual reports, opened up databases and files containing scientific notes. There were formulae signifying amino acids and hormones and neurological effects, breakdowns of biochemical reactions, notes on culturing compounds designated SPrp and HPrp, in isolation and in conjunction, projected outcomes for experiments and write-ups of each step.

'It's Factor Q!' Sam could not take her eyes away from the screen.

Fei leaned in beside her. Sam hardly noticed. She was talking fast, heart thudding with exhilaration and horror. 'There – this sequence. And here. The amino acid chains correspond to the Factor Q in the JB case and Ben Chang's sample. And the same sequence from Chang's sample turned up in Hong Kong – I couldn't understand what the connection was then. But the explanation is here: they used the same compound, what they call generation 106, in both Chang and the chickens eaten by the guy called Chee. But somehow the distribution got messed up, the wrong chickens got to the wrong people on a vast scale.

And in JB they doctored the beef, that's how the prion – named gen105 – got into the kids wholesale.'

'But what is it, this compound?'

'They've been doing this for years like Ginny told you. They picked their victims at random. That's why Factor Q manifested so inexplicably. I was picking up their modifications. They've been engineering this compound through a hundred genera-tions.' Sam switched screens. 'Look – it derived from the grey orang-utans.'

'The ones at the Sanctuary?'

Sam clicked and scrolled in one of the files till she found the details again. 'The apes were found to have a naturally occur-ring prion that co-existed harmlessly in their brains. Morgane Lovelace came across it first. In moments of danger, adrenaline kicks in and reacts with the prions. Put simplistically, the protein bends in on itself and triggers other proteins in the brain to do the same. The brain enters a sudden trance-like state and the apes follow the actions of the lead male without hesitation – whether it's fight or flight. It was observed that in fight mode, they attacked with mindless ferocity and without fear. In flight mode, they moved at remarkable speeds and overcame obstacles that they would otherwise be unable to surmount. Evolutionarily, that's probably what helped them survive and also hid them so well from man up till recently.

'Wyndham – or Lovelace – extracted the prion and modi-fied it to respond to another hormone, chronotonin, which keeps the body clock in check. He began to use it on human subjects to change their behaviour through manipulation of the subjective experience. Once triggered by the hormone, the effect of the folding prion is to put the subject into a trance-like state that resembles deep shock.'

Fei interjected, 'And by using the digitally manipulated images and suggestive commands, as in normal hypnotism, they work on the subject's mind till they've remade him.'

'But there's a difference. A hypnotist cannot make the subject do anything they object to. In such a case, the subject comes out of the trance. But with this neurochemical mechanism, the subject is rendered brain-paralysed until the manipulations are over.'

'And the Asian Values Alliance is funding the Wyndhams.' Fei sank down in the chair next to her.

Sam flicked through the files. 'They started with SPrp but it's since been modified further to a version they call HPrp. They're upping the proportion of HPrp, which seems to have a better binding effect for a deeper trance state although it is less stable. Their main problem is stability – the compound's volatility manifests in the side-effects I've been identifying in my Q database, most often ending in death.'

The next item caught their attention at the same time. Sam felt her heart miss a beat. She was targeted for abduction on Ginny's recommendation for what the file termed 'Double Alpha reprogramming'. Fei pushed to her feet with a cry. Sam sat transfixed, reading on. There would be an experiment they called Phase Four, targeting a whole town: Rutan in the state of Kilming. Sam read out to Fei the proposal on the screen. They could not turn away from this. Not now.

The compound would be distributed through the town water supply, initially with doses of chronotonin. The visual and aural input would be transmitted through radio and television day after day, coinciding with the twice-daily release of chronotonin within the population's bodies. This experiment would be slow, in contrast with the intensive reprogramming carried out to date. Over months, the subjective lives of the population would change, bending to the AVA's will. It was expected that the mutations of their will would in the natural course of their daily interactions be reinforced in a feedback loop to reach a point where the process would speed up exponentially.

'What they call the Final Phase is after that,' Sam said. As she read on, she felt her mind whiting out. The Asian Values Alliance. The twisted horror of their vision seeping across Asia, infecting the living with the death of the will – she could not hold its monstrosity in her understanding.

She heard her own voice as if from far away. 'From what I

can tell, they plan to distribute the compound throughout Asia. The top ranks of the AVA and the scientific controllers would be protected by a chemical inhibitor injected into their system. It neutralises the effect of the hormone trigger, preventing the folding of the prion that is essential to trance induction.'

Fei gasped. 'Leaving a lucid, free elite in control of the mass of Asia, unopposed and unquestioned in their absolute power.'

'But there's a problem. They can't produce industrial quantities of the compound by their current means. I can't make out what that is from . . .'

'I don't want to know anymore!' Fei cried. She tugged Sam to her feet and pulled her away. 'What are we going to do? They want you. Ginny targeted you! Oh, God, Sam . . .'

'We've got to go to the police.'

'No! We can't trust them!' Fei pulled away again. She paced by the window and froze, staring out.

Sam came up to her. 'What is it?'

In the car park far below, a burly Chinese man was stepping out of a car. He looked like a boxer. Fei gasped, 'It's him – Han.'

'He'll help us . . .'

'No! He's with the security forces, they've got to be linked to the police. I don't know . . . I don't trust him.' Fei paused then cried: 'There was no file on Han in the mainframe, I'm sure of it. I would've copied it for sure.'

'If the police are in on it then Han . . .'

'We've got to get out of here!'

Sam was back at the computer. 'Wait!'

She worked fast, pushing panic and Han and Fei out of her mind. She had to save what was on the disk without trace. She called up an article she had stored from the *Wired* magazine website, extracting the photograph. It was of her favourite science-fiction author, Nicholas Bennett, his rugged features gazing confidently into the camera. She closed the files and directories on the CD and selected them all. Clicking into her encryption application, she encrypted the digital codes that made up the information on the disk into the photograph.

'Sam, we've got to move!' Fei called from behind her.

'Just a minute.' She switched windows, dialling up the Internet, the modem pinging and crackling, then inputting a web-based e-mail service. She had several e-mail accounts in different names as was common for experienced websurfers. It solved junkmail problems and eased mail management for different aspects of her work and personal life. At the site, she logged into her account, amended the automatic forwarding instructions and, switching windows again, downloaded the encrypted files. She typed in the receiving addresses, hit 'send' and exited.

'Switch off the mains.' Sam pushed away from the terminal.

'What?'

'Just do it.' Sam hauled the monitor off the hard-drive box. She had split the encrypted files into four and each quarter was being forwarded remotely by the e-mail application to four other different accounts. Even if anyone retrieved one part of the encrypted information, it would be unreadable without the other three.

The plug out of the wall, Sam heaved open the casing to the hard-drive box. Fei was staring in bewilderment. Sam scrabbled in her bottom drawer and found a screwdriver. Peering into the maze of slotted boards, studded with chips and meticulous grids of metal, she located the memory chips and motherboard. She jammed the screwdriver in and levered the plates out, throwing them on the table.

Back on with the casing, hauling the monitor on top. Scrabbling for the disk and boards, slamming the screwdriver back into the drawer.

'Let's go!' She headed out into the corridor, Fei close behind.

<hr>

Han made his way across the hot tarmac into the hospital. At the reception desk, he asked for Sam Ryder. He took in the directions and strode to the lifts.

Sam clattered down the fire escape stairwell at the far back of the hospital complex, Fei close behind her. They did not speak, their feet pounding in a manic rhythm. Round each landing. Round again. Lungs burning. Heart bursting. Down another flight.

They reached the basement. Sam slammed through fire doors, racing down the fluorescent lit corridors. Turning this way and that. Where was it?

'There!' she called to Fei. They pelted down to the end of a dimly lit extension and burst into a room. It was uncomfortably hot, bright red and yellow hazard signs all over the walls and machinery. Sacks of bedding, linen and rubber gloves spilled across part of the floor. At the far end stood the incinerator.

Sam found the hatch to the incinerator chute. She tossed in the CD and computer plates. Removing the chips from the hard-drive had been the simplest and fastest method of ensuring that nothing they had viewed on it could be retrieved. She slammed her fist on to the red 'process' button and a clattering began.

Hauling herself across the room, she dragged Fei with her out into the corridor again.

Han stood in the middle of Ryder's office. There was no one here or in the adjacent labs. He looked through into the neighbouring office. It was empty, too.

He flicked through the papers on the desk. Scanned the shelves of lever arches and folders. He went up to the computer. The screen was dead. He pushed the power switch. Nothing.

Moving away from the desk, he saw the plug out of the wall.

Han crossed to the window and looked out. In the car park below, he saw the running figures.

Qwong and a white woman. From his surveillance of Qwong, he recognised Ryder. He burst out of the room towards the lifts.

PART THREE

Spirit

Chapter Twenty-Five

Sam drove through the gridded streets of Petaling Jaya, circling roundabouts unexpectedly, taking sudden turnings. Fei twisted round to see if Han was following them. It was difficult to tell but none of the cars either ahead or behind seemed to be there constantly. Fei said, 'We're okay for now.'

Sam nodded. She found the junction for the intercity highway and took a lane at random. They were heading for Subang Jaya, a satellite town built round the old airport. She said, 'What are we going to do?'

Fei stared out at the speeding tarmac. She had to think but her mind seemed frozen by panic. She let the words take her, grappling for sense. 'Han said he was after Dean. He never said anything about the AVA, and whenever I pushed him on the Wyndhams he never replied. Maybe he already knows what they're doing. He could even be working for them.'

'You think he's *not* a security forces agent then?'

'I don't know. If he's not and he's an AVA insider, he's probably trying to get a hook on what Dean's agenda is – and maybe find out what Ginny's link is with me.' Fei thought of the fanaticism of the Alliance members as they had rationalised their hatred of those they viewed as 'perverts'. Remembered Han's car ramming into hers, his cold face staring at her.

'But we can't be sure.'

Fei considered the alternative. 'If he is a government agent . . . My God!'

'What?' Sam shot a glance at her.

'If the security forces are part of it – and the police – then how high up does it go? The government, and maybe other Asian authorities – Han mentioned regional security.' Fei turned to Sam. 'They must *all* be involved.'

'Jesus!'

The car shot forward as Sam stared unseeing at the highway, her foot hard down on the accelerator. The truck in front loomed towards them. Fei cried, 'Sam!'

She rammed on the brakes, pitching them both forward. The truck ahead sped on. Sam was breathing hard, slowing to seventy. She took the next exit, looping back to KL. Fei swallowed painfully. The enormity of it was almost impossible to take in. She had laughed at the Alliance for their fantasy of perfection but all along their dream had been attainable. They had the means to remake the world in their own image and no one was stopping them.

Except Dean. Fei gasped, 'He's our only chance – Dean. He's CIA. The Americans want to stop the Wyndhams. They must know about the AVA and they're trying to find out about the experiments and their ultimate objective. *That's* why Dean is here. Why he tried to get to the Wyndhams through me.'

Fei's head was spinning. Images of Dean flashed into her mind, things he had said, how she had trusted him. And the hurt she had felt at his betrayal. What was real and what had been coloured by her own bitterness and anger? 'Maybe I misjudged him. His goddamn' ego and cack-handed attempts to seduce me! And the blackmail! All this . . . this garbage getting in the way. And I gave him away! Promised to help Han get to him. Shit!'

Sam reached out to Fei. 'Are you sure we can trust him?'

Fei searched the highway as if for an answer. 'I don't know – I hope so. I did once. If only he'd been straight with me from the start . . .'

'All right. How do we find him?'

Fei scrabbled for her cellphone. She dialled the number he had given her. An electronic voice came back. His cellphone was switched off.

Sam said, 'Keep trying till we get him.'

Fei said, 'He gave me an address.'

'Last resort. His place might be watched.'

'What now? We can't drive around forever.'

In the next hour, Sam pulled up by shopping malls, banks and stand-alone ATM machines. Between them, they withdrew all the cash from their various bank and savings accounts. Passports were next. Sam had hers on her from her Hong Kong trip. They headed to Fei's condo.

Sam parked the car in a side road to the back of the building. They entered the block by the tradesmen's entrance, glancing into the reception hall as they hurried up the stairs. The porter at the front desk caught Fei's eye but looked away, ducking his head as if wishing he hadn't been seen. She frowned. Hassan was usually friendly.

They took the lift from the second floor. Arriving on Fei's floor, they sensed something was wrong from the start. The corridor was sealed off from natural light by the apartments running off it. But now, pale daylight at the far end met the soft electric glow. An apartment door stood ajar.

Fei's door.

She exchanged glances with Sam. There was silence but for the hum of the air-conditioning. Should they run or go on?

Sam began to inch her way towards the door. Fei followed. Her every nerve was tight. She hovered, ready to run, checking the fire exit to the stairs.

The door had been rammed and levered open, the lock hanging from it. No movement. No sound. Crouching low, Fei flat against the wall behind her, Sam nudged the door open. She peered round and then beckoned to Fei.

The living room was empty. The electricity had presumably been cut, to disable the alarm. Sam tested the light switch. Nothing. The place had been ransacked, books and papers thrown across the floor, furniture pulled out, cushions slashed, drawers and bookshelves dismantled. Shock and disbelief slammed into Fei. She felt tears rising in spite of herself.

Sam checked the kitchen, bedroom and study. 'No one

here. But the place has been turned upside down.'

'But why . . .' Fei could hardly speak.

'There's money left lying around. And they didn't take this.' Sam held up her passport.

Fei stood immobile in the middle of the devastation.

Sam saw the piece of paper first. On top of the upturned coffee table.

The phone rang.

Fei looked at Sam who hesitated then nodded. Fei picked up the phone as Sam reached for the paper.

Hassan was on the line. '*Mem*, they coming again.'

'Who?'

'I couldn't stop they all before.' He sounded frightened. The line went dead.

Fei grabbed Sam. In the corridor, the numbers above the lift were lighting in slow succession, rising from the ground floor. Fei crossed to the fire exit, slamming out into the bright day, Sam behind her.

———

Dean sat in the back of the Daewoo. It was sealed from the front by dark opaque glass. The tinted windows cast the world beyond into murky gloom. Silent goons jammed him in to either side, their eyes gashed slits. They were big for Asians, muscle-bulked like boxers. His eye was swelling and his face was stiff with pain. The ache in his gut and groin was easing but not much. His tongue, swollen still from Fei's bite, was thick and throbbing against the cuts to his gums and lips.

They had come for him within minutes of his arrival at the pick-up point. Taken the photos from him as they hustled him round the back exit of the mall. Roughed him up in the stair-well in the few seconds between punters passing, taken his phone and weapon from him. Disabled both. Dragged him out to the waiting car as he retched and hung against them.

Fucking goons always had to show who was in control.

But he'd got the go-ahead from his bidders before he had made the meet. Whatever these fucking tough guys played at, Dean knew he had a deal for Wyndham that was his ace. The bidders wanted Wyndham so bad, the bastard could call the goddamn' shots whichever offer he took and Dean would get paid either way. Everybody would be a fucking winner, he thought sardonically.

<hr />

Sam closed the shutters against the lights of Petaling Street. The noise of the night-market grew muffled but the music still thudded through the slatted wood. Fei flicked the light on. The bulb cast a feeble light on the cracked walls. There was just enough room to stand between the narrow twin beds. Fei slid the flimsy door shut and threaded its hook through the eye on the frame. That was as much security as they would get.

The piece of paper had been a search warrant. On the back, someone had scrawled: 'This is only the beginning.' The signature was bold and clear. Han. Fei had felt sick.

She and Sam had abandoned the car in a back street in Setapak, an old Chinese area on the trunk road to the East Coast. They had planned to lie low here but Fei had been conscious of Sam beside her, the only white on the street. Instead, they took a bus into Petaling Street. It was early-evening by then. Chinatown was thronged with night-market stalls, Western backpackers and locals strolling the streets. Sam and Fei would hardly be noticed here. After scouring the stalls for what they needed, they checked into the East Star rooming house. It was typical of the hostels in the area – a nineteenth-century shop-house that had been left to run down, chipped paint inside and out, antique tiles on the wall cracked and missing.

Fei was exhausted. In silence, she began to change out of her suit. She tied a cloth money bag to her waist, then pulled on the jeans and T-shirt she had bought from a stall. Crammed against her, Sam exchanged her clothes for cotton tie-dyed leggings and a loose top, her money also carried against her skin. Neither met the other's eye as their limbs and bodies brushed in the tiny space. Fei slipped into Bata trainers and began to wipe off her make-up with toilet tissue. Sam jammed a baseball cap low over her eyes and laced herself into hiking boots.

Outside in the warm night, Fei might have been any one of the young local girls who ran the music stalls or served noodles at a coffee-shop. Sam looked like any other traveller, a cheap day-pack strapped to her shoulders. They ordered rice and roast duck in a shophouse caff, sitting in a dark corner at the back. Fei had been trying Dean's phone every hour. She tried again. It was still disconnected.

She called her mother's house. Her brother answered. Fei felt a surge of emotion. Johnny's voice seemed to come from another reality. She said, 'Are . . . are you all right? All of you?'

'Yeah. Hey, why you don' call for so long-lah?'

'I've been busy. Is everyone okay?'

'Sure-lah. I'm just home from Klang these last two days. I go back first thing in the morning. Why don't you come have dinner with us all tonight?'

'Nothing's happened? No problems?'

'No – why? What's going on? You don't sound good.'

'I'm fine. Just tired.' Fei sank back in relief. They were all right. No one had come for them. She didn't know what she had expected, hadn't even wanted to consider the possibilities. But they were safe. For now at least. 'Be careful, okay? Tell Mum, Kit, Anita – they must be careful.'

'Don't worry-lah. Fei, are you okay?'

'I've got to go. Be careful. Be safe. I love you all.' She hung up.

Sam was watching her. 'We'll stay here till we get hold of Dean. By tomorrow, I'm sure we'll speak to him. He'll know what to do. He'll help us. We'll be safe, and your family too.'

I am safe, Fei wanted to say suddenly. *I am safe with you.* Relief and exhaustion hit her sideways on. She felt a strange upsurge of emotion. She wanted to touch Sam, curl up in her arms like they used to do. But she did not move.

That night, she crept into Sam's cramped bed. The mattress

was thin and the wooden frame jammed into her bones. She burrowed her face against Sam's cheek, smelling the familiar vanilla and honey scent. A part of Fei seemed to open up again like a lotus to the sun. Sam's hand caressed her back. They did not speak. Their kisses were fond with familiarity. It was like coming home. Like never having left. Fei fell asleep cuddled against Sam, her back easing to Sam's soft stroking.

<hr />

Dean sat with Piers in the cosily furnished counselling room in the Secure Unit. Curtains were drawn against the barred window. They might have been friends sitting down to a game of cards at the baize table – only its legs were fixed to the floor as was the other furniture. A pile of thousand-dollar bills – US currency – lay on the table, taken off Dean by Wyndham's goons. Dean drank from a glass of beer, its clean taste easing the pain in his mouth. Wyndham was leaning back in his chair, watching him.

Dean gave a lop-sided grin against the swelling of his face. 'We should have got to this point earlier. It would have saved a lot of trouble.'

'What do you want?'

Dean tutted at his lack of humour. 'Justin Lovelace used to be fun, I hear. What happened to you?'

'You know what happened.' Wyndham held his gaze.

Dean nodded. At least the guy had stopped playing games. 'There's two million here. A deposit if you like. I am your ransom against the good faith of my – ah – business associates. But if I don't call them in twenty-four hours, they know where I am, they know everything I know, and won't have any hesitation in taking you and your precious Centre down.'

'They'll need more than a dirty photograph.'

'That was just the ice-breaker. If they can't have you, no one else will. You're not dead because that hasn't yet been on the agenda. But if they make it their agenda, you and Ginny and

Siew and anyone else you care to think of will have no more than a day left to live. And the Centre . . . fire, gas explosion, terrorist bombers. Who knows? Anything might happen to destroy your life's work. A shame, don't you think?'

'That's the threat. Now what's the incentive?'

'My business associates could get the charges dropped against you. You could come back to the States, carry on your work where you left off.'

Wyndham snorted, indicating the Centre with a jerk of his head. 'What's my work to your "business associates"?'

'Professor Crane told them about your hypothesis.'

Wyndham looked thoughtful. 'He was the only one at the Carl Heinsmann who supported my research proposal. Tried to get me funding. But the experiments would have been too "politically sensitive", apparently.'

'He'd've got it for you, you know. But not from the usual channels. If only you'd sat it out a couple more years.'

'What do you mean?'

'As one of the top neuropsychologists in the States, Crane was invited on to the panel of Burman Pharmaceuticals. They were very interested in your ideas when he told them about you. But that was a year after you'd disappeared. They called me in to find you.'

'And who are Burman?'

'A drug company, like any other.'

Wyndham cocked an eyebrow. And waited.

Dean smiled. 'On the outside at least. Behind the scenes, they're a division of Newland Defence.' The largest manufacturer of arms and strategic weapons in North America with a billion-dollar contract with the US government. 'They had the FBI and police files on you closed, issued a press statement that Lovelace had been found by police but shot and killed resisting arrest. That got you out of the public domain and you became exclusively mine.'

'*Now* it's making sense.'

Dean slugged more beer. 'Biological warfare is all the rage. Newland diversified from hardware a decade ago. Burman develop nerve gases, toxins, viral-based infectants – you name your poison, they've got it. Trouble is, all their current technology kills or maims or paralyses or turns subjects into babbling vegetative retards. Nothing like your wonder serum – leaving the body fully functional and twisting the mind just how you want it. Although, judging from the Johore Baru therapy, you've still got some fine-tuning to do.

'Burman have sold the Pentagon a contract on the basis of your ideas. They want you to come in and work with them. All charges dropped. They'll give you whatever you need to iron out the current glitches. They'll pay whatever price you name.'

Wyndham shook his head. 'No deal.'

Dean laughed. '*Any* price. As many noughts at the end as you want.'

'You Americans,' Wyndham sneered, and lunged forward suddenly like a cobra. Veins bulged in his neck and brow. 'Everything is there for you to take or buy, isn't it? Instant gratification, that's what life is to you. "Gimme food now, gimme an easy life, gimme money for nothing, gimme sex, gimme love, gimme your soul and your body." Well, mine's not for the taking. You took my child, you took my wife, you took justice from me. No more! You created an evil like *him*, you fed *his* desires and taught *him he* could do anything. *He* did what *he* did to my Katie, laughing in your faces. And you let *him* go. All the while mouthing about political sensitivities and individual freedom and respect for personal liberties in the face of what I was once willing to offer you. *He* is the American Dream and I don't want any part of it

'My life is here now. Here they understand what is worth hanging on to – loyalty, family, community, decency, hard work, endurance. They welcomed me and made me one of them. Trusted me with their souls. And you think I would come back with you just because you offer me any number of noughts?'

Wyndham was breathing hard, his face close to Dean's over the table. He had expected a diatribe. With men of principle, you always got this sanctimonious horseshit. He waited a beat, then said calmly, 'Burman can also offer you Logan Connelly.'

Wyndham's features worked for an instant but he managed to control himself. He eased back, still standing. Dean went on, 'Connelly's got a two-bit engine workshop on the Lower East Side. Doing pretty well, I hear. He's got a woman and a couple of kids now. He still goes off for weeks at a time, no one knows where or what for. Kids go missing all the time in New York, their bodies turning up in junk yards and down sewers. The cops have hauled Connelly in a few times but nothing ever sticks. Maybe he even *is* innocent. Or just too fucking smart.'

Wyndham was shaking now. His face was white, a sheen of sweat glistened on his forehead. He sat down again. Dean said, 'You could do whatever you wanted with him. Burman will get him for you. Nobody would ever know what really happened if one day, *his* body turned up in the Hudson.'

Wyndham slammed his fists on to the table. Wood splintered. Blood poured from his knuckles. The glass of beer jumped but the table did not move. He was yelling, 'No! No! You goddamn' bastards! Not even for that satisfaction. Not for Connelly's life. Not for anything.'

Dean sat still but every muscle was tensed. He had thought Connelly would be his ace. Had not been prepared for Wyndham's refusal. 'Why not? It's what you've wanted all this time, isn't it? It's what you tried to do yourself.'

Wyndham glared at him in anguish. 'I believe in what we're doing. This is beyond personal gratification. This is the future. Not just for Asia but for us all. For humanity. Out of horror comes perfection. That is my sacrifice. This is for Katie and all the Katies yet to come. Not the fucking American Dream but true universal values – Asian Values.'

Dean stared at him. Wyndham really believed all this shit he was spouting. He saw himself as some Messiah come to save the world, ennobled by the poor kid's death. It was sick. But still it led comfortably into Dean's alternative offer.

'Take it easy,' he said. 'I'm just the broker. Sit down. Relax. Hear me out.'

Wyndham did not move.

Dean shrugged. Leaning back, he outlined the offer from his second bidder. The Americans did not know about their competition but that did not matter to Dean. Whichever deal Wyndham made, Dean would get paid.

He finished, 'Whoever you go with, the other will order you killed. But your new employers will have the resources to protect their expensive new asset so I wouldn't worry about it.'

'And you?'

'Your concern is touching. If Burman loses, I throw up my hands and say, "Goddamn it, I tried." If they don't kill you first, they'll send me out to renegotiate. As for the second bidder, they came in late on the deal so they know the risk's beyond my control. I just lose my final fee. There'll be other deals, other games to play.' Dean shrugged.

Wyndham stood up. Blood dripped from his fists. A dark pool stained the carpet. 'How long do I have to think about it?'

'How about breakfast tomorrow?'

Wyndham nodded. Dean stood up. He knew Wyndham would play ball. Wyndham buzzed the door. There was a pause while the security guards on the other side opened it up.

Wyndham did not look at the four burly men who swept in, but stepped aside as they grabbed Dean. Dean found his arms pinned down, twisted back against his shoulder blades. Jarring pain as he was lifted off the floor. A bag over his head. Cold metal against his wrists – handcuffs. A prick in his arm, the cold liquid shooting into his veins. 'Hey! What are you . . .'

Chapter Twenty-Six

Dean arrived back at his apartment block late in the afternoon the next day. He felt heavy with frustration and defeat. Every inch of his body ached from the assaults of the last few days. His head was pounding with a migraine. He hauled himself up the stairwell. The graduate block was a low-tech sixties building, functional and soulless. A noticeboard displayed university activities and house rules.

Dean let himself into his set of rooms. Leaving the door ajar, he crossed to the wall behind the TV. Moving the set aside, he slid open a false panel. From among the weapons, forged identity papers and surveillance equipment, he pulled out a laptop. It was slightly larger than standard commercial models with a built-in encoder and satellite transmitter. He left the panel open and set up the computer on the desk to begin typing up separate reports to his bidders.

After all this time scouring Asia for Lovelace and being so damn' sure that he was on a hot trail with the Wyndhams, he had been proved wrong. His meeting with Wyndham had been intensive and detailed and, at the end of it, Dean had had to admit that Wyndham could not be and was not Lovelace. Wyndham had known Lovelace, though, Dean recalled. Wyndham had treated Lovelace after he had tried to kill himself while in hiding in Malaysia a few years before. Wyndham had at first been reluctant to say more, Dean remembered, but the two million US dollars had clinched it. Wyndham told him that the Red Tiger had brought Lovelace to him and sworn him to secrecy on pain of death. On Lovelace's recovery, Wyndham said, the funding of the Centre had been assured through an anonymous donor. Wyndham had told Dean that Lovelace was now working out of Buenos Aires, giving him the name of a Red Tiger contact there.

Dean did not pay attention to the four removals men who came into the flat as he worked. They were big men for Asians, uniformly dressed in overalls, security tags at their lapels. They closed the door and stood waiting, empty boxes and trolleys beside them.

Dean finished the reports. He advised his bidders that he would be leaving KL within twenty-four hours and making his way to South America to pursue the lead Wyndham had given him. He would re-establish contact once he had secured a foothold in Buenos Aires, hopefully within ten days. Signing off, he encrypted the messages and transmitted them.

Dean closed the applications and switched off the power. He sat back in his chair. His headache was blinding. He closed his eyes but the pain assailed him still. The removals men took the laptop from in front of him. Dean did not move. They cleared the cubby-hole behind the TV set. Then they worked through the flat, checking the walls and floorboards, the ceiling tiles and electrical equipment. They leafed through papers and books. Everything that remotely hinted at Dean's being anything other than a graduate student was removed and placed in the boxes.

He sat at the desk staring ahead. The men left the flat, closing the door behind them. They trundled their load to the service lift, exited by the trade door and placed the boxes in an unmarked van. As they pulled out of the car park one of them called Dr Wyndham on a cellphone. 'We got everything-lah, *tuan*. We heading back now, boss.'

In the apartment, Dean sat unmoving at the desk. He did not know how much time passed. He had nothing left to do. It meant nothing to him either way, sitting here for a while. If only his goddamn' head wasn't killing him. He thought about getting a beer but it seemed too much of an effort to get up. He was vaguely aware that it was getting dark. After some time – five minutes or five hours, he didn't care – he had to piss but that, too, could wait.

Just after four in the morning, the other symptoms began.

Fei and Sam spent most of the next day cooped up in the cramped lodging room, the shutters closed. Fei kept trying Dean's cellphone until the battery on her own phone died in the afternoon. In the tiny cubicle, she felt awkward with Sam, their intimacy of the night before filling the space between them. They did not meet each other's eyes. Sam could not sit still, tapping, drumming, striding back and forth in the small space at the foot of the beds.

They went out briefly to get something to eat. At a hawker stall, they sat at a tin table screened from the street. A television was on an upturned box by the wok and stove. Its portable satellite aerial protruded high up from a nearby lamp post. A forest fire had started in a remote logging area in Borneo, smoke and flames engulfing the jungle. There were flash floods in Bangladesh, shacks and trucks floating in mud, wide-eyed children staring out of make-shift shelters. An anti-American bomb had exploded at the consulate in Nigeria, killing scores. Scenes of twisted metal and shattered concrete filled the screen. People were sobbing, being helped from the rubble. Others shouted and threw rocks, amassing into a sea of angry faces. In Jakarta, women wailed, victims of rape; men with bleeding heads were carried through fighting crowds. Currencies were plummeting, stock markets bottoming out, businesses collapsing. There were more muggings and violent crimes.

Fei felt as if she was witnessing the end of the world. Stranded here, she might never again find the reality she had once known. Fearful of every eye contact, dreading discovery, she seemed to be watching everything collapse around her. She and Sam stared at the screen but no one else paid any attention. The sense of disorientation was like vertigo.

Sam touched her arm. No more than a brushing of finger-tips. 'Are you okay?'

Fei nodded.

'I'm sorry.'

She was confused. 'What for?'

'The last time we met – I got on my one-track agenda. You didn't need that. I didn't mean for us to end it like we did . . .'

'Shh,' Fei said softly. 'We've gone beyond that, haven't we?'

Sam studied her for a long moment. Her eyes were bright with emotion. Her smile wavered then stayed. She touched Fei's hand under the table. Fei curled her fingers round Sam's. She felt a surge of exhilaration and hope, happiness as pure as a child's. It seemed to rock her like a wave.

On the TV screen, surreal scenes flashed up of figures in bright yellow body suits and thick rubber boots. They were masked. Sam glanced across at the set. Fei followed her gaze. The figures moved amid piles of corpses, mottled fowl stacked high. Officials were supervising the slaughter of millions of chickens in Hong Kong and in parts of mainland China, the commentary stated.

Fei stared in revulsion. She pushed away her plate of noodles. Sam said, 'I followed one of the medical teams the other day. The smell . . .'

Fei glanced at her. 'What about the Q lead you told them about?'

She shook her head, frowning. 'I don't know. Grossman's been the only one who's taken it seriously so far. Hiew, his senior consultant, dismissed it – wouldn't let me follow up my enquiries.'

'What are we going to do if we can't get hold of Dean?'

'We will. We have to.' Sam stared grimly at her. 'After all the trouble he's gone to to pin you down, he's not going to pass this moment up.'

Fei began to make calls from public phones, slipping out of the hostel every hour and going to different booths. Her nerves were fraying. She didn't know how long she could bear this waiting. How long they had before Han or the police or the Wyndhams' security people found them. They would have to do something soon if they kept drawing a blank with Dean.

———•———

The men circled Ryder's house under cover of darkness, watching the doors and windows. There was no movement or light from inside. One of them picked the lock on the kitchen door and in moments six men were in the house, their weapons concealed under their T-shirts. Two carried handcuffs and duct-tape.

The house was empty.

The leader made a call on his cellphone. 'No sign of Ryder or Qwong. Looks like Ryder never made it home from the airport.'

'Find her. And Qwong. Don't fuck up.'

———•———

Piers slammed down the receiver. He was back at the Centre, waiting with Ginny in the office adjacent to the labs. The Red Tiger had missed Ryder at both the airport in Hong Kong and KLIA. By the time they had got to the hospital, she had been and gone. Someone else had also been asking for her, they discovered: a man who had flashed an official badge at the reception desk. They had found out nothing more. They had staked out the lab but she had not showed again. Now they had screwed up the swoop at Ryder's house.

Piers had sent men round to Fei-Li's and they had come across the devastated apartment. The authorities had shown a search warrant, the porter told them. Fei could not be found and had not shown up at work. There was no sign of her at her mother's.

'Where the hell have they both gone?' Piers glared at Ginny.

'We can trust Fei, I swear it,' she said. But Fei's cellphone was disconnected. There was desperation in Ginny's eyes.

'The Red Tiger will bring them in. Then we'll see if your faith is justified.'

'They mustn't hurt Fei, whatever they do. Promise me, Piers? She hasn't gone to the authorities. Why else are they still looking for Ryder and searching Fei's apartment?'

'Why have they both gone missing at the same time?'

Ginny looked as if he had skewered her heart. 'Fei wouldn't do that to me. She loves me. She wouldn't betray me. She's not with Sam – she can't be. God, she mustn't be! Find her, get them to find her. God knows what danger she's in out there alone!' Her voice was rising higher. She paced in an erratic circle. 'She'll be safe with us, doesn't she know that? Maybe I should go and find her. She trusts me.'

'I want you here.' Piers did not want Ginny out of his control in her manic state. Her self-indulgence had caused enough damage already.

She grabbed him, screwing his shirt into a knot. 'What will the authorities do to her if they find her before we do? They might use her to get to us. We have to bring her home! Piers, help me. Help her. Bring her home to me safe and I'll do anything, I swear.'

He pushed her away.

He had no stomach for histrionics. They were working frantically to increase production and stabilise the latest version of the compound for use on Rutan. Siew had come and gone in the night, cursing and threatening Piers and the teams. His blazing wrath had seared through them all. Even as he had watched Dean's programming, he had blasted Piers. Why had he allowed Dean to come so close? Piers had not told him of Ginny's part in it all, only that Dean had located him somehow and offered a deal. His sister was safe for now but Piers did not know how much longer he could go on protecting her.

Their successful elimination of the American had not satisfied Siew. Piers had also promised him Ryder and she was still beyond the Centre's reach. They could not fail him now. Could not let a few maverick individuals put their great cause at risk.

Ginny reached out to him again but he pushed her roughly aside. 'Get out! Go to your trance suite and stay there.'

He ignored the hurt in her startled eyes. She scurried away, head down to hide the inevitable tears.

He glanced at his watch. By morning, Dean would be dead. Piers had used an early version of the compound on him – SPrP34gen21 – a highly unstable generation. A large dosage guaranteed severe and escalated effects within twenty hours. As a Double Alpha, Dean was a difficult subject to control completely but Piers had managed to implant a false memory of their exchange and its outcome. Dean would retain it for long enough to send misleading reports back to his two employers – wrong in fact but believed to be true by Dean himself. By the time he failed to report again in ten days, the Red Tiger would have ensured cremation of the 'unclaimed' body and there would be an independent doctor's certificate stating natural causes as the reason for death. Dean's people would follow the trail to South America and be off Piers's back. The Red Tiger contacts in Buenos Aires were being instructed to lead any of Dean's successors on false trails and kill them if necessary.

Piers went back to the frenetic activity of the labs, checking on Ricky's team who were working to finalise the scripts for the Phase Four town experiment. This was a new departure, tailoring their program to a mass, diffuse target instead of the individually tailored transformations of previous experiments. They needed to structure the nuances more carefully while retaining a generality in the program. Assuming they managed to produce the required amounts of the compound – and that was becoming more of a problem with each day – controlling the dosage through the water utilities plant would be difficult but not insurmountable. They needed more time but the schedule Siew insisted on gave them no margin. The only thing that was certain was the twice-daily cycle of chronotonin in the subjects and that had nothing to do with any of the scientists. Piers smiled at the irony of it. It was as if in their supreme hopes of controlling humanity, they could really control nothing at all.

⟞⟶⟶•◄⟵⟞

Fei stood with Sam under a banyan tree across the road from Dean's apartment block. A steady drizzle blurred the morning light. They carried umbrellas, tilted to obscure their faces from the crowd outside Dean's building. Parked cars and the awning of a hawker stall added to their cover. Fei's shoes and trousers were already sodden.

Police cars and an ambulance stood outside the building. A curious crowd had gathered in spite of the rain, heads and umbrellas bobbing as they tried to get a view. Reporters milled about. Police barred the way at the top of the steps. Fei felt her heart stick in her throat. Somehow, she knew that this had something to do with Dean.

An unmarked car pulled up. An athletic-looking man got out, others behind him. His shirt was instantly soaked, his dark muscular bulk visible through the wet fabric. His face was grim and hard, eyes cold slits as he glanced about.

Fei instinctively drew back. 'Han,' she gasped.

He did not see them but jogged into the building with his men, flashing a badge at the police guard.

Sam said, 'We have to find out what's going on. Stay here. I'll go and have a look.'

'No, wait . . .'

But Sam was already crossing the street. Fei waited for an eternity, watching Sam as she mingled with the onlookers, slowly moving through them, engaging them in conversation. The police were inches away but were caught up in their tasks, questioning neighbours and witnesses, keeping reporters at bay, and did not notice Sam. Figures came out of the building – a doctor, pushing his way through the journalists, then a laden stretcher, entirely covered by a sheet. It looked heavy from the way the bearers moved. The entourage made their way to the ambulance and slid the body into it.

Sam pushed her way to the vehicle. She used her umbrella to shield her face from the building, rain soaking her. She had recognised the doctor as one of the physicians from the National Hospital. He was surprised to see her, squinting through rain-spattered glasses. He hauled himself up into the ambulance. 'What are you doing here?'

'Came to see one of the students in the building.' Sam clambered up, closing the umbrella. 'Do you mind? Looks like no one can get into the block.'

She nodded at the body. 'What have we got?'

Dr Kee wiped his glasses and studied her myopically. He glanced out at the rain as if deciding something. Finally he said, 'One of the graduates, supposedly an Australian. Went crazy in the middle of the night – shouting, screaming, tearing up the place. I'm the campus doctor so they paged me. The students in his hallway tried to contain him. They also called the police. By the time I got here it was just after six. The police were already there. He was in an active state of delirium and he was a big guy. After a while, he collapsed. He had a fever – 104 and heading upwards. He complained of abdominal discomfort and chest pain. Increasing stiffness of the neck and back. He was raving. Paranoid delusions – people were trying to kill him, use him for experiments. Kept calling out a woman's name – Feng-Lee or something. The police wanted to arrest him so we had this stupid tussle about whether it was going to be jail or hospital. It was the strangest case I've ever seen. All the classic symptoms of meningococcal meningitis, including alteration of consciousness. But there were no rashes and the deterioration rate was unusually rapid. He died at 7.04 a.m.'

Sam half stood in the interior of the ambulance and stepped closer to the body. Kee lifted the sheet. It was Dean.

'And the police?' She sat down again.

'They came round to my way of thinking in the end. But they needed to verify there were no unusual circumstances before I signed off on the death certificate. That's routine in such call-outs. They got this new gadget and some bright spark patched through the deceased's fingerprints. The database came back with a match for an American called Carson Dean but this fellow's papers said he was Kyle Laddman. So they called in the security forces – something about Dean being that spy who was deported some months back.'

Sam nodded.

'What do you know about all this?' Kee said.

'What do you mean?'

'A security agent, Han – he asked if I was from the National Hospital. When I said yes, he asked if I knew you and if I'd seen you recently.'

'What did you say?'

'Yes, I knew you, and no, I hadn't.'

'What are you going to say now?' Sam studied him.

'He won't ask again.' Kee met her gaze. 'I don't want to get involved in your personal business.'

Sam touched his knee. 'Thanks.'

'He's in there checking the scene. You'd better get out of here.' Kee turned away and began fiddling with an oxygen mask.

Across the road, Fei saw Han appear in the shadows just inside the doorway. He paused, talking to a colleague. She stared at the ambulance. Come on, Sam, hurry up!

She saw Sam slip out into the drizzle and duck round the side of the ambulance. She appeared at the bonnet of the vehicle and was about to head back across the road when Han stepped out into the rain, facing the banyan tree. Fei caught Sam's eye under cover of her umbrella and shook her head. Han hesitated and then turned to come down the steps towards the ambulance.

Fei jerked her head. In the moment that Han sank down into the crowd, Sam began to move across the street, her umbrella screening her head and shoulders. His view of her was already obscured by the on-lookers and the body of the ambulance.

As Sam reached the parked cars on Fei's side of the road, Fei moved away, meeting Sam diagonally some yards from the front of the building. They carried on walking without breaking step, heading round a corner. Out of sight of Dean's building, they broke into a run.

———————⊃●⊂———————

Fei and Sam stepped out of a taxi along the sheltered sweep of parking at KLIA's departure gates. The drizzle had turned to sheets of rain. Fei's wet clothes chilled her. She glanced around her anxiously. She was not sure what – or who – she expected to see. There were families unloading luggage from their cars; limousines dropping off Japanese executives. Sam glanced at her and they made their way into the sleek interior of the airport, the air-conditioning icy against their damp clothing.

Fei was trembling – whether from cold or fear, she did not know. They had not thought beyond finding Dean. They had run for several blocks in the rain, weaving through back streets, and finally taken shelter in a coffee-shop. Downing hot sweet coffee, they had tried to work out what to do next. Sam had wanted to try the US Embassy. Fei had hissed, trying to keep her panic under control, 'We won't get past the police.'

'The British High Commission?'

'I want to get out of here. Leave the country.'

'The High Com—'

'We can't risk going all the way over there and finding the police or Han's people waiting. Let's just get a flight out of here. Go to . . . I don't know, the CIA or MI6 or whoever. Direct.'

Across the airport's shiny marble floor, the ticketing counter seemed a long way away. Fei strode beside Sam awkwardly, conscious of their bedraggled state and trying to project an air of confidence. She whispered, 'We should pay by cash.'

Sam muttered, 'They'll be suspicious. Who pays for airline tickets by cash?'

'But they'll trace our card payments.'

'I'm hoping that by then we'll be out of Malaysian airspace.'

'They could make the plane turn around . . .'

Sam turned to Fei. 'We don't have much choice right now.'

Fei nodded. Her chest hurt from the tension. She could not think clearly, could not use tactics in a game without rules. There were threats wherever she turned, whatever they did. There was no safety, no certainty but the closing off of all their options. She felt as if they were already trapped, that it was only a matter of time before Han or the Wyndhams or the police caught up with them. But they could not give up, could not stay put till then. They could only try and keep trying, like birds fluttering against a glass cage.

At the counter Sam spoke to the ticketing officer, a pretty Malay girl in Malaysian Airlines groundstaff uniform. Her name tag told them her name was Noridah. The next flight to London was via Frankfurt, leaving in two hours. There were only first-class seats left, Noridah said, looking at Fei and Sam's wet clothes, 'For two seats, *mem*, it will be eighteen thousand and thirty *ringgit*, including tax.'

Sam gasped but suppressed it.

'How do you wish to pay?' Noridah peered to the side of them. Fei knew she was registering that they had no luggage.

Fei slid over her Gold American Express card.

'Passports, please.'

One Malaysian. One British. Noridah took them from the counter and ran each one in turn through the electronic reader. The charge card lay untouched on the counter. The data came up on her computer screen. It was turned away from them. Noridah stared at the screen for a long moment. She tapped some keys and checked the screen again. Fei exchanged glances with Sam. Her mouth felt dry. In their panic, they had not thought about passport control.

They had their backs to the man in the seating area two aisles across from the ticketing counter. He folded his newspaper casually as he muttered into the microphone under his lapel. Its earpiece was unobtrusively flesh-coloured. Both were connected to the cellphone in his jacket pocket which was on conference mode. He stayed on-line as he stood up. The other men in place around the airport acknowledged his alert. They were making their way over.

Noridah had called over her supervisor. They were both looking at the screen. Fei said, 'Is there a problem?'

'Just one moment, please, *mem*.' Noridah flashed her a smile.

The supervisor moved away and picked up the phone. He spoke urgently, not looking at Fei and Sam. Sam nudged Fei, her head turned away. Fei followed her gaze. A man in a denim jacket was making his way over to them, a paper under one arm. From either side of him, a hundred yards away, several other men were converging. Fei looked behind her. Figures coming from all sides. Men. All casually dressed, all affecting indifference. But all aiming for the ticketing counter.

Fei stared beyond the luggage belt and the curve of the counter to the departures hall. Airport security police were striding towards them. Noridah turned away. The ticketing supervisor caught their eye and nodded.

Sam reached across the counter and swung the monitor round. Their passport details had police notifications against them, the alert flashing silently beside their names.

'Hey!' Noridah spun back. Fei pushed herself back from the counter as Sam twisted round. They ran.

Behind them, Fei heard shouting. She glanced round. The police were breaking into a run. There were throngs of people ahead of them. Businessmen. Families. Luggage. Trolleys. Crowds of Australian backpackers. Fei pushed through, dodging flight bags. Sam was ahead of her now, weaving in and out. Faces staring. People shouting as they were jostled. In the corner of her vision, the men were also running, fanning out to cut them off.

Fei's breath rasped in her lungs. Her legs thudded heavily, as if beyond her control. She did not know where they were going, blindly following Sam ahead of her. Slamming into a trolley, pressing on. Exit doors in front of them, cars and taxis beyond. Hammering footsteps behind her. She did not dare look round. Pelting on.

An Indian family crossed their path laden with boxes, bags and baskets. Sam leapt over a suitcase. The family stumbled to a halt in surprise. A woman in a sari stepped back. Fei slammed into her. Tried to recover, the momentum carrying her out of control into a trolley piled with boxes. The woman was yelling in pain, her sari a tangle as she fell. Pain jarred into Fei's hips and legs. The floor smashed into her shoulder. Winded, she tried to get up, hawing for air.

Arms grabbed her. Men all around her. They blocked her from the Indian family. From view of Sam. Fei fought against them but they were too strong. Too many of them.

She caught sight of Sam a long way away. She stood frozen, it seemed for a long time, staring back, her face distorted as she shouted Fei's name.

There were other men closing in on Sam. Moving fast as she stood still. Fei was hauled off her feet, pulled along even as she struggled. She screamed, 'Go! Go! Get out of here! Sam, for God's sake!'

A hand slammed into her face. Cut off sound. Cut off air. Fei fought it but they had her arms pinned. She kicked out, made contact with legs, but still they hauled her along. Her jaw was caught at a painful angle, the pressure stopping any biting movement. Red flashed before her eyes. Her lungs were bursting. Her heartbeat roared in her ears. She sucked against nothing.

Chapter Twenty-Seven

Sam turned and threw herself at the exit doors. The air outside was warm. Rows of taxis faced her. She raced along the parking bays. The men were still chasing her. Twisting round, she saw far behind Fei was being pushed into the boot of a car, the bonnet slamming down hard. Turning back, Sam caught a movement out of the corner of her eye. Ahead of her, a security officer emerged from an exit door. She was trapped.

Close by was a Proton. A woman stepping out of the passenger side. A man unloading bags from the boot. The key dangling high up on the boot bonnet. Sam pushed the man out of the way, grabbed the key, slammed the boot. She dived into the driver's seat and started the engine with a roar. The woman screamed. The man picked himself up, stunned. Sam's pursuers pushed the woman aside. One of them grabbed the passenger door.

She shot the car out of the bay, clipping the vehicle in front. The man let go of the door handle, the momentum catapulting him over the back of the other car. Sam scraped the parked vehicles ahead, fighting for control as she accelerated. The BMW they had shoved Fei into loomed in her rearview mirror and rammed into Sam's bumper. She jolted forward against the steering wheel but held the car steady. The BMW's tyres screeched as it passed parallel with her on the right, then swung into her front bonnet. Sam fought for control as the car heaved to the left against a parked coach, sparks spraying as metal skidded against metal.

The BMW accelerated, overtaking her.

She pushed the car to the limit of second, slammed it into third and took the curve out from under the parking bays at fifty. Rain unloaded onto the windscreen. She scrabbled for the wiper switch, not slowing down. The BMW was a black smudge ahead, its powerful engines outstripping the grinding whine of the Proton.

Another car suddenly coming up behind her. A Merc. Bumping her. Pulling alongside and ramming into her. Sam bounced in the seat, her head and neck jerking painfully, back straining to keep upright. The rain whited out the vision beyond a few feet. At a junction ahead, the BMW pulled right, speeding towards the highway. Sam pushed the Proton on. She could not lose Fei.

The Merc swung out to cover her flank, smashing into her as she tried to turn right. Vehicles all around hooted and screeched past. Sam spun the wheel left, avoiding a head-on collision with a white car. The Merc reversed and pounded into her again. Sam slid into first and forced her way round the white car. The Merc followed. Fuck! She had no choice but to speed on.

The road was single-file, a barrier down the middle. The Merc was forcing the pace, pushing her up against the slower vehicles ahead. Sam flashed and hooted, scraping past as each car pulled over to the side as far as it could. A Japanese jeep refused to move out of the way. She rammed it. It pulled aside slowly. She pushed by, gouging its shiny metalwork. The Merc followed.

Sam spun the car off at the next junction. It was an old trunk road connecting the new airport highway to a nearby town. Traffic was heavy but, Malaysian-style, moving fast along the single-lane road. This time there was no barrier in the middle. Spray and rain blurred the windscreen. The wipers worked frantically to little effect.

Sam made herself take a long breath. What now? It wasn't over yet, the Merc sitting hard on her bumper. There were no turnings off the road, uncleared forest to the left, thick oncoming traffic to the right.

Then she saw it. A gap in the oncoming traffic. Difficult to judge the distance or how much room she would have. No time to think now.

She held the car steady at sixty. She'd never done it at this speed before. The gap zipped by. She would have to wait for her next chance. Pray for it.

There, in front of a goods lorry! One and a half turns to the right, the back of the car spinning round to the left. Spray fanning out. The car juddering from the water on the road. The Merc appearing suddenly by her side window. Slamming on the handbrake. The car flying backwards as it skidded into the gap in a 180-degree turn. The truck honking and flashing her, thundering towards her rear, its huge bulk unstoppable. Slipping into first, revving with the clutch down, rolling the steering wheel straight. Handbrake off. Clutch off. Wheels catching just as the grille of the truck nudged her bumper. The Proton took off straight ahead. The Merc was a flash of movement just out of sight, still heading in the original direction.

Sam picked up speed and cruised on. She had a few minutes' headway at least even if the Merc managed the same manoeuvre. Enough time to get back to the junction and detour up on to the highway. Then she would decide what her next move would be.

Complete blackness. No crack, no seam. Fei clamped down hard on her panic. She was curled awkwardly in the confined space, her body aching from where the men had grabbed and shoved her. She did not know how long they had been driving, the swinging of the car steadying now to a roaring hum. She guessed they were on a highway. The sound of the rain was strangely muffled. She heard no other traffic, only the rasping of her own breath.

At first she had pounded on the bonnet but its thick padding swallowed the sound. Her screams had rung back in her ears.

But she could not stop, could not give up, slamming her palms until they were raw, straining her voice until exhaustion had stilled her.

Exploring the confined space with her hands, she found it empty. Every inch was padded – insulated against sound. There was a tiny vent through which a trickle of air flowed across her fingers. The boot had been custom-designed for abduction.

Fei sank back. She felt no terror, only an overwhelming sense of despair. She did not know who her captors were. Did not care. She could not fight them. Could not outwit them. She could not trust her grasp of reality anymore, nor her own judgement. There had been Ginny. And Dean. They had been constructs, no more real than their own imaginations. Had any of it been real? Here in this padded coffin it was easy to believe that none of it had happened, that everything she remembered had no basis in reality. That perhaps she had always been here in this cocoon of nothing, living out in her own mind images that had been born out of nothing and nowhere.

Fei cried out, her own voice startling her.

Sam was real. She clung on to that like a lifeline. Sam was real and out there somewhere. She had to have got away. Please, God, Sam had to have escaped. She would know what to do. How to get through to the American or British authorities. Get help. And she would find Fei. They would see each other again.

They had to see each other again.

Fei felt it with a certainty she had never felt before. It sat inside her like a clear diamond embedded in rock. At each moment, she had always sought out Sam and Sam had always been there. For everything that was real, everything that had any meaning, she had found it in Sam. Fei understood it all suddenly. She had been so afraid. So afraid of Sam. So afraid of what love really meant. Of its demand for her whole self. And so she had worked to own Sam and control her. But Sam in her own reality had always been there, had refused to surrender to Fei's power. Fei felt as if she saw Sam for the first time. For who she was and who she had always been.

The car swung to the side and the engine noise changed.

They were slowing. Going uphill, veering to left and right. Then down again. Rising again. Silence suddenly. Muffled doors slamming.

The bonnet whipped open. Bright painful light. Rain pelting Fei's face. Hard hands grabbing her and hauling her out.

⸺➤●◄⸺

Ginny pulled Fei into her embrace. They were in a windowless underground cell, comfortably furnished with a bed, table and chairs, side lamps and curtains. Fei was barefoot and stripped of her accessories.

Ginny's grip was tight around Fei's neck, her kisses stifling. Her voice was sharp with tension. 'Where have you been? I was so worried about you. Why couldn't I get through on the cell-phone?'

'The battery ran down.' Fei tried to ease away from Ginny's hold but could not. Ginny stroked her hair, clasping her head to her breast. Fei felt a rising sense of claustrophobia.

'But they found you. You're safe now. We have you safe now.' Ginny held Fei's face in both her hands and peered into her eyes. Fei made herself meet her intense gaze. Anxiety had made Ginny's features taut. Her lips were hard in spite of her comforting words. There was a glint of rage in her eyes. 'Why did you disappear?'

'I . . . I needed some space. To – to think.'

'About us?'

Instinctively, Fei knew she had to keep up the façade of their love affair. If only to buy herself some time. 'Everything: Dean, our future. It was happening so fast.'

'Who were you with?'

Fei feigned puzzlement. 'No one. I was just driving around.'

Ginny's face was pinched and harsh. 'Why didn't you come to me?'

'You said we needed to keep our distance, we would be safer apart . . .' Fei floundered. Ginny's gaze was like a drill through

405

her skull. She had to turn this staccato interrogation another way. Keep it away from Sam. She said, 'Dean's dead. I tried to see him but they said he'd died suddenly in the night. I was scared. There were police at his building and I panicked. Took off. But it's over now, isn't it? With Dean dead, there's no more blackmail threat, right?'

'You were with Sam.'

'I . . . no . . . look . . .'

Ginny shook Fei suddenly. Her head snapped back. Ginny cried, 'Don't lie to me! They saw you at the airport – you were trying to leave the country. You ran away from me and back to Sam. You thought you could leave me, abandon me. After everything I've done for you . . . for us. You love me, how could you try to escape me like that?'

'No . . .'

'We're bound together now, don't you understand? You're part of all this. You're part of our future.' Ginny's face was right in Fei's, veins angry like snakes across her forehead. Rage flashed in her eyes.

Fei tried to pull back but Ginny's claw-like hold trapped her. Sharp fingers dug into her flesh, breaking the skin. She struggled but Ginny was bigger and stronger. Ginny shook her again, pushed her hard against the wall. Fei gasped, 'I was saying goodbye to her. She was going back to London. I told her it was over.'

Ginny's grasp relaxed. Fei squirmed aside, wrenched herself free. Blood trickled down her arms. Fei sucked in air. Ginny's manic eyes followed her, assessing, thinking. Her hands were streaked with blood. Fei felt a chill of terror. She rushed on, 'I told her it was you I love.'

In one stride, Ginny was on her. A back-handed blow across the face. Fei reeled backwards, her ears ringing. She sprawled on the floor, blood clogging her mouth.

'You're lying!' It was a wail. Tears streamed down Ginny's face. She knelt and reached out. Fei flinched but could not move. Ginny began to wipe the blood from Fei's face with her handkerchief. Her touch was tender. She was crying. 'How can you love me? After all that you know about me. After all the things I've done and all the killings I've been a part of. How can you love me?'

Ginny's hands caressed her face, traced the curve of her throat. They were strong hands, smeared with blood. Fei knew her life depended on her next words. She worked to control her trembling. Her voice was hoarse. She spoke as if to Sam. 'I love you, Ginny, don't you get it? I love you. Whatever you've done, whatever you're doing – I'm here. I'm yours. You didn't have to send them for me, I would have come back to you. Whatever you do to me, I will always love you.'

Fei could not stop shivering.

Ginny did not move. Her hands froze, fingertips against Fei's skin. She searched Fei's eyes with a desperate gaze. Fei looked back, seeing only Sam, giving to Ginny everything that belonged to Sam.

Ginny closed her eyes. It was as if the Fei of her intangible hopes had taken on flesh and substance. She had longed for such a moment in her loneliness. To be loved by another absolutely and without question. To be loved by Fei. She could not believe it. Did not believe it. She opened her eyes. Fei was watching her with a liquid gaze that melted the core of her. It was a look totally without guile, a look of trust and devotion. Was this really happening? Her breath faltered. It was everything she wanted. Everything she needed. It would be so easy to believe this truth.

Fei's voice was rich with emotion. 'Let's get away from all this. Leave now, go somewhere safe. We can be who we want to be, take on any life we choose. They'll never find us. Take me away from here, my darling Ginny. We don't have to be caught up in all this. I know it tears you apart. I know your grief and your pain. I know how much you long to be free. We *can* be free, I promise you, my love. We'll live the life you've always wanted, I'll make sure of it. We'll get a little place, with roses and a garden. Just the two of us. No one will know us, no one will come between us. Just you and me, for the rest of our lives, being there for each other, happy, alone – and safe.'

Fei was stroking Ginny's hair, the touch of her fingertips

electric. Her long eyes were fixed on Ginny, never leaving her face, never looking askance. Ginny nuzzled into her palms, kissing the soft flesh. Her body seemed to sway to a rhythm of its own, as if luxuriating in the very air that embraced her. The steel wires that had twisted inside her for so long melted away. She felt only exhilaration, the energy of release. Curiously, she thought, was this what happiness was like? In her mind, they were already there in that image Fei had offered her, its colours infusing them both, its textures of warmth and delight brushing against their skins. She would find a way to get Fei out of here, past the nurses and the guards, past Piers. They would vanish as if through the looking-glass to another reality. She could do it, she had the resources, all the skills that the years in hiding had taught her. She could rescue Fei, rescue them both.

She kissed Fei, felt the yearning in her response, let it drown her. Ginny gasped, 'I'll get you out of here . . . I need to think. We'll get away, just you and me. Trust me. I'll get us out.'

Piers's voice spoke suddenly from the blank walls, so clear he might have been in the room. 'Ginny, your time is up.'

<hr />

A bank of CCTV monitors showed Fei and Ginny in the cell from different angles. The sound and picture quality had been custom-designed for clarity and might have been those of superior broadcast television. Piers watched from the control room as two security staff entered the cell and drew Ginny from Fei. Ginny scanned the walls, her professional eye picking up each tiny camera and mike one by one. She stared into the last one with hatred and terror, her gaze seeming to lock with Piers's. He had promised her time alone with Fei. 'You bastard,' she said.

The guards escorted her out. Fei rushed to the door but it locked electronically behind them. She circled the middle of the cell. She could not see the devices. Each lens and mike was the size of a screw head, embedded in the plaster and lost amid the bumps and imperfections of the wall. Her face was contorted with fear and frustration. 'What do you want from me, goddamn you? Why are you doing this?'

Her voice broke and her legs seemed to give way. She fell to her knees, hanging her head, sobbing.

Piers turned down the sound. Ong buzzed through on the intercom. 'Mr Siew and his party have arrived. They are coming to shore now.'

Piers had been waiting for word on Sam Ryder. Nothing yet. They had run out of time on the Double Alpha programming he had promised Siew. But Fei-Li would do just as well. He switched intercom channels and spoke to the mission control teams. 'Stand by with the Qwong files.'

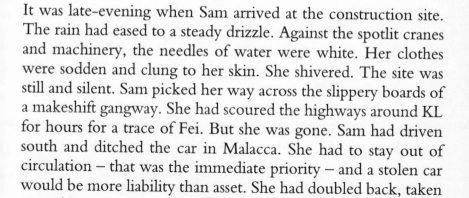

It was late-evening when Sam arrived at the construction site. The rain had eased to a steady drizzle. Against the spotlit cranes and machinery, the needles of water were white. Her clothes were sodden and clung to her skin. She shivered. The site was still and silent. Sam picked her way across the slippery boards of a makeshift gangway. She had scoured the highways around KL for hours for a trace of Fei. But she was gone. Sam had driven south and ditched the car in Malacca. She had to stay out of circulation – that was the immediate priority – and a stolen car would be more liability than asset. She had doubled back, taken several buses and taxis. Finally she arrived in Klang, the port west of KL.

There was a light on in the Portacabin at the side of the site. Sam felt an urge to cry suddenly. But she was not there yet. She had no time to rest, no time to think of herself or her terror. She had to keep going, keep strong. Action, take action, that was the way forward. The way to find Fei.

She pushed herself on to the cabin, stumbling up the steps. She banged on the door, leaning against the frame, feeling her energy ebb away. She had to hold on, not give in yet. She banged hard, calling out, 'Johnny! Please, Johnny! Open up!'

The door was wrenched open. Fei's brother stood in the light.

<hr />

Piers was making his way along the tunnel to the beach to meet Siew when Ginny caught up with him, grabbing his arm. She was gasping for breath, tears choking her. He did not break pace. The momentum of her distress gave her raw strength. She yanked him round to face her, gripping his arm. 'Don't hurt her, Piers, for God's sake, please!'

'We need her healthy, Ginny. She'll be fine.' He stared coldly down at her.

'Just give me one thing. One thing only – that's all I ask from you.'

He waited.

'Don't make her forget me.' Ginny pleaded as if for her life. 'Everything else is yours. You can have me next. Two subjects for your audience – they'd like that, wouldn't they? Only let her remember me and let me remember her. Like two best friends. Like it should always have been. She with her new life, her husband and children, whatever future you give her. Me with you, our work, the centre. But best friends always. Please, Piers, don't take that away from me. I've given you my whole life and all of myself. Leave me just this one happiness, I beg you.'

She began to weep in spite of herself. She clung to him, buried her face in his chest. Slowly, she felt his arms curl around her. His lips on her hair. She closed her eyes and whispered, 'Thank you.'

Then he was gone, striding down the tunnel. Ginny stared after his straight back. He was on his way to meet the future without her. After all the long years of waiting, the moment of her transformation was here. She did not care if the new version of the compound was still imperfect or not. No one could know for sure until it had played out its reactions in Fei's system. But her life and Fei's were bound together and wherever the Cure took Fei, Ginny would be there also. It would purify their love through fire, burn off its degradation and sickness, leaving only the sacred meeting of mind and spirit. They would be saved, fit citizens of the New Asia and content at last.

Ginny turned and made her way back down the tunnel towards the underground labs.

<hr>

The invited audience settled in the auditorium which had the intimacy of a private viewing cinema with luxurious furnishings and soft carpets. The audience was made up of leading members of the Asian Values Alliance and the top benefactors of the Centre's secret work. Among them were powerful business tycoons, politicians and military leaders whom Siew had persuaded to the Alliance cause. With such slow progress on the development of a usable compound, they had demanded to see for themselves what results their money was buying.

Siew Kei-Win sat in the place of honour next to Piers; Ginny and the computer and psych teams were in mission control. They were linked to the auditorium by live video hook-up, the scene at mission control taking up an inset box on the cinema screen. Audience reaction was monitored by Piers on one of the many TV screens in the control room. The control teams all wore radio-linked headsets to allow them freedom of movement.

The lights dimmed in the auditorium. A picture faded in on the screen. It was Fei in her cell. She was half-slouching on the bed against the wall, a blanket pulled around her. Food and water were untouched on the floor nearby. She stared dully ahead of her.

Piers spoke to the camera relaying his image to the audience. He told them about Fei. The screen flashed up images of her and her life: smiling at public functions with the Wyndhams, confident and sleek at the inauguration ceremony, arguing

fiercely at the negotiations with the JB school, lists of her qualifications and degrees. Through N-Sat, Piers had obtained
interviews from her colleagues, friends and family under the
guise of a documentary on high-flying Asian women. The
portrait that emerged was of a woman who was independent,
stubborn, wilful, intelligent, quick-witted and articulate – a
feminist and a liberal who fought men on their own terms in
their own territory. And a pervert. A picture of Fei kissing Sam
flashed up. There was a ripple of surprise that turned to murmurs
of disapproval. The photo had been snapped by Ginny from
pictures in Fei's apartment, using a tiny digital micro-camera.

Siew took over at this point. 'Modernity is a disease of the
mind. It began in the West and for generations it bred there,
spreading like a cancer. Asia held it at bay for a time, but with
education and travel, networked communications and populations who have learnt to think for themselves, the infection of
this region has begun. We are at crisis point.

'To ensure the success of our region, in business and
commerce, for productive economies and effective armies, we
need more and more people who are creative and intelligent,
skilled and educated. Yet the more highly tuned and independent their minds, the more dangerous they are. Such minds are
most at risk to the corruption of self.'

Piers glanced at Ginny. To his surprise, a rush of emotion
caught him. He felt an ache of compassion for all she had
suffered. They had been through so much pain and horror
together. He knew how intensely she carried her guilt.
Whatever future he negotiated for himself with Siew, it made
him happy to be able to give her what he had promised her so
long ago – freedom from her own mind.

Piers picked up his cue. 'All of you here tonight believe in
the Cure. Over the next few days, I will show you how we will
cure the mind of modern Asia. I will show you a miracle.'

Chapter Twenty-Eight

Sam ate the Maggi instant noodles hungrily. She sat with Johnny in his tiny rented apartment, the blinds drawn. Between mouthfuls, she talked, trying to capture in words everything that had happened. To her own ears, her story sounded crazy and paranoid. But the stark reality told them both more than she ever could. Fei was gone.

A sound. Sam stiffened. Johnny turned his head to the door. It had been a shuffling sound, like feet brushing the floor.

The door smashed open, wood splintering. Dark figures exploded into the room. Masked. Rifles to the fore.

They swarmed round Johnny and Sam, shouting, 'Police! Freeze!'

Johnny was half-out of his seat. A bristle of rifles aimed at his head, inches away. A barricade of men stood between him and Sam. Other figures hauled her up, the bowl of noodles splashing across the floor. They pinned her within a tight circle.

There had been no time even to scream.

Fei stood in the middle of the cell, listening to the voices broadcast from the auditorium. She searched the wall for the concealed cameras but saw nothing. She had recognised Siew's voice and Piers's. Their contempt had stirred her, goading her on to her feet. Anger churned in her gut. She had shouted at them but the mikes had not transmitted her cries. Their voices droned on. She stood rigid with frustration. She was exhausted and hungry. Her head throbbed. Her mouth was painfully dry. She looked over at the glass of water. She could almost feel the liquid on her lips, washing over her tongue. She turned away.

She was their experimental subject. The prion Sam called Factor Q was in the water – or in the plate of congealing Chinese stewed pork next to it. It had to be. She had touched neither since the tray had been slid through a flap in the door some time ago. She did not know how long she had been in the cell. She reached out to the walls as if to make solid the disembodied voices.

'Miss Qwong.' It was Siew. 'Be patient. It's only a matter of time now.'

'Let me go, damn you!'

'You had such promise. I thought you might join us of your own choice. You played your part well that night we were in Chow Kit. As I said then, the Alliance needs strong women like you. But on our terms.'

'Is *this* Asian values?' Fei shouted. Words were the only weapon she had. 'Locking me up like this? Playing God? Ben was right – he tried to warn me. You killed him. And Deng, *he* was telling the truth in all his madness, wasn't he? You locked him up . . .'

'He's dead too.' Piers's voice.

Fei closed her eyes. They would kill her if they needed to. It hit her for the first time.

Siew again. 'Why do you reject Asian values? They can heal your sickness. Fill your empty life.'

'Why?' Fei opened her eyes. White walls and ceiling glared back. She had nothing more to lose. Her laughter was harsh. 'The Asian Values you preach are a mockery of the spirit of all the ordinary people who try to get by the best they can. The values that we all muddle along with are not about fear and control and hatred and contempt. We work hard, we love who we love, we do our best for our families, for our futures – those are the ordinary values lived by ordinary Asians. Your version is wrong. And the proof of that is that you have to do this. You have to make robots out of us because you won't win us any other way. I say, fuck your Asian Values! Fuck you all!'

Fei slammed her hands against the walls. She was losing it, she knew. She had to hang on, wrestle back control from her fear and rage. The cell roared with a hubbub of voices, transmitted from the auditorium.

A woman's voice rang out above the noise. 'You don't believe that-lah. You studied in the West. You fell in with Western women. This sickness of yours is not an Asian thing. Asian women aren't – um – they don't do such things-lah. You just got corrupted. We take you away from the Western influences, make you properly Asian again, and then you can be happy.'

Fei searched for the cameras. She wanted to see the woman's face. Look into her eyes. These people understood nothing.

She could not control the emotion in her voice. She stared up at the blank wall. '*I* am Asian. Whatever *I* do is Asian. Whatever love *I* share is Asian. Whatever thoughts *I* hold, whatever beliefs *I* live by, are Asian – because *I* am. You cannot choose which parts of me to take or leave. You cannot choose who is to belong and who is not. This is my home and I am a part of you.'

Voices rose in outrage. Fei sat down on the bed, her strength gone suddenly. She could hardly remember what she had said. It was as if her fury and despair had spoken for her, bursting out like genies from a bottle.

In mission control, Piers switched the head-mikes to the private channel. He said, 'She hasn't ingested any of the food or liquid. She's not stupid. They contain a solution of generation 107 of the compound and a dose of chronotonin. Once the compound takes hold in the brain, reaction with the hormone will induce the state of deep trance. We will need to administer the Cure and the triggering chronotonin by force.'

'No!' Siew cut across him as Piers began to give the orders. Piers paused.

'I want this done as it would happen in the real situation. Phase Four depends on the distribution of those two elements in the water system. We can't afford any slip-ups in the event.' Siew's glare added the unspoken addendum: there had been too many fuck-ups already.

'I'll have an orderly administer the water by force.'

Siew nodded. Then something occurred to him. 'Wait!'

He flicked the head-mike channel over to open transmission and addressed Fei. 'Why don't you have a drink of water?'

Fei looked up. She was about to answer. Then stopped. As if assessing her choices. She said nothing.

Siew snorted, 'You think you have a choice, don't you? Choice – the ultimate prize of the liberal. Freedom of choice. Freedom of the individual.'

Fei ignored him.

Piers watched Siew. Fei's silence was goading him, pale fury tightening his face until it resembled a skull. It was as if Fei was making a fool of Siew and the Alliance by her bloody-mindedness. It would be simple to force the water down her, Piers thought. But some inexplicable impulse in Siew was making this stand off symbolic somehow. This telescoped for all of them – Siew, Piers and the Alliance devotees – the battle they had sworn to fight all their lives, with all their energies and resources. Fei had a choice. To drink or not. To speak or not. So far, Piers and Siew had been in control of her physical body, bringing her here by violence, locking her up. But that was not enough. It would never be enough. They could not control her freedom of choice. That failure had mocked them all their lives and would mock them to their graves. No one had ever been able to, nor ever would, control another's choice.

But the Cure would change everything.

It was as if, by her silence, Fei mocked even that sacred hope.

Siew cupped a hand over his mike and leant towards Piers. He wanted to show Fei in the most absolute terms that he controlled her, no matter what aberration made her think other-wise. His eyes were wild with fury. Piers offered him an ace that would give him the power he wanted over Fei. Siew smiled with sadistic pleasure. He said, 'Do it.'

He spoke into the mike again. Anger made his voice hoarse. 'This wilfulness is characteristic of a disease of the mind. For generations the wise and good have had to waste endless energy and resources in persuasion of the masses – through inducement, force, pain or argument. None of that works. History has proved it time and again. There will always be upstarts who think they know better than those superior to them. These people destabilise worthy government and threaten the common good for their own agendas. The Cure will rid us of such wilfulness once and for all. With a drink of water you will see the waste of resources required by the old methods, and afterwards the simplicity and ease of the Cure.'

In the cell there was a low hum and a panel slid open. A huge screen emerged, encased in a reinforced glass shield and taking up most of the wall. From it Siew was looking straight at Fei. There was a furious satisfaction in his face. He said, 'We found your Sam.'

Fei felt her heart stop.

He said, 'Switch to outside link.'

His face vanished and on the screen was a black-and-white image of two figures against a background of thick trees. Fei found herself on her feet. A man in black, his face smeared dark, held another figure in front of him. It was night. A clock at the bottom right gave a date and time, the seconds clicking on. It was a live transmission. The figures were white in the beams of light – car headlights? The smaller figure was a woman with a boyish figure, her loose tunic and leggings torn. She was blindfolded, her hands behind her back, pinned awkwardly by the hold around her throat. It was Sam. The man held a pistol to her temple.

A cry escaped Fei. She moved to the monitor, fingers reaching for Sam's image. The cold glass kept her from the screen. The camera zoomed in shakily, hand-held. Sam's face filled the screen. Her mouth was open in a grimace of pain. She was breathing hard.

'Sam!' Fei could not stop a sob of terror.

Her head jerked. The gun pushed her back into position. 'Fei?'

'Oh, God, Sam . . .'

Piers now spoke over Fei, addressing Sam. 'We're holding Fei here at the Centre. We couldn't find you in time for you to join us. She's taking your place. So you're of no use to us any more.'

'What are you going to do to us?' Fear tore away Sam's breath but it was a demand, not a plea.

'That depends on Fei.' Piers switched gear. 'Let Ryder go,' he ordered.

The man pulled away from Sam. The camera zoomed out. She stumbled and regained her balance. Turned. Moved sideways. Trying to find her bearings. The camera followed her. Piers commanded, 'On her knees.'

The man barked the order to Sam who ignored him. He backhanded her across the face. Fei cried out, throwing herself at the screen. The shield bruised her. Sam fell. The man shouted at her to get up on her knees. Retching, choking, she struggled against her bound hands. She hunched over, head on the ground, gasping and spitting. The man pulled her torso up. She swayed. Blood ran from her nose and mouth.

'What do you want? For God's sake, what do you want?' Fei was screaming. 'Leave her alone! Let her go, you've got me, what the hell do you want with her?'

'Drink.' Piers spoke as if to a child. 'Or she dies.'

Sam croaked, 'No . . .'

Fei stepped back. This wasn't happening. Just to make her drink? Were they so desperate to control her? Or was it gut-kicking revenge? Just because they had the power to do it. Just because they wanted to do it. She backed away.

But was this Sam? Fei blinked. She remembered Ginny's manipulation of the photo. The horrors that Chee had been forced to watch featuring his wife and child. The scenarios that had been played to the JB boys. Was this just another mindgame?

She moved back to the screen, staring hard. Nothing to tell

her whether it was fake or real. The camera zoomed in to Sam – head and torso. Every curve and indent, the shape of her shoulders, the outline of her face, was Sam. She called out, 'Fei, are you all right?'

It was Sam's voice. Fei's reply was shaky. 'Yes.'

'Don't eat. Don't drink. Q . . . they'll put Q . . . Be careful . . .'

'I know. Don't worry, Sam.' Fei was weeping against the cold glass.

Piers said, 'She drinks or you die, Sam. It's simple. If she drinks, she is ours and we will let you go. By the time you find her, she won't know you.'

Fei stared at the image on the screen. She knew suddenly what her Sam would say. Her Sam. The Sam she knew like her own heartbeat. What would this Sam do? Whatever she did, Fei would know if she was real or not.

Sam was panting, swallowing. The blood was drying on her face. She shifted, her head turning this way and that. Assessing the options. Fei searched the image. It was so like Sam.

She seemed to muster all her strength and called out desperately, 'Fei, they're going to kill me anyway. Don't believe any of their bullshit. Don't give up, do you hear me? Whichever way you choose, they'll kill me, don't you get it? There's no way out but your freedom. You have your freedom, whatever they do!'

Fei screamed through her tears. It was Sam.

'I love . . .'

The bullet caught Sam in the side of the head. She collapsed like a sack. It was a clean shot, leaving her features intact. Blood spewed from the exit wound as she fell.

<hr />

The first mouthful was easy. The water was tepid but soaked her parched mouth like balm. Fei emptied the glass in moments. She sat on the floor, propped against the wall. The tumbler slid from her hand and rolled in an arc. Sam was dead. The horror of it exploded again and again. There was nothing else. The pain was unbearable and she had no more tears.

She did not have the strength to fight them any more. Sam was dead. Whatever they did to her now, whatever they did to others beyond these white walls, it did not matter. They had won. They would always win. Freedom and choice and her own self held no meaning for her any more. To defy them, to hoard her soul against their destruction – for what? Sam was dead.

The lights dimmed in the cell. Fei crawled on to the bed and curled up. She felt tired. The cell was thick with silence. Sleep closed in on her. It felt good, a release from the reality she could no longer face. She didn't fight it. She closed her eyes and surrendered herself to emptiness.

Chapter Twenty-Nine

A few days before, Han had stood in Qwong's condo, the search warrant in his hand. He had followed procedure to keep *Bapa Tua* happy. He and two Snakes were accompanied by a local police officer. He made sure that they trashed the place. He had had no time to pussyfoot around any more. He scribbled his message to Qwong on the back of the warrant, signed his name and tossed it on an upturned table.

He still had not managed to get a location on Dean in spite of a tracer on the e-mailed photo – the trail had led backwards through several ISPs via which Dean had re-routed the trans-mission but had come to a dead end at source. All that the tecchies had been able to tell him was that the e-mail had been sent via a satellite connection originating within a fifty-mile radius west of Kuala Lumpur. That area encompassed the outskirts of KL proper and several of its dormitory towns, the aggregate population of which amounted to over half a million. Qwong was Han's only connection to Dean.

She had not told him everything that night, Han was sure of it now. Qwong was also his only link to the Wyndhams. He was less certain now of her involvement in the activities he was investigating but suspected she knew more than she was saying – or perhaps dared to say. Standing in her living room while his men systematically tore her things apart, he remembered her evasiveness and defiance. It did not surprise him. He en-countered it on every job. It was up to the Snakes to win their contacts' trust or find some other way to get the information they needed. Raul was a fucking softie and usually sweet-talked his way in. Han hated that side of the job. He preferred to work in other ways. Inducement and threats were the currency of his negotiations. They cut through the crap and got down to basics. Self-preservation – everyone had a stake in that.

It was time Qwong truly understood what was at stake here.

'Look what we got.' Raul came up to him with a sheaf of papers and photos. Love letters and photographs of two women: Qwong and a doctor named Sam Ryder.

Ryder was the lever they needed on Qwong. Han said, 'I'll take her.'

The other Snake, Yusoff, turned up a scrawled note. It had been tucked into the lining of Qwong's Filofax. It was Dean's address and phone number. Han clenched his fist in a shot of triumph, but his face was hard. 'Raul – get a warrant and check it out.'

By the time Han had rushed down to the National Hospital car park again – eight floors down from Ryder's office, the crowded lift taking its time, getting out at the fifth floor and racing up the stairs the rest of the way – Ryder and Qwong had disappeared.

He got a licence plate number for Ryder's car through police files and had them put out an alert for the vehicle, his fury loud over the cellphone secure channel. Yusoff, whom he had sent to Ryder's house, reported back that the place was deserted. Han said, 'She won't go home right away. They must have seen me. Go back tonight. Who's watching Qwong's apartment?'

Yusoff hesitated. 'No one . . .'

'Get the fuck over there!'

Han slammed the phone shut in frustration. Mokhtar had authorised the job but he was still holding Han back with a limited team. The go-ahead had been a sop to Han: Mokhtar guarding his own back in case this turn of events produced a lead. But he had not taken his eye off the politics-play of the goddam' Suits: to them, Han was a loose cannon and they were taking no risks, whatever he told them.

At Qwong's apartment, Yusoff and the police missed the two women by a breath. By the time they had worked out which way Qwong and Ryder had escaped and got their arses back downstairs, the women had gone. Hassan the porter had seen them, Yusoff said, but was playing dumb. Later that afternoon, police on patrol located Ryder's abandoned car in an alleyway in Setapak. Enquiries in the area threw up sightings of two women – one white, the other Chinese – earlier that day but no one could say where they had gone.

Raul called in to Han's cellphone. More fucking bad news. No sign of Dean. Han was in the office the police had given him at their main station. He stalked the floor. 'Fucking shit!'

Raul said, 'We searched his flat, though. Found his equipment. We got a tecchie here – he's hacked into Dean's laptop and working on the decryption.'

An hour later, Raul called back. 'We got what we need on Dean. He's an ex-CIA agent, working freelance. According to the information on his laptop, he's being paid by the Americans to persuade Wyndham – aka Justin Lovelace – back to the US to work on mind-control programming. The Centre appears to be a front for secret experiments to alter consciousness, personality and the behaviour of mass populations.'

Han threw back his head and closed his eyes. At last he was getting at the truth.

Raul was saying, 'Using Wyndham's technology, the American game plan looks set for targeting foreign non-friendly states – altering their mindset to a pro-US outlook and shifting their peoples against their native traditions, religions, whatever anti-American bias they may be clinging on to.'

'That's the link with the AVA. The Alliance want the same technology to control us through Asian Values.' Han stared through the fortified windows at the blazing day outside. It was stuffy in the room but he suddenly felt a cold certainty. 'Asian

Values or the fucking American Dream. There's no damn' difference.'

'Dean's notes and files talk about colonisation. Empire building based on the Victorian British model: only, the subject populations of South America, the Middle East, Asia, Eastern Europe, would have no thought for revolt or independence. America – and its Western European allies – would be great again, not to say rich.'

'Goddamn it!' Han sat down. It was as if an armoured vehicle had slammed into him at full fucking speed.

'There's more. They propose to use it on their domestic population – and those of Western Europe. To control dissent, strikes, upheavals, and all anti-social and anti-government activities.'

Han's rage stirred.

Raul went on, 'Dean's also working for Beijing. He's the Chinese contact we've been looking for.'

'A fucking double agent!'

'Whatever the US offers Wyndham, the Chinese are willing to top it. They'll give him all the resources he needs – hospital complex, experimental subjects, orang-utans. And the highest level of protection.

'Beijing's prepared to bring on board the Alliance and Siew Kei-Win too if that's what Wyndham wants. They couldn't make headway negotiating with Siew direct. He wants to run the show but in Beijing's game there can be only one master and they'd rather it was them. Their take on Wyndham's work is: Asian Values, sure, no problem – but with a Chinese flavour.'

'Meaning?'

'From what I can make out: communism began in the fields – that's where the golden age of China's psychological history lies. All this recent dabbling in capitalism is an experiment and a necessary evil. But if Beijing could give the people back the solidarity and brotherhood of those lost years . . . Think of it, billions of needy souls at Beijing's beck and call. It's the Long March all over again, but this time no dissenters or counter-revolutionaries to spoil the plan down the line.'

Han was on his feet now. He had been right all along to keep this op going. The Suits had been going to sit back and let the AVA and the goddamn' Americans and Chinese steal control of all their power and all their people right out from under their noses. He swept his arm across the desk in fury, sending the lamp and telephone crashing to the floor.

———◆———

The police were on red alert to locate Dean and the two women. Yusoff headed for the Centre, slipping into the surrounding forest to mount as intensive a surveillance as he was able with long-range cameras and mikes. Raul approached by sea, in the guise of a day-tripper on a hired motor launch. The sea route had failed before, the Centre's patrol boat ushering Han off. But this time, Raul stayed beyond the Centre's private waters. He watched the coast and grounds with powerful digital video cameras, trying to map out the detail of the shoreline.

Han battled with Mokhtar over the phone with requests for more Snakes to back up the operation. In the meantime, he had a senior plainclothes detective trying to pin a location on the whereabouts of Siew Kei-Win.

Han threw his cellphone on the desk in frustration. Whatever his next move, a simultaneous swoop on all of them would be the only sure way of seizing control of the situation. And right now, all the key players were just within his reach yet nowhere to be found. Mokhtar had finally agreed to give him a handful more Snakes. The tecchies were working on getting him satellite picture of the Centre and its environs. But essentially he had fuck all.

A return visit to Ryder's house that night found the place ransacked. Yusoff called Han. 'There's no trace of who did this.'

Han was at the hospital again, talking to Dr Govinda. He was beginning to piece together Ryder's hypothesis on Factor Q and the details of her search for its origin. Govinda had shown him her hard copy files on Ben Chang, the JB school children and scores of other victims affected by Q in the last few years and across the region. The doctor had indicated that Ryder held a database of thousands more Q cases. But they had not been able to access her computer – a blank screen stared back at them. Han stormed out of Ryder's office. He had to find her. Who else wanted her? The AVA. The Wyndhams. Dean's people. All possibilities. It was a race and he had no idea if he could win it.

Forty-five hours later, Dean was dead.

But someone in the crowd had seen a white woman talking to the doctor in the ambulance. Han cornered Dr Kee in the confined space by the corpse. It didn't take long for the medic to blurt it out. 'It was Dr Ryder. She told me to keep quiet. I don't know where she went. She was on her own . . .'

Several hours later Han got the call from KLIA security police: Qwong and Ryder had disappeared in separate vehicles. The airport police had stayed on their patch, radio-ing the highway police and the local force to give chase to the vehicles that had sped off. By that time, the cars involved had all vanished. Who were the men who had intercepted the fugitives?

Han stood out in the driving rain in the airport car park, scouring the blurred landscape as if it held the answer. He turned suddenly and slammed punches into the side of his car, the violence a release from his grinding frustration.

Later, Yusoff radio-ed in to report that a car had arrived at the Centre. The description seemed to match the one seen at the airport driving off with Qwong although there had been no licence number caught for the KLIA vehicle. Yusoff had not been able to see any of the car's occupants.

That night, the Klang police called. The watch Han had placed on John Qwong had seen Sam Ryder arrive. The detective said, 'They're heading back to JQ's apartment.'

⟫●⟪

In mission control, Ricky slid off his headset. The black-and-white image on the main overhead screen was frozen where Sam

Ryder had fallen. On the sound stage, the actor picked herself up from the floor. On one of the monitors at Ricky's control panel, Sam seemed to rise from the dead. The actor who had played the man began to take off the wired suit, assistants coming to his aid. On the screen, his image wobbled and melted eerily. On stage, he reached out to the woman to congratulate her, hugging her. She was grinning, pleased with her performance.

There was an air of euphoria in mission control. The Red Tigers who had been at KLIA had given Ricky a detailed description of how Ryder had last looked to Qwong, down to the leggings and boots. Ricky slapped high-fives with his team, moved over to the psych guys and punched their shoulders. 'Good touch, that double bluff thing!'

'The file on Ryder was thorough. From our analysis, we figured she wouldn't have just given up.'

Ricky popped a can of beer from the stash in the cubby hole under his control desk. He tossed a couple to the other guys, sat down and stretched his legs up on the panel. They had time for a breather before the next session. He was pleased with the composite night sequence he had put together from the image library. The secondary team had built up a substantial variety of scenes, settings and mood tones for use with or without the compound. The different elements overlayed on to the blue screen background and the basic figures of the actors had become a seamless whole.

Ricky toasted himself. 'Damn' fine work.'

<hr />

It was four in the morning.

Han sat at the kitchen table of John Qwong's apartment, Ryder opposite him. Her hands were free, placed on the table. Behind her, one of Han's team of Snakes stood watch. The others had positioned themselves at the weak incursion points — windows, door, outside landing — with additional police at the building entrance, across the street and on the roof.

Ryder looked pale and drained. She had filled in the gaps on Q but had refused to talk when questioned about the Wyndhams, Fei-Li or Dean. She was on the verge of breaking down at any moment, controlling herself with a superhuman effort. Han had separated her from John Qwong, letting him stew in the bedroom for now. Han pegged Qwong as an innocent in all this, his bravado in marked contrast to Ryder's tense wariness.

Ryder studied Han from under her brows. 'Who are you?'

Han did not answer. He could not tell her who he really was. Nor could he tell her about the Family.

Han took out a pack of 555 cigarettes and lit one. He took a drag, his eyes never leaving Ryder.

His authority came from PACS, the Pacific Asian Congress for Security, made up of the nations of South East Asia, India, Australia and New Zealand. Its Regional Intelligence Unit had been set up to tackle both extra- and intra-regional security issues and was headed by the foreign ministers of member countries. They were the Suits, doing their jobs within the remit of regional treaties, their manoeuvrability and power checked by the laws of the democratic states that had elected them. Publicly, members co-operated on military exercises and police investigations of ordinary crimes. The RIU was PACS's top-secret operations arm. The Unit monitored region-wide organised crime – triad activities, drug smuggling, prostitution rackets – and covert threats to Asia's stability through assassination, insurgency plots and conspiracies against the established governments. Headed by an elite team of military and police commanders drawn from member states, the RIU did more than merely collect information. The Family implemented active operations to combat the plots and networks it uncovered. Its Director was known to insiders as *Bapa Tua*, the Old Man, and its field operatives called themselves Snakes.

These tags were meant to preserve the RIU's nebulous and anonymous character but to Han, they bound him to his colleagues and rooted them in the lands that made up Asia. They were the heroes – the guys who did the real work, whose lives were in danger from moment to moment on secret missions for the safety of the region. But it was the regular police and armed forces who always took the credit, coming in at the final moment to make the bust and front the whole damn' thing from there on. The Snakes would melt away again, moving on to the next job even as the crime scene was secured. It suited them, the men and women like Han who wanted only to get the job done and to hell with the glory.

The cigarette in his mouth, Han showed Ryder his badge. It was the same one he had shown Fei-Li. Aloud, he gave her the standard cover. 'We're a special branch of the police, dealing with security issues. We cooperate across borders with other Asian police forces.'

'Like Interpol?'

'If you like.' He sat back.

Ryder hesitated. Then, 'Fei was warned about the police. That you're in on the conspiracy.'

'Who warned her?'

'Ben Chang.'

'He was under the Centre's control. You found Q in his brain tissue.'

Ryder's eyes widened. 'My God, they planted that warning?'

'Or it was real so far as Ben knew in his own self. After Govinda told me about him, I talked to his widow. She was scared and wouldn't cooperate at first. But finally she told me that Ben arrived home in a terrible state of paranoia the last time she saw him. She called the Centre for help and they arrived with police – they wanted Ben on criminal charges and had placed him under house arrest under Wyndham's care, it seems. I checked the incident logs on the police computer database. No call-outs on that day correspond with what she described.'

'They weren't real police, is that what you're saying?'

Han nodded and stubbed out the cigarette.

Ryder searched his face in anguish. She was working out if she could believe him.

Han said, 'I'm your only chance of finding Fei-Li.'

She bit back her emotion. 'Where is she? What have you done with her?'

'We don't have her,' he said. 'And time's running out. Whoever's got her – we don't know what they're doing to her. Or what they've already done.'

Ryder covered her face with a hand. She was breaking. Not long now.

Han softened his voice. 'Tell us what you know. Everything Fei-Li might have told you. I know you're thinking you can't trust me. There's no one you *can* trust. Fei-Li is in danger. So are you. You both know too much. She about her clients and about Dean. You about Factor Q. We don't have long. These guns are here to protect you, not harm you. If you want Fei-Li back, I'm your only hope.'

Ryder looked up at him. Tears were streaming down her face. Her whole body shook. 'All right. I'll tell you what I know.'

———◆———

Fei sat facing the screen on the wall. Someone had come in to wake her and put her in the chair. Monitoring pads were attached to her temples and chest. She did not know what time it was. She had a vague awareness of where she was but did not really care.

She felt light-headed. The gouging pain had disengaged. It floated like a cloud above her body, dissipating into nothing. Fei breathed deeply, soothed by the rising and falling of air. She was aware of a voice but did not follow the words. She wanted more water. But she wasn't thirsty, she thought curiously.

The person with her gave her another glass of water. She drank it. He left her alone, disappearing through the door. He did not shut it. She saw the corridor through the open door. She took it in as a fact. She did not want to leave.

Pictures began to appear on the screen. But no, they were not pictures, they were real. She was amongst her family. At home. Her father was there, just as he used to look. He was back with them. He had not died after all. Fei felt an ache of elation.

She had stepped back in time and they were all young again. She was seven. But was such a thing possible? Fei frowned. Struggled to work it out in her rational mind but she could not reach abstraction. There was only the present moment, the sensation of being home, seven years old and happy to be with her father – even though she knew it could not be.

She heard the voice suddenly. Bursting out of her subconscious. She did not take in the words. It was only a fraction of a moment. But she heard its tones, its pitch, the way it rose and fell. It was a voice that frightened her, stirred a loathing that snapped her back into the cell. It was Ginny's voice.

She looked wildly around her. She was in the Centre. An experimental subject. Sam was dead. Ginny was part of all this, alive still. Killer. Manic. Mad obsessive. Her voice was pounding on, rising in desperation. It seemed to scream in Fei's head, invade every inch of her. She cried out, saw the open door, pulled herself out of the chair. The voice told her to sit down, be calm, go back to her family. Fei felt the impulse to obey. A desire to sit down, to give in. She fought it. The door was swinging shut on its own. Fei struggled towards it, screaming against Ginny's presence in her head.

The door clicked shut, locked electronically.

Fei crumpled to the floor, slamming her hands over her ears. Ginny was still there, hardly muffled. Fei felt sick with terror and hatred. She flailed out against the disembodied voice, crying, 'You killed Sam! You killed all those people! Get out! You can't ever know me, you can't be me! I never loved you, I never loved you . . .'

It was a chant of defiance. Fei clung to the reality of that memory. She had never loved Ginny. Fei shouted out the chant, wielded it like a weapon of exorcism.

***

It was light. Sam felt drugged with exhaustion. Han lit another cigarette. The stale air was giving her a headache. Han seemed fresh. Invigorated, almost. She had told him everything she could think of that Fei had told her about the Wyndhams, Ginny, the Centre, its strange goings-on: the mad patient who had grabbed Fei, the boat in the cove through the haze, the revelations about Ginny and Piers's past. Sam had also told him about the data and files that Fei had copied from Ginny's computer. She explained the scientific details and the proposals for what had been called Phase Four and described the use of the orang-utans as a source for the compound.

'It had formulae and techniques on it?' Han had cut in.

'Yes.'

'They were Wyndham's notes on his experiments and on the perfection of the compound?'

'Yes.'

'Give me that disk.'

'I threw it in the incinerator.'

'There's no back up copy? What happened to your computer?'

'I incinerated the memory chip as well.'

Han glared at her, his lips a hard line. Sam did not tell him that she had encrypted and divided the data in her web-based e-mail accounts. It was her bargaining tool, if she ever needed one against him. It would be obsolete the moment he found the formulae from elsewhere but for now it was the only power she had.

She demanded to hear from Han what he knew. After a pause, he told her about America and China's bids for Wyndham through Dean. Sam could hardly take it in. Dean had been a double agent working for money. He would have used whatever she and Fei might have given him for terrifying ends. It shook Sam to the core. Fei had been taken in by Dean's veneer, in spite of the blackmail and manipulation. She had rationalised it: he had resorted to desperate means for a just cause. Fei's residual warmth towards the Dean she had once known had obscured the real man. Sam had wanted to believe in Fei's version of Dean . . . because . . . because – why? Because he had been white. An American. Swamped in all the

AVA's anti-Western polemic, they had instinctively turned to the man who had been other. They had fled from Han because he had been Asian. He spelled out violence and bullying in their minds and they had acted out the distrust of Asian authorities and police that their liberal Western education had instilled. In opposition, Dean had stood for all that was good and free, democracy and heroism, one man battling against collective evil. It had blinded both her and Fei to their doubts about who he had been and what he might really have wanted.

'The Wyndhams have got Fei.' Han's voice was decisive.

'How can you be sure?'

'They have targeted you for programming – you know that from the disk. Fei got in too deep with the Ginny Wyndham affair and the photograph Dean took. Out on the loose, she was a risk to them. The men who've been on your trail have to be their people. The Centre were involved in Dean's death – we got a forensic report back late last night. His brain tissue contains a compound similar to the Q compound in your files. His encrypted files reveal contacts who've helped him on surveillance and weapons supply but none of them checked out as anything other than small-time hoods. I have no information of anyone else backing him up from the US or Beijing.'

Sam spoke over him, panic lifting her from her seat. 'They're going to programme her. They had a file on her on that disk. It was so detailed . . . You have to do something. Stop them. Please.'

In mission control, Piers cut the sound transmission from Ginny's head-mike. The remotely controlled door to the cell was now locked again. Ginny was hysterical, leaning towards the image of Fei on one of the screens. Her directive voice had become shrill commands, faltering now as she fought for breath against her panic. Desperation and anger corded the veins of her neck and temple. Fei's chant, still coming through from the cell, drowned out Ginny's faltering voice.

The psych team, Ricky and his programmers, the actors and back-up assistants, stood frozen in position, staring at Ginny. Piers silenced the transmission from Fei's cell. The silence was absolute. He reached out a calming hand to Ginny but Siew stepped forward and in one rough movement tore the headset from her and pushed her aside. She collapsed into her chair, sobbing.

He jerked his head at the assistants and they started forward. Ginny grabbed his jacket. 'No, please! Let me stay. Let me finish it.'

Siew tried to break her hold but she would not let go. Her pleading was pitiful. Piers ached for her. The assistants grabbed her, swiftly levering her off Siew. She cried, 'I know her like I know myself. Let me go on. Change the voice, that's all. No one else knows her like I do. Let me finish.'

Piers stayed the assistants. He turned off his head-mike and spoke quietly to Siew. 'She's right. We've always expected Double Alphas to be difficult. Her intimacy with the subject – whatever you might think of it – puts her in the best position to be the directive voice. We'll overlay Ginny with Ryder's voice.'

Siew hesitated. 'It'll work. I promise you.'

After a beat, he nodded.

The assistants let Ginny go.

Slipping off his headset, Piers drew her to him. He had always stood between her and Siew. This would be the last time. He had wanted the refuge and salvation of science but her presence could only remind him of their shared past and the pain of love. Whatever she had done to their lives, whatever her guilt, he still loved her. In a week or so, after they had finished with Fei-Li, this woman who had always been a part of his life would be gone. He would make her anew and she would be perfect.

But she would never be his sister again. These were her last days in her old consciousness and he had granted her her last wish. He kissed her on the brow.

On the silent screen, Fei lay on the floor. She had stopped shouting and flailing. Her body heaved as she sobbed.

Chapter Thirty

Fei-Li's abduction and Dean's death had given Han the ammunition he needed. He still had no proof of direct links to the Wyndhams but the circumstantial evidence was strong. Strong enough to get the go-ahead from Mokhtar for decisive action against the Centre.

He snapped his cellphone shut and said to Yusoff, 'Get a warrant. Suspicion of kidnap and homicide.'

'What's Mokhtar giving us?'

'The old team – plus you, Raul and me – and back-up operatives for security, recovery and specialised activities. Mokhtar's contacting police headquarters in KL and the coastguards. Have their team heads on standby. I'll give the briefing as soon as our people get in.'

Yusoff grinned, already at the door. 'That's more like it.'

Han stood up. He turned to Ryder. 'There'll be two police officers night and day with you and John Qwong. There are already officers with the Qwong family in case the Wyndhams make any moves against them . . .'

Ryder caught his arm. 'I'm coming with you.'

'We don't take civilians on ops.'

'You need me. I'm the only medical back-up you have who knows Factor Q inside out. You have to take me.'

'No.' Han signalled to his men to move out and shook her off.

Ryder stood in his way. 'I'm the only one outside the Centre who's seen the scientific notes and reports, all their data and projections. I'm going to be there when you find Fei. No one else can help her then but me.'

After a beat, he said, 'I cannot guarantee your safety.'

'I know that.'

He hesitated. Then nodded.

The men began to secure the exit route, radio-ing their movements to the others around the building.

Johnny emerged from the bedroom, looking bewildered. Sam rushed to him as Han began to usher her out. 'Don't worry, we'll find Fei.'

Sam hurried down the stairs, armed men ahead of her and behind, their bulky shapes blocking Johnny from view. A last glimpse of him as she turned the corner, the police guards behind him. One reached across and shut the door.

She felt a pang of fear. Had she done the best thing, throwing in their lot with Han? She did not entirely trust him still. But he had been right about one thing: for now, he was her only chance of seeing Fei again.

Fei sat up sleepily on the bed. She rubbed her eyes with the heel of one hand. Ginny bent over her. Fei looked up with the openness of a child. Her face was soft and she smelt of sleep. Ginny wanted to kiss her but did not. Fei's bright eyes took her in. She was trying to work out who Ginny was.

'Are you my friend?' she asked.

Ginny felt a rush of emotion. The guilelessness of Fei's voice and manner made her ache with love. She brushed her fingers through Fei's hair, speaking as if to a little girl. 'Yes, I am. It's time to get up now.'

'Okay.' Fei slid over and got out of bed. She was in the outsize T-shirt the nurses had put on her the night before. Ginny helped her into jeans and a top, wiping her face with a flannel while Fei squirmed. The experiment was to be conducted in as close a set-up to normality as possible. Only,

Fei's mind was at a stage where she believed herself to be a child.

'What's your name?'

'Ginny.' She searched Fei's face. Again the eyes narrowing as if she was trying to remember.

Then: 'It's a nice name.'

Fei froze suddenly, eyes screwed shut. A cry of pain escaped her. Her hands went up to her head. She doubled up. And then it passed. She was breathing hard, shaky on her feet. She stared at Ginny in terror. Sweat sheened her brow. A tumult of emotions skidded across her face. Momentarily, a fully conscious, intelligent adult woman looked out of her eyes. 'Ginny . . . what . . .'

And then she was gone. Ginny could not move. This was the typical relapse they had often encountered with Double Alphas – a subconscious resistance to the manipulations that manifested in a flip-back to their original personality.

The moment had passed from Fei's present mind. She smiled. 'My name is Fei-Li. Do you think it's a nice name, too?'

Ginny nodded.

Fei saw the breakfast tray on the table. Her eyes widened with delight. 'Wow! Coco Pops, they're my favourite.'

'I know.' Ginny grinned so widely her cheeks hurt. She drank Fei in with her gaze.

'Mum doesn't let me have them all the time. She says the sugar's bad for my teeth. Only on special days.' Fei settled excitedly at the table. 'Is it a special day today? Do you like Coco Pops? You can have some!'

Ginny would have to administer the booster shot of chronotonin soon. In the limited time they had, they could not rely on programming a difficult Double Alpha case on the natural hormone rhythm. The booster was a hand-held device with the look of a mini staplegun. The chronotonin was injected by an intense pressurised gas pump action without breaking the skin or bruising it. It was faster than a syringe injection and left no visible trace. The booster weighed heavy in Ginny's pocket.

Their work would start again then. Meanwhile Ginny savoured this precious hour with Fei. She sat with her, eating cereal as Fei fed her alternate mouthfuls, both of them giggling at the milk they spilled. Fei told her all about the things she believed had happened to her – memories implanted the day before. They were remodelling her ambition and competitive nature, giving her a father who loved and praised her without the need to perform IQ tricks. She talked about baking a cake for his birthday, how he had been so funny, making 'yummy' noises with every bite he took. Fei bounced happily in her chair. 'When I grow up, I'm going to marry a man like Daddy.'

'You'll make a wonderful wife.' But Ginny could not smile anymore. She studied Fei. Her pleasure was so genuine. She had never seemed more beautiful – her woman's body moving with the simplicity of a child. Her eyes were bright, taking in Ginny with an innocence that made her almost weep with desire.

Today, they were going to switch to a simulation of Fei's father for the directive voice in the programming sessions, to be spoken through one of the Chinese psychiatrists. Till now, Ginny had done it in Sam's persona, improvising on and texturing instructions fed to her by the psych team for maximum effect. It had gutted her as she had worked, to see Fei respond with trust and obedience to that voice. But a strange fascination held her to the task. Whatever Ginny had told Fei to do, she had done it. Whatever feeling Ginny had implanted, Fei had felt it. Ginny had never known such absolute power nor such charged eroticism. Being with Fei now – the woman-child so dependent on her, so keen to be her friend, looking up at her for adult acknowledgement – it was as if Ginny was living at last her most secret fantasies. Tears welled to blur her vision. A jagged rock seemed to lodge in her throat.

Fei looked anxious. She reached out and took Ginny's hand. 'Why are you sad?'

Ginny shook her head, unable to speak.

'Please don't cry. Don't be sad.' Fei was flustered, squeezing Ginny's hand. She looked around, not knowing how to make things better. She came to Ginny and knelt in front of her. She touched Ginny's face, stroked her arms and lap. 'Will you be my best friend? Please? Please say yes.'

Ginny felt the tears burst from her then. She embraced Fei as a mother might a child. 'Yes, I'll be your best friend, of course I will. I'm not sad, I'm happy, don't you see?'

With her free hand, Ginny reached behind into her back pocket for the booster.

———◦———

Sam waded out through the shallows. They were moving quietly in the darkness. Ahead of her the silhouettes of Han and another man led the way; behind her two more followed. Two others had already gone ahead as a recce party. It was two nights after they had left Johnny's apartment in Klang. Sam had pressed Han to move earlier but he had refused to be hurried. 'We're going into this thing half blind. I want the best shot at it we can get.'

He had collated all the data he had on the Centre's topography, comparing satellite pictures with what they had observed from the sea and from the times they had been in the grounds. The detailed satellite photos had shown a cove to the north of the headland where the water seemed deeper. Artificial shapes also appeared there which Han had guessed to be boats. Correlating the location with Fei's anecdote of the launch and men with rifles she had seen, he had hypothesised that there was a hidden entrance to the grounds via that cove with the Secure Unit on the headland as cover. He was chancing the whole operation on being right on that count.

It was low tide, the air roots of the mangrove rising out of the swamp like snakes. The dank, fetid smell of the sea hung close. Sam was hot inside the armoured vest Han had made her put on over her dark clothing. Her face and hands were smeared with mud to hide her pale skin as were the men's. Han's team carried guns and ammunition – what looked like automatic rifles in their hands and pistols in their belts. They had other tools and gadgets she could not identify. They each wore earpieces and body-mikes but she did not. With open water close by, sound would carry a long way and so far there had been no talk through the radio channels. Communication was through hand signals. Han kept in contact with the other teams gathering round the Centre's periphery through pre-arranged clicks on the transmitters.

Everything was on course.

The mangrove thinned as they rounded the curve of the shore. Rocks and boulders scattered out from the headland forming a natural barrier between the delta and the open sea. The water inland lay sluggish, while beyond the sound of waves lulled the still night. Han and the men began to climb stealthily across the slippery stones. Yusoff stayed close to Sam, steadying her and easily lifting her over crevices and outcrops.

Finally, down the other side, Sam was sweating heavily. Her legs ached from the task of climbing and sliding over the steep, treacherous terrain. The sea swelled and churned around her legs, its energy amplified in the funnel of this narrow sound. They began to wade across, Sam half-swimming in the deep water, her body vest pulling her down. Water engulfed her, poured into her nose and mouth, the taste of salt making her choke. She was lifted off the rocks underfoot, swept towards shore, then sucked out again, only Yusoff's grip keeping her anchored.

By the time they reached a small patch of sand, upshore from the rocks, she was shaking and drained. She felt sick but controlled her retching, churning up bile in silent spasms. They were very close now and they could risk no sound.

The recce party was waiting for them. They communicated silently with Han about what they had found. The stars were bright in a cloudless sky. Sam saw the Orion constellation, heard the sea splashing on the rocks. Up on the high ground, the jungle noises creaked and hummed. Ahead, boulders and the jutting cliffside reached out, forming a black embankment into the sea against the sky. Beyond there was a hint of light and voices, barely distinguishable from the surrounding noises. They had reached the cove.

Han signalled to the men and they scooted up and ahead,

disappearing into the dark. He steered Sam by the shoulder to a rock near the embankment. In the dim light, she could just make out men clambering up over the boulders to the ridge from which she guessed they would have a view into the cove. Han gestured to her to stay put. She nodded.

There was another sound now, almost indistinct at first: the hum of an engine, tinny music and voices carried over the water from a long way away. Then a muffled electronic alert on the other side of the embankment. It shut off and there was some kind of activity in the cove.

A speed boat's engine roared, echoing off the cliff. It revved and then sped off, decreasing into a distant buzz.

Han and the team fanned out and headed up the embankment, climbing up the cliff face and over the ridge by that route. In moments, the night swallowed them and Sam was left alone.

―――――

The two pleasure boats were inside the bay. The Centre and its grounds lay ahead, lights brilliant in the dark. Passing through the electronic beams criss-crossing the line of buoys, the craft would have set off the alarms. Raul stood alert on the deck even as he grinned stupidly and whooped like a drunk. All the lights were on on both boats and music blared. Several of his men were on the decks wearing Hawaiian shirts, beer bottles in hand. To anyone who saw them, they were just a bunch of lads on the piss-up of their lives. He heard no sound of alarms above their noise but knew it would only be a matter of minutes before the Centre's security patrol arrived – that had happened when Han had chugged into the bay on a fishing boat on their first recce months before.

The two boats slowed, circling.

There it was – as Raul had expected: the motor launch heading towards them from the direction of the concealed cove, its spotlights dazzling. He muttered into his body-mike, 'Stand by.'

The party swung upbeat. Concealed from the approaching launch, the ambush team slipped into the water from the far side of Raul's boat.

The patrol closed in on them, the security guards on board waving and gesticulating. Raul feigned deafness, cupping his hand to his ear. They did not use megaphones, as Han had briefed Raul – the proximity to the sanatorium meant such sounds would carry across the water and possibly alarm the patients. The patrol boat pulled up close alongside as Raul waved to one of his men to turn off the music. Noise still blared from the other boat, bobbing behind them.

There were two guards on deck and one at the wheel. All wore automatic rifles slung across their shoulders. The one in charge said, 'This one private property, sir. I ask you please-lah leave.'

Raul played the cheerful but unapologetic drunk. 'We're having a party, man. Don't spoil the fun. You wanna beer? We got plenty . . .'

The guards were engaged in keeping an eye on the second boat while talking to Raul. They had not yet reached the stage of getting heavy.

His ambush team were up on deck behind the patrol crew before they knew what was happening. Two operatives struck their heads with silenced pistols, a third took care of the one at the wheel and a fourth slipped below deck to check the rest of the craft.

In moments, the guards had been handcuffed, their mouths taped. They were tossed over into Raul's boat which had pulled up alongside. On the other side, the second boat sandwiched the patrol. From both crafts, teams of special police, Snakes and Family-trained medics and psychiatrists poured on to the patrol boat. Once emptied, the two boats pulled away and headed out of the private waters, music turned up.

Raul, at the forward helm, picked up the radio. 'They going. Just crazy guys-lah having a party.'

'We copy. Okay-lah, come back.'

Raul switched off the spotlights. The coastguard officer steered the launch towards shore, as close to the shallows as he dared. The party lads exchanged their bright clothing for black assault outfits and strapped on their weapons and gear. They slipped into the water, followed by the medics and shrinks, heading for the beach, swimming and wading in the darkness. The coastguard officer and a police special team operative would take the launch back to the cove. Raul stepped into the water. The objective of the beach teams was to secure the main Centre building and protect the patients, preventing them from being used as hostages, and to identify and take the security control base.

On shore, Raul and his teams moved towards the main building, stealthy shadows merging swiftly into the cover of darkness.

———————

At the main gate, the police car pulled up, siren wailing and blue light flashing. The four officers stepped out and surrounded the security booth.

Sergeant Hamid said, 'We have a search warrant. Let us in.'

'Sorry, sir, I got no authority. Please-lah come back in morning,' the guard said impassively.

Hamid brandished the paper. 'I don't care what your authority is. We have a warrant. Open the gates.'

'Everyone asleep. No one to help, sir.'

The police made an ostentatious show of taking out their weapons. The guard swallowed, fingering the revolver at his holster. Hamid knew that the firearms licence the guards had did not permit them to be used against the forces of law. 'Give me your pistol.'

The guard hesitated.

———————

In the Centre's security base, the guard on duty had alerted Ong. The gate officer had sent the signal through a discreet alarm wired under his desk as the police cars had drawn up. The security chief watched the CCTV monitor showing the gate and entrance way. It was on a bank of screens that gave the security base a view of sensitive parts of the grounds. Ong radio-ed for a back-up team and made his way out into the night.

At the gate an argument raged, Ong and his team of men standing their ground against the furious police. They would not hand over their weapons nor open the gate. Hamid and his officers ranted and bellowed, threatened and brandished their weapons in turn. The brief was to cause a distraction and to continue it for as long as possible. With a convincing show of incompetence and indecisiveness, Hamid focused Ong's attention on the charade. He radio-ed HQ for instructions, argued with Ong, demanded to see Dr Wyndham, refused to give details of the warrant.

Behind him, down the slope and out of range of the CCTV cameras in the trees, police reinforcements and armoured vehicles waited.

The patrol launch skimmed into the cove at full speed, its spotlights bursting full on suddenly. Taken by surprise, the other guards in position in the cove stared in amazement.

Sam had crawled up to the ridge of the embankment, peering down from behind a rock.

The momentary distraction was enough for Han and his team. Diving out of the shadows, they took the guards from behind. Rifle butts to the heads, arm-locks, more blows and the cove was secured. Han stood over one man and hauled him up. He had swung his own rifle over his shoulders and now shoved a silenced pistol into the man's temple before stripping him of his weapons.

Yusoff muttered instructions into his body-mike, the barrel of his rifle holding down a guard who gasped and groaned beneath his feet. The coastguard and police back-up teams would now move in from the sea to secure the scene one step behind Han's assault team.

The launch cut out and Raul's men came up the beach in the meantime to hold the guards while Han's group moved on to the next stage.

Sam clambered down the embankment, tumbling part of the way and landing in the sand.

Han held his hostage in front of him, gun to temple. 'Where's the entrance?'

The man was gasping, his silence defiant.

Han shifted the weapon to the man's thigh and squeezed off a shot, ramming his other hand over the man's mouth to muffle the scream.

He collapsed, sobbing and whimpering. The gun was back at his temple. Han hissed, 'This can take as long as you choose.' He jerked the man's head back by the hair.

Sam stared in horror.

The prisoner managed a weak gesture. Han hauled him up. A wail escaped him. 'Show me,' Han ordered.

They found steps hacked into the cliff face, leading upwards. Han smashed the butt of the pistol into the man's head and dropped him to the sand. He signalled to Yusoff who prodded his hostage with his rifle. This man scuttled up, terrified. He scooted over to Han, hands up, body abject in submission. Yusoff followed, rifle ready. They stepped over the first man's body and began to climb the steps.

The rest of the team moved with them, leaving the guards to the securing group. Sam hurried after them. She could hardly move, her whole body shaking with shock.

At the top of the steps, Han gestured to them to keep back. He leaned hard back into the wall. Sam followed the men. There were probably cameras covering the entrance. She looked out towards the sea. The line where water met sky was just visible. She heard nothing but the sound of her own breathing. Tremors of shock ran through her. She had not expected such violence. Han frightened her – there was an intensity in him that was lethal.

The hostage guard stood in front of the door alone. Han trained his gun on him and gestured to him to open it. The man punched a code into a panel by the door and stepped back. Han knocked him out with one blow and they were moving again.

The other members of the team hurried ahead. Yusoff spoke into his mike. 'We're in.'

That was the signal for the land unit to make their move. On the slopes on the delta, the police vehicles and armoured cars revved into action. At the front gate, Hamid stopped his play-acting and his team held their guns still and steady aimed at the security guards. 'Throw down your weapons!' he ordered.

Ong moved to bring his pistol up. The other guards followed.

Hamid squeezed off the first shot. His men fired. They aimed to injure and disarm rather than to kill, diving for cover as gunsmoke filled the air.

The first armoured vehicle roared up the slope and rammed into the rear of the police car, shunting it into and through the gate even as the Centre's guards tried to throw themselves out of the way.

Running down the tunnel into the secret labyrinth beneath the headland, Han grabbed Sam and pulled her behind the cover of his body. 'Stay close.'

Fei was showing resistance in spite of their reworked programming techniques for Double Alphas. Ginny stood over the control panel monitor, gripping the back of the chair. Piers beside her was grimly silent. Siew sat behind them, a brooding ominous presence. On the display panel, Fei's heartrate and oxygen intake showed panic. Her brainwave pattern was erratic. On the screen, her features twitched in a succession of rapid emotions, body contorting against the narrative command to stay still. Her father's voice spoke, trying to calm her.

Piers said, 'All right, stop.'

The directive voice stopped. The psych team doctor who was performing the role spoke through their headsets in his own voice. 'We have to go back to Ryder's voice. It's the only one that works.'

Piers sat back, face creased with strain. They had scripted Ryder out of the reworked memories they were implanting. They had brought Fei into adulthood with a false construction of her past – the trick had been to maintain key events in her life that would have been shared by others while structuring inside her a new interpretation that consolidated the remade personality. In Ryder's place, they had moulded a clean-cut but sensual young Chinese man who embodied the legal career that Fei had had. Her experiences in London and her work were being re-shaped into drudgery and bitterness in contrast with the fulfilment and satisfaction of her domestic life with this perfect Asian man. Her life and energies were being shifted from a focus on self to an absolute concentration on his welfare. The scenario would end with his leaving her for a better model woman. Fei would be embedded with an obsession to heal this hurt and loss with a new, good man of Asian Values for whom she would be always the perfect companion.

And still Ryder's voice maintained its power over her.

Fei calmed in the silence. She looked around, confused, striving to orientate herself.

A piercing electronic alarm sounded throughout the complex. The security base came through on the overhead intercoms. 'The police smash through the gate! Intruders via tunnel! Level One alert! Dr Wyndham! Level One!'

Siew hurled himself out of his chair. His personal guards swooped into position around him. He was white with rage. 'How did this happen, Wyndham?'

Piers was on his feet, bellowing into the intercom. 'Who are the intruders? Where's Ong? Give me the locations of all activity . . .'

'The main building, sir – intruders. Police all over the place . . .'

The intercom cut out.

'Hello! Hello!' Piers cursed, pulling his head-mike off.

On the split screen, they could see the auditorium. The AVA guests were in a panic. Security personnel were trying to calm them for an orderly evacuation. Women were screaming; businessmen shouted and pushed. The armed forces elite demanded to know the situation, trying to take charge.

In mission control, the psych team and actors knew the drill. They grabbed weapons from concealed cabinets beneath control panels and edging the sound stage. As they evacuated, guards poured in to secure the area and move the Wyndhams, Ricky and Siew out.

Siew stormed up to Piers, pistol levelled at his head. 'I've put up with your delays and mistakes for long enough. You've failed on all your promises. This latest fiasco with Qwong is the final insult . . .'

'Oh, God, no, please!' Ginny cried out but did not dare move.

One of the bodyguards said, 'Sir, we got to leave. Now.'

Siew jabbed his gun furiously. 'How did this intrusion happen? Who are they? What the hell is going on?'

Piers stared back coldly. 'I don't know. But you should leave. I have to deal with this and would prefer not to lose any more time.'

He turned from Siew and opened the weapons cabinet. He handed a pistol to Ginny, taking the other two himself. Behind him, Siew's gun was still trained on him. The bodyguard who had spoken moved closer. 'Sir, he is right. Please-lah, come.'

Siew lowered the gun. He was trembling with rage. The ring of men round him began to hustle him out. Ginny hesitated. Piers switched the giant screen up front to split-image mode and tapped through to the security base. The CCTV screens flashed up and most showed swarms of police and armed men moving through the Centre's grounds. The one in the security control room itself showed intruders checking through the panels and monitors while the security guard was handcuffed and bundled into a corner.

Piers glanced over to Ricky at his station.

'Fucking Armageddon, man,' Ricky said. He held Piers's gaze. 'Suicide scenario?'

Piers nodded. Ginny knew what he was thinking. All that work. Eleven years, new identities, scurrying from hiding place to hiding place. They had come so close. And now this. Suicide scenario yet again – as they had had to set in motion out of Shanghai. As Piers had had to do all those years ago in New Jersey. But he showed no emotion.

Ricky said, 'I need five minutes to get through the security levels and activate the auto-delete function.'

Piers stuffed the guns into his belt. Only he could activate the destruction of the complex. For that, he needed to access what he called the suicide room – a box space built like a safe where the detonation program could be launched. He looked over at Ginny. It was a moment they had encountered in the hideout in China and the warehouse lab in another life-time. But this time, Ginny knew she would never see him alive again.

Piers turned and made for the door. Several guards followed to cover him. Others stayed, circling Ricky as he worked.

On a small box on the screen, Fei glanced wildly around, the alarm panicking her. Ginny backed away. A guard began to follow. 'No, stay with Ricky. I'll be fine!'

In the corridor, she broke into a run. She had to take Fei with her. She would protect Fei. They would escape together. Escape the police, Piers, Siew, the AVA. She saw it so clearly now. After this, no matter what happened, the Alliance would have enough to distract them without hunting her and Fei down. Whatever had been made of Fei's mind – whoever she had now become – she and Ginny would have the chance for freedom together. As friends, as lovers – it did not matter any more. There was only Fei. Ginny would be there between her and the world for all their lives. The gun felt heavy in her hand as she ran, fingers curled around the trigger guard.

Han took down two guards. Others returned fire down the corridor. All around there was running and screaming. He pushed Sam into a doorway, covering her with his body as he shot off more rounds. They had to get out of this firefight.

He hauled her aside and fired at the electronic lock. The door creaked open and he propelled her through. Turning, he saw the metal cabinets by the door. One-armed, he slammed the door shut and pushed them over, shoving them across to block it.

Sam stood frozen in the middle of the cavernous space. She stared in horror at the figures that filled the room. Men in lab coats were hurrying up, drawing weapons, shouting.

Han spun and fired off shots at the moving targets. The technicians fell, neat rounds of blood on their white clothing.

It was then that he saw what the room contained.

Chapter Thirty-One

The room was the size of a warehouse hewn into the rock. Three levels opened up above them. Nearest to Sam, the grey orang-utans lay in their cubby-holes, wired up to monitors, tubes and drips. There were no bars or restraints on the animals. They lay very still. She moved closer. One of the monitors showed slow pulse rates. On another, the pattern revealed very little brain activity. It was then that she noticed the tubes were inserted into the animals' skulls through neat punctures drilled into the crowns.

Sam looked down the length of the warehouse. There was silence. Only the regular bleeping of monitors could be heard.

She began to walk down the aisle. On both sides were cubby-holes containing apes – different ages, different sizes. Some had been skinned, their pink mottled flesh giving them the appearance of deformed children. Drips were attached to varying parts of their bodies. Some lay on their fronts, tubes emerging from their spines. Sam stood frozen in front of a group of apes which had been dissected, exposing spines, abdominal organs, ribcages missing. Out of their bodies, tubes again emerged.

There were groups of severed heads, the brain exposed like an egg in a cup. The heads were suspended in solution and fed blood, oxygen and nutrients through tubes. The eyes were open, following Sam as she approached.

Pregnant females were suspended on their backs, some with their bellies opened, the skin peeled back to reveal the womb. Tubes fed out of the mother as well as the foetus.

Another section housed foetal sacs and baby apes.

With a cry, Sam shut her eyes, twisting her head away.

Han was behind her, his voice hoarse with shock. 'What the hell is . . . all this?'

It was only then that Sam realised she was crying. She smeared the tears from her eyes with the back of her hand. She felt as if she would never be warm again. She could hardly speak. 'It's the SPrp factory. This is how they make the compound.'

Her eyes followed one of the drips. Clear liquid was being fed into the baby orang-utan. There were other tubes, through which brownish liquid was flowing out from the animal in a glass rod which led to a pipe. Other tubes from the same group linked to the same pipe. She traced its length to a compact vat, sealed and marked with numbers and formulae. Sam forced herself to be clinical. 'These animals are brain dead but they're being kept alive and drip-fed nutrients. Their bodies are the cultivating ground for the compound and these other tubes are siphoning off the finished product – collected in that vat over there.'

Sam turned to Han. 'Wyndham's notes said that they had problems manufacturing the compound through chemical manipulations in the lab. They need to grow it, so to speak, in its natural environment – the apes' bodies. They've been trying to find the most effective way of producing mass amounts of the compound but the natural processes are slow.'

Han looked around. 'So they're trying any which way.'

'Keeping the animals alive means the bodies can keep processing even as they extract the compound.'

Han reloaded his automatic rifle. He held out a handgun he had taken off one of the technicians. 'Take this. You might need it.'

Sam hesitated. 'I'm a doctor . . .'

'In the scrum out there, I can't play nursemaid.' His face was fierce. 'This fucking set-up is bigger than anyone ever imagined. They're not going to get away.'

Sam felt claws tighten in her gut. Han's focus had never been on Fei. She had given him the way in, that was all. Sam did not know how to find her. She did not know how vast this complex was. In the gunfire she could dimly hear, any one of the shots might take Fei. She said, 'What are you going to do?'

'Siew's been seen in the complex. We've got him after all these years! And Wyndham has to be around somewhere. They're both mine now.' Han was already heading for the exit, his sights set on his prime objective. 'Let's move!'

A wave of bodies rushed for the tunnel to the cove. Actors wielded weapons as did the psychiatrists and technicians. There were also those who were unarmed, including the AVA elite, orderlies and nurses, trailing in their wake. Siew and his tight huddle of bodyguards were among them.

The tunnel had been secured by police troops, a flank of armoured and helmeted figures dark against the lightening sky beyond. Their weapons bristled at the ready. A loudhailer crackled. 'Stay back. Throw down your weapons and you will not be harmed. Place your hands above your head.'

The group jostled and shunted as those at the back rammed up against those at the front. People were shouting, dithering. The voice over the police hailer repeated its orders. 'Do not attempt to resist. Throw down your weapons.'

Some at the back began to retreat, running through the maze of corridors. Others dropped their weapons to the floor and raised their hands. There were many who still stood their ground, rifles and handguns twitching tensely in their hands. An actor swung his rifle up and fired at the police. Others around him followed. They charged forward, rattling off shots. Deafening volleys reverberated through the confined space. The police returned fire.

In the chaos and noise, Siew's huddle dived back down the corridor. Everywhere, people were running. There was gunfire and shouting. Alarms rang at the gunsmoke and in some sections sprinkler systems kicked in to drench the corridors with water.

There was no knowing how many gunmen had penetrated into the labs, their heavily-armed dark figures now seen, now not, in the midst of the mayhem. Siew's bodyguards covered him with volleys fired at the armed police, reloading on the run. Siew stepped over the bodies of security guards, passed walls smeared with blood. Along one corridor, he saw through windowed doors experimental subjects still in their cells – some alone, others in dormitories – oblivious to the panic outside. Others, sensing the fear on the other side of the electronic doors, were pressed up against the glass panels, eyes wide, mouths screaming. Siew ducked as a shot cracked out behind them. His men returned fire and hustled him round a bend.

They were pelting across the labyrinth to the only other escape – the exit several levels above into the scrub by the Secure Unit.

In mission control, Ricky worked quickly, his fingers flying over the keyboard. He paid attention only to the prompts and data flashing up on the screen at each step. There was no time for any thought but the security codes and procedural commands. He blocked out any sense of the guards behind him, watching the door. Tuned out the noise of the alarms and of muffled gunfire in the distance.

His objective was to set the auto-delete and get out of here. Auto-delete was a fail-safe function. Even if Piers did not manage to arm the detonator, all data would be wiped from the computer's short- and long-term memories. There would be no recalling them in any form. A rifle balanced precariously on his lap while he worked.

An explosion of noise behind him. The electronic security on the door had been broken. Gunmen burst into mission control through the smoke. The guards were ready for them, firing off rounds as the dark figures poured through. Gunshots cracked around Ricky.

He did not look up. He was almost there. His heart was pumping, his fingers trembling. It was like the best and highest level of a video game. He was almost at the treasure and his lives had run out. Ricky felt a strange dizzying elation. What a fucking way to go! He had spent years of his life here, living through the scenarios he had made real on the screen. A passing regret stung him that all that work would be wiped. That no one would see now the genius of what he had done.

Voices behind him were shouting. He did not take in what they said. The guards were still there, holding the gunmen back, but not for much longer. Two of them slumped across the floor. The air smelt of gunsmoke and explosives.

Ricky hit the last key. The screen began to scroll, its speed increasing. It was the list of files and programs being read by the deletion program. As each item slid into the cursor's light, it vanished. In moments, there was only a blur of movement, unreadable to the human eye.

'Game fucking over!' Ricky whooped, grabbing the rifle and spinning round as he dived from the chair.

The bullet slammed into his shoulder, throwing him back against the panel. It did not hurt but blood sprayed across the instruments. He stared at the gaping wound in astonishment. A snort of bewildered laughter escaped him. Ricky swung the rifle up and pulled the trigger, firing off a round at random.

The second bullet caught him in the head.

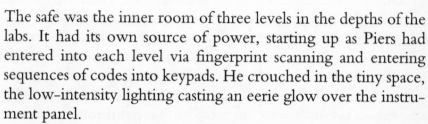

The safe was the inner room of three levels in the depths of the labs. It had its own source of power, starting up as Piers had entered into each level via fingerprint scanning and entering sequences of codes into keypads. He crouched in the tiny space, the low-intensity lighting casting an eerie glow over the instrument panel.

He took off his glasses and positioned his right eye for iris scanning. The beam of light focused and the processor hummed. The beam clicked off. After a pause, the panel fired up. He was through.

He inputted the commands to program the detonator. Explosion points were fitted to the key structural ballasts of the lab complex. Additional impact areas included the several mission control rooms and the prion cultivation units. Fuel would also be released upon detonation to ensure that fire would destroy anything that remained after the explosions.

In New Jersey, he had amassed grenades and petrol cans against an emergency evacuation. This was no different – just more sophisticated.

He keyed in the final code and the detonator was armed. He took a tiny device out of its slot under the instrument panel. It was the size of a pager. He clipped it to his belt.

Fei had slipped back into deep trance. Ginny searched her glazed eyes. Their dark pupils focused, wavered, slid back towards an internal world. Ginny said, 'I'm your friend. Do you remember? Your best friend.'

'Since we were young . . .' Fei's voice came from a long way away.

'That's right.' Ginny grinned in relief. She drew Fei up. 'Don't be afraid, Fei, whatever happens. You're with me. Nothing can harm you. You trust me.'

'. . . trust you.'

Ginny felt the comforting weight of the pistol in her hand. She would not hesitate to use it if she had to, to protect Fei. She had grabbed the booster as she had run from mission control and it was tucked into her pocket. If the current generation of the compound proved stable, it would remain in Fei's system for years, if not the rest of her life. Ginny would need the chronotonin booster to complete Fei's programming if – when – they got out of this. She made herself focus on the moment but could not help a thrill rippling through her. Fei's destiny was entirely hers.

She took Fei's arm and led her out of the cell.

———⟫●⟪———

Han and Sam raced through the corridors. The pistol Han had given her jostled in her belt against the small of her back. Han barked staccato commands into his body-mike, taking in the return transmissions from Raul and the various teams. From what Sam could work out, the main building had been secured by the beach party. The land units were swarming the grounds in fire-fights with security guards. The land teams had not yet managed to gain control of the headland and reported that scores of the Centre's personnel were getting out under cover of sustained fire from the Secure Unit area. Leading AVA figures had been arrested trying to escape down to the cove and there were apparently others in the grounds.

Han stopped suddenly. 'Repeat . . . I'm on my way.'

He turned to Sam. 'Yusoff's engaged Siew on the next level.'

'Fei?'

Han shook his head. He was already hurrying away. 'I'll be back.'

Sam kept moving. Heading down to the end of a corridor, she found herself caught up in chaos. There were people running, some shooting at dark-clad police troops. The officers held fire where they could, unwilling to risk stray shots ricocheting into the unarmed. They manoeuvred to separate those who were armed from the rest of the crowd but in the narrow space control was almost impossible. Sam ducked and weaved through the people, making her way down corridors, trying doors where she could. But they were impenetrable and windowless. Fei could be behind any or none of them. She was calling out for Fei, trying to see her in the confusion.

She followed a stream of running bodies. The corridors were disorientating and several times she seemed to end up where she had started. She grabbed passing men and women, shouted Fei's name at them, but no one seemed to know. Or care. Some pushed her aside, beat her off. One man whipped out a pistol and held it at her as he backed away, leaving her frozen till he was round the corner. She tried to stop one of the police officers but he was working with his team to herd the panicking crowds towards an improvised pen at the junction of two interlocking corridors.

And then she saw Ginny. A flash of paler hair above the Asian faces. Beside her, Fei. They were in the far distance, away from the crush of people, ducking through a door. Sam pushed her way against the bodies, sliding along the wall, propelling herself to the door as it slowly swung shut.

She slipped through and heard footsteps receding. Followed. The corridor was quiet here. Another open door. Sam hurried through. The smell of animal fear hit her.

The storage room was enormous. There were pens of orang-utans stacked high and crowded close. The apes screeched and chattered, their spindly arms reaching out through the cages. These had to be the fresh apes, waiting to be processed. Sam ran down the narrow aisle. She could see Ginny and Fei now, their figures tiny at the end of the vast hangar-like space. She picked up her pace.

At the far end, they disappeared behind a stack of crates.

By the time Sam got there, they were gone.

In front of her stood two doors. Both shut. Sam hesitated. Then chose the one on the left.

Three of Siew's men were down. Han glanced over at Yusoff. The Snake was drawing fire from the remaining two as they covered Siew's retreat. Siew jabbed the code into the door panel and ran through as it slid open. Yusoff fired a sustained burst, sending Siew's men diving for cover. Han skimmed round the junction of the corridors in which they had contained the firefight, throwing himself through the door after the retreating figure.

In three strides, Han was upon him, his bulk and momentum slamming Siew to the floor. Siew struggled against the restraint that Han forced on him, rifle drawn across Siew's shoulders, knee in his back. The bastard in his expensive suit was sweating now, face contorted with pain and exertion. Han allowed himself a moment of grim satisfaction. The little fucker was not going to politick his way out of the Family's hold now, Han would make sure of that.

Han glanced up. What he saw made him ill.

The room was filled with vats and pipes and tubes such as he had seen in the first prion production warehouse. Only instead of apes, human bodies were lodged in cubby-holes and shelves, some suspended upright. There was the same silence but for the bleeps of monitoring equipment.

Han hauled Siew one-handed to his feet, twisting his arm into a rigid lock. He jammed the rifle barrel under Siew's chin, holding him captive, and moved down the aisle, forcing Siew along in front of him.

There were all racial groups here: dark Tamil skins, Japanese, Chinese and Vietnamese, Hindus, Malays, Pakistanis and Sikhs. They were mixed in some batches, sorted by race in others. It was as if the production process had been trying to ascertain if there was any efficiency bias in particular racial hosts.

There were all age groups but subjects were predominantly males who might once have lived on the street. There were children among them. Han swore out loud. There were young girls too, their pregnant bellies round and full. He saw the elderly, the disabled, severed heads, foetuses, torsos hanging like meat, brains and their stems floating in tanks.

Han could not control the shudder that shook him. He had seen the violence that street battles and military skirmishes could do but never anything like this. There was a madness here, a sickness of the mind. He remembered what Ryder had told him she had seen on the disk. Wyndham had used the simian product at first but its binding quality was weak inside the human system, she had said. It all fitted now. S denoted 'simian'. H had to indicate 'human'. Wyndham must have devised a way of producing a human version of the prion which co-existed more stably within the programmed subject. This was HPrp. The notes Ryder had analysed said that they were currently using a combination of simian and human products to maximise hypnotic effect which the H version lacked, and increase stability which the S version failed to provide.

There had to be thousands of bodies in this one room. How many more had passed through? How many more waited? In the increasing momentum of the raid, Han had had no time to think beyond each strategic move. Now, suddenly, the monstrosity of these underground labs slammed into him. Rage fought against an overwhelming sense of horror. His grip slackened.

Siew could not break out of Han's hold but new energy filled him. He barked out, 'Who do you work for? Who are you? Identify yourself.'

Han pulled himself back under control. He jerked the arm lock hard. Siew cried out involuntarily.

He smelt of expensive cologne. The stink was an insult to Han's nostrils. This was Siew Kei-Win, the manipulative sick bastard Han had been chasing down for all these years. Sweating, trying to bully-boy his way out of this. But Han had him now. Han had him and his evil right here. Triumph burned in his gut. He shouted, 'I don't fucking answer to you!'

Siew was breathing hard. Defiant still. 'You people have no courage for the future. That is why your governments need Asian Values even as they make a pretence of posturing against us.'

Han rammed the rifle harder into Siew's jaw. 'Are these your Asian Values? My God, children, pregnant women . . .'

He shoved Siew's face into an open belly. Siew strained against it, eyes looking aside, face contemptuous. Han's voice was hoarse. 'Is your ambition worth this?'

'It was mothers who sold their children to us,' he said impassively. 'It was families who gave their unwanted girls to orphanages. It was parents who disowned their pregnant daughters and their *pondan* sons, parading in make-up and girls' clothing. The rest begged on the streets or robbed for drug money. They are all surplus to society, born for no good purpose but this. All we've done is make use of them.'

Han hauled him back up and hurled him out of the arm lock, smashing the rifle butt into the side of Siew's head. He felt himself losing control. 'For what? For your madness?'

Siew stumbled, blood gushing from his temple. Han punched one fist into him, holding his rifle in the other. Contact was satisfying, the crunch of bone breaking and flesh parting. Siew's head snapped back as his body caved in. He fell to his knees.

He was down on all fours like a dog, retching and gasping. Han held the rifle muzzle hard against Siew's head. It would be so easy to pull the trigger. He felt its hard curve under his finger.

Siew glared up at him with contempt in his eyes. He said through the blood and spittle, 'You would never understand – people like you. You and your governments are nothing but toadies of the West. Slaves. You don't have the moral strength for greatness. Sacrifices have to be made by the few for the many. Asia has a choice. It can stay forever a colony at the beck and call of the West or it can be great again through Asian Values. To be strong and pure and know no fear – what price is not worth paying for that?'

Han dragged Siew up and rammed him against a wall, rifle barrel angling his head to one side. Han was close up against him, Siew's every bead of sweat and drop of blood clearly defined. It would be the triumph of Han's career to blow the bastard's brains out. For all these victims, for all the Snakes who had died over the years in failed operations against the Alliance, all those AVA members who had turned fatally against their beliefs, the innocents who had stood in the way of Siew's ambitions. For all Han's failures. Every muscle was rigid with fury and the lust for vengeance as if a demon grappled to possess him. Han swore through gritted teeth and rasped,

'Whatever fine words you try to use, these lives were never yours to take.'

He looked around. He could not drag Siew with him nor did he have the time to take him into the custody of the back-up team. There – some cages in the corner, emptied of their human cargo. They were the size of large crates. Han pulled Siew over and shoved him into one of them, slamming the bolt and clipping on the lock. Siew had to sit, knees curled and head tucked down to fit. Han pocketed the key. He radioed the back-up team to give them Siew's location.

The voice crackled in his ear. 'Roger. We've found a load of prisoners. Look like experimental subjects. They're spaced out of their heads. Cells and cells of them. Some of the rooms are like the fucking black hole of Calcutta. We're evacuating them, got the paramedics on standby in the cove.'

'Qwong among them?'

'No, sir.'

Han began to move away.

Siew shouted, 'Don't leave me here! How long are they going to be?'

Han turned. This sudden display of panic was a surprise.

Siew rattled the cage. 'Get me out of here! Now! God-dammit, please!'

'What's the hurry?'

Siew hesitated. His face was sheened with sweat. 'Wyndham's going to blow the place! The suicide scenario. He's setting the detonator.'

Han stepped back to the cage. 'Where is it?'

Siew blinked rapidly. He said nothing.

Han began to walk away again.

'All right! Jesus Christ, I don't know how long we've got!'

Siew's directions were garbled. Han made him go over them again. 'But there are three levels. Only Wyndham can access them and only he can disarm the detonator – the security codes need his fingerprints and an iris scan. It's automatically set to blow in twenty-four hours as a default unless he triggers it before.'

'How's he going to trigger it?'

'There's a portable device. Like a pager. Its range is world-wide – it piggybacks on the mobile phone networks. For God's sake, get me out of here!'

Han strode away. Siew rattled the cage harder and shouted. Han turned at the door. 'Start fucking praying.'

Stairs. Leading up and down. Sam headed up, two at a time. Round one corner, up another flight. Another. She was breathing hard. Finally, the stairs opened into a corridor. There at the far end she saw Ginny dragging Fei along.

Ginny turned. Sam called out Fei's name. Fei did not react. She looked at Ginny as if for a lead. Ginny spoke urgently to her, guiding her through the door. Fei obeyed without protest.

A yell exploded from Sam. It began as Fei's name and ended in a scream. She pushed herself on, fighting the swamp that seemed to churn at her legs. What had Ginny done? The blank stare that Fei had given her terrified Sam. She wanted to tear Fei away, pound into Ginny all her rage and desperation.

Ginny shoved Fei through the door and slammed it. Sam hurtled on, hauled it open. More stairs. She began to climb, following the sound of their footsteps.

Wyndham dived through the exit by the Secure Unit, guards and armed personnel covering his escape with fire out to the land unit and back against Han and his men. Ducking down a corridor, Han paused, checking positions over the radio network. It would be a matter of moments before a wave of the Centre's armed men pushed back into the corridors to pick off his team's scattered members. Yusoff and others were already down with gunshot wounds, some of them dead. From the cove level, police troops were heading up while back-up teams were moving in to deal with the injured and move out the captives they had discovered.

Han cursed. He had radioed the alert to all units. A bomb disposal unit was flying in by helicopter with additional back-up. But no one knew how long they had before Wyndham triggered the detonator. He had to be apprehended alive at all costs. Whatever time Han's men might have to complete the evacuation was purely at Wyndham's whim. Han suspected that not all the Centre's personnel were aware of 'the suicide scenario' – there was a zeal in their defence of the lab complex that made no sense if they knew it was going to be destroyed within the day. That ferocity was giving them an edge over Han's professionals. An added advantage was their knowledge of the complex. It had given them manoeuvrability and better tactics where their weapons skills had been limited and amateurish.

Han felt a surge of fury. So many months wasted, so many years spent chasing the Alliance down. Battling Mokhtar and the Suits for the resources and go-ahead. And all along his gut suspicions had been right. He had got this far and it might yet vanish in an instant.

Han gave the order for the all-out assault. He reloaded his rifle then pulled out the lightweight mask from its sling on his belt and slipped it on. In his free hand, he held a gas grenade. On the count over the channel, he hurled it into the group holding the exit. Other grenades flew, hissing, into the crowd from members of his team. Among them were smoke crackers, harmless but noisy, set to explode at random to maximise confusion.

'Go!' Han commanded.

His men, hooded in their gas-masks, launched themselves into the mayhem, crouching low and returning fire. At the same time, the land unit moved on the forward group, drawing their focus away from Han's upcoming team.

His men were gaining control. Shouting into his mike, Han handed the lead over to another Snake and knifed through the skirmish after Wyndham.

Chapter Thirty-Two

Han wove his way through the trees away from the Centre. Wyndham was running along the cliff edge, heading inland towards the mangrove. The perimeter fencing lay between him and the forest. To his left was the sheer drop into the sea, to his right wooded scrub beyond which the Centre's grounds lay. Han picked up speed. Behind him, the sounds of gunfire and shouting receded.

Wyndham launched himself up and over the first layer of fencing, stepped across the middle ground and up over the next. He disappeared from view into the forest.

Han followed, slinging his rifle over his shoulder. He leapt down the slope on the other side, crashing through thick under-growth, tumbling and skidding down the steeper stretch, trying to head Wyndham off. Han was gaining, his physical fitness giving him the advantage.

Wyndham was staggering through the mangrove, slowing in the muddy shallows. The tide was coming in. Sunlight dappled through the trees and dazzled off the water. Wyndham turned and fired random shots. They were wide and Han kept on charging him. He swung the rifle into his hands. Shouted, 'Stop! Police!'

Wyndham kept on moving. As Han had expected him to. Drawing the rifle up to take aim, Han squeezed off a single shot.

The bullet zinged into the water inches away from Wyndham. Another shot. Clipping a mangrove trunk just as

Wyndham placed his hand there to push off from it.

Wyndham froze. The last echo of the gunfire faded.

Han was upon him, churning through the shallows, rifle aimed. 'Throw down your weapon!'

Wyndham turned round slowly. His pistol was levelled at Han. It would have been easy for Han to have taken him with another clean shot. But he bit down hard on the impulse.

'Don't come any closer!' Wyndham held up a small device in his other hand. It was the pager. His thumb hovered over the single button. His eyes were wild. He was breathing hard. 'This will trigger . . .'

Han interrupted him. 'You're not going to destroy all you've worked for.'

'You know about the detonator!'

'Siew told me.' Han did not shift his aim. He had to talk Wyndham down. Find a way back to disarming the detonator. 'Your sister is still down there. And your people. Your life is down there. It doesn't have to end like this.'

Qwong was still unaccounted for and Han had left Ryder in the complex. None of his team had reported seeing her again. He felt a bead of sweat trickle down his brow.

Wyndham waved the trigger. 'I'll do it! Goddamn you, I'll do it! Drop your rifle! Now, fuck you!'

Han hesitated. Then slowly lowered the weapon and let it fall into the water. 'It'll blow anyway, I know that . . .'

'Shut up! The pistol! Now!'

Han lifted the Beretta out of its holster and dropped it into the shallows. 'The authorities don't want to destroy you. We can work with you. It's Siew we want. Siew and the Alliance.'

Wyndham was backing away, slipping in the mud underfoot. Han inched forward. Wyndham's aim was erratic as he moved. 'Stay where you are!'

Han kept moving. 'What does it matter now? I'm un-armed. After all you've been through – New York, Shanghai, the last few years here – what's two minutes more? Just hear me out.'

Han stopped an inch from the barrel of Wyndham's pistol.

'At this range, this body vest might as well be silk. Listen to what I have to say. Then do what the fuck you want.'

Han saw the shift of focus in Wyndham's eyes. It was infinitesimal but enough – a settling of the gaze, a decrease in agitation. He had the sucker's attention. It would be no effort to disarm him from this distance. As for the trigger device – Wyndham was holding it up and behind his left shoulder – that would be trickier. But at least Han had bought himself a little more time.

He went on, 'Siew's already sold you out. He's putting the blame on you. With his connections, he might still wriggle out of this. But you – who have you got but him as your protector? Everything you've got, he gave to you, isn't that right? How far can you run? Whatever resources you might have, whatever safe house you might hope to get to, he gave them all to you. He's going to fucking give it all out to us, if he thinks it's going to save his skin.'

Wyndham swallowed.

Han had hit a nerve. He had been weighing up likely scenarios and this one had struck home. He pressed on. 'After New York, you set up your work again. How? Because Siew was there. After Shanghai he got you out and set you up here. After today – what? You got so close this time. The perfect stable compound is in those labs, isn't it? If you blow this place, you're going to have to start from nothing. And with what? The clothes you're standing in? Hiding out, on the run? You're finished if you hit that trigger. You might still walk away with your life. But what is your life without your work?'

'Shut up! You don't know anything about my life or my work!' Wyndham rammed the pistol into Han's chest, pushing him backwards. Wyndham kept on coming, even as Han backed up, stumbling in the shallows. His features were contorted with despair and grief, fighting against spasms of wild fury.

Han kept talking. 'Give us Siew and we'll give you your work! Give us enough to put him away for murder, conspiracy, extortion, abduction, treason – that's all it takes. And you'll get the funds, the personnel, the equipment, the bodies – whatever you want – to carry on with your work.'

'You're lying!' Wyndham stopped. 'You don't have the clout to make such a deal!'

'As a Special Forces operative, Regional Intelligence Unit of the Pan Asian Congress for Security, I am authorised to broker an amnesty in return for your co-operation with the governments of the PACS region.'

'Jesus Christ!' Wyndham stepped back. His gun was still raised but the tension eased from his body.

Han slowly reached for his ID – his real one – and held it up to Wyndham. 'We would require you to divulge all knowledge and information relating to the compound, all details of your experiments and projections for its practical use as a military weapon and any desirable objective. We would also require you to develop the compound for such use exclusively by PACS.'

Wyndham stared at Han, taking it in, reassessing. Would he believe the offer?

Han said, 'Now give me the trigger. Nice and easy. We'll settle this – the right way for you. The right way for PACS.'

Han held out his hand.

Wyndham did not move. He seemed to lose momentum. His gaze slid momentarily away from Han as if seeing the swamp for the first time. 'I've been here before. Too many times.'

Han frowned, uncertain where this might lead.

'There's no one left to trust. They all turn on you in the end, one way or another. Susan was the first. But she's gone, as good as dead.' Wyndham moved away, stumbling through the muddy water. He was agitated, waving the gun. He was working something out, his words only the surface of a violent internal battle. He ranted, 'Then Deng, Ben . . . They were at the heart of it, trusted even by Siew. And Ginny – I had hopes for her. A rebirth, a new start. But she and Fei – that was the first crack. Now Siew. I believed in him. He was the hope of all our futures. I thought we could win this time. The Alliance and my work – together we might yet beat back the demons. We were going to win. Against *him*. But *he*'ll always win, won't he? *He*'ll always go free. And it's the innocents who die.'

Wyndham turned to Han. He had the look of a man standing

on the edge of an abyss. 'You want my work. You want my mind. Like the Americans and the Chinese, you think you can buy me with infinite resources. Only Siew understood. He gave me a vision to live for. He gave us all the dream of our better selves, how the world might be in another purer reality. He gave me back Katie from all the darkness that lives out there. There's no going forward, no going back. No escape but one. If I had known what *he* was going to do to Katie, I would have killed her myself that morning.'

Even as Han launched himself at him, Wyndham glared up beyond the trees towards the headland and clicked the trigger.

The stairs opened out into a maze of narrow tunnels. The lighting was dim, the occasional low-wattage emergency bulb casting patches of grey into the gloom. There were no doors leading off any of the corridors, some leading to blind alleys, others criss-crossing again and again. They seemed to have been designed for no purpose other than to confuse.

Sam followed the sound of the footsteps but they echoed from all around her. They were growing less distinct and she knew she was being left behind. Panic struck her. Every stretch of corridor looked the same, every corner identical. The dark seemed to intensify. She would not even be able to find her way back to the stairs again.

She made herself stop. Stay still. Listening. Closed her eyes. Behind her.

Sam turned and traced the receding sounds that seemed to thread through the tunnels. They stopped suddenly. She stopped. Inched her way on. Listening beyond her own breathing. Fei's voice, distressed. Then Ginny's, reassuring.

Sam called Fei's name.

An answering cry.

That was all she needed. Sam raced on. Ginny's voice, angry, trying to keep Fei quiet. Fei's voice, rising in confusion. They were getting louder. Then she heard the sound of grinding metal, heavy iron fighting rust.

A sudden spray of light to her left.

The hatch was of thick iron, mechanically opened from the inside with a wheel like a naval hatch – no doubt a fail-safe against power failure in the complex. Sam guessed that it had been built as an escape route, known only to the Wyndhams. It was close to the ground, the size of a large drain.

She began to crawl through. Her body vest caught against the frame. She struggled, working herself free. She did not budge. She pushed herself backwards and slid back into the tunnel. Fumbling at the buckles, she took off the vest and slipped through the hatch into the bright morning.

The freedom of movement was a relief. Air on her torso chilled the sweat dripping from her. She looked round. She had emerged below the fence edging the Secure Unit on the bay-side slope of the headland. The incline was gentler here and covered with thick undergrowth and trees. Through the cover of vegetation, she saw the beach and bay below. In the water, anchored beyond the shallows, was a police speedboat. She could not tell if anyone was on board.

Noise and movement below indicated where Ginny was taking Fei. Sam began to pound down the slope after them.

On the beach, Ginny was dragging Fei across the sand. Sam emerged from the trees and quickened her pace. Without the body vest, she was moving fast. The speedboat seemed unmanned and Ginny was aiming for the shortest stretch of water to it. To their left, in the distance, Sam was aware of shouting and gunfire from the Centre's grounds.

She called out to Fei again.

Fei looked back, slowing. Ginny jerked her arm, dragging her on. Sam called again. Fei pulled against Ginny, turning her whole body now. Sam kept on calling. Fei struggled against Ginny, digging her heels into the sand. Staring at Sam. There was confusion in her face. She shook her head as if to clear it. She was frowning, fighting now with a new energy. Ginny had to stop, turning to deal with Fei. They struggled, splashing into the surf.

Fei pulled away and began to wade towards Sam. Ginny cried, 'No! Fei, this way . . . we have to go, it's not safe here . . .'

Sam headed into the water.

Fei said, 'Sam?'

'Yes. It's me. It's Sam.'

Fei hesitated. A wave rocked her. She was struggling as if against her own mind.

Behind her, Ginny shouted, 'Stop right there!'

She was speaking to Sam, aiming a handgun, double-handed, past Fei, level with Sam's chest.

Sam splashed to a halt. Her lungs heaved. Blood pounded in her ears. She was five paces from Fei, Ginny ten paces beyond.

Fei was staring at Sam, her face bewildered. Sam forgot Ginny, forgot the gun and the danger. Suddenly there was only Fei, alive and in the flesh so close to her. She said gently, 'Fei, it's all right. I'm here now. You're safe with me.'

Something inside seemed to drag Fei away from the present moment, her face blanking out even as she strained to make sense of what was happening. Sam suppressed a cry of despair as reality hit home. She was too late. They had worked on Fei and Sam did not know what was left of her.

Ginny's aim did not falter. Her voice strained for softness as she addressed Fei. 'Don't be taken in by what you're seeing. She's not real. You don't know who she is. I'm your friend, your best friend, remember? We made that promise years ago when we were children. You asked me to be your friend. You wanted me to be your friend. Remember? We were eating Coco Pops . . .'

Fei twisted round, the voice and the memories drawing her back to Ginny. Sam felt a chill in her gut. What was Ginny saying? What lies had they made Fei believe? The pistol that Han had given her was hard against her spine, tucked in the back of her belt. Could she reach it without provoking Ginny? But even if she could, what then? Fei stood between her and Ginny. Sam had never handled a weapon before. She could not risk Fei in all this.

Ginny took a step forward. Fei started. A gasp of fear. She

staggered away. Swivelled her gaze back to Sam. Her whole face and body pleaded for help. But she did not move. It was almost as if she could not. Sam felt as if she was drowning. The guilt she had been holding back overwhelmed her. There had been no time to think, no time to feel in the last days, all her energy poured into action. Find Fei – that had been the litany that had kept her struggling on. And now Sam had found her and it was as if who Fei had once been was dissolving into nothing.

Sam burst out, 'I let them take you. I could have stopped it but I ran away. I left you. I'm sorry. God, I'm sorry. They wanted me and I let them take you. I couldn't find you – I drove for hours – but I lost you.'

Sam reached out both arms in a plea. But she did not dare to move. Fei stumbled, crossing into Ginny's line of fire. Her eyes were fixed on Sam, taking in the look of her, working out what she was saying.

Ginny hurled forward and grabbed Fei from behind, one arm tight across her chest and shoulders, the other training the pistol on Sam still. Fei cried out, struggling. Ginny began to drag her backwards, her larger build easily controlling Fei's light frame. Sam took a step.

'Stay where you are!'

Fei saw the gun. Looked at Sam. It was a heartbeat. Her gaze locked with Sam's. It was Fei in her whole self who looked out in that moment. Saw Sam for real.

And then Fei stopped pulling against Ginny, let herself be hauled along. She cried out, 'Ginny, my darling! Ginny, help me, get me away from here.'

Ginny loosed her grip, startled. Fei pulled free and twisted around. She threw herself at Ginny, cupped her hands to Ginny's face and kissed her with a terrible, desperate passion.

Fei felt a hideous nausea tasting Ginny's lips. She hardly understood what she was doing. She moved as if in a dream. Nothing made sense. And yet everything had a logic of its own that she did not – could not – question. Her mind seemed to spin in neutral even as her body acted as if in the control of something other. All she knew for certain was that Sam was alive,

Sam was real, and she could not watch her die again.

Fei's arm reached down and back, grabbing at the pistol in Ginny's grip. She pushed it into a downward swing as the momentum of her weight against Ginny's caused them to stagger.

Sam propelled herself forward. The shot rolled across the water even as she drew breath to scream.

Fei and Ginny fell into the waves, tendrils of blood spiralling out to engulf them in crimson.

The explosions came in waves, shaking the ground across the bay.

Inside the complex, walls and ceilings collapsed. Tons of rock slammed down into the corridors. An inferno raged through the tunnels, each burning section igniting the next as petrol poured down through the sprinkler systems. The bodies of apes caught fire. Vats and tanks exploded in the immense heat. The hundreds of people still in the complex were engulfed in fire or crushed by tumbling concrete and rock.

In the human prion room, Siew screamed as the fire caught him. Rattling on the wire cage, face twisted in an agony of fear, he felt first the searing heat, then his clothing began to burn. Fire wrapped around his head, licked into his mouth, poured into his lungs. All around, the warehouse collapsed under rock and rubble.

At the topmost ridge, the Secure Unit burst into fragments, the earth beneath it heaving up in a spray of rock and flaming gasoline. Bodies were flung up, dismembered by the violence of the blasts. Flesh caught fire. Trees and soil were forced up from several points along the headland, boulders and fireballs blasting out of the chasms. Lower down the slopes, explosions deep underground did not reach the surface but collapsed struts and ballasting walls of rock. Sections of the headland sheered and slumped like crumbling chalk.

In the shallows, Sam was flung off her feet, falling headlong into the water.

She struggled up, hauling herself over to Fei and Ginny. Rocks and debris rained down. She hunched over Fei, shielding her with her own body as she dragged her up above the surface of the waves.

Wyndham's eyes were wide and staring as the thunder of the explosions rolled across the cove. He turned suddenly to Han as he took a step forward. Wyndham rammed the pistol against his own temple.

He blinked once as he held Han's gaze. And squeezed the trigger.

On the beach, Fei sprawled on the sand, gasping for air. She was watching Sam as if she watched a stranger. There was no fear, no emotion. Only curiosity.

Sam knelt over Ginny. The wound in her side was large and bleeding profusely. She was semi-conscious, her breathing erratic. Sam tore off Ginny's shirt and shoved it hard into the gaping hole, trying to stem the flow of blood.

With her free hand, she searched Ginny's pockets for other weapons. She pulled out a device the size of a handgun. From its appearance, it looked like a booster fitted with a full phial of liquid. Sam tucked it into her own back pocket.

There was little she could do for Ginny without medical equipment. She glanced around. There were two dark figures moving towards them from the grounds – Han's men. On the horizon, boats were approaching, sirens wailing. The sound of helicopters grew louder. Against the bright sky, she could see the five rotor-blades flashing in the sun.

She was aware of Fei beside her and looked up. Fei's face was very close, her long eyes taking Sam in. She was focusing out from somewhere far away, like someone emerging from anaesthetic. She said, 'Sam, it is you, isn't it?'

She nodded. Drew Fei away from Ginny. They knelt on the sand, the surf spraying salt over them. Its drumming seemed to tune out the distant sounds of engines and gunfire.

Fei touched Sam's face, ran her hands over Sam's body. 'I couldn't lose you again. I thought they'd killed you, I saw it. But it's you, tell me it's you?'

'It's me, Fei, I'm all right. You won't lose me again, I promise.' Sam stroked her hair, cupped her face in her hands. The touch of her warm skin made Sam ache with relief.

Fei's voice was choked. 'I don't know what's happening to me. I've had dreams . . . Or maybe they were real . . . My father – he's alive. But he can't be. Sam, I'm so scared. I see you and I know you. But I can't remember so many things about you. Yet I know you. Is this real? Is it?'

Sam took Fei's hand and held it to her face. Tears blurred her gaze in spite of herself. She tried to speak but could not. How could she convince Fei with words of a reality that was as ephemeral as her senses? Words had lied to Fei. Images and sounds and feelings had deceived her. Her knowledge of her own life, her experiences and memory, all had failed her. Only Fei herself could decide if anything she saw or felt now was real.

Sam felt herself melt in Fei's liquid gaze, as if soaked in Fei's pain and doubt. She thought of how Fei had been in all her contradictions and sensuality – stubborn and passionate, am-bitious, cheeky, fervent in her love. How they'd stormed at each other and ambled through the ordinary days; how they'd made love with the intensity that only came with trust. The woman kneeling in front of her seemed a tired phantom of the Fei she had always known. But Sam could not let herself believe that they had lost, not after all this.

She said Fei's name, clinging to it like a talisman.

Fei leaned in and kissed her, her lips salty from the sea.

Chapter Thirty-Three

Han and his men found mass graves in the grounds of the Centre, thousands of bodies from experiments that had failed and human culturing vessels who had become obsolete. Among the genuine patients and staff at the Centre, there had been discarded subjects like the keeper Deng who had died in the Wyndhams' charge. Over the next year, the authorities sifted through and pieced together the horrors of what the Centre had hidden. The AVA participants who had survived, including the elite benefactors, the psych team and actors and back-up personnel, were painstakingly interviewed, their statements compiled for the complex prosecution case. The senior levels of the Alliance – tycoons, armed forces top brass, the rich and influential – were investigated all across Asia. Members of the Red Tiger were arrested and the gang blown apart through the inevitable betrayals. The far-reaching grip of murder, abduction, extortion, blackmail and violence was finally exposed. AVA moles who had been manipulating agendas and policies within media, political, business and military organisations were rooted out. Witnesses, informants and conspirators named names and tried to strike deals in the scramble to save themselves.

Ginny Wyndham – aka Susan Lovelace – co-operated fully with the authorities from the prison hospital, giving them detailed accounts of her brother's hypotheses and experiments. She offered full descriptions of the psych scripts and the technology behind the computer-enhanced dramas. With the Centre and all its data, computers and culture factories destroyed, she became the focus of relentless questioning. The security of the region depended on Asia taking control and neutralising the power of the Alliance's Cure. But Ginny was unable to give them more than an outline of the chemical and biological formulae and methods Piers had used to manipulate and control the prion to his own ends: 'I left that all to him. He was the neuropsychologist. I didn't want to know all of it.'

Han's triumph was palpable but that one failure still raged in his gut. He had not secured the knowledge that had died with Wyndham. He hounded Sam Ryder in the first months, grilling her on what she remembered of the information she had read from the destroyed disk. She gave him sketchy details, half-recollected formulae, incomplete rationalisations. He impounded her Factor Q data and samples but when the police arrived at her labs, she and her staff were in the middle of an office move. In the chaos, everything on Factor Q had apparently been lost. Threatened with charges of destroying evidence and obstruction of justice, Sam shrugged helplessly, tears in her eyes, 'It was everything I'd worked for. Find it and give me back my life!' Charges were never filed. Han melted back into the shifting colours of Asia with his team of Snakes.

The control the Alliance had once had over the region unravelled. It was as if their ordinary followers had woken from a trance, confused and shaken, not knowing how they had arrived in this place. They drifted back to their lives, no longer the heirs to a mythical all-powerful Asia. They were unremarkable again, struggling like everyone else to make the best of their futures. In years to come, they would wonder how it was that they had been swept away by such fantasm and they would shrug and put it down to the madness of the times.

The call of the muezzin drifted over the late-afternoon. It seemed to come from across the centuries, out of the mystic lands of Arabia into the muggy tropical heat. The sinking sun cast the day in solid amber and for a moment time seemed suspended. The fronds of the palm trees were motionless against the sky. Hibiscus and bougainvillaea deepened in the mellow light, the perfume of frangipani thick in the air. Even the midges and bees seemed transfixed by stillness. Birdsong paused and dogs lay quiet. Human voices trailed away in the peace of the park.

The lake at its heart was still as polished pewter. Beyond, the city skyline rose out of it like a mirage. The Petronas Twin Towers gleamed gold in the sun. Beside them, dwarfed by distance, the space-age KL Tower blinked in the sunset. Fei sat with Sam on the grassy bank, palm trees behind them, gazing out at these emblems of the future, as if born out of the depths of the water. The lakes in the Titiwangsa Gardens had once been tin mines, fathoms deep amid sand picked clean to whiteness. Tin had been the making of Kuala Lumpur, a settlement clawed out of the muddy delta of two rivers. The tin was gone now but hope remained.

Fei curled her arm around Sam's waist. She could feel the dampness of Sam's T-shirt and, beneath, the warmth of her body. Sam smelt of vanilla and honey and a trace of sweat. Fei felt as if they sat at the meeting place of time, the present and past uniting amid the trees, the future within sight.

A flash of pain caught her. Her vision blurred. It was as if jolts of electricity cracked through her skull, throwing her mind across a gulf of consciousness. The world around her seemed to erupt and her sense of herself caved in. In the void, there was only pain and a terrifying aloneness.

When it was over, Fei was sweating, shaky. Her heart was racing and she gulped in air. She found Sam holding her hand. Watching her. There was no panic or anxiety in Sam's eyes, just a calm that seemed to contain Fei. She never knew when each one would happen but these seizures had become a part of her life. As her body returned to normal, Fei tested her vision and movement, sensation and control, as Sam had taught her. So far, there had not been any muscular or functional deterioration. Mentally, Fei had remained alert and cognisant in the last months, carrying on her legal work at the office, her reduced hours and caseload slowly building as her health improved.

She smiled at Sam. Normal recovery again today. 'So far so good.'

Sam squeezed Fei's hand. She made herself breathe again. She never showed it to Fei but every seizure she witnessed was like a freefall. In the seconds it took, Sam waited a lifetime to see Fei open her eyes again, to see her look in full conscious-ness, present still in this reality. It had been a year and these spasms had been the only indication of the alien presence in Fei's brain. All this time the prion had remained stable. That was all that mattered. Fei was still Fei, healthy and alive. But for how much longer? How long before muscles might start to spasm, co-ordination fail? Before dementia might emerge? Months? Years? Perhaps never? God, perhaps never. Sam said the words into her own silence.

She had told no one of the chronotonin booster, bringing it home tucked inside her jeans. That first night she had accessed the four fragmented files in her web-based e-mail, decoded them and reassembled Piers's data. Sam combed through every file, every word, struggling to understand it all and commit the programming procedure to memory. She was at the screen for almost twenty hours solid. Afterwards, stiff and bleary-eyed, she deleted all the files from the e-mail accounts and her hard drive, emptied the Recycle Bin, went deep into the software foun-dations of the machine and wiped all traces from its long-term memory. No one would ever know that the files had existed.

And then she had tried to give Fei back everything Sam had ever known about her.

Day after day, using the booster in conjunction with the diurnal natural releases of chronotonin, Sam sat with Fei through the trances, talking, telling her who she was, what she had done as a child, how she'd lived her life as an adult, who she loved and what made her laugh. Sam scavenged in her mind for all the things that Fei had ever shown of herself – not just stories and words but every nuance and look that had indicated the woman beneath; she spoke with Fei's family, shared their intimacies and knowledge of Fei and gave them all back in the narrative of who Fei had been.

In the fading light, Sam studied her. Was she doing the right thing? The question haunted her. She had tried to give back to Fei all of the woman she had been – not just those parts of her Sam loved but also those others that had made them clash so often before: Fei's ambition, pride, fierce independence, impatience, hard-headed business smarts. It had been the hardest thing to do. To narrate for them both with enthusiasm and unwavering belief all the things Sam had once criticised her for. In those moments, it was as if she had had to become Fei, to look out at the world from within Fei's mind. She had had to reinterpret the facts in the language of Fei's reality. She had to learn to feel Fei's world, live with her values and emotions. Sam experienced almost tangibly the reality of what it was to love. It was a beholding and a separation, an acceptance of a beguiling otherness.

But had Sam tried to temper those things she had not liked, sought to improve on them? She told herself she had not. But the temptation had been there, she had known it, nudging her deep behind the armour of her integrity. Had she given in and not admitted it to herself? Had she changed Fei to her liking and not realised it?

Were any of Fei's choices really her own? Her ease now, slipping her arm back round Sam's waist. This new relationship they both seemed to flourish in, each a co-partner in the other's life. Fei's more relaxed attitude to her work. Her new closeness with her family. Did she choose these new states of mind because she wanted them? Or only because of some embedded signal Sam had unconsciously given her?

'What?' Fei shook her gently. She was smiling.

'You never used to do that before.' She indicated Fei's arm around her.

Fei shrugged.

'We used to argue about it. You used to be so afraid. Ashamed. I wanted you to be different. Have I . . . have I made you different in this last year?'

Fei stared out over the lake. A breeze had risen out of the sultry heat. It toyed with a lock of her hair. 'I don't know. I know I don't want anything else. Maybe we'll never be sure. But I make the choice each time. To give up my consciousness to you.'

Choice. Like a frontier of freedom. Sam savoured the cool air on her face. The day was fading fast. Beside her, Fei caressed her back with light fingers.

Author's Note

The novel is set against a critical watershed in South East Asian history. The Haze and many of the background events of the economic crisis are real but time has been telescoped for the purposes of dramatic effect.

Conversations with my brother, Dr Yang-Wern Ooi, gave me the basis to the medical background to this story – so: thanks, bro! Additionally, I am indebted to Nicholas Bennett for sharing his scientific and IT knowledge with me: in particular, for helping me devise the interactive trance process and for inventing the fictitious hormone 'chronotonin'. All my most lavish thanks are due, too, to Dr David W Grossman for reviewing the medical aspects of the text and for his cameo appearance in Chapter 22. I am grateful, moreover, to my uncle, Dr Meng-Hooi Lim, for talking over details of psychiatric treatment, diagnosis and practice and for his wonderful encouragement and keen support throughout. The compound Factor Q is inspired by scientific fact. However, literary imagination has taken the bare facts into the fictional realm, bending the science where narrative dictates and making imaginative leaps to enable the drama of the story to be emphasised. All discrepancies, errors and inaccuracies are entirely mine.

The grey orang-utans exist only in my imagination.

My most heartfelt thanks are due as always to my ever amazing parents and my sister Yang-Ming – and to the usual suspects: Terry Bailey and Helene Nowell. Also to Alina

Rastam, beng hui, Ben Page, Paul Carter, Rosemary Hart, Simon Jamieson, Marianne Aston, Sam Mason, Andrew Bennett and everyone who has offered help, friendship, morale-boosting and light relief during the writing of this book.

Yang-May Ooi
London 1999